An Old-Fash

MW00390139

BY RICHARD LAWS

for Mum and Dad

First published 2019 by Five Furlongs
© Richard Laws 2019
ISBN 978-1-9164600-4-1 (Paperback)
978-1-9164600-5-8 (EBook)

This book is sold subject to the condition that it shall not, by way of trade or otherwise, be lent, re-sold, hired out, or otherwise circulated without the publisher's prior consent in any form of binding or cover other than that in which it is published.

This is a work of fiction. Names, characters, businesses, places, events, locales, and incidents are either the products of the author's imagination or used in a fictitious manner. Any resemblance to actual persons or organisations, living or dead, or actual events is purely coincidental.

Published by Five Furlongs 2019

Other horseracing stories by Richard Laws:

The Syndicate Manager;
Gimcrack.

One

July 2016

The Scotswood Bridge towered into the night sky above him as he emerged tentatively onto the riverside footpath and stared eastward in the early hours of Sunday morning. The moon was bright tonight. It could have lit the scene beside the River Tyne without assistance. Streetlights also cast their glare onto the A6085 every fifty yards, a ribbon of yellow dots which stretched into the city.

The dog sniffed the tarmac as he crossed the deserted dual carriageway. A recent rain shower had brought forth pungent and aromatic new smells. Above him, a lorry rumbled across the bridge and caused the stray mongrel to stop in the centre of the road and glance up into the concrete columns.

The car weaved erratically as it approached. Its engine noise came to the dog too late. Streetlights and headlights merged and reflections bounced off the wet surface. Momentarily dazzled, the dog tensed, unable to decide in which direction he should bolt. The approaching mechanical noise soon ceased, blocked out by screeching brakes and tyres tearing as friction bit into them.

The car left the scent of burnt rubber as it slid past the stray, careering over a curb and into the riverside bushes. It mowed the light shrubs down, skidding and gouging furrows into the earth before striking upright black posts on the edge of the riverbank. The dog scampered off the road, picking its way up the embankment, away from the shouting.

A metallic clang was followed by the sound of scraping. A human scream forced the dog to pause at the crest of the banking. He turned, flicked his ears forward, and peered curiously at the star-lit scene. Only the rear of the car was still visible, hanging over the edge of the manmade riverbank, caught on the remains of the railings. There were more human noises, but the dog lost interest. He turned and was soon slinking away through undergrowth, placing distance between himself and the smell of rubber and petrol.

Two

With the party already well under way, Charlie Summer let himself in through the farmhouse's back door. He was looking for one specific girl, that special someone. She was the person he had travelled three hours from Leeds on a Friday night, through driving snow, to be with in Inkberrow, Worcestershire. Nothing would have stopped him. It was her big night, the one she would remember for months, maybe years. He found her in the large, beamed front room, wearing a fairy costume and sitting in a ring, along with fifteen of her six-year-old classmates.

Poppy's small round face and puppy fat cheeks bent into a glorious smile as soon as he stepped into the room, and she jumped to her feet. He reciprocated with wide eyes and both eyebrows high on his forehead.

'Uncle Charlie, you came!' the little girl screamed excitedly, rushing over to him with arms outstretched. Charlie gathered her up from a kneeling position before lifting her effortlessly off the ground and twirling her around. The rest of the girls watched entranced, as the tall, muscular stranger in his late twenties wearing a Paul Smith three-piece suit and Burberry brogues, danced around the room with his god-daughter. One or two of the young girls shot their own hands in the air as he passed, hopeful of receiving similar treatment. A smattering of adults on the periphery found a smile creeping onto their lips, the little girl's delighted giggling becoming infectious.

'Happy Birthday, Poppy,' Charlie told her gently, just for her to hear, and was rewarded with a rubbery kiss on his forehead.

'Glad you could make it, Charlie, eventually,' scolded a female voice behind him, laced with sarcasm. He swung round to find the girl's mother standing with a large gaily-wrapped parcel in her hands.

'Ah, have I arrived at a bad time?' he ventured, allowing his face to drop like an admonished schoolboy and immediately placing Poppy's feet carefully back onto the polished parquet floor.

'There's never a bad time for you to arrive as far as Poppy's concerned,' Laura conceded with a grin, 'But we were in the middle of a game…'

She spun the oversized, light paper parcel between two fingers and Charlie was momentarily struck with how her features matched the little girl's: curly blonde hair, cheeky lips which quickly curled into a smile, and assured azure blue eyes which projected a fierce intelligence.

'Understood,' he responded before helping to arrange the excited troop of girls back into a seated circle. As the game recommenced, he drifted to the side of the room and watched a few rounds before disappearing into the kitchen in search of a drink.

Being a horseracing yard, the farmhouse was generally full of people, but this evening every room was bursting at the seams. Charlie excused himself through a doorway and two corridors of chatting guests before managing to squeeze between a gaggle of diminutive jockeys at the entrance to the kitchen, casting an eye around the large space. Despite there being close to twenty people in the kitchen, his brother was an easy spot. Like Charlie, he stood at over six foot three and the two of them locked eyes above the sea of party guests and exchanged a smile.

'Beer for me!' Charlie called across the room. Tommy nodded and busied himself in order to have a bottle of Charlie's preferred brand ready by the time he reached him.

'You managed to beat the snow then,' Tommy noted as he clinked bottles with his twin brother a minute later.

'Nothing was going to keep me from Poppy's sixth birthday. Quite a popular little girl I see!'

'We've got all the yard staff, a few owners, and friends on top of Poppy's entire year at school, plus their parents. It's bedlam,' Tommy declared with a shake of his head.

'Well Poppy seems pretty happy with it,' Charlie grinned.

'She's just like her mother. She loves a party,' he replied with a roll of his eyes. Whereas me, I'd…'

'…rather be out in the stables seeing to your horses. Yes, we know!' Charlie interrupted.

'How can we have been born just three minutes apart and be so different?' Tommy stated in mock bewilderment.

Charlie considered his elder brother's statement by placing an index finger on the end of his chin and adopting a puzzled expression. In return, he received a playful dig in his ribs.

It was certainly true about their personalities. The twin brothers were of a similar height, but that's where the similarities ended. Right from childhood Tommy displayed practical tendencies. He was good with animals, rode well, was quiet, thoughtful, and driven by an obsession to continue with the family business of training racehorses. Charlie had never been drawn to his father's passion for training, although he enjoyed the sport itself and was a keen racegoer. His passion lay in technology, people, and business. He was a wordsmith, a communicator and he'd like to believe, an innovator; someone who read situations and made things happen. If, as a result of his involvement a powerful client bought expensive services or products, so much the better.

'So you're a salesman,' Tommy had surmised when Charlie had trotted out this job description to his brother upon joining the advertising and promotions agency in Leeds.

'Yes, I suppose I am,' he'd eventually replied with an air of one having their pomposity popped. It was the last time Charlie had used such a pretentious description for how he earned his living. He was a salesman.

The boys had been nineteen when their father died on the farm from a heart attack. Their mother had gone quickly to a virulent cancer two years before. There was only one possible outcome when their father died, Tommy took over the yard, and Charlie went to university.

'How are the horses running at the moment?' Charlie asked tongue in cheek, knowing full well Tommy had sent out three winners in the last six days. Tommy regarded his sibling and read his enquiry correctly.

'Oh, just rattling along, making a few quid where I can.'

Charlie snorted into his bottle of beer. 'Don't kid a kidder, you're smashing it at the moment!' he insisted, 'That mare you ran the other day in the bumper at Stratford looks useful.'

'Yeah, she's nice. She could be right for the Aintree bumper in a few weeks time. We'll see,' Tommy replied in a low voice and a meaningful stare.

His brother responded with raised eyebrows and an impressed nod.

'And you?' Tommy asked, 'I've not seen you for about three weeks, have you made another million since we last shared a beer?'

'Oh, two at least,' Charlie smiled, but there was something in his brother's reaction. Tommy sensed a hint of negativity. The marketing and advertising agency business was a world away from training racehorses. However, his brother was easy to read, at least for him. Some of the stories Charlie told of how business was won and the demands from clients made him realise why his brother would have been bored with the family business of training racehorses. However, this was the first time since he'd started his meteoritic rise through the ranks of the famous Leeds based marketing agency there had been any intimation everything wasn't perfect in Charlie's world.

'Really, that good?' Tommy ventured with a raised eyebrow.

Charlie shook his head. 'It's nothing,' he replied, still smiling but inwardly kicking himself for allowing his guard to drop.

Tommy allowed the conversation to stall, watching his brother peer uncomfortably over the heads of the guests in the kitchen. He'd seen that look before; at school in the second year of sixth form, and again in Charlie's last year of university; he was becoming bored. Charlie didn't cope well with boredom. It could be the job, the people, personal relationships, or any combination of the three. But you could be sure, whatever it was, Charlie wouldn't stand the boredom for too long. Big changes were probably around the corner, Tommy could tell.

Tommy didn't ruminate on what could be the driver of his brother's grey mood, as he already had the perfect, ready-made distraction for him - and it was sitting, waiting for him down the corridor.

'I've got to admit, I'm impressed that you've made it down here for Poppy's birthday, however I did have an ulterior motive for dragging you back to Inkberrow from your expensive executive Leeds flat on a wintery Friday in March,' Tommy announced, then lowered his tone, 'The game's afoot...'

Charlie turned and examined his brother's face intensely for signs of tomfoolery; he found none. This was unexpected. The 'game' was Tommy's way of referring to a horse which he expected would win its next race. Not just that, the horse was laid out for a *specific* race. Charlie imagined it must be a bit special if he'd brought him all the way down from Leeds to discuss it. It was Poppy's actual birthday on the following Monday, and although he had planned to come down for that small family celebration, when he thought about it, Tommy had been very insistent he make his way here specifically for this evening's children's party.

Tommy couldn't help letting out a rattling chortle at the sudden interest and change in Charlie's body language.

'Yes, one of my owners is waiting to speak with you,' Tommy continued. This was greeted with a frown.

'Yes, yes, I know,' said Tommy, waving away the stack of questions he knew Charlie wanted to fire at him. 'Let me introduce you to him and he can explain. Besides, this chap is pretty rich...'

'Pretty rich?' Charlie repeated incredulously.

'Keep it down!' Tommy hissed, rolling his eyes in silent rebuke, 'Come on, he's in the summer room.'

It was Charlie's turn to stifle a laugh. 'Blimey, he must like it cold. The last time I poked my nose in there during winter you could have gone ice skating.'

The summer room was an adjunct to the end of the farmhouse, consisting of a medium sized swimming pool which was only ever used in the summer months. Its walls and ceiling were constructed of heavy transparent plastic, so heating it in winter was too costly to consider. The two brothers had spent virtually every day of the summer holidays in and out of the water enjoying what their parents had insisted was 'The best investment they'd ever made', and Poppy and her friends were now its primary users.

Charlie followed his brother out of the kitchen and down the familiar route to the end of the farmhouse before being cautioned to wait outside the summer room double doors.

'What, he's already in there?' Charlie joked.

Tommy cocked his head to one side, pursed his lips, and nodded apologetically as he opened the door and beckoned for Charlie to enter.

Charlie stepped inside the room. The light wasn't on, so he immediately started to feel the wall for the switch.

'Just go on in,' Tommy insisted, bustling his brother into the cold, dark space with a gentle push. The change in temperature hit Charlie immediately, condensing his breath and prickling his cheeks.

6

'Good evening Mr. Summer!' said a lilting Geordie voice from somewhere low down. Charlie examined the area the words had been spoken from and caught the outline of a face and the hint of a silvery beard, lit by the dim light from the open door.

'Please! Do switch the light on, it really won't matter to me,' the voice offered.

'Charlie, this is Sam Lewis and Harvey. Sam owns five horses with me,' Tommy announced, flicking the light on from the doorway. 'Okay, Sam, I'll be in the kitchen. You and Harvey can come find me after you've had your chat,' he added before clicking the door closed.

Looking down, Charlie found a man who could have been aged from his mid thirties to late forties. He was sitting well away from the pool, on a yellow sun lounger. There was no sign of his colleague, Harvey.

Sam Lewis peered up, blinked a few times, and stuck his hand out in greeting from his seated position. Charlie bent over and grasped a dry, soft hand which he shook while looking directly into the man's eyes. One of them was slightly closed and he got the impression the irises were larger and darker than they should be. Short silver hair, thinning in places, was matched to a well-kept silvery beard on a round face which Charlie could only describe as jolly. Laughter lines creased around Sam's mouth and his smile was dominated by one wonky front tooth that seemed strangely in keeping with the rest of the man.

Charlie broke eye contact after they shook hands and he cast his gaze around the room on the lookout for a seat of some sort. In the end he pulled up an ancient lawn chair and carefully eased himself into it, for fear it could collapse. He noted a huge number of plastic pool toys in a variety of colours surrounded Sam Lewis's chair, and jumped slightly when one of them appeared to move. He'd missed the mainly black and tan German Shepherd which lay motionless at Sam's feet. He realised his mistake; *this* must be Harvey.

The dog wore a glowing yellow harness and he was gazing sleepily up at Charlie. Sam must be blind he thought, before modifying his view; the man had moved his hand to shake his, perhaps he was partially sighted.

'Looks like I'm in the cheap seats, Mr. Lewis,' Charlie said as he gripped the arms of his rickety chair and turned it so he was on a non-confrontation angle diagonally opposite the man and his dog. As he maneuvered the chair he smiled inwardly at himself. They did say a salesman was always selling.

'Please, call me Sam. I've no time for formalities. I think you tend to get more that way the older you get,' Sam replied with a hint of sadness.

'Well Sam, I'm guessing this is Harvey?'

'Ach. My apologies. Yes, this is my constant companion,' he said, reaching down to pat the dog's rump. 'As you've probably guessed I'm pretty much blind, so Harvey is used to sitting in the dark. I'm in the dark

7

whether the lights are on or not,' he added in a self-deprecating lilt.

'We can switch the light off for Harvey, if you wish,' offered Charlie awkwardly.

Sam paused, considering the offer. 'No, there's no need. Besides, I'd like you to read my face with the tale I have to tell.'

'Really? I thought you'd just wanted some advice on how to place a few bets. Tommy doesn't get involved in that sort of thing, with the rules of racing being so tight, so he drags me in to help some of his owners.'

Sam leaned back on his lounger, which necessitated him drawing his knees to be almost up to his chest and gave a growling laugh. His face creased and for the first time Charlie realised how rotund the man was. It seemed miraculous to Charlie that the sun lounger was capable of supporting Sam, as his midriff was copious and currently bouncing in unison with his laughter.

'No son, this is a bit bigger than just a bet,' he commented happily and without condescension, 'I'm hoping you might be able to help me with something altogether more… stimulating.'

Charlie felt a smile creep across his face. He was beginning to enjoy this encounter. Sam was certainly a little different to the rather stiff, well-heeled racing set Tommy usually attracted as owners.

'So what do you have in mind for me?' he asked.

Sam's slightly off gaze settled to the left of Charlie, and again, he blinked rapidly a few times before answering.

'I want to pull off a coup!' he said excitedly, slapping his thigh as he finished his exclamation.

Rattled by his master's sudden movement, Harvey jumped to his feet and let out an indignant woof, the hairs between his shoulder blades standing proud. A second or two of alert listening and the German Shepherd turned his head to stare mournfully up at his master, finally slumping back down and resting his head on the man's foot.

'Sorry, boy,' Sam said quietly, reaching down to scratch the dog behind his ears. Charlie noticed his hand had to work its way up Harvey's back in order to find the sweet spot for the scratch.

'I hope you don't mind me asking…' Charlie started.

'About ninety-five percent gone, I'm afraid,' Sam interrupted. 'I've still got a little peripheral vision, so I can just about watch my horses run as smudges in the distance. I assume that was your question?'

Charlie couldn't help smiling. The man may be virtually blind, but he was still as sharp as a tack. Just the inflection of his voice must have told Sam which topic his query concerned.

'It does, Sam, thank you. So I'm guessing you want some sort of assistance with this horse Tommy has ready to win for you?'

It was Sam's turn to crack a smile. 'Actually, your brother has *two horses* he tells me are ready to win.'

8

Three

It was Sam's backache which eventually forced the two men to curtail their conversation after twenty minutes with an agreement to reconvene elsewhere. Charlie had noticed the odd grimace from Sam during their conversation and when the older man started to unconsciously caress the base of his spine and shift uncomfortably in his inappropriate seat, Charlie suggested they find somewhere just as private and ideally with more robust furniture.

The sounds of the party rushed at them when they opened the summer room door and Charlie left Sam in the corridor, hopeful a search of the upstairs would secure a bedroom to occupy. However, after scouting around the rambling farmhouse it soon became clear that Tommy had reserved them the only room in the house not awash with six and seven year olds.

So far their conversation had danced around a little, with the two of them giving each other a bit of background. Charlie had explained that he was an Account Director with one of the biggest marketing agencies in the country, which meant he pitched, sold, created, and managed large media campaigns. Sam Lewis had nodded his understanding and explained he too had a relatively demanding job; he was on the board and part owner of the biggest independently operated food businesses in the country, boasting a turnover of over a billion pounds a year. As Sam had put it, Lewis the Baker created a loaf for every household in the country, every day. Charlie had gulped down his surprise and had realised *this* Samuel Lewis was a member of one of the United Kingdom's leading entrepreneurial families of the last two decades. He'd been relieved his companion hadn't been able to see the shock register on his face. However, this information also served to intensify his curiosity. Why would a man with such personal wealth be interested in taking bookmakers for a few quid? Surely it would be a very insignificant drop in the ocean.

Charlie was still baffled by Sam's reasons to enlist his help as he picked his way back down the stairs. He found Sam and Harvey standing where he'd left them, up against a wall at the foot of the stairs, trying to avoid the constant stream of children running up and down the hall playing some sort of searching game.

'No room at the inn I'm afraid,' he told Sam above the hubbub.

Sam nodded, looking slightly askew once more, as if he was peering over Charlie's shoulder.

'Then we should try the stables.'

Charlie gave a snort of mirth, before quickly realising Sam was serious. The portly, silver-haired heir to a billion pound business set off toward the back door, Harvey guiding his master expertly through the mêlée. The two men stepped outside into a cold, cloudless night and Charlie felt the goose pimples rising through his thin work shirt within seconds. The remains of a snowfall earlier in the day lay half-melted and had subsequently turned crispy in the sub-zero temperature. They crunched through the farmhouse garden, passing between evenly spaced ancient apple, plum and pear trees standing bare, waiting for the warmth of spring to wake them. Charlie opened a small wicket gate and almost immediately they were back under lights and a wooden roof, at the entrance to the first and oldest of Tommy's three stabling barns.

'I love that smell,' said Sam, breathing in the aroma of fifteen horses, most of which were now looking down the barn toward them from over their stable doors. Charlie nodded, before realising Sam wouldn't have picked up his gesture. Instead, he replied 'Yes, I know, it reminds me of my childhood.'

'This is the main barn isn't it?' asked Sam, not stopping to wait for an answer, 'Jumble Sale should be two up from the right.'

He gave Harvey a slight shake of his harness and the German Shepherd stepped forward, guiding Sam around a few bales of woodchips and a straw steamer. Charlie followed, fascinated by the relationship between the man and his dog. As they reached the bottom of the barn, Sam slowed and cocked his head slightly.

'The music,' he pointed out, with a nod to a battered old radio which was sitting on a small plinth up on the wall of the barn. It was set on a low volume, currently providing the equine residents and passing humans with Radio Two's brand of music. 'It helps me get my bearings,' Sam explained. He altered direction and approached a stable occupied by a strapping chesnut gelding with a large, crescent blaze down one side of his forehead.

'This is Jumble Sale,' Sam told Charlie proudly.

The gelding moved over to the door of his stable and Sam raised a hand and held it there, palm up. The horse dutifully moved his head into the path of Sam's hand. Once contact had been made Sam released his grip on Harvey and shuffled closer to his racehorse, running his open hand up the horse's jaw line until he could scratch him behind his ears and provide a soft pat on his neck. Harvey immediately planted his backside onto the barn floor and looked up at the horse as Jumble Sale's head emerged over the stable door above him.

'He's impressive,' Charlie admitted. 'And he seems to know you quite well.'

Sam beamed, 'I've owned him for four years now, Tommy bought him for me as a yearling. He's not top class or anything, but he tries hard and has a great temperament. Look at him, he loves the attention,' he said, blowing air up the gelding's nose. Jumble Sale reacted by flaring his nostrils, but remained stock still, apparently enjoying the sensation.

The two men spent the next minute or two discussing the gelding, Sam revealing he made the trip down to the yard at least once a fortnight to spend time with his five horses trained by Tommy. During their conversation he rubbed the gelding's chin throughout, with Jumble Sale's jaw eventually lowering to sit dotingly on his owners shoulder.

Presently, Sam turned to Charlie and suggested they needed to move on.

'Ah, I know, we'll go into the tack room, there's a bench and a heater,' Sam suggested. 'I've spent quite some time chatting with the work riders and stable staff in there.'

A few minutes later the two men were sitting side by side on a slatted wooden bench warming their hands on an old freestanding propane heater, which quickly filled the tack room with enough heat to take the chill away. Harvey was sitting at Sam's feet, his chest facing the fire, lifting his head from time to time to warm his neck and chin. There was a musty tang of leather from the dozens of saddles, cloths and riding gear around them which mixed with the smell of the heater to deliver a strangely comforting atmosphere. Charlie watched the heater turn its elements orange and flower with a tinge of red before turning to Sam. However, Sam sensed the movement and spoke before Charlie could restart the conversation.

'You're wondering why I would want to pull off a gamble, aren't you? I freely admit the money would mean nothing to me.'

'It had crossed my mind.'

Sam stifled a half laugh. 'There are some things which simply bring great joy. I love being at the track when my horses race, the feeling of anticipation on the night before the race, the excitement when you wake on a race day and that rush of adrenaline when the race is being run and you realise the animal you know intimately is coming to challenge and is being competitive in a sport it was bred to excel in.'

Sam was smiling as he spoke, gazing into the rafters of the tack room. He paused and slowly his warm expression fell from his face, to be replaced with a look which was tense and determined.

'It's not the monetary gain which matters, it's the execution of the plot which will thrill me,' Sam explained. 'I want to give the bookies a good rattling, and for one bookmaker in particular our actions should rock him to his core. I suppose it's the challenge I'm interested in, you know, taking on a business which you shouldn't be capable of beating. After all, that's what bookmakers do; they construct a 'book' in each race and balance it so that they don't lose whatever the outcome.'

Charlie didn't reply. Even though he still had no idea what Sam was planning, he was already feeling exhilarated by the prospect of being involved. He reflected for a moment that he used to feel this sort of excitement in his current role, starting after university as a lowly account executive six years ago, leaping deftly through the corporate ranks, each achievement thrusting him forward on a wave of enthusiasm. But just lately, the excitement had faded, to be replaced with a type of boredom he couldn't quite fathom.

Charlie pushed these thoughts away, instead returning to consider a betting coup which could be of gargantuan proportions, given the resources Sam could potentially place at his disposal.

'And my role in this endeavour would be...?'

A grin sprang upon Sam's features, puffing his cheeks out and creating symmetrical creases across his face. 'I require the services of an accomplice. Someone I can trust, who understands racing and betting and who also possesses one or two other... attributes.'

'Such as?'

'You use speed and pace ratings don't you?' queried Sam.

'You must have been speaking with Tommy. Well yes, I do.'

'And that's profitable for you?'

'I see a long term profit by using them, yes.'

'Very good. I also understand your line of work brings you into contact with the media, which will be useful. You will have other people from your business you can bring in to help us, and I believe you've done some amateur dramatics, which could also come in handy.'

'Well the media work is one thing, but the acting was a long time ago,' Charlie admitted. In fact, he'd thoroughly enjoyed the two pantomimes he'd been involved with aged seventeen and eighteen before university. Quite how that experience would aid the execution of a betting coup was puzzling and once again, strangely enticing.

'Your brother speaks very highly of you. Having spent a little time with you, I reckon we could work together and I'm guessing this is something you would be interested in pursuing. Am I correct?'

Charlie regarded the silver bearded man at his side, with his skewed vision and that one wonky tooth, waiting patiently for a reply. Harvey turned an intelligent head toward Charlie as well, his deep brown eyes gazing dolefully up at him as if both man and dog were hanging on his answer.

'Certainly,' he stated positively. 'My only reservation would be...'

Again Sam broke in, preempting Charlie's query. 'You have my word that at no stage we will break or even bend the rules of racing. Tommy will train my horses to win and we will obey the rules each bookmaker has in place. In fact, I would imagine it's essential we follow their rules to the letter for my plan to succeed.'

'I was going to say my reservation would be handling so much stake money!'

'Ah!' said Sam, scratching his beard. 'Sorry, I do have a tendency to assume I can read people's minds from time to time. Something to do with a heightened sense of hearing, I think. It means I can jump in too early.'

'Not a problem, it's nice to know you're going to keep everything on the right side of the law. I assumed it would need to be, given your business interests.'

Sam shrugged, 'Well I don't know about that. Being involved in a large business makes me feel like a villain at times. But you'll be glad to hear that you will have as much stake money as you need, in cash if required. I will place myself entirely in your hands, should our little enterprise go ahead.'

Sam rubbed his thighs and stood, followed obediently by Harvey. 'I'll explain my requirements in more detail tomorrow. Which brings me to my final query: what are you doing in the next ten days?'

'It's happening that quickly?'

'I'm afraid the horses are ready and we need to be too.'

Charlie stood up to face Sam and pursed his lips in concentration, trying to remember what he had in his diary for the next week. Then he realised he didn't care.'

'I'll make it work,' he replied positively.

Sam held a hand out and went to pat Charlie's arm, and just about connected. 'That's grand lad. I'm staying in Inkberrow. I didn't organise it, I think it will be one of the pubs. Come and find me after breakfast and I'll run you through my thoughts on the matter.'

'So we're on then?' asked Charlie, 'An old-fashioned betting coup?'

Sam reached out, touched, then gripped the younger man's shoulder and rocked him slightly. 'We're on!' he confirmed.

Four

It was getting on for ten o'clock in the evening by the time the adults at Poppy's party finally started to head for home and the Summer household returned to normality. It was standard practice for the farmhouse to provide sleeping accommodation for at least one or two stable lads or lasses. They would make use of one of the many spare rooms and this evening's party meant a couple of owners were also staying over. This still left several bedrooms empty, so Charlie had a choice of rooms to deposit his overnight bag and the various bits of technology that accompanied him wherever he went.

He found his childhood bedroom occupied and, instead, made himself at home in a large double room next door. He couldn't help firing up his laptop as soon as he was in there and taking a peek at Sam Lewis's online profile. It was a bit of a shock to learn he was only thirty-seven; Charlie had assumed he was at least ten years older. It seemed time had not treated Sam Lewis well.

His current role as an executive board member of Lewis the Bakers, the largest bakery brand in Europe still in private hands, had followed a two-year stint as a Managing Director starting in 2008, during which time the company's fortunes had remained fairly static. His father, Reginald Lewis, the eighty-year-old retired founder of the company had been rumoured to be steering Lewis's during Sam's short tenure, despite his advancing years. Charlie found two lengthy interviews with Reginald Lewis, who had been an outspoken business leader in his time. One contained little substance. It was full of compliments and read like an advertorial, the second interview was quite different.

This was an independent piece by a consultant to the bakery industry in the nineties. It stopped short of calling Reginald Lewis a rogue, but Charlie was left in no doubt the author believed Sam's father to be a tyrannical business leader. The author had questioned Reginald's hard line with suppliers, unions, and even his employees. In return he'd received stark responses to some queries and a refusal to answer to the rest, however it was Reginald's condescension that had riled the writer most. A further, detailed internet search by Charlie found a couple more press reports and an illuminating article in *The Financial Times* which painted Reginald Lewis as a ruthless businessman who wasn't afraid of being disliked.

The Lewis company's current fortunes started to improve hugely in 2009 when they radically altered their range of products to satisfy the burgeoning take-away boom and started to expand their own retail base under a brand new management team.

Charlie moved on to investigate Sam's business background. He

14

was seemingly well respected and kept a relatively low profile in the business community, despite his father's notoriety. The Lewis family was listed prominently in *The Sunday Times* rich list each spring, estimated to be worth a touch over a billion. Sam had become a keen racehorse owner in the last ten years and as well as horses with Tommy, he had a number of flat horses scattered around the country.

Sam's philanthropic activities pervaded most of his reports, with mentions of his charitable donations to all manner of good causes. Charlie noted with interest that he was involved with several racing charities, including the *Retraining Of Racehorses* and *Racing Welfare,* as well as two of the biggest charities who helped people deal with depression. However, this was the tip of the iceberg, as the latest reports were all about his significant donations to several sight loss charities, both on the medical research side and those providing hands-on help to those afflicted. Charlie considered Sam's charitable activity. The sums were impressive; fifty thousand here, twenty-five thousand there… but compared to his income and net worth, these amounts were very small beer. Charlie felt a cold wave of self-righteousness pass over him and he closed his eyes tight and reprimanded himself. He'd worked on several projects with major charities in recent years, developing a jaundiced view of the sector, believing them to be quite cutthroat and morally questionable when it came to their methods of attracting donations. He shouldn't paint Sam with the same brush. The man had seemed genuine, and his donations were sizeable, despite looking distinctly like tax write-offs to Charlie's suspicious mind.

His Wikipedia entry, an adjunct to his father's, told Charlie that Sam had lost his eyesight suddenly at the age of eight, was unmarried, and lost his mother, a bipolar sufferer, to suicide a dozen years ago. Tragically, his brother had died in a car accident two years ago, aged thirty-two. It seemed the Lewis family had seen its fair share of bad luck during the same period their business had soared to new heights.

After half an hour of web surfing Charlie jumped down the stairs two at a time, as he had done throughout his childhood, and went in search of Tommy or Laura in the kitchen. In his experience this was always the first place to look for a trainer. He found Laura busy making homemade hot chocolate for her houseguests, and the sounds of Tommy pouring the last set of merry party guests out of the front door and into waiting taxis reached him from the other side of the house.

'Is the birthday girl in bed yet?'

Laura smiled and stifled a yawn, 'Oh yes, she was shattered.'

'I'm guessing you're a bit sleepy too?' Charlie said as he rescued a pan of milk off the oven ring just before it boiled over.

'Go sit down,' he instructed, 'You look like the walking dead, I'll make the chocolate,' he added, busying himself with mugs, spoons, and chocolate powder.

Tommy joined them and one by one, the houseguests and staff all gave their compliments to their hosts and headed to bed. Laura sat with her husband and Charlie for a few minutes, quickly realised they wanted to be alone and told Tommy not to take too long as she too climbed the stairs.

'Come on then,' Tommy said across the kitchen table once the brothers were alone. 'You've got that twinkle in your eye Charlie. Let's have it, spill the beans.'

'Do you know what Sam is planning?' Charlie asked.

Tommy shook his head. 'Beyond the fact that I have two horses of his which have decent chances of winning races in the next week or so, no.'

'So why did you recommend me, and why no warning?'

'Yeah, not so sure on that either. Sam asked about you months ago, I thought he was just being friendly, y'know trying to show an interest.'

Tommy gave an expressive yawn before continuing, 'He called me a few days ago and wanted to know more about you, and then asked if he could meet you at the yard. So I invited him to the party.'

'And the reason for keeping me in the dark?' Charlie queried. He could see his brother was tired, reddening eyes were the giveaway, but he needed a few answers.

'Oh right, yeah. Sam asked me not warn you who he was because he didn't want you to judge him on his background. I guess he's that rich, some people might find it difficult to see beyond the pound signs. So what has he asked you to do for him?'

Charlie frowned. 'Help him with a coup, so he says. We're meeting again tomorrow. I think tonight was more of an interview, to see if I'd fit the bill.'

'You know I can't be involved, apart from getting the horses ready to race,' Tommy stated earnestly.

'Yeah, don't worry. I somehow don't think it's going to be the sort of venture which strays into criminality. He made that very clear.'

'Yep, that sounds like Sam,' Tommy said through another yawn. 'It's always by the book all the way with him.'

'I assume he's a good payer?'

'Always bang on the nail. Wish I had a few more like him.'

Charlie was out of questions. He pondered the possible reason a man worth a billion could have for pulling off a coup which might net him a few tens of thousands, possibly a hundred thousand if his bet was big enough. On the other side of the kitchen table he caught his brother's chin slowly dropping to his chest and his eyes closing.

'Does he like a bet?' Charlie asked, rapping the top of the table with his knuckles to wake his slumbering interviewee.

Tommy sat bolt upright and his eyes flashed open. He grimaced once he caught the scampish look his brother was giving him.

16

'No, Sam's never spoken about betting and I've never seen him checking odds or having a bet at the races. I think he loves the animals for what they are. Never just dumps them: they always go for retraining.'

'Okay, Tommy,' said Charlie, smiling at his brother's inability to keep his eyes open. 'Go on, get to bed. You've got runners tomorrow?'

'Two at Chepstow, if the meeting is still on,' he replied tiredly, pushing his chair beneath the table.

'Thanks, Tommy,' Charlie called after him. He received an amiable grunt and dismissive wave from his twin as he left the room.

Five

Charlie walked into The Old Bull, his own preferred pub in Inkberrow, at nine thirty on Saturday morning and was unable to find any trace of Sam Lewis. It took a phone call to Tommy in order to work out that Sam's 'local pub' was in fact The Grove, a five star hotel and country club a little way out of the village. Sure enough, he found Sam sitting in one of the huge high-backed leather chairs in the expansive foyer of The Grove a few minutes later. Sam struggled ungainly to his feet as Charlie crossed the ornately inlaid marble floor of the foyer.

'Charlie, good to meet you again,' he said in greeting, Harvey at his side once more, 'I've booked a room for us, so we can discuss the er... project without being overheard. It's called the Gretton Room, perhaps you can lead the way?'

It must be my shoes, thought Charlie as he followed the highly polished brass signs to the Gretton Room. Sam must have recognised my steps on the marble, or can he see more than I'm giving him credit for?

The room turned out to be a good-sized ground floor suite with a view onto the golf course though a large set of patio doors. Fresh coffee and pastries were waiting for them, set upon a Victorian table, and two armchairs, as was a chalkboard, flipchart, and instructions for accessing the WiFi. Charlie set up his laptop, poured coffees and the two of them settled in. Sam let Harvey out of his harness and the German Shepherd poodled around a little before eventually stretching out on a piece of carpet catching the weak winter sun, no more than a few feet from Sam.

They endured a minute of small talk before Sam cut it short.

'Perhaps if I run through my little plan and we can get on to the main event,' he suggested. Charlie detected a hint of glee and smiled inwardly as he felt the same butterflies of excitement in his own stomach.

'Of course, I'm keen to find out what you have in mind.'

'I told you last night there were two horses your brother has ready for me, well that's only half the story really. I've actually got three horses which should win next time out...'

'Really! Three?' Charlie blurted, 'Will they all run on the same day?'

'No, no. I think that's one of the issues I'll need your help with. You'll quickly realise I know *about* betting, but I'm not a betting man. I love my horses and especially enjoy watching... well, *listening* to them race: however I've never needed the extra excitement a bet generates... until now.'

'Perhaps we can put names and dates to these horses?' Charlie asked, getting up from his chair and crossing to the flip chart. 'I hope you don't mind, but I tend to work best when I write things on walls.'

18

'Whatever works for you Charlie. However, bear in mind it will all be just a blur to me. I can see a little in the distance, but this close I have to work from sound.'

'Understood. So where do we start?'

'My aim is to win around one hundred million pounds, half of which I want to win from one bookmaker in particular,' Sam stated in a steady voice.

Charlie's jaw dropped open. He had been standing, marker pen at the ready and now was a statue of astonishment.

'Problem?' Sam ventured, a slight curl of his mouth hinting at possible amusement, or was it a query over the resounding silence his announcement had elicited.

'Erm… well, that's a very significant amount, Sam. To my knowledge the largest sum ever paid by a bookmaker…'

'Ah yes, the maximum payout, so what's that?' Sam broke in.

Charlie hesitated, ordering the words in his head to make his statement as clear as possible. It seemed Sam really didn't know anything about the world of betting.

'In theory most bookmakers allow a maximum win of one million pounds per customer, per day.'

Charlie paused, allowing this information to permeate before he continued. 'That's not your only problem. You'd need to stake tens of millions to win that sort of cash, and I doubt there's a bookmaker in Britain who would accept such a bet.'

Charlie watched as Sam's upturned face crumbled from a look of excited anticipation to one of disappointment.

'It would mean approaching each bookmaker one by one. You'd have to request specific odds for each horse, which means your bet would be shot down before you started… every bookmaker would slash their price to virtually nothing.'

Silence descended on the room as they both considered the reality of the situation, Sam staring toward one of the walls from his armchair and Charlie, with a hand rubbing the back of his neck, inspecting the paisley design on the carpet. It seemed to Charlie, the fun was about to be squeezed out of the adventure before it had even begun.

Sam cleared his throat. 'Come and sit down, Charlie. I need to tell you a story.' From being buoyant and engaged, the older man suddenly appeared tired, and quite possibly, defeated. Charlie thought he looked smaller in his chair, more vulnerable, and tried to lighten the atmosphere with a bright acknowledgement which he realised didn't quite hit the mark.

'I've no doubt you've looked me up on the internet and you're well aware of my background and the extent of my family's wealth?'

Charlie found himself nodding and produced a quiet 'Yes,' when he realised Sam wouldn't be able to process the usual gestures which act as the grease to a conversation. He made a mental note to try and be as vocal as possible.

'I had a brother,' continued Sam, 'My younger brother Laurie died when he was thirty two, just over two years ago. He'd been running the family company for about ten years before he died.'

Charlie found himself frowning. The brother, Laurie, was hardly referenced in the pages he'd read on the internet the previous night. He could kick himself. It was always dangerous to believe everything you read on the internet. He should have known better.

'My brother was a brilliant businessman, just like my father,' said Sam sadly, 'Truth be told, I struggled when I took over from my father, but Laurie breathed new life into the company. He took over after me, we didn't make it public. He preferred it that way. He recruited a new team of people, and developed the business into a modern retailer, rather than just a producer of bread. His only small vice was that, like me, he loved horses and the races. He'd always been conservative in his betting, more of an enthusiast really. That's until he met Mick Kowalski.'

'You mean Michael Kowalski from BetMick?' Charlie queried.

'Ha, he wasn't *Michael* in those days,' snorted Sam, his fingernails biting into the leather arms of his chair as he spoke.

'Mick Kowalski was nothing more than a small time Newcastle bookie with a spit and sawdust betting shop in a rough area of the city, until he met my brother.'

Sam's bottom lip trembled slightly and Charlie detected a sense of rigidity in him. He sat motionless beside Sam, not wishing to stem his flow.

'They started going racing together and before too long they were inseparable. Laurie learned the bookmaking business and helped Mick take over a couple of failing betting shops in the city and got him going on the internet, just as online betting was starting to take off,' Sam paused to lick his lips, as if something distasteful had crossed them.

'Mick Kowalski has a reputation for inviting potential high rollers to his fancy private boxes at the big race meetings, where he encourages them to gamble, giving them bonuses or bigger odds, all designed to tip them into chasing their losses. My father and I believe this is what happened to Laurie. Our father set trusts up for both of us and once Mick Kowalski got his hooks into my brother, we're sure he bled Laurie's trust fund dry. He took Laurie for a couple of million,' Sam stated bitterly, squirming in his chair, the mere description of the man proving powerful enough to create a negative physical response.

Sam took a sharp intake of breath. 'It shredded his dignity and eventually killed him,' Sam said quietly as he exhaled. He leaned back in his chair and released his grip on the arms, seeming to crumple into the back of his chair. Harvey lifted his head from his mid-morning slumber and lazily regarded Sam for a few seconds before settling his chin back onto the carpet, apparently appeased by what he saw.

'Mick Kowalski is still doing this. In fact, I understand he employs a group of people whose only job is to identify, recruit and then financially ruin people, and I have evidence that they adopt tactics which aren't just unethical, but border on criminal.'

'Are you sure?' Charlie queried seriously, 'I thought the gambling commission seized upon anything like that?'

'Hah, I wish!' Sam spat contemptuously, losing his composure and populating his laughter lines with a grimace. 'I reported him and the authorities found nothing. They said there was no case to answer. It was just a whitewash.'

Charlie shook his head. He knew Tommy was closely scrutinised, both in his yard and at the races. If any member of staff stepped out of line on the racetrack a fine would land on Tommy's doorstep. Racing was so keenly administered you could be punished just for waving your arms at a horse in order to encourage it to go to the start. The integrity team at the British Racing Authority was considered essential to keep racing straight, yet it caused trainers no end of work and headaches. Charlie considered - perhaps this relationship was as it should be. However it seemed apparent that individuals with gambling addictions weren't being protected from dishonest bookmakers with the same fervour.

Sam rubbed the top of his head with flat hands and eyes closed, his mind filling with memories of his brother; his warmth, brilliance and also his fragility. His own personal regret bubbled to the surface too. His head rubbing turned to scratching, reducing his perfectly combed silvery hair to an unkempt mess. Finally he dropped his hands into his lap and cast a glance in Charlie's direction. From Charlie's point of view this gaze appeared to fly a few feet over his left shoulder. The older man sighed long and low before he coughed, sat upright, and seemingly emerged from his funk.

'I was hoping to serve Mick Kowalski with a body blow to his business, or at least dent his confidence and bank balance enough to reduce the impact he has on people like my brother. It's taken over two years for this opportunity to arise, now it looks like it won't be possible,' he lamented in his gentle Geordie drawl.

Charlie cupped his chin in his hand and tapped his cheek with a finger, considering.

'You said there was a third horse?'

'Ach, yes. I've a four-year-old miler who I'm told is going well enough to start the season in the Lincoln Handicap at Doncaster. He should go very close according to Joss Faraday, his trainer,' Sam confirmed. 'However he won't race until the very end of March, about four days after the other two.'

21

'Are the two with Tommy both expected to race at the same meeting on the same day?'

Sam looked bemused for a few seconds, finally crumpling his face in thought before replying, 'Market Rasen for both of them...' He didn't sound sure though, his statement ending with an upward inflection which Charlie took as a question rather than a certainty.

'I'm pretty sure, but you'll have to check with your brother,' Sam added.

Charlie made a note on his laptop whilst nodding, caught himself, realised his mistake and replied, 'Yes, I will.'

'It's not about the money, it really isn't,' Sam insisted as Charlie continued to tap on his keyboard.'

'Mmm...' muttered Charlie, still typing. He looked up from his computer and asked, 'I'm guessing you want to win fifty million from BetMick?' he asked.

'It's the size of the working capital and deposits BetMick has reported in their accounts. If he had to pay out that sort of sum, his business would be severely restricted.'

Despite being heir to a fortune and wealthy in his own right, Charlie had a good feeling Sam Lewis had a healthy disregard for the trappings of wealth. Whilst a modicum of revenge formed part of his reason for pulling off a coup, his wish to protect future potential victims of Mick Kowalski came across as being far more important to him. Sam was quirky for sure; especially when discussing Mick Kowalski, however he struck Charlie as incredibly centred, given he'd been born into a life of privilege.

He closed his laptop and assessed the man seated a few yards from him, his guide dog asleep at his feet. He needed to apply serious thought to this situation, there had to be an angle which could at least deliver some of what Sam was aiming for.

'Do you need some time to think about it?' Sam asked evenly.

Charlie couldn't help but laugh. 'You're going to have to stop doing that, Sam,' he scolded happily. 'You seem to know exactly what I'm thinking!'

'It's one of the benefits of being almost blind!' said Sam, smiling broadly, losing the grimness which had gripped him moments before.

The atmosphere lightened and Charlie watched the laughter lines deepen on Sam's face. Harvey lifted his head once more, checked out Sam and once he was satisfied, sent a snort whistling down his nose. Stretching out on the carpet, he ensured as much of him as possible was in the sun, whilst maintaining contact with Sam's boot with one of his toes.

****

Charlie left Sam at the country club, with a promise to return later that evening. Sam was due to leave for Newcastle on Sunday morning, so any plan needed to be agreed within the next twenty-four hours. To make this deadline he had to speak with Tommy, and also needed time to conduct further research and consider the options.

He got back to Middle Bouts Farm, the home of Tommy Summer Training, a few minutes after midday. A few stable staff milled around the yard, finishing off morning stables. Charlie acknowledged them with a wave as he crossed from the hay store to the house. His breath condensed in the freezing conditions; however, the spots of snow in the orchard from the night before were noticeably smaller. The yard had an empty feel to it as horses relaxed at the back of their boxes. He reasoned that a good proportion of the staff would have left for the races. Tommy was fielding three runners at two different meetings.

He found the farmhouse deserted apart from one of Tommy's older stable lasses making a coffee. She quickly disappeared, so he set up his laptop in the kitchen and went to work.

He accessed the *Racing Post* website and checked on Tommy's declarations and quickly found the two horses owned by Sam. As he had thought, they held entries in two races at Market Rasen on Wednesday March 27th; only four days away. The first was Jumble Sale, the gelding Sam had petted the night before. He was a twice-raced five-year-old novice hurdler who had finished mid-division on both attempts. His entry was in a two mile novice hurdle race at the start of the card. The second was an eight-year-old mare with a racing name of Loafing Around. She was similarly unexposed, despite her age. She looked as though she must have had problems as a younger horse, having been off the track for eighteen months and only raced the odd once or twice each season before that. However, her form prior to her layoff was a fourth and a third in maiden races. She was in a chase race over two and a half miles, the last race on Market Rasen's afternoon card. There were plenty of entries in both races, over twenty in each, so a full complement of ten to fourteen runners could be expected to declare on the Tuesday, the day before the race.

Satisfied he had enough on both Sam's National Hunt horses, Charlie searched for the Lincoln entries. Due to be run at Doncaster on March 30th, only three days after the other two, the Lincoln was one of the oldest handicaps in the racing calendar, and a major betting race. He found the list of entered horses and searched for the Faraday runner. There was only one in there, and it belonged to Sam. Cool Blue was his name and turned out to be a four-year-old with half a dozen runs under his belt and two wins. His form had tailed off hugely in the middle of his three-year-old season. He was rated toward the bottom of the huge set of declarations, and just on the cusp of the likely cut-off from his official rating of ninety-six. It looked touch and go whether he would get a run, but if he did make it into

23

the line-up of twenty-two horses, he'd be carrying a low weight.

Having made copious notes on his laptop regarding Cool Blue, Jumble Sale, and Loafing Around, Charlie started new searches on Sam Lewis, his brother Laurie Lewis, Michael Kowalski and BetMick. He then spent time visiting each of the major bookmakers' websites and finally made a few phone calls. It was three o'clock when he closed his laptop, and realised his stomach was rumbling. He rummaged around the kitchen and found a few slices of bread, butter and an apple and took them upstairs to his bedroom.

After polishing off the bread and butter, Charlie lay on his bed crunching on his Granny Smith, staring at the familiar wallpapered ceiling and woodchip walls. Every now and again he would lift an arm, point a finger and draw imaginary figures in the air, letting out tiny exclamations or snorts of disgust until finally, an hour after lying down, a smile extended across his lips and he clenched both hands in fists, mouthing a silent, 'Yes'.

Moments later Charlie became aware Laura was calling his name from the foot of the stairs. A quick glance at his mobile phone revealed it was four thirty.

'Yes?' he shouted down from the landing.

Laura was leant up against the bottom rung of the stairs and gazing hopefully up at her brother in law when he appeared on the landing above.

'Ah, I thought you were in. I've got a few people around, do you fancy a cuppa?' Her words sounded slightly strained and she rolled her eyes and pulled her face to one side as she gazed upwards.

Charlie recognised the request: this was Laura asking if he would come down and help her entertain. A few owners must have pitched up unannounced and she wanted a bit of help keeping the conversation going.

'Sure, down in a second,' he promised enthusiastically, indicating with a thumbs up that he'd understood the subtext.

When he entered the kitchen a minute later he was surprised to find a gaggle of elderly women pitching in to help make teas and coffees. Most were well-dressed country types in their late fifties and Charlie noticed there was a liberal use of scarves and sensible shoes. Laura was doing her best to maintain her patience as two of the five elderly ladies were jostling her, and each other, in an attempt to provide unwanted coffee making assistance.

'Ah, here's Charlie,' Laura told the group, relief showing in her voice. 'He's the man responsible for that supermarket advert on television with the Dachshund puppy. All the ladies turned their faces up to greet him and a couple let out a cooing noise.

'Good afternoon, ladies,' Charlie offered to the group and received a number of appraising looks up and down and beaming smiles in return.

'Charlie is here visiting for a few days, but I'm sure he'd love to tell you about all the famous people he works with,' prompted Laura.

Charlie slid into a chair around the table and went to work, charming, winning over, and holding the interest of the group. He was good it. Charm came easily to him. He soon discovered this was a delegation from the local Women's Institute, hoping to secure free use of one of Tommy's grass paddocks for a flower and produce show in the summer. However, he had been mistaken in assuming all the ladies were elderly. Leading the little clan was a vicar from Inkberrow, a lady called Sharon Stone. Charlie had tried not to react when he learned the twenty-something's name; however, a flicker of recognition must have escaped as the buxom clergywoman flashed him a smile and as an aside quietly assured him she was no relation to the actress. Sharon's ability to laugh at herself shone through and Charlie found himself enjoying her company. The Rubenesque, blonde bobbed vicar turned out to be great fun and he thought she'd make a pretty decent advert for the Church of England should they ever be in need of one. The two of them sparked off each other, much to the delight of the older people around the kitchen table who swapped knowing glances and exchanged a few playful nudges.

The next half an hour flew by, as Charlie entertained and was equally engaged by the four ladies and the vicar, almost forgetting he had an appointment to keep with Sam Lewis back at the country club. It was early evening when Tommy walked in, buoyed by a winner at Bangor earlier in the afternoon and he soon agreed to the delegation's requirements in June. It was as the group were heading out the back door and making their way towards their cars that Charlie struck upon an idea and caught the vicar before she left, asking a question. Having provided a succinct reply Sharon peered up into Charlie's face with a troubled expression.

'Why would you want to know if a vicar is allowed to gamble?'

Charlie gave a slightly embarrassed grin. 'Oh, you know, just one of those things I've always wanted to ask a vicar, but I've never had the opportunity.'

'So why do I get the impression there is more to it?' she pressed, displaying an inquiring raised eyebrow. 'You seemed rather pleased with the answer.'

Disarmed and also a little fascinated by her directness, Charlie admitted he was indeed rather pleased with her answer.

'I will certainly be in touch with you should your revelation help deliver the result I'm looking for,' he told her, his tongue firmly planted in his cheek.

'Oh, I don't think you could count me as a revelation,' she countered before jumping into the passenger seat of the waiting car. Charlie watched her car reverse and trundle down the drive before heading toward Inkberrow, all the while wondering whether there had been an element of coyness in Sharon's parting comment.

Six

Charlie got back to the country club just after seven o'clock and found Sam and Harvey still occupying their private room. It was as if the man and his dog hadn't moved since he'd left them there hours earlier. Sam looked around when Charlie entered and once again called to him.

'Charlie, good to have you back lad. Ha'way, sit down. Did your few hours of contemplation provide us with any headway?'

Charlie would normally have raised an eyebrow and shot Sam an encouraging look, but he was starting to get used to altering his communication for the virtually blind man.

'Hi, Sam,' he answered quickly as he walked down the room toward him, putting aside his heightened curiosity as to how Sam had managed to identify him by the way he had entered the room. 'I do think I could have a possible solution to the sum of money you are trying to win, and the person you are trying to win most of it from, but you'll need to agree with the method I'm going to suggest to achieve it.'

'Ah! So you have a solution?'

'Mmm… I think so.'

'Oh dear, you don't sound so sure. We won't be breaking any rules will we?'

'Break, no. In fact, I want to use some of the bookmakers own rules to bend things to our own advantage.'

'Come on then, explain how you can do it,' Sam demanded. A tinge of excitement gave his voice a slightly wavering quality.

This excitement transferred itself to Charlie. He didn't bother to sit down and instead crossed over to where the flipchart was still standing displaying a blank page.

'Can you see any of this?' Charlie asked, after he'd written 'The Bet' at the top of the page in large capital letters.

Sam cocked his head to one side and leaned back in his chair. 'Maybe, I've got to sort of squint and see it out of the corner of my eye… Nope, I'm sorry, it's just a grey smudge. It's far too close.'

'No need to worry, I'll explain as clearly as I can. The writing is for me really. I work best with a pen in my hand.'

Sam shrugged, offered a nod, and so Charlie continued.

'There are three horses, two racing next Wednesday, the 27th of March. They are Jumble Sale and Loafing Around. Then you have Cool Blue's entry in the Lincoln, on Saturday 30th at Doncaster.

Charlie created a list and then returned to write odds of 12/1 and 20/1 against the first two horses. Then he wrote odds of 66/1 against the third. He repeated aloud each of the horse's names and prices for the benefit of Sam, adding a warning that he was only providing educated guesses at what the prices of the horses would be on the day of each race.

'The good news is that Cool Blue runs in a big race where the betting is already available, a week ahead. He would be an *antepost* selection. That means we can place him in the same bet as the other two,' Charlie explained, adding a line between the three horses to link them.

'However, there is a bigger issue,' he added.

'The maximum an individual punter can win from most bookmakers when betting on horse racing in one day is one million pounds. Virtually every single bookmaker has this written into their rules, which are displayed inside every betting shop in the country,' Charlie informed Sam, whose brow was furrowed in concentration. 'More importantly, every bookmaker's rules state that if there is a group of customers acting together who have backed the same combination of selections, and therefore colluded, they will refuse to pay out.'

Sam slumped in his chair and bit his lip on hearing this news. 'Well lad, that sinks us doesn't it? As soon as the bookies see the three horses on different betting slips, they'll refuse to pay.'

'Yes… and no.'

Sam let out a laugh. 'Your brother said you always have an answer, and he was right by the sound of it. Come on then, hit me with the big idea.'

Charlie wondered for a second how much his brother had let slip about him, but quickly pushed the thought away. 'Yes, Tommy's probably right. I don't like to be beaten by the system!'

For the next hour Charlie and Sam discussed, argued, agreed, and laughed. As their conversation developed, so did the excitement in both men until Charlie reached his fifth page on the flip chart. He underlined the words '*Shame them into paying*' which he'd written in capitals. After a short explanation Sam let out a squeal and slapped his thigh so enthusiastically, Harvey jumped to his feet, wagging his tail and barking.

The two men parted at eight o'clock in the evening with a promise to meet again at Market Rasen the following Wednesday. Just as Charlie was turning to walk back to his car outside the country club, Sam called him back, asked him to wait, and took a mobile phone from his pocket. It had large, easy to push buttons and a voice command facility. Thirty seconds later a smartly dressed man came out of the country club and handed Sam a briefcase.

'Fifty thousand pounds in a mixture of notes,' Sam told him, handing the case to Charlie. 'If you need any more, just let me know. And make sure you charge me for your time. I don't expect professional services for nothing and I'm guessing you'll need some help.'

Struggling for words, Charlie eventually gave a weak, 'Thank you,' in reply and self-consciously crossed the car park with the case, suddenly nervous the entire hotel might be watching his every move.

Seven

Charlie winced at the sound of his tyres squealing as he took another left-handed turn at speed. He checked the time again on his dashboard clock and felt the frustration rising in him as he reached yet another set of red traffic lights on the Leeds ring road.

In his first week of commuting to work in Leeds he'd lamented about the traffic in the city to a colleague at work and had been told a story about the man who designed the original road system for the city in the sixties. After the multi-million pound project had been completed it emerged in the local press that the architect of the inner city road system hadn't been able to drive and had never passed his test. As a result Leeds was the most intricate and counter-intuitive city to navigate by car in the whole of Europe. Whether this was just an urban myth, Charlie was unsure, but just at the moment he could believe it was entirely true.

He set off again, his engine screaming in far too low a gear.

A shout of 'Next left!' came from the back seat and checking in his rearview mirror he watched as two members of his young marketing team struggling to remain upright among a significant stack of cardboard boxes.

Charlie barrelled the car around another corner and caught sight of a road sign stating, 'Leeds Central Sorting Office'. Another two left-hand turns later his executive SUV came to a grinding stop, sending one of the boxes between the seats, spilling some of its contents.

'Six twenty seven!' he snapped at the young man and woman who jumped out of the car as soon as it came to a stop. Stan Dexter and Suzie Wu, the cream of Charlie's account executives, ran across the post office car park, each carrying a large cardboard box in front of them. Meanwhile, Charlie scooped up the lost envelopes, balanced the remaining two boxes on top of each other, and leaving the doors of the car open, he too scuttled across the tarmac. Stan reached a large red door and balancing the sizeable box in-between one hand and his chin, he placed his other hand on the handle, wrenching it down, and outwards. To his relief, the door swung open.

Five minutes later Stan, Suzie, and Charlie closed their car doors and flopped back in their seats, exhausted. After ten seconds of silence Charlie rearranged himself in his seat so he could examine the two members of staff he had called upon to help him. They had worked from noon on Sunday, right through the night and up until Monday evening, surviving on coffee, takeaways, and the odd snatched nap.

'We did it. Well done you two,' he told them, tiredness taking the exclamation he'd been aiming for, out of his voice.

'Yeay!' Suzie managed in a tone which only accentuated how drained she was after only a couple of hours sleep in the last two days. A twenty-two year old university graduate, she had long black hair cut in a severe horizontal fringe and usually sported pixie perfect facial features. Just now, her eye shadow looked smudged and there was the start of dark rings under her eyes. However, she was able to produce a wry smile for Charlie's benefit.

Stan, a brilliantly analytical young man with a deadly dry sense of humour, was a little older but appeared to have aged a decade in the last day and a half. He lay slumped in his seat, unruly black hair rumpled, and his brown eyes half closed. The wrinkled bags beneath them seemed desperate to force his eyelids shut.

Stan managed a feeble, 'Yeah, thanks boss. Remind me never to pick up the phone to you on a Sunday morning again.'

He added a floppy wave of his wrist as he fought off the effects of the sudden drop in nervous energy created by the frenetic journey from the office in Shipley to the main sorting office in Leeds.

'Ah, come on, Stan. This has been your type of project,' Charlie cajoled, 'Complicated, time-sensitive, and innovative.'

He stumbled over the last few words, fatigue forcing his tongue to run them together. Stan smiled crookedly from the backseat, however once his lips parted his grin developed into a yawn. 'I'm so knackered, I can't even be bothered to poke fun at your inability to speak,' he admitted.

'Pub?' Charlie suggested half-heartedly.

There was no response from either of them. Finally Stan piped up with a quizzical, 'Bed?' and a raised eyebrow, which was received with a grudging acceptance and tired smiles from his colleagues.

It had taken half of Sunday and all Monday to pull the first phase of the coup together. Charlie had managed to convince his two best Marketing Executives to come into the Shipley office on Sunday and between the three of them they had identified over seven hundred target recipients. They had appropriated their names, postal addresses, and created an approach and offer that Charlie believed would be totally unique. The office had been empty on the Sunday when they'd got started in Charlie's first floor office. The following day their activities had garnered some interest from other staff, but by closing the blinds of his all-glass office walls, and plastering signs warning of dire retribution should anyone enter, their secret project had managed to remain pretty much a mystery to every other employee. This included Graham Sutton, Charlie's direct boss, and the Managing Director of the firm.

In their attempt to complete the whole job, they had missed the last post from their building, busy pulling the last hundred letters together. This meant seven hundred letters, each with a hand affixed stamp, had to be hand delivered direct to the sorting office in Leeds before the six-thirty deadline in the evening in order for the letters to arrive the following day, or on Wednesday, the day the first horse would race. Now that this had been achieved, there was a day to recover before Market Rasen.

Charlie drove back to the office on the outskirts of Leeds at a leisurely pace and to the sound of both his Marketing Executives snoring quietly in the back seat. After plying both of them with more strong coffee ahead of their drive home, Charlie reminded them that they needed to be in the office for ten o'clock the next day to field any telephone enquiries received as a result of their missives arriving early on Tuesday.

'I'll be doing the same,' he assured the two of them before sending them home with their windows down and the cars radios playing loudly.

He traipsed back upstairs to his office with no objective other than to ensure Sam's briefcase was safely stowed away and his door was securely locked, but heard a familiar voice calling his name once he reached the first floor.

'Ah Charlie, I'm glad I caught you. You got a minute?' asked Graham. Charlie recognised the tone, it wasn't a request, his Managing Director wouldn't take no for an answer.

'Sure, Graham,' Charlie replied in as lively a voice as he could muster, 'In my office okay?'

In fact, it did look as if Graham was just about to leave, he was wearing his suit jacket, and his coat was folded over his arm. In his other hand he held a trilby, his constant companion. Charlie led his boss into his office, which still had envelopes, scrap paper, and the strips from self-seal envelopes covering most of the surfaces, including the floor.

'Been busy I see,' Graham noted as he cast his sharp sparkling blue eyes around the office. Charlie scraped some paper off one of the chairs around a small meeting table onto the floor and offered him the seat, then did the same for himself.

'I see we have a new client, Charlie,' Graham said, eyeing the Sam Lewis company letterhead which was scattered across the low table. He lifted his gaze to lock eyes with Charlie and after a second or two of hard stare, raised a quizzical eyebrow.

'Yes, it's all been a bit of a rush, so I've not actually been able to go through the normal client acceptance procedure I'm afraid.'

'Oh, I'm not worried about that,' Graham said, wafting Charlie's apology away with an open palm, 'I'm more interested in who this customer is, given you've been working all the way through Sunday and Monday, apparently without sleep and behind closed doors, in order to meet what I can only assume is a tight deadline.'

The query was light enough in tone, but beneath it Charlie knew there was a serious edge. Graham was one of the shrewdest men he'd ever met and could read people and situations incredibly well. He gave his people room to work and would support them, but he did like to know what was going on in his own company. He'd recognised Charlie's abilities and propelled him up the corporate ladder with alacrity. He was indebted to Graham. He also liked him.

'It's Samuel Lewis,' Charlie said flatly.

'*The* Samuel Lewis?'

'Yep, I'm afraid so,' The son of Reginald Lewis and heir to the largest privately owned retail bakery business in the country.'

Graham's face registered a mixture of shock and amazement. He blinked a couple of times before frowning at Charlie.

'I think I can see why you've worked like a dog for the last two days, but why not get the rest of your team involved? Why not get me involved for that matter, this could be huge!'

Graham's eyes had taken on a new level of brightness to which Charlie had rarely been witness. He was gaping incredulously at Charlie.

'Ah, well now,' Charlie started, holding up a single finger, as if trying to slow his boss down, 'The matter he has asked me to manage on his behalf isn't quite standard advertising or promotional work.'

'So you have *met* Samuel Lewis?'

'Err, yes,' Charlie answered with a frown, a little thrown by the question, 'I spent most of Saturday with him.'

'You do know that Mr. Lewis rarely grants meetings or interviews related to any sort of sales pitch? Neither does his father, Reginald Lewis.'

Charlie shook his head slowly and Graham looked to the ceiling and whistled. 'I've been trying to get an audience with that man for a decade! He sees hardly anyone, yet runs one of the most profitable businesses in the country. Getting work from him is like cornering a unicorn! And you've spent a *whole day* with him!'

Graham slapped his hands on both his knees and let out a huge guffaw, taking Charlie a little by surprise. Then his boss jumped up and taking Charlie's hand, proceeded to pump it up and down.

Charlie did his best to appear as excited as Graham, however, a combination of lack of sleep and bewilderment reduced his reaction to a simple, self-deprecating shrug of his shoulders and a goofy grin.

Graham seemed not to notice, lost in his own fervour created by the prospect of having an 'in' with what could be a potentially huge new account. Charlie was quick to re-emphasise the project he was working on was outside the normal remit of a marketing and sales promotion agency, but Graham remained undeterred. He left the room still voicing his admiration for the 'win' and promised any additional help Charlie needed would be forthcoming.

Charlie leaned back into his funky plastic chair, put his feet up on the highly polished table, placed a hand over his face, and gave a frustrated groan as soon as he knew Graham was safely out of earshot.

Eight

Joss Faraday examined the well-dressed man and his expensive car rather dubiously as he approached the front gate to his stables at Coverham, just outside Middleham in the Yorkshire Dales.

It was eight-thirty on Tuesday morning, already about three hours into his working day and he didn't welcome unannounced interruptions. With only three members of staff, including him, there was enough to cram into his day without dealing with cold callers.

Charlie watched Faraday make the two hundred yard walk from his stabling block, along the right-angled dirt road which cut through grass paddocks, flush with the first green shoots of spring. He leant against the substantial wooden gate and Faraday loped athletically toward him, striding out in polo shirt, jeans and knee high riding boots.

'You selling something?' Faraday queried in a light southern Irish accent. He was young, younger than Charlie had expected, probably no more than twenty-eight years old. An inch or two smaller than Charlie, he had an angular gait which made him appear to momentarily leave the ground with every step he made towards him.

Charlie smiled and held his hand over the gate, 'No, don't worry, I'm not here to sell you anything. Apologies for not calling ahead, I'm here to have a quick word with you about your Lincoln horse, Cool Blue. My name is Charlie Summer. Sam Lewis was supposed to let you know I was coming.'

Faraday met Charlie's hand with a muck-soiled palm and shook it whilst studying his visitor with a pair of sharp, blue eyes. He reminded Charlie of the character Rodney from *Only Fools and Horses*, only a sportier and more upright version.

'Nope, not had a call. You work for Mr. Lewis?' Faraday asked, twisting a key in a padlock, removing a chain and opening the gate.

Charlie considered his answer before replying. Sam was paying his employer for his team's time, so he supposed he was working for Sam in a roundabout way, but he certainly didn't feel like his employee.

'I'm helping Sam with a few things on a short-term basis,' he said, realising how bland this sounded as soon as the words left his mouth. He quickly added, 'Don't worry, it's just a courtesy call. I'll be at Doncaster on Saturday with Sam.'

Faraday nodded, but didn't look convinced. 'You want to see the gelding then?'

'Yes, that would be great, but it's really you I wanted to meet.'

Faraday grunted an unintelligible reply and set off walking. Charlie fell into stride with him and despite being a roughly similar build to Faraday, found he was required to stride out in order to keep pace with the younger man.

It emerged that Faraday's yard was a parcel of land and stables which had been split off from a bigger training centre. As they approached the building he explained to Charlie that originally the huddle of buildings and farmhouses had all been part of the David Hellis yard, which had been one of the top northern flat yards in the late fifties and sixties.

'There's a hundred and thirty boxes all together,' Faraday explained. 'It's split three ways now, and I have twenty boxes, with fourteen horses in at the moment.'

The stables were in decent enough condition, but old-fashioned and worn. The horses were housed in two stone built lines of stables, set at right angles to each other, complete with red tiled roofs. A cobbled area, with a small drainage channel cut into it, lay outside each stable door and everywhere Charlie looked there was evidence of decades of mismatched repair work. It was very different to Tommy's recently upgraded, modern yard back in the Midlands. Charlie couldn't help feeling the whole place jarred somewhat with what he imagined Sam Lewis would demand from a training establishment.

Faraday caught sight of Charlie's less than impressed look, tightened his jaw and crossed his arms.

'It's not perfect, I know that, but old Mrs. Hellis gives me a fair rate per stable and I've trained plenty of winners from here since I started last season,' he stated defensively, 'The horses are well treated and we've got the best set of gallops in the country over that hill.'

Charlie turned and saw resolute determination in Faraday's eyes and was immediately disappointed in himself for having judged the young trainer on the state of his stables.

'I may not have all the fancy equipment the big trainers in Middleham insist on having, but my horses are well looked after and win races. If you keep them fit and happy, they'll win for you. Bluey will prove that this weekend,' Faraday added scornfully.

Charlie put his hands on his hips, bowed his head, and let out an exaggerated sigh. Tilting his face back up, he locked a tired gaze on Faraday and shook his head.

'Look, I didn't come here to judge you. I've had a couple of long days and I guess I let my tiredness betray my initial feelings about the place. I just wasn't expecting a small yard. Sam doesn't strike me as the sort to support a yard of this size.'

Faraday pushed his bottom lip upwards as he assessed Charlie, eventually breaking into a grin.

'Yeah, I know what you mean, this isn't exactly millionaire's row.' He set off past Charlie and gestured for him to follow.

'I used to be an assistant trainer in the town and I looked after a four of Mr. Lewis's horses. I reckon he must have liked me, 'cos when I left to set up on my own, he sent me two of his youngsters.'

Faraday reached a stable half way down the line of boxes and picked a head collar off a nail in the wall.

'I was lucky,' he said over his shoulder as he opened the box. 'One of them was this lad.'

He kicked the bottom lock out and pulled the bolt back at the top of the half door, disappearing into the large, dark space beyond. Charlie waited and a few seconds later Faraday stepped back into the morning light ahead of an almost black gelding. The four-year old stepped lightly through the stable door, came to a halt, shivered, and snorted before turning an intelligent head toward Charlie.

'He's... impressive,' Charlie admitted, running a hand down the Cool Blue's neck.

'He's a bloody prima donna, that's what he is. Got real class, but not shown it properly on the track yet.' Faraday imparted as he picked wood shavings from the horse's mane.

'Can he win the Lincoln?'

Faraday pursed his lips, considering. 'If he gets a run, yes, I reckon so. We'll need luck with the ballot, but I'm very hopeful he's ahead of the handicapper. That's what I told Mr. Lewis.'

Faraday went on to explain that there were only twenty-two runners allowed to race in the Lincoln, even though there were sixty-four entries. Because of Cool Blue's handicap mark of ninety-six, he would need eight horses with ratings higher than his mark not to declare on Thursday, at the forty-eight hour declaration stage.

The trainer was a different person when discussing his racehorse. He relaxed and Charlie found himself enjoying the conversation. Faraday was clearly an astute and dedicated trainer, despite his tender age. However, as their conversation developed he displayed a good sense of humour combined with a touch of self-deprecation which Charlie found engaging. Starting in racing at sixteen, he'd climbed the ranks quickly, spend two years as a barn manager, and a further three as assistant trainer in a leading Middleham yard holding several hundred horses, and this small yard populated by largely moderate horses was Faraday's attempt to make it on his own. Charlie admired the man for following his dream.

'I told Mr. Lewis to buy this chap,' Faraday explained, 'He stood out at the yearling sales and happened to win on his debut the week I was leaving. Sam told me to take him with me. He's easily the best horse I've got.'

As if on cue, Cool Blue lifted a knee, stamping on the concrete surface and produced a snort and a shake of his head, his ears pricked.

'Bluey's ready,' Faraday confirmed, staring earnestly at Charlie. 'He's hopefully my golden ticket; a way to take my yard to the next level,' he added, before leading the gelding back into his stable.

'Who will ride him?' Charlie asked, pretty certain he already knew

34

the answer. The gelding had won twice last season with an apprentice jockey on board called Ben Plumber. The young lad seemed to get on with the horse well. The two runs with alternative riders had resulted in disappointment.

'Ben has been in every week to ride him out since January, so he'll get the ride. Besides, his three pounds apprentice claim will come in handy,' Faraday replied as he emerged back into the sunlight.

Faraday and Charlie continued to discuss the gelding's chances for the next ten minutes over Bluey's stable door, until two older horses walked around the corner of the drive and into the yard, fresh from breezing on the Middleham Moor gallop. Their riders, both young looking girls, dropped off their mounts and set about removing their tack and washing the horses down.

'Chelsea and Brittany,' Faraday said with a nod in their direction. 'Chelsea is due to lead Bluey up on Saturday.'

Charlie went over to the two stable lasses and introduced himself, explaining a little bit about his involvement, before returning to Faraday.

'Has Sam told you anything about what's going on this week?' Charlie ventured, 'About a bet he's planning?'

Faraday shrugged. 'I've told him Bluey's a bigger price than he should be and to back him, but that's all.'

'Well if things go to plan, you and Bluey might get a bit of attention on Saturday.

'Suits me!' Faraday chuckled, 'My yard could do with a bit of positive advertising. Besides, the horse likes any attention he can get.'

Chelsea led her mare past and into the vacant box beside Bluey. She was still wearing her riding helmet, which made her face appear almost childlike. Golden blonde curls poked out a couple of inches and over the collar of her jacket. She locked the stable door, walked over, and placed a hand on Faraday's back. Charlie clicked that the two of them were an item before the trainer provided confirmation.

He rolled his eyes toward his girlfriend, 'We're getting married in a few months. We've more than one reason for wanting Bluey to do well in the Lincoln!'

Charlie offered both of them his congratulations, guessing there was more to this story, but didn't pursue it. Instead, he thanked Faraday again, and made excuses to leave. He was a few strides up the drive when he stopped and spun around. Faraday was tidying up with a brush and looked up from his work when he noticed his visitor returning.

'Have you backed him?' Charlie called back.

'Of course we have!' Faraday shouted in response, a broad grin brightening his face, 'We took 125/1 a month ago. He's going to pay for our wedding!'

Nine

'Jeanne! Post!' bellowed her husband.

Jeanne waited, her eyes clamped shut, and her face crumpled. The front door slammed loudly, the sound reverberating around the high ceilings of the hall, through the back room, and into the kitchen, as it did every weekday morning at seven minutes past seven. The slam heralded the start of her husband's trek to the newsagent to pick up his daily paper, usually his only outing of each day.

Jeanne Stream opened her eyes slowly, searched for the right derogatory words to describe her husband's slavery to his watch, but they didn't come. She allowed the thought to drift away in the beautiful silence he had left behind him. Leaving her iPad propped up on the kitchen table displaying *The Racing Post* website, she dutifully padded out of the kitchen, across the back room, over her terracotta and blue tiled hall, passing a lifetime's worth of photos, artwork, and ornaments until she reached the ornate wooden banister. She glimpsed sight of herself in the huge, full-length Victorian mirror which hung on the wall at the bottom of the stairs and shrugged; no one looked their best before nine o'clock.

Her slippers slapped quietly on the hall tiles and as she covered the last few yards, she bit into the slice of marmalade toast she'd brought with her. Her bathrobe billowed as she approached the door, but at sixty-seven she wasn't too worried if someone caught sight of her less than flattering nightie. Holding her toast in her mouth, she scooped up the small pile of post from the floor, careful to bend at her knees. Still biting on her toast, Jeanne thumbed through the letters.

Two interested her. They were both addressed to her small charity. She tossed the other bills and junk mail onto a small mahogany occasional table and slipper flapped her way back to the kitchen.

The first was a handwritten letter from a man in Dorset, asking for advice on how to become one of her registered helpers. She was used to this; there were still people out there who shunned the immediacy of the online world. A fifty pound note fell out of the second envelope, which made her smile. She started to read the accompanying letter and frowned, then read further, and smiled again.

****

By the time Joel Barton swung his bicycle into the high street, many of the shops had already come to life. He took a quick look at his wrist and pedalled a little harder; he was late. A little way down the street he purposely splashed through a puddle before angling the bike toward a piece of flattened curb, using the pelican crossing to ramp up onto the pavement. Thirty yards later his brakes screeched as he brought the bike to a halt outside the charity shop he managed. Joel received a look of distaste

36

from a passing pedestrian he'd almost clipped on his way past, sneering insolently back at the elderly man.

Leaning his handlebars against the shop window, Joel spied the forest of mail on the floor on the other side of the glass door and groaned to himself, pushing the door back through the mass of marketing missives. He wheeled his bike over them, leaving wet tyre marks on the envelopes.

The shop should have been open a few minutes ago, so he left the door unlocked and concentrated on stowing his bike and flicking the switch on the kettle in the back of the shop. He reentered the shop to find a waspish middle-aged lady at the counter holding his letters at arm's length.

'Found these on your doormat,' she told him, smiling brightly. She deposited them on the worn wooden counter between the lollypop dispenser and a box of pencils with the charity's name emblazoned on them in gold capitals.

'Er, thanks?' Joel said, eyeing the woman balefully, before switching his gaze to the crumpled pile of paper and cellophane.

The woman didn't react to his passive-aggressive tone. Instead she gave a tight smile and turned to start browsing around the clothing area of the charity shop. Joel sifted through the post which bore the name of the huge chain of branded charity shops, for which he was a salaried manager. He binned most of the items immediately as junk mail. However, one manila coloured letter with a wet tyre tread mark running through it looked like it might be worth opening.

His intuition was correct. He quickly scanned the covering letter and checked the envelope again, delighted when a fifty pound note dropped onto the counter. He looked up to see where the pale looking woman had got to. Good, he thought, she was deep into the clothes section, sizing a jumper against herself. Joel turned his back to the shop and smiled greedily as the note was quickly tucked into his trouser pocket.

'Thank God for the little extras this job brings,' he thought as he went to make his first coffee of the day, his mood greatly improved.

***

'We've had a letter. It says it's from Samuel Lewis. There's a fifty pound note inside,' the woman related excitedly into the mouthpiece.

The phone line crackled. He was still there though; she could faintly hear his breathing. Presently, Harrison Saddington answered.

'What does it say?'

'It says we should have a bet... for our charity.'

'That's... rather intriguing.'

'What should I do?'

Saddington pondered a few moments, sighed, and responded, 'It's *so* weird, I think we should do it.'

37

Ten

Charlie arrived at Market Rasen racecourse with Suzie and Stan just before noon on Wednesday. A light breeze was filling the numerous flags dotted around the course and bright spring sunshine saw the three of them unzipping their winter coats as they wandered down from the Owners and Trainers entrance to the pre-parade ring and winners enclosure.

'When do the horses run?' asked Suzie excitedly. She was a racing novice, whereas Stan was a relatively seasoned racegoer, albeit a small stakes gambler.

Stan inspected his racecard. 'The first race is at ten past two and that's when Jumble Sale runs. Loafing Around runs in the last race of the six races, at ten past five.'

Charlie had discovered Stan's interest in racing the Sunday before. His knowledge of racing terms had come in handy when they were composing the letters. That said, he'd needed Suzie too: her input had been invaluable to make sure the letters sent on Sam's behalf could be understood by every recipient, regardless of their knowledge of the intricacies of racing.

'I should know the times of the races, shouldn't I?' Suzie admitted, 'I must have printed the horse names and times of the races out hundreds of times.'

'Don't remind me. My fingers are still blistered from all that keyboard work,' moaned Stan, flashing Suzie a cheeky smile.

The three workmates leant up against the white plastic railings of the pre-parade ring for a couple of minutes and took in the sights and smells of the racecourse as it readied itself for the six races that afternoon. A couple of fast food vans up against the back of the stands made the air taste of fried oil as the breeze swirled around, and in the background the burble of two male voices running through the card and giving their selections over the public address system produced a feeling of anticipation.

Charlie's mobile phone tingled an alert in his pocket, instantly killing the atmosphere. He checked the incoming text message.

'Come on then,' he prompted, 'It's time to meet the client.'

Charlie led his two young staff members off toward the grandstand and once inside, he guided them up several flights of stairs until they were halted by a member of the racecourse staff who insisted on checking their badges before allowing them to enter a corridor with doors evenly spaced apart. Each door had a small nameplate inserted into a metal frame in the middle of the door. Charlie checked each in turn before finding what he was looking for and nodding back at Stan and Suzie. He gave a small knock and pushed the door open a crack.

A voice from inside called Charlie's name and the three of them entered a spacious private box containing one man and his dog. Sam looked his usual, well turned out self, wearing a grey suit while Harvey sported a set of high-visibility straps and handles.

'Charlie, come in and join me,' Sam said in a friendly, welcoming voice. 'Oh, and I am pleased. It sounds like you have one or two others with you to enjoy the action?'

Charlie waved his two members of staff into Sam's private box for the day, a square room with blank, painted walls and a low ceiling. It was furnished with a couple of round tables covered in white tablecloths, each with a modest centrepiece consisting of a small vase of flowers. Sam was seated at one of the tables along with Harvey, who was sitting by his side, his tongue lolling out. Sam opened his eyes wide and stared meaningfully in the direction of Suzie and Stan. Suzie read his request and immediately introduced herself, before bobbing down to give Harvey a pat and a scratch. Stan did the same introduction but kept his distance from the dog. Suzie's efforts with Harvey were rewarded a few seconds later when the German Shepherd's back leg started involuntarily slapping the ground in delight as she scratched him behind his ear.

Sam crackled with a throaty chuckle. 'You must have the special touch! You're an animal lover?'

'Absolutely, we've three dogs at home, all re-homed greyhounds,' she answered enthusiastically.

'Well in that case would you accompany me down to the stables to meet Jumble Sale in a few minutes time ahead of his race?' Sam asked. Suzie glanced over to Charlie, seeking guidance. He answered her unspoken query with a little nod and she quickly accepted Sam's offer with an excited wavering in her voice.

'Before you disappear, I need to update you on the betting situation, Sam,' said Charlie, pulling a chair out from under the table. He beckoned for Suzie and Stan to do the same. The wide smile fell from Sam's face and he adopted a serious expression.

'We managed to despatch seven hundred and fifty two letters on Monday, all of which should have been delivered yesterday, or this morning at the latest,' Charlie reported. 'Each letter contained a fifty pound note, a covering letter with an explanation, and the instructions for the bet. I've checked the odds every thirty minutes this morning and so far there's been no major change in the predicted prices of any of the four horses. Now, that either means none of the bookmakers have registered the bet as being of any consequence, or only a few of the bets have been placed.'

Charlie paused for a few seconds. 'We have to hope that it's the former reason and not the latter.'

Sam pursed his lips and cocked his head slightly to one side. 'I think the three of you did a fine job given the time constraints. And I think your solution to my, er… volume issue was inspired. Hopefully the people receiving your letters will act accordingly.'

'Well, it's done now. We have to sit back and see whether the horses can deliver their part of the bargain. For now, it's over to my brother – the pressure is on him!'

Stan had been silent to this point, but was now clearly bursting to say something, leaning over the table and flicking his eyes between Charlie and Sam. Charlie gave him an encouraging smile.

'I, well, *we* were wondering…,' he indicated Suzie with a twitch of an index finger. '…whether we could place the same bet in the manner we've encouraged everyone in the letters?' he asked.

'Sam?' queried Charlie in a tone which was clearly aimed to place the decision in the older man's hands.

Sam broke into a smile once more. 'Oh, I think we can allow another two bets to be placed. There must be a high street bookmakers' betting shop on-course.'

'How about *three* bets?' Charlie ventured.

'What, you haven't had a bet yourself?'

'It wasn't part of the plan,' Charlie pointed out with a shrug.

Sam leaned forward and dipped into his suit jacket, removing a thin leather wallet. He pulled a few notes upwards and started to rub them, before extracting three fifty pounds notes.

'There you go. I think it's only fair I provide your stake, given you three did all the work.'

Charlie knew better than to argue with a client and so the three of them humbly accepted the offer. Stan and Suzie did so in tones tinged with excited anticipation and Sam picked up on this undercurrent of fervour.

'Just promise me, win or lose, you don't allow this episode to cause you to develop a gambling habit.'

Sam's warning was delivered in a mainly good-natured manner, however, there was a serious edge to his voice which caused both Suzie and Stan to immediately provide positive assurances. Seemingly satisfied, Sam stood up, grasped Harvey's handle and the four of them set off to the stables via an on-course bookmaker.

Rather fortuitously, the on-course betting shop turned out to be a BetMick, which amused Sam no end. After consulting the racing pages pinned out on the walls Stan, Charlie, and Suzie filled out their betting slip and approached the cashier, asking for an ante-post price on the Lincoln runner. Suzie watched entranced as the lady behind the counter wrote 100/1 against the name Cool Blue and ringed it. All three of them each took a photo of the large rectangular set of betting rules behind its Perspex frame with their phones before they left.

By the time they reached the pre-parade ring it was half past one and they found Tommy with Jumble Sale and a stable lass in one of the pre-race saddling boxes. The gelding looked even more statuesque than he had in the stables a few days before and Suzie and Stan were hesitant in getting too close to the gelding who Charlie estimated was standing at about seventeen hands.

Tommy gave Sam's little group an acknowledging wave as they approached, but continued to tack up the gelding.

'Big day today, I reckon,' Tommy called as he bent under the gelding to tighten his girth, 'Don't worry about this chap, he'll do us proud.'

'No pressure Tommy,' Sam called back. 'If it doesn't go well, there won't be anyone to blame except my own, daft self for believing the best horse always wins!'

He turned to Charlie and the other two and added 'And that goes for you too. If for whatever reason things don't work out...'

'We know, Sam,' Charlie said in quiet assurance, when Sam couldn't find the right words to finish his statement. 'I think we're all just really excited to be a part of it, win or lose.'

Sam scrunched his face up, 'Yes, but I do hope we come out winning!' he exclaimed in good humour, shaking a clenched fist theatrically as he spoke.

'Okay, we're ready to go,' Tommy told Sam. The group dutifully backed away from the stall to stand on the pre-parade ring grass. The stable lass headed off toward the walkway which would mean leading Jumble Sale on a circuitous route around the other side of the racecourse to the parade ring in front of the stands. Tommy joined his owner on the walk straight down the hill, through the lines of touting independent bookmakers, and further downhill to the large Market Rasen parade ring.

Charlie looked back up to the stands and decided it was a decent sized crowd for a midweek meeting in March. The grandstand wasn't full, but it was busy enough for the track to have that essential buzz around the enclosures. That was good. If the results went their way it would help if there were a number of racegoers still around later in the day. Stan and Suzie seemed to be enjoying themselves, currently being entertained by his brother. Sam and Harvey were standing silently beside him, the latter sat looking up at his master.

About a minute passed during which the two men allowed their surroundings to fill their senses. Charlie surveyed the increasing number of runners filling the parade ring and looked out over the course and down the hill to the bottom turn, and Sam, with closed eyes, seemed to be in a state of meditation. Charlie was fascinated, eventually forced into asking a question.

'What do you see?'

Sam gave him a quizzical look, which quickly transformed into a smile of understanding.

'Seven horses are walking on a tarmac walkway, one of them has

41

no shoes on its back feet,' he began in a hushed voice, 'Tommy's telling Stan and Suzie why Jumble Sale is wearing cheek-pieces. I'm guessing there are a dozen bookmakers standing about twenty yards in front of us and there's an uneasy favourite, they keep calling the odds of several different horses as the odds flip-flop. There are a group of pigeons to my left that keep flying overhead and settling on a roof, I can hear the air going through their wings when they pass overhead and their feet make a tinny noise when they land on a steel platform. Oh, and the racecourse announcer has a slight cold.'

Charlie spun around, eying up the various items Sam had mentioned. He was impressed. Shaking his head, a smile soon broke through the astonishment his face initially displayed. He gave a low whistle.

'That's... pretty impressive,' Charlie said, hoping Sam would pick up the sensation of surprise he was experiencing.

'Not much compensation for loss of sight,' Sam pointed out flatly. 'But a heightened aural awareness seems to come with the territory.'

'So can you see the horses when they race?'

Sam shrugged and focusing over Charlie's shoulder, replied 'They are just smudges, but from about thirty yards away I can just about make out my jockey's colours. Close up, I'm useless.'

'Well we'll stay in the parade ring to watch the race, you might be able to pick them up on the course after they jump the last.'

'Sounds good,' Sam said with a nod. His expression changed and he added, 'He's here, Jumble. I can recognise his walk.'

Charlie looked up, and sure enough, Jumble Sale strode past, his feet making a loud clopping sound as his racing plates met the tarmac walkway. Charlie listened intently but couldn't discern any identifiable difference. Jumble's hooves made a noise no different to that made by any of the other eleven horses. However, the way Jumble Sale moved was clearly individual on some level, and could be picked up by Sam.

Charlie wanted to quiz Sam further, however a gaggle of brightly coloured jockeys entered the parade ring, and the opportunity was lost. Duncan Foss, Tommy's apprentice rider popped up in front of the group with a serious, workmanlike expression. He greeted everyone with a handshake and concentrated hard when Tommy gave him a few last minute reminders of how the gelding needed to be handled.

Charlie was struck with how young Duncan appeared. He'd met him a few times when returning to his family home on short visits, and found him to have a quiet, almost demure air about him. He was regarded as something of a loner in the yard. In Sam's yellow and blue silks and with his riding helmet displaying only the essential elements of his face he looked much younger than his nineteen years. Weighing in at nine stone thirteen and standing five feet seven inches tall, Duncan was the ideal shape for a jockey, finding weight management relatively easy. His riding style was still a little rough around the edges, however he'd ridden thirty-five winners during the last winter and was being touted as a serious contender for the conditional title the following year. It was his people skills that let him down and was something Tommy was trying to help Duncan improve. In the modern sport, maintaining a good working relationship with the media was essential, and providing succinct, meaningful reports after a race to owners and trainers helped ensure you retained your rides and acquired new ones. At the moment Duncan was on fire in the saddle, but a bit of a damp squib out of it.

As Charlie expected, Duncan retained a concentrated face for the two minutes he stood in the parade ring. He said very little before being spirited away by Tommy to get the leg up on Jumble Sale.

'Does it matter what odds he is?' asked Suzie as they watched the gelding cock its head upwards a few times once Duncan was on board.

'Yep, the prices are key to the success of the bets,' responded Charlie.

'I saw a bookmaker offering thirty-three to one as we walked past them into the ring,' Stan offered brightly.

'Yeah, but it's the official starting prices which matters to us today. The only price we've got guaranteed is Cool Blue in the Lincoln on Saturday, all of today's horses will get prices determined by the betting markets. The returned starting price for Jumble Sale should be over twenty to one hopefully, but we'll have to wait and see.'

Facing the track, Charlie watched Jumble Sale canter past, Duncan crouching high in the saddle. The two of them dropped to a walk and turned a sharp left before heading over the middle of the track toward the two miles start down the back straight.

'Of course, they actually have to win their races as well,' Charlie stated in a slightly downcast tone. Stan and Suzie shared a look and an amused shrug. However Sam started to chuckle and shake his head.

'Oh ye of little faith Charlie,' he managed to squeeze out between his mirth, 'You're just like your brother, you must see half-empty glasses everywhere you look.'

Suzie wasn't able to suppress a giggle, which only served to make Sam laugh out loud. The heir to a billionaire bakery business rolled from one foot to the other, swaying as he enjoyed the shared joke.

'I think I'm more nervous than the three of you put together,' Charlie complained lightly.

Tommy rejoined the four of them and they all turned to watch the large video screen which lit up the middle of the track.

'Best of luck everyone,' Charlie announced as the field of eleven kicked off and the race commentary started.

In line with his riding instructions, Duncan allowed the gelding to miss the kick and he settled Jumble Sale at the rear of the field on the inside rail as they jumped the first hurdle. He cleared the obstacle like a seasoned pro and found himself in mid-division as a result of a couple of untidy jumps from runners in front of him. Duncan had to maintain a tight rein on the gelding for a few strides to ensure he didn't clip heels. However, the runners settled and found themselves space on the run to the second hurdle and Jumble Sale sailed over with plenty of space in front of him.

As the field turned into the home straight for the first time Charlie took the opportunity to switch his line of sight to Sam. He looked well turned out in his three-piece suit, complete with a yellow and blue tie to match his racing colours. The outfit did its best to hide Sam's waistline though Charlie felt masking such bulk would be a challenge for any tailor. Sam was standing upright, his head tilted upward, as if he were examining something skyward, although his eyes were unfocussed. Facing the bottom of the course, the only indication he was engaged in the race was his grip on Harvey's harness, which he kept rolling between thumb and forefinger.

Sam managed to catch a smudge of dark blue and yellow in the corner of his eye as the eleven strong field jumped the hurdle in front of the stands. The gelding was travelling in midfield and the thin ring of sight which was left to him in one eye suddenly danced with colour as the riders lifted their mounts over the hurdle which would be the last in a circuit's time. He smiled as he became aware of his heart banging harder in his chest and the sound of hooves cutting into the ground became distant as they rounded the top turn and set off on their last lap of the racecourse.

'Do you want me to tell you what's happening to Jumble Sale,' asked a quiet female voice by Sam's side.

Sam turned toward the speaker, who spoke again before he could reply.

'I'm sorry, I should have said. It's Suzie.'

'A few little updates would be wonderful, Suzie,' Sam replied, smiling, 'The commentator has only mentioned him twice so far.'

'Oh, good. Well, he's in about sixth place on the rails at the moment. They are just about to jump another fence and… yes, he's over and passed one who didn't jump as well.'

She paused and cleared her throat, 'I'm not too good at this, I'm afraid. It's the first time at the races for me, so please forgive me if I get the racing terms wrong!'

'Don't you go worrying about that, lass,' Sam told her. 'You'll be better than the commentator, that's for sure, because you're concentrating on just the one horse, my horse.'

Suzie gave another three short reports as the field went down the back straight, delivering the news to Sam that the gelding was into fourth as they travelled two by two into the bottom turn.

44

'There's a few of the riders starting to push now,' Suzie whispered to Sam. 'They are coming around the bend and they'll be into the home straight soon.'

The commentary over the public address system announced that Jumble Sale had taken third position on his own, with the fourth placed horse starting to lose ground. Suzie stepped closer to Sam and linked her arm into his. His hand stuck into his pocket.

'Duncan is pushing him now,' she told him excitedly. 'I think there are two err... hurdles left and he's about five yards behind the front two.'

There was a roar from the crowd and Suzie reported again immediately.

'One of the leaders made a mistake at that fence, the rider got thrown up the horse's neck, but Duncan is level with the one in second now, oh, hold on... he's in second and it looks like he's about ten yards behind the leader now.'

Suzie shouted, 'Come on, Jumble Sale,' and started to hop up and down on the spot, jiggling Sam's arm out of his pocket. Grinning, Sam bellowed his own encouragement, trying to focus his one crescent of smudged sight on the last hurdle.

'He's coming up!' Suzie screamed with both hands on Sam's arm as she continued to hop excitedly from foot to foot. 'They're both over together!'

Sam caught a flash of blue and yellow on the nearside and tried to follow Jumble Sale as the gelding challenged the long-time leader up the long run-in. He seemed to be alongside the leader, but then Sam lost them both as they became unrecognisable blurs in his peripheral vision.

'He's getting there, Sam!' Suzie screamed above the sound of the public address commentary and the crowd.

Close by, another two shouts, male and guttural went up from Charlie and Stan together. Sam could see in his mind's eye the gelding pushing his nose in front. Behind them, the grandstand was in full voice too, as the favourite was run down by Jumble Sale in the last three strides.

'Duncan's pushing him still; he's level, he's going... he's won!' reported a laughing Suzie, who planted a spur of the moment kiss on Sam's cheek. The businessman dropped Harvey's harness, raised both arms in the air, gave a hoot of delight and started a little celebratory jig. Harvey looked up, cocking his head on one side as if having trouble attempting to understand his master's actions. He gave a muted whimper but was immediately comforted by Suzie who delivered a calming pat and stroked the dog's head for a few seconds, while Sam received congratulations from everyone in his little group.

'He's done that with a bit in hand,' Tommy told Sam. 'I think Duncan knew what he had under him and just did enough without showing the handicapper too much of his ability.'

45

Catching his breath after his little jig had finished, Sam eventually replied between intakes of breath, 'That's not what my apprentice commentator told me. She made it far more exciting!' Suzie, already wide-eyed, began to colour in her cheeks. As her excitement abated, Charlie got the impression she had become slightly embarrassed, perhaps due to her loss of inhibition. He was relieved when moments later, she laughed once again when Sam asked her for a final friendly hug.

Charlie beamed, delighted with the result, but also pleased to see his two account executives overtly enjoying the experience, especially Suzie. Along with Tommy, he watched as Sam, Suzie, and Stan all congratulated each other, laughing and joking. Presently they looked back to Charlie with silly grins still plastered on their faces and eyes ablaze, clearly thrilled by the experience.

He clapped his hands together, 'Come on, let's get to the winners enclosure!'

As they walked up the hill Charlie gently took Sam's arm and shared a few words with him:

'One down, three to go...'

Eleven

Mick Kowalski was doing what he did best; putting the fear of God into his betting shop staff.

Standing on the uneven West Yorkshire pavement, waiting for a pause in the traffic in order to cross the busy road, he cast a disapproving eye over the exterior of his newly acquired bookmaking shop, the third he had visited that day. He found an unannounced whistle-stop tour kept staff on their toes and it kept him in touch with the grassroots of his business. This shop had been part of a bookmaking group called 'Sutherlands'. He'd bought six of their shops which would soon be rebranded to 'BetMick'. He grimaced at the sight of the deep green façade, encrusted with road dirt, and the blanked out windows displaying ancient sporting scenes. The Sutherlands branding was way out of date, and would be the first thing to go.

He smiled inwardly. Actually, signage probably wouldn't be the first thing to go. If the staff here were anything like the shoddy excuse for cashiers he'd encountered at the first two shops, the employees would be the first casualties. Their dismissal would be closely followed by the latest BetMick makeover; new signage and a cheap internal revamp would lift the premises and deliver him the profitable customers he could then convert to his online business.

Beside him, his Commercial Director, Frank Best, shivered as another lorry thundered by, part of what seemed to be a continuous flow of heavy traffic. The fourteen-wheeler was hauling aggregates and its backdraft spewed a cutting shower of dust into their faces. It left Frank spitting specks of chalky dust from his lips and trying to blink his eyes clean. He could feel the greasy dust sticking to his gums and screwing his face up, he rolled his tongue over his teeth. Mick's eyes hardened as he watched his stumpy, balding colleague struggle. He blinked away his own dust motes and waited for Frank to regain his composure.

'What do you think of it, Frank?' Mick asked in a raised voice, indicating the betting shop on the other side of the two lanes of noisy speeding traffic. The bookmaker's was sandwiched between charity and greetings card shops, on a street which would have been full of family run retail businesses forty years ago, but now it was dominated by the same national brand names that clogged up the centre of every small British town.

Dabbing his face with a pearl white handkerchief, Frank scrunched his face up and peered over the road at the drab exterior of the premises emblazoned with an old, well-known family name in bookmaking. Frank was trained to observe and weigh. He analysed Sutherlands; he saw square footage, capital outlay, on-costs, and revenue followed by profit. However this wasn't Frank's first love; that was all things digital. A Masters in

Business Information Technology followed by ten years growing an internet software startup saw him eventually on the board of his first company. He was a techie at heart, and he'd been head hunted and offered a lucrative deal to head up the internet expansion of BetMick. Part of his role was also to ensure the bricks and mortar side of the business made money.

'One hundred and sixty square feet. It does forty-five thousand a week and should be capable of a little more with a refit. I assume an upgrade to its technology is out of the question, so we'll be pushing as many of the punters online with offers,' Frank answered in a flat, monotone drawl. He was going to continue, in order to regurgitate the demographic analysis for the catchment area but another lorry thundered past at speed and he turned away, covering his face with his forearm.

Mick remained still, the diesel fumes and road dust blowing over and around him. He allowed a contemptuous sneer to curl the side of his mouth for a moment, but wiped it from his face before Frank could spin around and look him in the eye. Frank was certainly physically soft, even vulnerable, but when it came to squeezing profit from a betting shop he was a cold-hearted, amoral wolf. These were traits Mick valued, and actively encouraged in his staff. It was also an act put on by Frank for Mick's sole benefit.

These site trips were not Frank's idea of fun. He much preferred a quiet, clean, air-conditioned office where he could sift the daily revenues, calculate the over-rounds, and control the risk. Quite apart from the fact that it was noisy, cold, and dirty outdoors, being in close proximity to Mick Kowalski for an entire day tended to make him nervous, prone to self-deprecation and bouts of frustration. He eyed Mick's large frame which seemed to loom over his five feet six inches and examined the face of his employer. Mick wasn't a looker. His chin jutted out too far, and his cold blue eyes were placed too close together. He may have had a boyish charm as a younger man, however in his late thirties Mick now exuded a hard, life-weary demeanor which wasn't helped by his coarseness. Coils of lank black hair fell unkempt from Mick's receding scalp until they lay lifelessly on his shoulders, a nod to his passion for heavy rock music. Presently Mick was gazing down at Frank with a faintly amused expression, the flattened end of his nose displaying a shock of black hairs which were twitching from contact with the road dust.

'Those trucks carrying gravel and sand will deliver our profit,' said Mick, pointing a pudgy finger vaguely up the road. 'They're building a new housing estate up on the hill there.'

Frank nodded 'Yes, the demographics are…'

'Okay, Frank,' Mick cut in, holding a hand up and then taking a half turn away from him. 'I know you've done your homework, you always do. Let's see if the staff are up to snuff. Let's hope they're better than the last two shops.'

Frank bit down on his lip and followed Mick across the road during a lull in the traffic. As he crossed two strides behind, Frank made a mental note to try to stop biting into his lip as a means of remaining silent in Mick's presence; he'd spent four hours with the man and was sure he could taste the tang of blood on his tongue.

When the reinforced door to his shop was pushed open and Mick Kowalski walked in, John Ford, the shop manager recognised him immediately. John made eye contact with Mick Kowalski and noted he was wearing his trademark black rider boots, jeans and checked shirt. These items were topped off with a heavy, expensive looking black overcoat with a high, upturned collar whose perfectly sculpted lines swept down to his calves. In conjunction with his long, straggly hair, the coat gave Mick the look of a wizard. The small man behind him had a receding hairline and wore a grey pinstriped suit, a thin raincoat and was carrying a large briefcase. He was rubbing his eyes. Kowalski appeared to be sneering as he appreciated the décor. Neither man made a move to introduce themselves. Instead, they halted at the middle of the public area of the shop and spun slowly around three-hundred and sixty degrees, mumbling a critique to each other as their eyes travelled the walls, floor and ceiling.

A minute later the two of them approached the counter. John rose and came out from behind his settling desk, taking a few steps to stand behind his sole cashier with him on this Wednesday afternoon, Linda, who was seated at the only open till on the counter.

'John Ford and Linda Fry,' Frank Best informed his boss surreptitiously as the two of them approached the counter. John caught a snatch of his accent; he sounded like a character from an episode of *'Bread'*. It was nasal, abrupt, and faintly amusing.

Mick locked eyes with Linda through the inch thick reinforced glass and asked gruffly, 'I know who you are, do you know me?'

'No love, should I?' Linda retorted in a purposefully disinterested tone. John nibbled nervously on the inside of his cheek. In her fifties, divorced and with thirty years experience of working in betting shops Linda didn't suffer fools gladly or for that matter, bullies. She fluttered a pair of false eyelashes at Kowalski and leaned forward slightly to examine him more closely with her darkly hazel eyes which matched her dyed hair. She knew full well who was standing in front of her, and wasn't in the least bit intimidated.

Mick scowled at her and his gaze switched onto John.

'Let me in,' he demanded quietly.

'I'll need to see some ID please, Mr. Kowalski.'

'So *you do* know who I am.'

'Yep, but I still need to verify your ID please,' John insisted in a pleasant tone, 'After all, it's your company's policy.'

'You realise I own the company?' growled Kowalski.

It was mid-afternoon, and despite the racing being in full flow, the shop was sparsely populated. Even so, a couple of the regular punters started to take an interest. Two men dressed in painting and decorating overalls moseyed over the worn carpet to the counter and enquired after Linda's wellbeing, whilst giving the two strangers a filthy look.

'It's okay, Cliff, this chap reckons he's Mick Kowalski, y'know, BetMick? He owns this place now and is here to find fault and sack us, if he fancies,' Linda announced matter-of-factly. She was sat on her high stool, glaring wide-eyed at Mick through the scuffed glass screen.

This made Mick smile. The jungle drums must have been banging as a result of his altercations at the other two shops earlier in the day. He produced a grin and turned his attention to the two punters.

'Don't worry, boys, I like my staff to have a bit of fire in their bellies. This one's safe as long as she doesn't get too bossy with me!'

His switch to self-deprecating humour worked, and after receiving a pacifying purse of her lips from Linda, the two punters retreated once more to the back of the shop.

Mick dug deep in the back pocket of his trousers and produced his company ID, pushing it photo first, up against the glass and glared intensely at Linda.

'That do you, *pet*?' he asked quietly.

Linda tapped a front tooth with an index finger, clearly unimpressed, and raised an eyebrow at John. He perused the photo of a younger looking Mick Kowalski for a few seconds and then moved to the corner of his little domain to unlock the staff door. He let the two men in, being sure to secure the door behind them. Then he returned to his settling desk.

Mick stood, hands on hips evaluating the shop from this new perspective. He liked a streetwise cashier with a bit of steel in them, this one would do. Even better if they were divorced and had a few kids at home; cashiers couldn't afford to walk out if they had to put food on the table. But he admired her no nonsense approach; it would keep the punters in line. The manager was young, probably twenty-two or three, bright enough to have the shop in good order and certainly capable of coping with the cosmetic changes he'd be making.

'This place is in the dark ages,' Mick informed Frank in a voice loud enough to ensure the entire shop could hear. Frank scanned the area under the counter and crossed to the shop safe.

'Am I going to find this open?' Frank asked the two members of staff in his flat monotone. John shrugged, 'I hope not,' he replied amiably, 'Isn't it a sackable offence?'

Frank smirked and bent over to grip the steel bar which operated the locking mechanism on the front of the three foot square safe. He encountered resistance, signalling the safe was indeed locked, sniffed, and straightened.

'Your figures for this week?' he enquired with a hard stare.

'Where they always are,' returned John with a wan smile. He groped under his desk and produced an A3 sized three-part form with half of it completed. He'd received two warning phone calls from other managers in the last hour, so he'd made sure everything was up to date and pleaded with Linda to be on her best behaviour, which incredibly, she was.

'Tills and cameras separate, still settling all the bets in the shop and the accounts are done by hand each night,' Mick grumbled. 'I was hoping a fresh paint job would do, but it looks like we need to spend a bit on this if it's going to deliver anything more than flat returns.'

He cast an eye around the customer area once more. 'Thank God for the fixed odds betting machines,' Mick added, gesturing to the line of three flashing boxes currently occupied by a sole punter. He sighed, 'I've seen enough if you have, Frank.'

Frank looked up from the daily accounts, surprise registering on his face.

'I was hoping to balance the accounts and have a further look around the premises to determine...'

Mick gave a deep sigh and held up a hand to silence his employee.

'I think we know what we need to do here. The place needs dragging into the twenty-first century. There's nothing else to be done at the moment. Besides, these two haven't even offered us a cup of tea.'

Behind Kowalski, Linda issued a snort of derision and crossed her legs in order to position herself with her back to him.

Kowalski slid himself along the counter and tilted his head until he was looking up at Linda, drumming his fingers on the laminate surface. 'And you lady... you better buck your ideas up or I'll have you out the door,' Kowalski added with a hint of menace.

Frank cleared his throat. The last thing he needed was another court case brought against Mick for constructive dismissal. This situation could so easily head south quickly. A cock-sure cashier baiting Mick only ever ended one way; badly.

'Okay Mick, we've another two shops to see anyway,' he grunted in acceptance and made for the door in the hope that Mick would follow.

John considered saying nothing, but youthful exuberance got the better of him. As the two men let themselves out of the staff door he called after them.

'There is one rather odd thing about today's racing, only if you're interested...'

He left the statement hanging, his head down as he continued flicking methodically through the pile of colourful betting slips heaped into a neat pile in front of him. It would be interesting to discover whether they would bother to react.

Mick Kowalski spun round and swallowed the irritation which was rising within him. 'This better be good kid.'

'It's these bets here,' he said, indicating two betting slips which were separated from his main pile. 'Take a look.'

Mick travelled the five yards back to the manager's settling desk and leant on it with both hands, examining the top bet. His long straggly black hair fell down like a string curtain to cover his face.

'Okay, so the first one's won. We just need to keep an eye on it, nothing to get worried about son.'

'Look at the second bet, it's exactly the same. Different customer. Both of them from first-time punters in here.'

Mick flipped the first betting slip over. The same four horses, instructions and staking were evident on the second betting slip.

'Okay, so it's the same bet, which isn't too strange. But the two people who put them on have never been in here before and were...' John's brow furrowed for a few seconds as he searched for the right phrase, '...quite different to normal punters,' he finished.

Frank was now peering at the bets from behind Mick's hunched back. He picked one of the slips up. 'When would you normally call this off?'

'Oh, not until the run on is capable of taking out more than two thousand. She'd need another good priced winner before I'd get worried, and the next horse to run is a favourite.'

'And the final selection must have no chance, they've taken odds of 100/1,' Frank noted, addressing his comment to Mick rather than the young manager. Mick grunted his agreement and tried to make a mental note of the horses' names on the slips.

'You'll be fine, son,' he told John. 'They've had a bit of luck with the first one at 25/1, the rest will go down. You just watch.'

'Well, we'll find out soon enough,' replied John brightly. He indicated a flat screen monitor on the wall. 'The Southwell race is just about to go off.'

Twelve

The unfamiliar jangling of nerves had started half an hour ago. Charlie reflected that his primary contribution to the betting element of this plot was rapidly approaching, and for the first time in many years he was experiencing sweat seeping into his shirt under his arms. With Jumble Sale having completed the first leg of the bet in admirable fashion an hour earlier, he was aware that if his own selection was the only one to let the bet down, it would feel like he'd failed, even though Sam had assured him of no ill feeling in such circumstances. Also, there was the depressing likelihood his brother would certainly never let him live it down.

He tried to brighten his outlook by reminding himself that the bet had needed four selections, it was the only way he could see it working the way Sam wanted. And it had required a certain type of selection. So a fourth horse had to be found and Sam had asked him to supply it.

The bet Charlie had chosen was a Lucky Fifteen, one of the most popular types of multiple bet. With the tens of thousands of lucky fifteens being placed every day, Charlie had figured theirs might go unnoticed, at least until the second or third selection had run, allowing the prices to remain on the larger side. But for the Lucky Fifteen to deliver the big money return Sam was looking for, all four horses had to win. So Charlie's selection *really did matter*.

He'd chosen a race at Southwell in the middle of the afternoon, and now there were only a few minutes to the off. Charlie watched the horses mill around behind the starting stalls on a small television screen mixed in with a bank of nine others displaying prices of several races and results from around the country. The BetMick betting shop at Market Rasen racecourse was only used on racedays, and it shared the same slightly weathered and forlorn look which characterised most on-course betting shops. Suzie was still on a high following Jumble Sale's win, chattering away with Sam who seemed to be thoroughly enjoying the spirit of excitement and intrigue the day's racing was creating. Stan remained on the fringe of the group, taking everything in; however his role would expand as the day wore on.

Charlie was paying just as much attention to the betting screen for this 3-10pm five furlong handicap at Southwell, as he was to the live pictures of the horses loading. He had spent hours that weekend, poring over the exact wording of every bookmaker's terms and conditions, both online and offline, trying to ensure he wouldn't be caught out. There had been a number of big wins from so-called coups over the last two decades and Charlie had investigated every one of them. Several had ended up going to court, with bookmakers claiming foul play and refusing to pay out.

Charlie had tried to imagine being the organiser of such a coup: planning, recruiting people to place the bets, doing dummy runs to get bookmakers to accept the bets when the coup is on, possibly all over the country. Then incredibly, the horses win and when the victorious punter arrives for his payout, the bookmakers refuse. The thought of this happening to Sam made Charlie shudder even now, which was why he'd trawled all the possible options with three horses and come to the conclusion he not only needed another horse, but that horse had to be unnamed.

As the betting flashed up with odds changes for the Southwell race, Charlie's heart started to pound a little louder. Its strident beat made him grin for a few seconds. He felt alive. His obsessive monitoring of the race betting reminded him of Suzie's query when she'd been printing the letters on that manic Sunday to Monday at the office: 'So there's a horse actually called 'Fav'?'

Stan had showed her a broad grin and explained to her that 'Fav' was shorthand for 'Favourite', which meant your selection for that race was whichever horse in the field started as the shortest starting price. It meant you were effectively selecting your horse based on what the betting market believed was the most likely winner.

'But isn't that a really vague way of choosing a winner? You could end up with a horse you don't think will win,' Suzie had questioned.

Stan had gazed thoughtfully at Suzie and added, 'And you don't know you've won until the starting prices are announced after the race has run...' After a pause, both members of his team had turned to Charlie for clarity.

'We need to have an element of sheer dumb luck thrown into the bet,' Charlie had explained, aware how brittle this argument sounded once he'd said it out loud.

This had been greeted with bewilderment from the two of them. True to form, Suzie had asked the awkward question which needed asking, and why Charlie valued her input into his projects so highly.

She crossed her arms tightly, pointed her chin, narrowed her eyes at him, and demanded, 'Why? It seems like you're throwing caution to the wind.'

Charlie had leant against his desk and thought hard before answering her, trying to ensure his explanation didn't end up confusing the matter further.

'Okay, if we only had three horses in the bet, and they were all owned by Sam Lewis, and all the bets were placed at the same time, the bookmakers could certainly challenge whether they should pay out. They've done it before, taking punters to court and successfully proving the bets were coordinated by a team of people, and timed with the intention of not allowing the bookmaker to adjust their odds. If, and it's a big if, all

54

four of our selections win, we need at least one winner the bookmakers can't claim is anything other than a pure gamble. By backing an unknown selection in our bet they will find it very difficult to argue in court they have been systematically set up.'

'I suppose there's no way all the Lucky Fifteen bets will be placed at the same time either,' Stan had pointed out.

'That's right. And apart from the last horse in the Lincoln on Saturday, Cool Blue, we're not asking for any guaranteed prices,' Charlie added.

In fact, Charlie had spent many hours analysing every race on Southwell's seven race card on Wednesday afternoon, knowing he needed to select an unnamed favourite in one of the races. The declarations for Wednesday's races had been announced at 10-45am on Monday and he'd pulled apart all seven races in search of the longest priced likely favourite which he believed would win. The result of this painstaking process, and the reason they had almost missed the post that evening, was a horse called Screaming Jimmy.

Trained in Malton, Screaming Jimmy was a consistent gelding, on the small side, but Charlie liked his attitude and felt sure this gelding was ready to run a big race. He was running into form, his speed ratings were the best in the field and he was the likely favourite. Most importantly of all, this six furlong handicap was competitive enough to ensure Screaming Jimmy's starting price would be around 7/2 or even 4/1, should he be returned the favourite.

He realised some flat racing aficionados might find a lowly heat at Southwell a rather obtuse choice of venue for such an important selection, however Charlie loved the racing on sand-based surfaces. His speed ratings had proved themselves to be a powerful tool on the artificial tracks and the change of code and type of racing provided the bet with that essential element of randomness.

The reason Charlie was feeling pinpricks of perspiration breaking out on his forehead with only a few minutes to the start of the ten past three race was due to another horse in the field being heavily backed. Screaming Jimmy had just been usurped as the favourite, contesting the top of the betting with a horse called Golden Charmer, which was trained by a yard renowned for setting up gambles.

Charlie felt slightly sick. Despite Sam's insistence that should his selection be a loser, there would be no recriminations, he was experiencing a level of nervousness which was contrary to his usual calm state. Sam had given him a free hand, so if his selection let the bet down, it could only be his own fault. Charlie scanned the betting shop screens and his heart beat harder within his chest. He purposefully breathed out slowly to try and stem the lightheadedness which was giving him the weirdest of feelings.

'So which horse are we shouting for?' piped up Suzie at his side.

'Yes, come on Charlie, give me something to shout for!' Sam pitched in.

Charlie hugged his sides and blinked to bring the monitor with the Southwell 3-10pm betting into focus once more.

Golden Charmer is currently 4/1 and Screaming Jimmy has just gone 9/2. The next horse in the betting is a horse called Dark Quest at 6/1.

'How long to the off?' asked Sam.

'Only a minute.'

'So we want Golden Charmer to win?'

'Errm…not necessarily,' Charlie replied, willing the betting to update, 'The favourite keeps changing.'

The stalls were almost loaded for the sprint. The television pictures showed the last horse behind the starting stalls being helped to join the line up by two stalls handlers. Stan and Charlie couldn't peel their eyes from the screens, while Suzie linked arms with Sam, providing him with a whispered description of what was happening. Harvey sat quietly at Sam's heel, sniffing at the floor. Two further customers were there to witness the race, although neither appeared to be particularly interested, both engrossed in the form guides pinned to the wall for the next race at Market Rasen.

'They're still trying to get the last horse into the stalls,' Suzie told Sam quietly, 'He's being a bit awkward and keeps stopping and holding his legs rigid before he gets fully into his stall.'

'Ah!' she continued a few seconds later, 'They're putting a blindfold on him now.'

Charlie, hugging himself even tighter now, glanced every few seconds between the live pictures and the betting market monitor. He watched in horror as the prices updated once more and Screaming Jimmy went out by one more point to 5/1. Golden Charmer eased to 9/2 whilst Dark Quest gained support and was in to 5/1.

'Any one of three horses could end up being the favourite. It looks like Screaming Jimmy is out of it,' he intoned grimly. He'd spoken to himself, but being at the centre of the small group, Suzie and Sam caught his prediction.

'So there *was* a horse you wanted to be favourite?' Suzie queried.

Charlie nodded, still examining the betting market and live pictures. The last horse was now being manhandled into its starting stall by no less than four of the handlers.

'Yes, I really hoped Screaming Jimmy would be favourite,' he reported sadly.

However, almost immediately his tone altered. 'Hold up, he's gone 9/2 again,' he added excitedly. 'The longer it takes to get this last horse in…'

Charlie was cut off by the sound of stalls opening and the betting shop was suddenly full of the sound of commentary from Southwell. The last horse had finally relented, entered its starting stall, and now the field was already half a furlong down the back straight, charging for the bend.

'What's the betting?' asked Sam in a slightly exasperated voice.

Suzie read off the first four in the betting to him. 'Dark Quest 9/2, Golden Charmer 9/2 and Screaming Jimmy 9/2… no, hold on, there's another number, it's in a different colour, it says 4/1.'

Charlie glanced back to the prices to check Suzie's revelation. 'Crikey, it looks like they came for him just at the off!'

'Never mind that!' Stan said, pointing a finger at the screen. 'He's still got to win it, and he's out the back at the moment.'

Suzie and Sam groaned in unison as a diminutive chestnut gelding in yellow and dark blue colours, not too dissimilar to Sam's own silks, travelled out the back of the field as the fourteen runners started to straighten up for the four furlong run to the finishing line. He was markedly smaller than most of the runners and seemed to be taking three strides to cover the same distance it took his rivals with only two. Suzie informed Sam sadly, 'Our little horse is behind I'm afraid.'

A line of three horses led and tacked over to the centre of the course, all three riders starting to push vigorously. In behind, a wall of seven horses spread out across the track.

'Screaming Jimmy is still last,' Suzie told Sam. However, this time she didn't sound so disappointed, adding: 'But the jockey isn't moving a muscle on him!'

Charlie smiled, impressed with her reading of the race. 'He's a stretch horse,' he commented quietly, eyes glued to the television monitor. 'He bides his time and saves his big effort for the last couple of furlongs.'

The commentator increased his volume and speed of delivery as the race started to change in complexion. The three early leaders melted into the ruck under strong drives from the saddle and several new challengers burst through and into contention from positions right across the track.

One of the disinterested punters in the shop screwed his head around as the volume of encouragement for what on the face of it, was a minor race at Southwell.

'He's coming through!' screamed Suzie. 'He's on the far side and his rider is just pushing him and he's coming through!'

This news elicited a shout of 'Ha'way Jimmy!' from Sam, but it could hardly be heard above the sound of Charlie and Stan bellowing for Screaming Jimmy and his jockey, Kimberly Jones. With a hundred yards to race, the gelding's rider crouched even lower in her saddle, took a look over into the middle of the track and gave the six year old a flick of her whip. The response was immediate; Screaming Jimmy found another gear, stretched into the lead and went half a length up.

With only fifty yards to cover, the race was seemingly won. But not complete. Screaming Jimmy was easily holding the horse in second, however, rallying in third, an unconsidered outsider started to make eye-catching progress. With each stride Screaming Jimmy's lead diminished. Kimberly Jones, recognising the danger, became more animated in her saddle, urging the gelding on. The duel looked terribly one-sided, Screaming Jimmy was at least a hand smaller than his new challenger who ranged up beside him and looked the stronger of the pair.

Charlie recognised the danger and became quiet, gritting his teeth. Nothing could have prized his eyes from the screen as the finishing post appeared on the right-hand side of the screen. With only three strides to the post the little gelding stuck his head down and eyeballed his competitor who had wandered left to challenge, now bang alongside him. Screaming Jimmy thrust his head forward once more, stretching as if he knew where the finishing line crossed the track. His nose struck the finishing line on the end of a neck stretched out at ninety degrees, such was the little gelding's desire to beat his opponent.

'He's got there. He's fended the challenger off by a nose!' Charlie announced excitedly, his clenched fist pumping the air.

Sam, Stan, and Suzie fell upon each other in a group hug which developed into a little circular dance as Suzie couldn't keep her feet still, jigging around excitedly. All three of them were bursting with exclamations of delight and beside them Harvey joined in with a couple of deep throated woofs and his tail seemed to be excitedly wagging the rest of his body as he circled the little throng. The objects of his excitement reeled around the centre of the betting shop, much to the amusement of the sole remaining punter who was watching the spectacle with a broad smile on his face.

Charlie stood apart, waiting for the full result to appear on the screens. His eyes flitted nervously between the monitor with the live pictures and the BetMick screen showing the text of the result, minus the starting prices and other dividend information. He scowled when the live pictures altered to a feed from Lingfield, crossing and uncrossing his arms in frustration. Finally, in a thirty second wait which felt like an eternity, the win for Screaming Jimmy was confirmed over the betting shop sound system by their anchorman, then there was a pause before a mild, West Country accented voice confirmed the starting prices.

'First at Southwell in the three ten was number nine, Screaming Jimmy, the 9/2… favourite. Second was…' Charlie gave out a cry of delight and joined the other three, ensuring the momentum of their little ring was increased as they twirled for the next thirty seconds. Once they had broken apart, Sam reached out and grabbed Charlie's shoulder.

'He *was* the favourite wasn't he, the little horse?'

Charlie was forced to swallow a couple of times before he could answer. 'Yes, thank goodness! He's been returned the 9/2 favourite. It's better than we could have hoped for. The other two must have lengthened in price while they were trying to load that last horse.'

Sam gave a celebratory bellow, and grasping Suzie's waist once more, resumed their little dance, Stan joining the celebrations to create a ring of three of them, pirouetting around the centre of the betting shop. Suzie was wide-eyed and excited, enjoying the celebration, but a moment later she caught sight of Charlie and her features took on a concerned expression. He had one hand to his breast and the other was fanning air into his face. There was a definite reddening of his cheeks and his forehead glistened with sweat. He was staring at the bank of monitors yet his eyes weren't quite focused on them.

Stan read the look of concern on Suzie's face and followed her gaze. He immediately dropped both arms from their celebratory clinch and strode over to Charlie.

'Hey, are you okay boss?' he asked, placing an arm around Charlie, worried he might need guiding to a seat, or worse still, faint on him. Charlie's eyes were still locked on the monitors, but it was as if he was looking beyond them.

'You look awful,' Stan added. 'Come on, have a seat.'

As if Stan's words had flicked a switch, Charlie snapped back, peering down at him. He raised a questioning eyebrow, apparently unaware he'd been the cause of any anxiety.

'Sorry, have I missed something?'

Relief filled Stan's face as Charlie seemed to return to his normal self and he dropped his arm from around him. Suzie and Sam soon joined them so there was a ring of three looking up at him.

'You were out of it for a moment. You just seemed to be… vacant,' said Suzie.

Charlie laughed, colour flushing his face with its usual healthy glow. Stan and Suzie shared a quick glance and relaxed.

'I was a bit nervous for sure, I've not been that relieved a horse won a race since I was actually riding them myself!' Charlie exclaimed, landing a friendly hand on Stan's shoulder.

'Sorry if I zoned out, I was actually trying to work out the bet,' he added.

Suzie's eyes widened. 'You used to ride… in races?'

'Oh, a long time ago, and I wasn't much good.'

'Come come, Charlie,' Sam chided. 'No false modesty needed here, among friends.'

Sam turned to face Suzie and shuffled a little closer to her with the air of someone sharing a secret. 'Charlie here rode twenty-two winners for his father from the age of sixteen to eighteen. The only thing that stopped him was the growth spurt that turned him into a seven foot giant…'

Charlie smiled down benignly at Sam and squirrelled a sceptical glance at Suzie. 'He's right,' he admitted with a heavy sigh, and after a short pause added, '…I am a giant.'

A minute later the four of them were back out in the fresh air, Sam and Stan both firing questions at Charlie and the buzz of excitement still evident.

'So what have you worked out after that winner? Surely you need all four of the horses to have run?' Sam queried.

'Yes, to get a proper total we need all the prices, but because we have already secured the price of your Lincoln runner it means there is only one price we're forced to guess at; Loafing Around. I was checking the latest prices in the betting shop and your mare is currently 16/1.'

Charlie paused, then, as if writing the math in the air, he did the calculation again, wafting his index finger as he settled the imaginary bet.

'If she were to win at sixteens later today, and Cool Blue, you know, Sam's Lincoln horse, was taken antepost at 100/1 as we did, each bet would win just over a million pounds…'

Stan let out an involuntary barking laugh which caught in his throat as he realised the potential value of the wafer thin betting slip in his inside pocket. The other two were silent, Suzie with her mouth open, staring at Charlie in disbelief.

Sam, in contrast, simply smiled. It was no ordinary smile though. It was one of those infectious sorts of expressions, delivered in such a genuine and joyous manner it melts your heart and forces you to adopt a similar look; of childlike awe. Charlie raised an eyebrow to both his young protégés and slanted his eyes toward his client. Stan and Suzie immediately fell under the spell of Sam's smile, trading silent, joyous looks.

The halcyon moment entrancing the four of them passed after a few seconds. As the bubble popped the sounds and smells of the racecourse rushed back at them.

'Well…' Charlie said, sucking in a deep breath.

'Two down, two to go!'

Thirteen

Mick Kowalski scowled as the official result of the Southwell race came over the shop loudspeakers. He snatched up the two betting slips and examined them both before handing them over to Frank who immediately went over to the settling machine on John's desk and started tapping keys.

'Do you know who placed these bets?' Mick enquired of the shop manager quietly.

'I was out banking yesterday's profits, Linda took them.'

All three men looked to the cashier, who they assumed had overheard the conversation. However Linda stared stoically into space. She waited just the right amount of time to wind up her employers without forcing them to ask for her help. Then Linda's chair swivelled round, wearing a benign expression and adopting a mock angelic pose.

Mick almost growled at her, but thought better of it. Instead, he stood with both hands out, as if he was ready to catch a tossed basketball, and waited with a heavily expectant look on his face.

Linda pursed her lips and tapped her cheek, as if she were casting her mind back the four hours to when she had struck the two bets. John's legs jiggled under his desk, finding his cashier's toying with the two men excruciating. Not for the first time he decided she must have broken plenty of hearts as a young woman, she had all the looks and moves, and was frankly wasted as a betting shop cashier. In desperation, he delivered a pleading glance Linda's way and she relented.

'You mean the three pound lucky fifteens?' she enquired in a gentle, almost soothing voice.

Mick tutted in irritation and rolled his eyes, which only resulted in Linda remaining silent. She sniffed derisively at Mick, before uncrossing and re-crossing her legs in a manner clearly aimed to establish who held the power in this situation. Mick eyed her pensively, not quite able to decide whether to acquiesce or come down on her hard. He concluded he rather liked this one; she was… interesting.

Linda made a point of clearing her throat and continued. 'The first was a lady of about forty and I reckon she'd never placed a bet in her life. I had to tell her what to do and which betting slip she needed.'

In the background, Frank's mobile phone started to chirp in his inside pocket and he extracted it and disappeared through a door into a tiny staff room at the very back of the shop.

'So you've never seen her before?' Mick asked.

'I've never seen her *in here* before, but I recognised her. She runs the charity shop next door.'

Mick's face crumpled into a frown.

'And the other bet?'

'Ah well, that was Father McCafferty.'

Mick's eyes grew wide and he ran a hand through his hair, pushing it back over his ears. 'What, he's a Vicar?'

'Actually, I think he's a Priest,' Linda corrected. 'He's always around the church hall just up the road here, runs the homeless shelter and…'

Mick had heard enough. 'Yes, yes… did either of them *say* anything about their bets?'

Linda's eyes narrowed once more and Mick held up an apologetic palm, gesturing for her to continue.

Taking a breath, she was about to start speaking when the staff room door burst open and Frank reappeared. Mick turned, looked Frank up and down, and winced. Frank looked worried, and when Frank looked worried there was always a damned good reason.

Fourteen

The third leg of the bet was about an hour away. Loafing Around would run at ten past five, the sixth and final race of the day. Meanwhile Charlie was using the time to try and explain to Suzie the Lucky Fifteen bet they had placed.

'It consists of four horses, and as you would expect, fifteen bets,' he told her as they sat around a small, oblong table in the Owners and Trainers lounge, cups of steaming coffee in front of them.

'There are four singles, six doubles, four trebles and one four horse accumulator, that's fifteen bets. You start to make serious money if you manage to get three or four horses winning at decent odds.'

'So, fifteen bets at a three pound stake cost everyone forty-five pounds, which is why we put a fifty pound note in each letter,' Suzie said, nodding. 'Okay, I think I understand. So if Loafing Around wins, we have a three day wait for Cool Blue to race on Saturday before the bet is complete?'

'Yep, that's right. But I expect we're going to be busy for the next few days, especially if Sam has another winner in the last race.'

'Won't the bookmakers realise that they could be paying out a huge amount of money and do something to stop it?'

Charlie produced a mischievous grin. 'I'm hopeful that the bookmakers we've had the bets with won't notice the potential payout because the killer horse with the biggest price is the last one to race. If the bookies are on the ball they will back Loafing Around themselves in an attempt to reduce her price, or maybe lay off some of the bet by backing both her and Cool Blue in a double. If they do, it will mean we will win far less.'

Suzie scratched her forehead in the manner of someone trying desperately to wrap their thoughts around a new concept, and struggling with it somewhat. Charlie waited patiently in silence, hopeful his words would eventually deliver enlightenment.

'So the way a bookmaker ensures he doesn't get caught having to pay out huge sums of money, is to cover the bet by backing the same horses with another bookmaker?' Suzie ventured uncertainly.

'If they're doing their job properly. Yes,' Charlie confirmed.

'However, we're banking on them *not* doing their job properly...' Suzie queried.

'I don't know if you'll be able to rely on that,' Stan broke in, his eyes surveying his mobile phone that was displaying the odds for Loafing Around's race. 'The mare has dropped to 14/1 in the last few minutes.'

Charlie sniffed and looked thoughtful for a moment, 'There's no need to worry, there's bound to be some movement, that's the nature of a betting market. Ninety percent of the bets will be placed within the ten minutes before the off, that's when we'll know whether most of the bookmakers are on the ball or not.'

'Besides, even if the odds tumble, we'll hopefully have Mick running scared,' said Sam, a degree of seriousness apparent in his voice. 'Remember, the plan Charlie has created isn't only about the bet, there are other…' he searched for the right word. '…*outcomes* to be achieved.'

This comment prompted an exchange of sobering looks around the table. Charlie was reminded that the mention of Mick Kowalski always brought a grey curtain of inner turmoil down upon Sam. Their discussions on that day at Inkberrow had struck a bad note every time the bookmaker's name was mentioned. Sam would become detached, consumed by a complex mix of emotions. Every attempt Charlie had made to question Sam to discover the true relationship between the two men had been fruitless.

Charlie hadn't saddled Stan and Suzie with the entire background to the coup, and he now saw the folly in their exclusion. His colleagues traded frowns and shrugs, quickly followed by both of them staring fixedly at Charlie, silently demanding an explanation. He managed to placate them both with a raised finger to his lips and a small series of nods which indicated he would explain, but not in front of their client.

Sam sensed the unease around the table. He tried to visualise what was going on between the three of them, producing a grimace when his imagination let him down.

'Perhaps I have strayed into a subject area which hasn't been properly shared?' he suggested.

Charlie held his head in one hand and eyed the virtually blind man across the table, staggered by his intuition. 'I continue to underestimate your capacity to read inflections of speech and the sounds around you,' he moaned, 'Your senses are… impressive.'

'And pretty annoying too, I would imagine,' Sam added wryly.

Charlie fixed his gaze firstly on Stan, knowing that the young man would be the most offended at not being privy to the entire back-story between Sam and Mick Kowalski. He also darted a glance at Suzie, ensuring she too was brought into his silent plea for forgiveness.

He checked the time on his phone. 'We've got a few minutes now. I can bring you both up to speed. Is that okay with you, Sam?'

'Fire away Charlie, there's no need for secrets as far as I'm concerned, not after I've shared a dance with the two of them,' Sam said, offering up a smile.

'In fact, I think I'll stretch Harvey's legs for a while before the next race goes off. Come find me when the troops are updated.'

With that, Sam left the Owners and Trainers bar, Harvey navigating his master through the sea of tables and chairs. Once outside the two of them headed up the gentle incline toward the pre-parade ring.

Charlie spent the next ten minutes running through Sam's recent history with Mick Kowalski and also his concerns over the death of his brother, Laurie. Suzie and Stan listened intently, heads bowed in concentration. When he'd finished it was Stan who was first to seek clarity.

'Sam wants to bankrupt BetMick,' Stan mused. 'Because he believes its founder was responsible for the death of his brother.'

'Yep, that's about it,' Charlie agreed.

'And to make that happen he's going to make other people wealthy.'

'Wow, now that is pretty cool!' Suzie cooed in amazement.

Charlie gave her a sideways look. 'It helps that he's one of the richest men in the country.'

'Well, not yet he isn't. But mmm, yeah, I suppose,' she admitted with a smile.

'I know he comes across as this rather benevolent and placid soul, but am I the only one who finds his thirst for revenge a little disconcerting?' Stan asked, clasping his hands together and rubbing them in what amounted to unconscious nervousness.

'He's a client,' Charlie said slowly, locking eyes with Stan. 'We've been employed to deliver a project and publicity campaign, nothing more. Granted, it's a little different to creating poster campaigns for dog food or TV adverts for energy bars, but let's face it, the dog food was low quality and those so-called energy bars were packed full of sugar. There's always going to be aspects of our business which make us question if we're doing the right thing.'

Two young, bright faces looked up at Charlie with a hint of condemnation and a good dollop of disappointment. After a few seconds of holding a false smile he grimaced and dropped his eyes to the table.

'Okay, yes, I agree. It sucks,' he added in a resigned tone. 'I don't like the fact Sam has an ulterior motive either.'

He looked back up at his two protégés and realised they were actually sharing a smile with each other. It only took him a moment to realise what was going on.

'Okay, how long have you two known about the back story then?' Charlie asked, after issuing a long sigh.

Suzie flashed a perfect row of teeth in his direction as she gave him a pitying smile. 'On Sunday. When you went out for the takeaway.'

'You didn't think we'd not research the client did you?' Stan asked, bursting with incredulity, 'He's almost a billionaire, the internet is full of all sorts of dirt on him.'

'So what do you think?' Charlie asked, sitting up in his seat and leaning forward conspiratorially. Stan and Suzie did the same.

'His business seems to run itself,' said Stan, 'Even when he was

Managing Director the rumours were that the executive team and his father, Reginald Lewis, actually did all the work. He's a bit of an odd-bod, never married, lives alone – if you count having five members of staff and your father living in your house, sorry..., mansion, living alone...'

Suzie took up the report, 'He's a classic recluse in many ways, doesn't spend much time with what family he has left. After his brother died he sort of retreated from public life, although he's maintained his philanthropic stuff. He was really close to his brother according to most accounts; they made big changes to the business together in their late twenties which helped take it to a new level. Oh, and Sam doesn't appear to have done any work for the family business for two years, ever since his brother died in that traffic accident...'

Suzie paused out of curiosity, as Charlie started to shake his head, his eyes becoming watery.

'What!' she protested, 'What's so funny?'

'And here I was, beating myself up because I thought I'd led the two of you astray! You've managed to research Sam deeper than I did before accepting the job!' he blurted.

'We knew from the beginning there was more to Sam than first met the eye,' Stan said, 'We thought you might be under a non-disclosure agreement or something.'

'No, nothing like that,' Charlie admitted, dabbing his eyes with a handkerchief and bringing his mirth under control. 'I just thought I'd let you two make your own mind up about him.'

'Well I think he's a bit of an old smoothy,' Suzie remarked, shooting a glance at both her colleagues, daring them to disagree. To her relief they both nodded a degree of agreement.

'I don't think his real objectives matters too much,' Charlie said, leaning back and checking the time. He glanced over his shoulder to make sure the subject of his next comment wasn't stood within listening range.

'Sam's never going to break BetMick. The chances are they will lay the bets off, or refuse to pay out and everything will go legal for the next umpteen years.'

'That's what we thought,' agreed Stan, 'It's a shame, a million quid would have been nice,' he added with a hint of bitterness. In the background, the commentary for the penultimate race of the day started up and the volume of conversation around them fell as the race grabbed people's attention.

'Well, the game isn't over, or even near completion just yet, and it's gone pretty well so far,' Charlie said, downing the last gulp of his coffee and getting up from the table. His two companions did the same, the three of them the only owners in the lounge not watching the race.

'We've still got a job to do today, and over the next few days. Go collect your kit from the car,' he instructed Stan, then to Suzie added 'And you need to get ready on the phone. Are we all set up?'

Both of them gave a positive response and were suddenly wearing serious looks; back in business mode. Outside the Owners and Trainers lounge Stan disappeared toward the racecourse exit and Charlie and Suzie went to hunt for Tommy in the saddling boxes.

The completion of the fifth race of the afternoon was marked by a sustained roar from the stands as three thoroughbreds fought out a close finish to a two miles chase, battling up the long run-in from the last fence. Charlie, Stan, and Suzie paid no attention to the action. They were concentrating on the build up to what could be the most important moment of their day.

Fifteen

Charlie found his brother in the stable yard at the back of the racecourse going through his pre-race checks with the mare Loafing Around. He and Suzie spent a few minutes chatting with Tommy about the eight-year-old's chances. A strapping individual, the mare was twitchy and nervous as she was being prepared and Tommy had to be quite deliberate in his movements around her in order to telegraph to the mare where he was and what he was doing. A young stable lad was at the front of the animal, whispering to her and rubbing her nose to try and keep her calm.

Suzie was watching Tommy and the mare in fascination, but Charlie felt himself becoming distracted as the race time crept nearer. He'd seen this many times before and was keen to get on with the rest of the day's work. When Stan arrived with bulky professional backpack strapped to his shoulders, Charlie made their excuses and made to leave.

Tommy called out to the three of them as they turned their backs to walk away. 'Hey! She's going to go close today. Just so you know.'

Charlie turned and called back to his brother, 'She'd better do. We've got a lot riding on her.'

'Just don't expect to see her get involved until after the last and remember she won't be touched with the whip,' he warned, 'She'll down tools if she gets the feeling she's not in charge.'

Charlie left Stan outside the winners enclosure, where he started to setup a laptop, camera and sound equipment. They didn't say a great deal, both men preoccupied.

With twenty minutes to the start of the final race of the day Charlie and Suzie walked through the two lines of bookmakers pitches and leant up against the parade ring rails, both thumbing through menus on their mobile phones. Charlie watched as Suzie switched her business phone off and produced a new one which she turned on for the first time that day.

'Ready?' Charlie asked after she'd checked the phone was operating correctly.

Suzie looked up at him pensively and nodded, brushing her hair out of her face and tying it back with a hair grip; the way she wore it in business meetings and when meeting most clients.

'It feels a bit strange,' she admitted shyly, 'I really want Loafing Around to win, but I have a sick feeling in my stomach that the world is going to go mad for a while if she does.'

Charlie responded with an understanding smile. 'I know what you mean. How she runs her race is out of our hands. How we handle the result is going to be down to the three of us, and we're just as liable to cock it up as she is!'

The two of them shared a nervy grimace and made their way into the parade ring where Sam was already standing with Harvey at his heel.

****

John Ford kept his head down as he sat on his high stool at the betting counter. He wasn't taking bets, his till was closed. He had been usurped by Frank, who had taken control of his settling desk. He exchanged a glance with Linda who rolled her eyes to the ceiling and back before slowly shaking her head.

'Trust this to happen on a slow Wednesday when I'm out of the office,' Frank muttered to himself angrily, thumping odds into a standalone settler, a phone clamped to his ear. Mick too was on his mobile phone, leaning against the back wall, intermittently screaming at staff back at his head office who, one after another, were unable to answer his questions with replies he wanted to hear.

Frank ended his call and simply by staring, indicated to Mick he wanted to speak with him. Mick removed his phone from his ear mid-sentence and shouted, 'What?' loudly across the room.

'Nine more of them, so far.'

'What's the take out now, then?'

'At the current price of 20/1, the maximum of a million per bet,' Frank reported flatly.

'What the hell!' Mick exploded, 'I thought it was 16's on the tissue.'

'It's not fancied, no one is betting it,' Frank said with a shrug, 'It's in the same ownership and trainer as the first winner on the bet, but there's no market interest.'

Mick nibbled on the end of his phone, deep in thought, having forgotten he was still on an active call.

'Who owns them?'

Frank tapped a few keys on a pad which controlled two monitors behind the counter. 'Mr. S Lewis,'

Mick's eyes narrowed. 'Who, Samuel Lewis?'

Again, Frank shrugged. Just at that moment Mick could have quite happily thrown the phone at his right-hand man's head, but instead he swallowed his frustration and started an app on his phone, tapping furiously though half a dozen menus.

'Bloody hell,' he whispered hoarsely once he'd brought up the ownership details for Loafing Around.

Frank checked the time; three minutes to the off. He cleared his throat. 'We should halve the price, just in case...'

'If it's a coup, why isn't it already down in price?' Mick demanded.

Frank bit the inside of his mouth thoughtfully before replying. 'I doubt many bookmakers will have picked up on it. There's only two of the four gone in and one was an unnamed favourite.'

Mick adopted a glazed expression, 'Or we're the only bookmaker to take the bets…' he stated under his breath.

Mick swept his palm through his hair and held it on the top of his head, staring at the odds for the ten past five race at Market Rasen.

'Throw a few thousand onto the horse at the track and get those odds down so the starting price is in single figures,' he barked.

Frank clamped his phone back to his ear and the instructions tumbled from his lips in his faintly Liverpudlian accent. He kept the phone there, speaking in monosyllabic tones every now and then as information was passed back to him.

Mick was watching the horses milling at the start on the live racecourse monitor and his hands found his hips. 'I don't see the price shortening,' he informed Frank, irritation heightening the pitch of his voice.

'They can't get through to our layer on the course.'

'Why the hell not?'

Frank held his hand up, listening intently. 'Okay, the instruction has been given,' he reported.

The eleven runners took another turn on the television screen and Loafing Around went to 16/1 on the monitors.

'Come on!' Mick yelled at the screen as the horses started to walk towards the starting line, 'Bring the bloody price down!'

The two decorators wandered up to the counter and asked Linda a few questions in hushed tones. One of them scribbled a bet out and flung it under the glass. It was followed by a twenty pound note. His betting slip was rung through the till just before the commentator announced the race was off. The price on the screens showed that Loafing Around's price had been reduced to 12/1 before the market was closed.

Frank placed the telephone back into its cradle and watched Mick's reaction to the final starting price. Mick grunted an acceptance toward Frank, Loafing Around's price having reduced by a few points. He turned to the bank of monitors and standing legs apart, arms crossed, Mick watched the live television pictures from Market Rasen like a hawk.

The early indications from the racetrack were promising for Mick. Loafing Around in her blue and yellow silks was in rear and the mare's jumping was slow and sticky at the first two fences. Despite her age she was showing her lack of race experience, her jockey giving the eight year old a small slap down her neck after the second chase fence, to which the mare responded with a swish of her tail.

Mick turned his head to Frank. 'This thing can't win. It's all over the place.' Frank didn't reply, preferring to give a non-committal twitch of his bottom lip and maintaining his gaze on the monitor.

As the race continued, Mick felt the need to start gnawing at the rough skin on his index finger. Loafing Around was gaining confidence as the race developed and after jumping the two fences up the home straight tidily the first time around, she set off onto her second circuit having made up three places and was now traveling kindly. She stood off the first chase fence on the slightly downhill part of the back straight and by five fences out had tagged onto the rear of the main group, who were kicking away from the rest of the field. By the time the leaders had reached the bottom of the back straight and started to make their final turn right-handed, the twelve runners had been reduced to nine. A group of four had broken away by a few lengths and Loafing Around was in the middle of the chasing group of five. However her jockey Duncan Foss still hadn't made any move on the mare, and as the runners straightened up for the three fences up the home straight, Loafing Around moved to the front of the second group and started to make progress towards the four horses ahead of her.

Mick was now making gutteral noises each time the mare reached another fence, willing her to make a serious mistake and crash out of the race. She was still ten lengths off the lead when they jumped the second last, at which stage she jumped into a share of fourth. Over the last Mick erupted with a growl as Loafing Around took third and her rider started to push his hands down her neck and become animated in his saddle, but not resorting to touching the mare with the whip.

'She can't win from there,' Mick stated. He realised after the words came out that he'd expressed this as a question and not a certainty. Unable to peel his eyes from the monitor, a cold chill slowly grew down the back of his neck, despite the fact he was sweating.

There is a long run from the last chase fence at Market Rasen to the finishing line. The run-in is well over a furlong in length and Mick began screaming for the line to appear. The commentator had been concentrating on the two leaders battling out the finish but now, many seconds after Mick had recognised the danger, he started to call Loafing Around's name and adding phrases like 'making progress' and 'finishing well' to his commentary. The mare swept past a flailing jockey in second place, still under a hands and heels ride, and within two strides was level with the leader. Her head hit the front and almost immediately her rider stopped pushing and stood up in his irons, his job done, his ride timed to perfection.

Frank spun away from the monitor, screwing his face up, rubbing it with a sweaty palm. He picked the phone up again and started to dial. Mick didn't move. From the other side of the glass wall one of the decorators was celebrating a win. Mick eyed the punter, realised that his last minute bet must have been on Loafing Around, probably after overhearing his own conversation. He shot a look of pure loathing the man's way. It only served to widen the decorator's grin even further.

Sixteen

Charlie shook his head in disbelief. He couldn't believe how late Duncan had left his challenge. The mare had made up about eight lengths from the last fence to pass the leader in the last stride and win going away under one of the most confident rides he'd seen for many years. The reaction around the course was muted; the mare had got up to beat a short priced favourite.

Suzie and Sam were having fun re-enacting their victory jig from a few hours earlier, but Charlie mentally shook himself and considered what he had to achieve in the next few minutes. There was a job to be done, and it was going to require tact and precision.

Gently breaking up their celebrations in the parade ring, Charlie guided Sam and Suzie up to the winners enclosure. Suzie caught sight of Charlie's determined expression, took a breath, and became more focussed with every step she took up the hill. As they passed through the lines of bookmakers there were hardly any punters going to collect. If only they knew, thought Charlie, as he surveyed the lack of winning queues. Well, they're going to get to know pretty soon.

Duncan and Loafing Around were already walking into the winners enclosure when Charlie and Suzie reached the small, railed enclosure. About thirty people gave the mare a polite round of applause as she entered the ring and Duncan slipped off her back and immediately started to relate the details of the ride to Tommy and Sam. Charlie looked around for the Racing TV crew and spotted them and their representative at the track doing a small piece to the camera. He spotted Stan, his own camera equipment in hand, just behind them. Charlie waited for the presenter to finish his piece and strode across.

'Stephen!' Charlie exclaimed, a few paces from the tall, well-presented, chisel jawed forty-five year old. Charlie knew Stephen Jones from his own short-lived stint as a jockey and even though there were flecks of grey in his hair now, the media man looked good for his age.

Stephen greeted Charlie with a broad smile, stuck out a hand, and seemed genuinely pleased to see him.

'Hello Charlie, how the devil are you?' he asked, removing his earpiece.

Charlie could see Stephen's cameraman starting to pack his kit away and decided he needed to hurry things along. He took Stephen by the elbow and sidled up to him so he was closer before he replied.

'I'm really pretty good after that result. Actually, I might be able to give you a bit of a scoop if you're interested?' he whispered conspiratorially. Stephen's eyes widened and he nodded for Charlie to continue.

'I could do with a short interview, so if your man here could...'
Charlie indicated the cameraman. Stephen stepped away and had a few
quiet works with his colleague. The man listened, looked over to Charlie,
and after tapping his watch, shrugged. Stephen returned to Charlie.

You've got two minutes,' Stephen told him. 'But come on, what's
all the cloak and dagger stuff about?'

Charlie took a breath and gave Stephen his pitch. It took forty-five
seconds and included gestures to Stan and then finally to Sam, who was
busy being presented with a small trophy on a wooden plinth at the back of
the winners enclosure. He finished by removing a betting slip from his
blazer pocket and then looked to Stephen who had a hand to his forehead
and whose eyes were flitting around as he digested Charlie's words and the
contents of his betting slip.

'One minute,' he begged, and reinserted his small black earpiece.
He picked up his microphone and barked a couple of names into it, asking
if they were still there. Charlie heard a crackling response but couldn't
make out what was being discussed. Over Stephen's shoulder he could see
Stan watching. He had both his shoulders and arms raised in a 'What's
going on?' type of pose. Charlie remained straight-lipped and shook his
head ever so slightly.

Stephen held his finger to his ear once more and Charlie could hear
him say in a half-demanding, half-pleading voice. 'Three bloody minutes,
that's all. Three minutes, and I promise you'll have the news story of the
week in racing, and you might even have one for national coverage.'

It went quiet again for ten seconds and then Stephen fixed a stare
onto Charlie before breaking into a grin. 'You better make this good,
Charlie.'

Charlie returned Stephen's grin and immediately stuck his thumb
up to Stan and called Sam over from his presentation. Suzie brought him
and Harvey over and Stan moved his tripod and camera, setting them up
just behind the Racing TV cameraman. Thirty seconds later Charlie, Sam,
and Harvey were lined up with Stephen, who stood at an angle to them.
Stephen did a quick sound quality test, asked if they were ready, warned
them all that this was going out live, and after a terse nod, began.

'I'm here at Market Rasen racecourse today,' Stephen started in his
smooth, mildly northern voice, 'We've had a good day's racing from this
North Lincolnshire track and there's nothing too strange about that.
However, I have just received information from a trusted source that a
betting coup of huge proportions is currently under way...'

Stephen paused, allowing the weight of his words to percolate into
his audience before continuing. 'With me I have ex-jockey, Charlie
Summer, now a director of a top advertising agency, and with him,
prominent racehorse owner Mr. Samuel Lewis, who is a director of the
high street bakers, Lewis's.'

He angled himself expertly out of shot now, and the camera pointed into Charlie's upper torso. Behind, Stan was filming from a slightly different angle.

'So Charlie, what's the bet? Stephen began excitedly, 'And how come we've not heard anything about this during racing?'

'Thanks Stephen. Well the bet is a Lucky Fifteen, so four horses need to win. At the moment three of the four have already won. For those in your audience who know a little bit about betting, it's a three pounds Lucky Fifteen costing forty five pounds and we've managed to pick three winners so far at 25/1, 9/2 and 12/1.'

'Wow, those are decent prices!' Stephen exclaimed. 'So how much do you stand to win?'

Charlie smiled. 'We've already won almost seven thousand pounds. However, we still have one horse to run. If that horse wins we could win significantly more.'

'Come on, Charlie, don't be coy,' Stephen chided in a friendly manner, 'Can't you tell us the horse and what you could potentially win?'

Charlie adopted a more serious expression, as if he was contemplating whether this was a good idea or not. After a short pause he replied 'Actually, Stephen, I'll be happy to tell you because I think we may need the help of your viewers to spread the word.'

Stephen raised an eyebrow, but said nothing at first. He judged Charlie knew where he was going with this and was keen for it to unfold with as much drama as possible.

'Okay, you have your platform,' Stephen responded encouragingly, 'Tell us about the bet and how Mr. Lewis fits in, and of course, your final selection.'

Charlie smiled once again at Stephen and then turned to face the black, square face of the television camera.

'This whole bet was the idea of Mr. Samuel Lewis,' said Charlie, gesturing to Sam standing beside him. 'He came to me last week knowing that two of the horses he owns would have a good chance of winning. People who know Sam will be aware he is a prodigious philanthropist and has given hundreds of thousands of pounds to deserving charities. He wondered whether his racehorses could potentially benefit some good causes.'

Charlie noticed Stephen was frowning, clearly wondering where he was going with this explanation, so he ploughed on.

'In short, Samuel Lewis tasked us to create and post over seven hundred and fifty letters to named individuals all over the country. Earlier this week, people working in carefully chosen charities received a letter from Mr. Lewis telling them to place a bet. It explained how to place the bet, the names of the four horses, and times they were running. Sam also placed a fifty pound note in each letter, telling each recipient that he hoped they would place the bet, but if not, they should take the fifty pounds as a charitable donation. However, he did point out that placing the bet could mean their cause would possibly benefit significantly.'

A light came on in Stephen's eyes, and a rush of relief flooded Charlie, as he hadn't been too sure where to go next.

'So you're telling us that there are potentially seven hundred and fifty of these Lucky Fifteens which have been placed with bookmakers?' Stephen said, allowing a little wonderment to seep into his voice.

'That's right. And already, those bets will have brought their good causes a donation of almost seven thousand pounds!' Charlie replied, allowing a benevolent smile to grace his face. He judged it was now time to go for the big finish.

'However,' he stated on a deeper, more serious note. 'If the last horse wins, we believe it will be the biggest payout in British bookmaking history, and all the proceeds will be going to charitable causes.'

'So please don't keep us in suspense,' Stephen cajoled, clearly enjoying himself now, 'What is the fourth horse and when does it race?'

'The horse runs in the Lincoln at Doncaster's big meeting on Saturday, the first day of the new flat season. His name is Cool Blue and the declarations for the race will be made tomorrow morning,' Charlie said slowly and as clearly as he could, 'The gelding should just about make the cut for the big race.'

Stephen was already grinning, but now his face broke into a full-blown smile as he realised the implications.

'Cool Blue in the Lincoln, you heard it here first everyone.' Stephen interjected, 'But surely that would be an antepost bet Charlie?'

Charlie almost laughed. Stephen knew his stuff and he'd set the interview up for a perfect finale.

'It is indeed Stephen, which means all our charities have already taken a price on Cool Blue. In fact, it was the only price which was taken across the entire bet...' Charlie paused, and Stephen waited. '...Cool Blue was around 100/1. That means each charity stands to win almost eight hundred thousand pounds each, if they placed the bet.'

Even the cameraman gasped. The little ring of people listening to the interview from the rails of the winners enclosure took an intake of breath and then started chattering loudly.

Clearly delighted with the way the interview was going, Stephen allowed the cameraman to flick around the enclosure to capture reactions from the crowd.

He asked his final question: 'Well, this is huge news for the racing world, and I would imagine for an even wider audience. Is there anything else you'd like to add?'

'Thanks, Stephen. Yes, there's just one more thing if I may. Mr. Samuel Lewis would like to invite every single charity who placed the bet to join him, at his expense, in a private suite at Doncaster Racecourse on Saturday to celebrate the win so far, and also to cheer home Cool Blue. It should be a fantastic day at the races. To attend, please contact us. The details are in Mr. Lewis's letter.'

Stephen gave Charlie a surreptitious grin, straightening his features before he spun around to deliver a final message to camera.

'There you have it,' Stephen said brightly, 'Possibly the biggest betting coup of modern times and it has been created for charitable reasons! Who would have thought that Market Rasen on a Wednesday in March would provide such intrigue? Of course the big question now is; How many of those seven hundred and fifty charities actually placed the bet? If they didn't, they'll be kicking themselves now!'

He paused in a rigid position for a few seconds until both he and the cameraman relaxed. Stephen pulled out his earpiece, filled both his cheeks with air before blowing it out through pursed lips. He turned to face Charlie, still exhaling his breath.

'Bloody hell, Charlie!' he said, eyes wide and holding out a hand in congratulations, 'That's a hell of a bet. How many of these charities do you think placed it today?'

Charlie shrugged. 'That's what I'm hoping to find out in the next few hours.' He nodded over to Stan and Suzie. 'These guys will be hard at it from now on making sure that we track everyone we can.'

Stan had placed his camera onto a tripod and was busy working on a laptop which he'd leant up against the rails of the winners enclosure. Suzie had a mobile phone clamped to her ear, a pen top in her mouth and appeared to be writing notes on a small, but thick, pad of paper.

Stephen laughed. 'Good heavens, the bookmakers must be pulling their hair out now, worried that the Lincoln horse is going to go in at 100/1. Can he win… what was it called?'

'Cool Blue.'

'But can it win?' he pressed.

'His trainer, Joss Faraday, seems to think so,' replied Charlie, 'First he needs some luck at the declaration stage tomorrow and then we'll have to wait until Saturday afternoon and see what happens. It's a big ask, which is why he is a huge price.'

Stephen's cameraman came up to them, a finger held to his ear.

'They want another interview,' he told Stephen excitedly. 'Get your microphone in, this one might be networked!'

Ten minutes later Stephen had completed another interview with Charlie and taken a short, thirty second video statement from Sam, with promises that they should see themselves on more than just the racing channels.

Charlie bowed his head a little closer to Stephen's, asking, 'Any chance we could get some coverage on terrestrial TV on Saturday morning, you know, the breakfast build-up show?'

'I'll be at Doncaster on Saturday, but I'm not doing the morning line myself, I'm just doing a few trainer interviews in the paddock,' Stephen replied thoughtfully, 'But I'll see what I can do.'

'Perhaps a couple of bookmakers giving a reaction might provide some good viewing?' Charlie suggested hopefully.

Stephen studied him, 'You didn't give any quarter as a rider and I can see now you've continued that in your new career.' He paused, rubbing his chin, considering. 'I could see that working, but I'm just a lowly microphone man. You'll need to speak with the producer. Here, I'll send you his contact details.' Stephen played with his mobile phone for a few seconds and Charlie's phone pinged.

'Thanks for your help today, Stephen,' Charlie said, looking down at a contact card for a Mr. Xavier Trent on his phone.

'Nonsense, I should be thanking you,' he said, producing a beatific smile. He clapped a big hand onto Charlie's shoulder and gave him a friendly shake, 'It's been a great scoop for me.'

The crowd around the winners enclosure had all but disappeared now. A few racegoers were ambling past on their way home and the horses had left the ring long ago. Charlie watched Stephen and his colleague head off and spun on his heel to locate Suzie and Stan. He found them standing in the lea of the weighing room, both engrossed in their post race activities. Suzie was responsible for phones and Stan was the internet and social media man. They looked equally harassed and Charlie approached them carefully, first peering over Suzie's shoulder to find her little notebook was filling with names and contact details, and then around behind Stan. He was uploading videos to YouTube but Charlie could see other windows on his laptop open to Facebook and Twitter, both of which seemed to be scrolling with activity.

Stan glimpsed momentarily at Charlie before burying himself in his computer once more. 'It's going mental online,' he managed before clicking into another window to type a tweet regarding the latest video he'd posted. 'We're up to twenty-five thousand views of the main video interview on YouTube and Cool Blue and Sam Lewis are currently trending on social media,' he added before another barrage of electronic comments tipped into view on the Twitter account they'd set up specifically for Cool Blue.

Charlie moved over to Suzie's side and she acknowledged him with a sharp nod, eventually winding up her conversation with an excitable caller. She tapped the hang up icon on her phone, checked the call had indeed dropped, and closed her eyes for a few seconds. Charlie waited, giving her time to find the words, however a moment later the phone started to vibrate in her hand, and after rolling her eyes and shooting Charlie a quick grin, she answered and was immediately lost in another conversation with a participant in the bet.

With Sam off enjoying a glass of free champagne with the racecourse dignitaries following Loafing Around's win, and both his protégés busy, Charlie sat down on the weighing room steps and took a moment to review the day's events. Tommy had delivered two wonderful runs from Sam's horses, which alone was a tremendous achievement, and the Southwell favourite, Screaming Jimmy, being returned a larger than expected 9/2 starting price was certainly a big bonus. Now it was a case of maintaining, and if possible, swelling the public knowledge of the bets.

Giving charities the responsibility for placing the bet had been a risk. Charlie couldn't be certain how many of the seven hundred and fifty charities they'd written to would actually place the bet. Just as imperative from Sam's point of view was the question of *with whom* they placed the bet. Charlie had purposefully chosen charities from a wide range of backgrounds, but roughly from two areas. Half of the organisations were directly to support people; such as hospices, medical care, food banks, support groups, church funds, and sports activities related community projects. The other half had been environmental causes; animal shelters, building preservation trusts and libraries and museums of all descriptions. The recipients were equally split between causes for children, adults and the aged, and across as many ethnic backgrounds as possible. However, the geographic split had been carefully contrived into certain pockets of the country.

Charlie was aware of Suzie's phone ringing once more as soon as she finished her latest call. He wondered how many charities tore the letter open and simply banked the fifty pound note? How many had planned to place the bet, but then forgotten? Would they have five people at Doncaster on Saturday or fifty? He wrinkled his brow and decided he'd make more use of himself and give Suzie a break. Jumping up, he waited until she'd finished her latest call and took the phone from her.

He was about to ask a frazzled looking Suzie how many people she'd spoken to in the last twenty minutes since their interview had aired, but the mobile immediately started buzzing in his hand. He inspected the screen and recognised a Bradford calling code and was about to accept the call when he also saw there were fourteen voice messages and half a dozen text messages which hadn't been touched.

'I think only having a single phone line for incoming calls from people who have placed the bet may have been a slight oversight!' he told Suzie, arching an amused eyebrow.

She produced a wan smile in return and in an unashamedly sarcastic tone replied, 'You think so?'

Charlie tapped the call receive icon and spent the next eight minutes trying to convince a terribly excited middle-aged lady that she had indeed already won almost seven thousand pounds for her youth centre.

Yes, there could be far more to come on Saturday, and no, it wasn't a fake bet and yes, the charity could keep all the proceeds. The lady, called Petula but 'Pet' to her friends, had insisted on regaling Charlie on the good causes the money would support, and how every penny would be well spent. Charlie wondered how many of those who had placed the bet would consider keeping the profit for themselves, then disregarded this line of thought. There were bound to be a few, and those individuals would just have to live with the knowledge they defrauded their own charity. Besides, he had no way to monitor it. You had to trust people.

He noted Petula's personal details in Suzie's pad, plus the name of the bookmaker she'd placed the bet with and rang off by telling her to take a few breaths, make a cup of tea, sit down, and look forward to a free day at the races on Saturday. Petula cooed in delight over every word he spoke and gushed her thanks. He couldn't help chuckling when he heard the lady squeal with unadulterated delight before she'd put the handset down, not realising he was still listening on the line.

The phone informed him there were now twenty-two messages and sixteen missed calls and it started to ring again within a few seconds. He handed it over to Suzie at his elbow, intending to do a tag team on the calls, however his own personal phone started to ring. He answered without looking to see who it was and reacted with genuine delight when Sharon Stone, the Inkberrow vicar announced herself.

'Sharon! Lovely to speak with you again.'

'Ah, Mr. Summer. I'm guessing you were responsible for the letter I received earlier this week?' she said without preamble, a stern quality in her voice.

Charlie had slipped an extra charitable letter into the pile which went into the post on Monday night, addressed to Sharon's church. He felt his conversation with Sharon at Tommy's yard had been instrumental in firming up his plan for Sam, and if there were benefits to be had, Sharon deserved the chance to share in them. He paused and the line went silent for a little longer than he'd wanted as he busied himself wondering if she was going to inform him she hadn't placed the bet.

'Mmm.. I guess you took the fifty pounds and placed it into the collection plate?' he finally enquired.

'Oh gosh no!' she replied, bookending her bright response with a throaty chuckle, 'I was straight down the bookies this morning and followed Sam's instructions to the letter!'

'Oh, I'm so pleased,' Charlie managed, caught a little off guard by her warmth.

'I imagine you are, it means you may have the pleasure of me pestering you at the races on Saturday.'

'Really?' he asked, immediately grimacing at how limp his response sounded. 'Er, I'm...'

79

'Oh don't worry, if I come, I'll be on my own this time. I won't have the women's guild posse with me,' she broke in, seemingly oblivious to Charlie's lack of guile, 'I assume you'll be there?'

'Yes, of course. I could give you a lift there if you wanted?'

This suggestion was greeted with a wall of silence, but Charlie had enough selling experience to wait it out for the answer. He eventually heard movement and paper rustling and realised Sharon was probably checking a diary.

'Go on, then,' she answered as if he was twisting her arm. 'I suppose I can postpone the engaged couple I was due to harangue with the sanctity of marriage if we happen to be late back.'

'Then it's a da...' he started and caught himself. '...day at the races!' he concluded.

She didn't reply immediately and he realised he'd not nearly been slick enough to cover his faux pas.

'Well done, by the way,' she stated, back into her warm voice. 'Even if Cool Blue doesn't win, the church will get its plumbing upgraded, which was well overdue, and the parishioners will be warmer in winter as a result of your kindness. Please thank Mr. Lewis.'

'No problem,' Charlie assured her, 'I'll be sure to tell Sam.'

They traded a few more remarks regarding times and arrangements and Charlie put the phone down in a state of fuzzy warmness. He was still standing with a crinkled smile when his phone chirruped at him again. He checked the number this time and saw it was a Leeds regional code.

'Is that Charlie Summer?' asked a light Liverpool accent before he could announce himself.

'Charlie Summer speaking,' he confirmed slowly, all the warmth draining from him.

'My name is Frank Best, I work for BetMick, the bookmakers. Mr. Mick Kowalski and I would like to meet with Mr. Lewis before his horse is declared for the Lincoln. Can this be arranged?'

Seventeen

Sam's physical response to the meeting request from his nemesis Mick Kowalski had caught Charlie by surprise. Sitting with Sam in the back of his car, Charlie was only dimly aware of the North Lincolnshire countryside scooting past the window as he was too busy pondering what possible meaning Sam's uncharacteristically cruel smile and a lick of his lips could mean for their imminent appointment with Kowalski. Sam's expression had stung Charlie; for those few seconds Sam had probably revealed more of himself than he realised. Charlie stole a glance at his client across the few feet of luxurious leather that separated them on the backseat of his chauffeur driven Range Rover; it did nothing to settle his growing concern.

They'd agreed to meet Kowalski and his colleague Frank Best at one of their BetMick betting shops in Scunthorpe at eight o'clock that same evening. Charlie guessed Kowalski must have caught his Racing TV interview, as he'd suggested a BetMick betting shop only forty minutes from Market Rasen racecourse. Just the two of them were to attend, Suzie and Stan were despatched back to Leeds in Charlie's car to manage the various communications which were pouring in by phone, email, and on social media.

Sam hadn't said more than a few words since they had left Market Rasen. His joy at having succeeded in winning two races at the track had evaporated as soon as Mick Kowalski's meeting request had been received. He had quickly become introspective and nervous.

Choosing his words and tone carefully, Charlie broke the silence.

'Am I an observer Sam, or do you have a role for me at this meeting?'

A hardened version of Sam's face acknowledged the question with a sharp twitch. He remained silent. After three heavy breaths expelled through his nose he finally answered with a question of his own.

'What would be the effect on our little coup if I was to instruct Joss Faraday not to declare Cool Blue tomorrow for the Lincoln?'

Charlie's heart missed a beat. He considered not answering and restating his own question, but thought better of it… for now.

'As far as the bets the charities have placed are concerned, Cool Blue was an antepost selection. If he doesn't run, either at the declaration stage, or if he's a non-runner on the day, he will be settled by every bookmaker as a loser. Each charity will still win about seven thousand pounds, but their chance of pocketing three quarters of a million pounds would disappear.'

Sam nodded thoughtfully, staring blindly ahead. His outline, framed by the car window caught the dying rays of the spring sun as it dipped beyond the horizon, causing blades of his short silver hair to glisten. Charlie waited; biting back the surge of frustration he sensed building inside him.

Suddenly Sam swivelled in his seat to face Charlie, the setting sun now at his back, forming a golden aura around his head and shoulders while his facial features remained largely in shadow. Charlie wondered if Sam could sense how commanding he appeared and decided he couldn't rule it out.

'I've waited many years to engineer this, er, *type* of meeting with Mick Kowalski,' Sam stated in a level tone. 'I need to beg your understanding and patience this evening, but most of all, your loyalty.'

He clasped his hands together and they rocked as he continued to speak, as if pressure were being applied to them.

'You and your staff have acted admirably so far. However, this meeting is very personal. You do not have to say or do anything. What transpires between Kowalski and me is outside your remit.'

Sam paused for a few seconds, allowing his hands to drop to his lap. 'Of course, I do have my reasons for dragging you along, not least for your knowledge of betting. But to be honest, I want you there to witness what is said and interpret Mick's reactions for me. I want you to be my eyes.'

'To help broker some sort of deal?' Charlie ventured.

'No, not really,' Sam admitted, leaning back into his seat and turning to stare ahead once more. 'I want you to make sure I don't kill the wily little shit.'

Charlie glared at the silver outline of the man, needing to ease the muscles in his cheeks that had become taut. Sam glanced over in Charlie's general direction wearing a waspish grin and added, 'I'm kidding, son.'

The rest of the journey was completed in silence. Charlie spent the time trying to fathom where he stood with Sam and kept coming up empty. Sam continued to sit quietly, lost in thought, his eyes half closed.

They reached the betting shop Frank had specified as the sunset was fading to grey. The car pulled into a makeshift car park on a rough piece of ground opposite the shop and the driver, a fit looking thirty year old, who Charlie guessed could double as a security guard, jumped out and went to the rear of the car to release Harvey. Left in the car alone with Sam, Charlie turned to face him with the intention of asking further questions. Before he could open his mouth, Sam beat him to it.

'You don't have to come with me.'

Charlie eyed Sam for a few seconds. He was sat rigidly upright and unmoving. His reply was slow and stern.

'Even with the limited knowledge I have about your relationship with Mick Kowalski, I couldn't allow you to go in there alone.'

'Harvey and I…'

'I insist,' Charlie stated bluntly.

After a short pause Sam nodded curtly. 'That's good,' he added with a positive inclination of his head.

Charlie detected the hint of a smirk around the corners of Sam's mouth as the older man swung his legs around and got out of the car. He wondered for a moment whether staying in the back of the Range Rover wouldn't be the sensible option. There was obviously history between these two men, and he didn't wish to get involved in any of their bitterness. Shaking negative thoughts from his head he jumped out of the car, inwardly scolding himself for being so melodramatic. Sam and Kowalski were businessmen; they were here to discuss business.

Charlie joined Sam and Harvey on the other side of the car and looked around this dimly lit corner of Scunthorpe. Sam shared a few short words with the chauffeur who returned to the driver's seat. They were standing on a piece of derelict land, consisting of square oblongs of concrete from long gone buildings interspersed with grassy areas embedded with brick rubble. It looked as though three houses at the end of a street had been bulldozed and the remaining flat land was being utilised as free parking by customers of a seventies style flat-roofed shopping arcade across the road. The headlights from Sam's car lit their ever-darkening path across the road and up to the end of the line of shops where a window and hanging sign advertised the fact it was a BetMick betting shop.

'I understand the betting shop is over this road...' Sam said, his last few words framing more of a question than a statement.

Charlie took Sam's arm in his. 'It's about forty yards away, you'd better let me lead, there's bricks and broken bottles all over the ground.'

In a small room above the betting shop filled with cardboard boxes containing betting slip stock, Mick Kowalski and Frank Best stood at a faded net curtained window and watched the two figures follow a circuitous route toward the shop. Backlit by the Range Rover's headlight beams the two men and their dog threw garish shadows against the shop's façade as they approached.

'He's always had a taste for the dramatic,' Mick said with a scowl. It's hard to believe he's as blind as a bat.'

He turned on his heel, making for the stairs at the back of the room. Frank lingered at the window, brushing the net curtains apart. He'd come across Sam Lewis before but he was keen to examine the face of Charlie Summer, the man who had executed what in Frank's view was a clever and carefully considered coup. He watched the strange trio until they were only a few strides from the shop door where they came to a shuffling halt. Charlie looked sharply upwards and locked eyes with Frank. Frank stared down and only a second into eye contact with Charlie, was struck by a sudden wave of nervousness and automatically stepped back from the window and out of sight.

'That's probably Frank Best,' Sam whispered, after Charlie had related the man's actions up in the window. 'You spoke to him on the phone. An intelligent, thoughtful man. Obsessed with business and wholly controlled in every aspect by Mick.'

'This shop doesn't look like it gets much love,' Charlie noted out loud for Sam's benefit, going on to describe the fading eighties sports scene set up behind the window, tastefully garnished with a carpet of dead bluebottles. The white paint on the windowsills had cracked and peeled many years before and rot was now invading the wood.

'He doesn't spend a penny on his properties,' Sam explained. 'He buys small, independent chains of bookmakers and then relies on his name and big bonuses to draw in punters. He targets the big money punters and lures them into problem gambling if he can. The rest he tries to convert to his website business, BetMick.com. The whole setup is geared to getting the punters signed up to his online business. The shops are just recruiting posts and when they've sucked up the new customers for the web, and run the shop into the ground, he closes the shops and lets the staff go.'

'You seem to know quite a bit about his business plan,' said Charlie, searching for the handle to the shop door and pushing it open.

'I should do, it was my brother who taught him how to do it,' Sam answered grimly.

Unsurprisingly, the air of neglect continued inside the shop. Sam and Charlie stepped onto a threadbare red carpet which was patched with a mishmash of silver coloured strips of adhesive duct tape. Charlie presumed the tape ensured punters wouldn't trip on rips in the carpet. On closer inspection they might be covering large stains, he couldn't be sure. There was a strong tang of cigarettes and Charlie guessed the ban on smoking wasn't being enforced too enthusiastically. Yellow betting slip copies littered the floor, something most modern bookmakers had dispensed with long ago. Thin fluorescent tubes shone down onto the walls from small wooden pelmets and underneath them, newspaper pages were tacked to green or blue felt boards. A steel shelf with a raised rim ran around the entire room at leaning height, covered in used and screwed up betting slips and stubby pencils. The whole room smelled of decay and Charlie was sure he caught sight of several silverfish out of the corner of his eye, as they darted for cover where the carpet met the paint peeled skirting boards.

The only faintly new equipment in the room was a bank of eight small flat screen televisions against one wall, and three betting machines displaying spinning digital roulette wheels. The machines blinked incessantly to each other, shoulder to shoulder in the recess created by the entrance Sam and Charlie had just walked through. The rectangular room had little in the way of furniture. A few stools screwed to the floor were the only apparent concession to comfort. At the far end was an old-fashioned betting counter encased in re-enforced glass. The ribbons of steel were clearly visible, running diagonally within the glass to advertise its strength to would-be robbers. A three-inch gap was left between the glass and the counter. To the right of the glass box was a dingy, poorly lit corridor. A sign on the corridor wall possessed a large pointing finger which informed the idle or possibly desperate customers that this was the way to the 'Gents'. It appeared women were not catered for.

Charlie hadn't been in a betting shop for some time, but had passed a number of the big brand high street chains during shopping trips and assumed their airy, open counters, seating areas and tea or coffee facilities were now the standard setup for a bookmaker. This shop appeared to be proudly maintaining the grubby, den of iniquity image beloved of the seventies and eighties. Despite the night racing commentary from Kempton burbling from the TV screens, the shop was eerily empty. There were no punters and no one appeared to be behind the counter.

Charlie watched Harvey for a short while. The big dog couldn't take his nose off the carpet, sniffing in big gulps of the various pungent aromas, eventually sneezing violently and lifting his head to reveal watery eyes.

Charlie was in the middle of relating their surroundings to Sam when there was movement behind the counter. A door into a back room opened and two men walked through. They positioned themselves side by side, the taller one leaning both hands on the counter and staring through the scuffed and scratched glass wall.

'Samuel Lewis,' Mick stated in an amused tone, 'I thought you'd be dead by now.'

Beside him, Frank hissed something and Mick returned a contemptuous glance and few sharp words to his colleague which Charlie didn't catch. He slanted a look at Sam and caught the twitch of a shudder from him; Mick Kowalski's words had plainly had the desired effect. Sam pursed his lips and sighed before speaking. 'And you, *Mick*, are just as despicable as I remember.'

Mick forced out a loud guffaw. His belly laugh reverberated around the small glass room and into the public area of the betting shop. As his laugh died he smacked a palm onto the counter, which made Harvey spring to attention and give a little whine of concern.

'We agreed we'd be conciliatory!' Frank said through gritted teeth and quietly enough to keep his comment private. Mick pushed his stringy black hair back with both hands and held it in a thinly matted ponytail for a few seconds. He sighed resignedly and releasing his hair, allowed his hands to fall limply to his sides. He watched with dull eyes as Frank tapped out the four-digit code on the security door leading to the corridor and let himself out of the glass box.

'Frank Best is coming over,' whispered Charlie out of the side of

85

his mouth. He waited for the small, virtually bald headed man to reach him and was puzzled when he smiled, but passed by and headed for the door. Frank produced a key from his trouser pocket and locked the shop door, turned and explained 'So we aren't disturbed. It's just the four of us. The staff and punters have been sent home.'

'I'm Frank Best,' he announced, returning with his hand held out. Charlie took it and swapped a sweaty palmed shake with him, but Sam made no effort to do the same.

As he was about to introduce himself, Charlie recognised his own voice coming over the shop's speakers. His face suddenly appeared on three of the small television monitors on the wall: Racing TV was broadcasting a repeat of Stephen's interview. Frank glanced up at the monitors and then tilted his head toward Charlie, a cockeyed smirk on his face.

'And you need no introduction,' he offered, followed by a raised eyebrow.

'Thank you both for coming this evening. I would like to speak on a strictly business footing with you both if I may,' Frank started, turning to face Charlie and Sam. The smirk had vanished, replaced with an earnest gaze.

'We have taken thirteen of your charitable bets today,' he continued, 'Congratulations on your... er, luck by the way, however Mr. Kowalski and I we were wondering whether you would consider a cash out offer?'

Charlie looked for a reaction from Sam, however he was standing in silence, wearing a sullen expression and giving no indication he was intending to reply. His only movement was a roll of Harvey's harness between his fingers. Charlie decided to take the bull by the horns.

'What sort of cash out offer?'

'Well, let's see,' Frank said, warming to his subject. 'Each of your bets currently stand to pay out just shy of seven thousand pounds, and we would be prepared to offer fourteen...'

'Firstly, they aren't *our bets*,' Sam cut in, 'And secondly, there is no way we can influence the final race on Saturday.'

'Come, come...' Frank said reproachfully, a sly sparkle evident in his eyes, 'You own the horse Mr. Lewis. You can instruct your trainer not to declare Cool Blue for the Lincoln tomorrow morning. He wouldn't run, and your last bet would be a losing selection. However, if that were to happen, we would be willing to pay each of your charities twice the value of their current winnings. Call it our way of... *supporting* your charities, if you wish.'

Charlie noticed movement from behind the counter and Mick Kowalski strode out into the public area of the shop, crossing over to sit on a small round stool screwed to the floor in front of the bank of monitors.

He threw one leg over the other and leaned back languorously so his hair hung like a limp black curtain from the back of his head. He studied the two men for a few seconds.

'You'll know, Sam and I have previous,' Mick told Charlie in a presumptive manner, 'He'll have *surely* filled you in on our little spats?'

Charlie watched Mick's eyes as they surveyed Sam's reaction intently. There was none, Sam continued to finger Harvey's harness and maintained an impenetrable stare.

'In fact, Mr. Samuel Lewis managed to hurt himself last time we met!' Mick added triumphantly. Again, Sam remained silent.

'He attacked me in my own office. Tried to strike me and managed to fall over his own feet...'

'You deserved to be struck,' Sam accused, his face finally descending into a mask of poorly concealed hatred.

His goading having achieved its goal, Mick broke into a broad smile. Charlie thought it made Mick's face look ghoulish. His receding hairline, the flattened end to his nose and the stark creases running from Mick's nose to his chin reminded Charlie of a villain from his childhood. He pondered this whilst being aware he was becoming physically repulsed by the man in front of him. Then realisation struck; Mick Kowalski was the child catcher from Chitty Chitty Bang Bang... The only thing missing to complete the transformation was a large crumpled black hat worn jauntily on his head.

Charlie and Tommy had loved the film as naïve youngsters, being enchanted by the flying car, wishing so much that they could have been those children, and scared beyond comprehension by the child catcher. Charlie realised as an adult how exquisitely Robert Helpmann had played the role, but it didn't halt the return of those childish fears in some small way. The comparison now made him baulk at the strangely similar figure reclining languidly in front of him.

Without any further reaction from Sam and Charlie, apart from glares filled with loathing, Frank joined the conversation once more. He felt he needed to repair the damage done by Mick.

'Looking at the chances Cool Blue holds in the Lincoln on Saturday,' he pointed out hopefully, 'I would have thought an enhanced payout would more than compensate for him not racing,'

It was Sam's turn to laugh. He chuckled, emitting an odd hooting noise from his nose, fighting for breath as his mirth continued and increased in volume. He laughed like this for a long time, so long the two bookmakers started to exchange frowns, uncertain what to make of the blind man. Sam's laugh struck Charlie as strangely unnerving. In one way it was pouring scorn on their belief he could be bought off, yet in another he was mocking Mick and Frank's ignorance.

'You two clowns don't have any idea do you?' Sam finally choked out as his laughing subsided. Mick stood up, his confusion and irritation showing in his brittle posture and indignant expression. He swivelled to face Charlie.

'You know he's mad, don't you?' Mick shouted, jabbing his pointed index finger toward Sam. 'He thinks I had something to do with his precious brother disappearing. He's had me followed, broken into my business premises and physically assaulted me! Now he's trying to ruin my business.'

'By picking winners?' Charlie queried smoothly.

He filed the accusations away for future inspection, but just now, in a grubby betting shop in Scunthorpe, late at night and with the doors locked, he felt he needed to diffuse the situation.

Before Mick could reply, Charlie added in the same serious tone, 'Surely, you can't believe you're the only bookmaker affected? If you think we only targeted you, then think again. You're one of many.'

This news stopped Mick's rant. The ramifications of their fourteen bets being only the tip of a coup iceberg gave him far less leverage. If there were plenty more betting slips out there with other bookmakers, his offer to cash out could be of no significance.

'How many others, Mr. Summer?' Frank asked.

Charlie looked over at Sam. 'Do I tell him, Sam?'

'Sure,' Sam said with a shrug. 'Tell him about *all* the others.'

'All?' Charlie echoed.

'Absolutely.'

Although it was Frank's question, Charlie faced Mick, aware that his reaction was likely to be the more explosive.

'We haven't finished collating the responses from the charitable causes, but at last count there were sixteen with BetMick and forty-two with other bookmakers.'

Mick's face slowly drained of its colour.

'Your cash out option is so small in the grand scheme of the bets, to be insignificant,' Charlie continued, '…and in fact, I'm surprised you're not aware that twenty-four of the bets from the other bookmakers are with Sutherlands.'

Charlie took a step away from Mick and toward Sam as soon as the word 'Sutherlands' left his lips, taking up what he hoped would be prove to be a protective stance, if required.

Mick didn't react. He looked stunned for a few seconds then stormed over to Frank, bearing down on the man.

'What does he mean?' he demanded viciously, spittle flying from his teeth as he spoke, 'That bunch of shitty shops we bought in West Yorkshire?'

'We only completed on them last week,' Frank reported weakly, cowering under the larger man's chest as Mick leaned in on him. 'They aren't part of our reporting network yet. I only included the two we knew about.'

Mick unleashed a torrent of abusive language at his colleague, expletives mixed in with numbers, as his brain grasped the enormity of their new position on the bet. Frank backed away to the wall, his face clasped in both hands.

Mick suddenly tired of berating Frank and stopped stomping on the spot. He glanced at the wall and lunged over to grab a handful of old fashioned two copy betting slips from a wall dispenser and spun on his heel. He went for Sam and Charlie, eyes wide and wild, and lifted his hand above his head two strides from them, set to throw the slips.

'Custodio!' called Sam in a clear voice.

Sam simultaneously dropped Harvey's harness and the German Shepherd sprang forward purposefully to meet Mick. The dog's muscles were suddenly taut, his docile nature transformed into savage rage in response to this one word.

Harvey's growl was truly impressive. Charlie watched in morbid fascination as the dog produced a deep-throated challenge to the advancing man, the dog's eyes never leaving its prey. Shocked, Mick tried to stop, but his forward momentum made him take a step too close. Harvey sprang up onto Mick's chest, snarling and bearing a set of needle sharp teeth which frothed and threatened serious injury. Mick saw a huge jaw rise up to his face and snap shut an inch from his nose. He involuntarily let go of the handful of betting slips and they fluttered down around him. The dog landed on all four feet and paused for a second, ignoring the betting slips, solely focussed on Mick. Harvey took two steps forward, raising his lips to display two neat racks of flesh tearing teeth, and emitting a deep, reverberating growl, forcing Mick backwards. The bookmaker held out his hands, fingers splayed, back bent low, and didn't take his horrified eyes from the dog's mouth. Harvey took a quick step forward and to Mick's horror he stumbled and fell onto his backside. Harvey leapt and landed his front paws on Mick's chest, still growling and baring his teeth. Mick covered his eyes with both hands and started to scream Sam's name, pleading with him to get the animal off.

Sam walked the ten feet to where his guide dog was standing, two paws still on Mick's chest, felt for the dog's harness and grasped it. However, he didn't pull the dog off the prone man as Charlie was expecting, instead Sam bent down.

'Want to save your business Mick?' Sam asked over the sound of Harvey's continued throaty growl. 'Tell me what you did to my brother the night of the accident. I want the truth. That's all I've ever wanted.'

Mick slowly removed his hands, revealing a face which had turned beetroot. He held his fingers only a few inches away from his angry skin, still fearful the dog would attack. Strands of matted hair fell across his face, some over his nose and into his mouth. The black hair blew left and right as he panted in short, hot breaths. He glared up at Sam from the shop floor, sweat trickling off his chin, making his throat glisten.

'You're a bloody lunatic,' he managed in a high-pitched whine. 'I've told you before, you fool; I wasn't there.'

'Now you know I don't believe you Mick,' Sam replied softly, his Geordie accent reasserting itself. 'Why would Laurie be driving your car? Tell me the proper story and I'll declare Cool Blue a non-runner. I get the truth about my brother's death and you get to keep your business.'

Mick bent his elbows and started to push himself up onto his shoulders. Harvey responded with another bloodcurdling snarl which was so primal both Frank and Charlie took an involuntary step away from the man on the floor. Mick shrank back. He pushed one cheek to the floor, both hands firmly guarding his face, the smell of dust and cigarettes from the carpet burning his nasal cavity. He could feel the dog's claws tensing; pulling at the skin of his abdomen and his knees reacted by bending and folding up.

Charlie realised he was watching the scene with an open mouth. This felt all wrong. He hadn't signed up for… he struggled to find the words at first. Torture, yes, this was what he was witnessing. He considered moving forward to try and part the man from the dog, but how? He was powerless.

'Well?' Sam queried, louder now.

Mick didn't reply; he lay quiet and unmoving for perhaps ten seconds. Charlie began to worry that Harvey would lose patience and strike. The dog was still snarling and reacting to every single movement Mick made, no matter how insignificant. Thankfully, Mick made a crackling noise which signified the clearing of his throat, and he spoke.

'Declare your horse a non-runner and I'll tell you.'

Sam straightened and threw his head back as if he was going to laugh, but instead he barked, 'Hah,' loudly at the ceiling. Harvey intensified his growling, eyeing Mick hungrily.

'It doesn't work like that Mick,' Sam said through a sneer. 'You think I'd fall for that one again did you?'

Mick didn't answer, not that he could, even if he wanted to. His hands were scrabbling around his face and neck, in response to Harvey moving further up his chest. The German Shepherd was now almost straddling the man, pinning him to the floor, so close to his head his growls wafted the strands of his unruly hair. Mick whimpered as the dog's saliva started to drip onto his upturned cheek.

'No,' Sam stated sternly. 'You have to tell me, and *if I believe you* you'll get your non-runner. You have until the morning of the race. I'll be at Doncaster races on Saturday. You can come and tell me what happened to my brother. If you convince me, you'll get to keep your business. If not,

90

well, we'll see which way fate takes us.'

Sam straightened once more and gave a quiet command of 'Cesso' to Harvey and the dog removed his paws from Mick's chest, padded behind Sam, and resumed his usual seated position at his master's side. All signs of the dog's anger were gone and replaced with a lolling tongue and soft brown eyes. Sam's hand went to his jacket pocked and he dropped a small treat into the dog's mouth.

'Charlie. It's time for us to leave. Mick has some thinking to do,' and he and Harvey walked to the door.

'Mr. Best, if you would be so good as to open the door?' Sam asked, his Geordie accent stifled for once by his overt courteousness.

Frank had his back to the wall, but after a quick glance down at Mick, he pushed himself away from the steel shelf. He rushed over, fiddled with his keys, clanked the hooked steel claw lock back, and pulled the shop door open.

Charlie picked his way past Mick, who was still lying spread-eagled on the floor, panting for breath between colourful expletives. He followed Sam out into the cool March evening air. The driver was waiting for them, having brought the car right up onto the pavement outside the shop and he helped Sam into the back seat. Harvey was placed in his cage in the back of the Range Rover.

Charlie walked round, climbed shakily into the back of the car, and slumped into his seat, dazed by the last few minutes. As the car set off he glanced into the shop's open door to see Mick back on his feet, busy remonstrating with Frank. Charlie turned and started to form a question for Sam, but the words wouldn't come. Sam sensed Charlie's astonishment and shot a hand out to try and pat him. Charlie caught Sam's arm; a defensive reaction.

'Please, don't be shocked,' Sam said as Charlie released his hand. 'Mick was never in any danger.' Then after a short pause he smiled before adding, 'I was actually very restrained; it would have been very different if I'd used the command 'Deleo'.'

Charlie swallowed hard. Plumbing his memory for his faint knowledge of Latin verbs gained as a fourteen-year-old schoolboy, he was pretty sure that 'Deleo' translated to 'exterminate'.

Eighteen

Frank had given up trying to calm Mick down. His boss was incandescent with rage and most of his words were unintelligible. He wasn't listening anyway. He concentrated on where Mick's fists, feet, and head were, ready to dodge anything that came his way. He reasoned Mick would have to calm down... eventually.

It took another thirty seconds. Mick started to struggle for breath and began to pant again. Standing in the centre of the shop he leaned over, his hands on his thighs, sucking in air so hard, Frank could see the rise and fall of Mick's spine between his shoulder blades. Mick's hair fell over his forehead and down his face and he finally ceased ranting.

Frank stopped cringing against the wall of the betting office and straightened. Mick was still bent double and Frank sensed it was time to try and build bridges once more. Sam Lewis may have the upper hand at the moment, but the game was nowhere near finished. Frank took a few steps forward.

'We don't have to pay out. We can claim collusion and group betting patterns...' he started, taking another few steps toward Mick. 'Come on, Mick, we can still fight this one, we've done it before...' he bent over and in a low voice said, 'We can sort this...'

Mick raised his head and looked into the smaller man's beady grey-blue eyes. For a split second Frank saw the danger lying there, but he was too close. He tried to back off but his reaction came too late. Mick straightened, stuck out a claw-like hand, and slapped Frank's face hard. Shocked, Frank tottered back a step, his arms wheeling as he tried in vain to regain his balance. Mick watched his colleague of ten years stumble backwards. Frank seemed to be regaining his balance when his foot became entangled with something on the floor.

Time seemed to slow down for Mick, watching in wide-eyed, open-mouthed fascination as the heel of Frank's shoe became stuck to a rogue piece of duct tape which had become half-unstuck from the betting shop carpet. With his momentum pushing him inexorably backwards and unable to plant his stuck foot, Frank toppled backwards, falling away. Mick grinned, anticipating Frank would land on his backside in slapstick fashion. His grin reversed into a frown when halfway through his descent to the carpet the back of Frank's head connected with the steel shelf on the wall of the betting office. A dull metallic thump saw Frank's jaw jolt into his chest and his eyes flew up into their sockets. His body hit the betting shop floor with none of the comedic effect Mick had hoped for.

'Frank?' Mick tried. He stepped tentatively forward, holding the bridge of his nose, trying to comprehend, fearing the worst. He squinted to the open door, then back to the unmoving body, taking two steps closer.

Lying awkwardly, Frank's face lolled to one side and an engorged, bloodied tongue hung out of his mouth; he must have bitten into it. Mick winced and his nose twitched with repugnance. He quietly, almost tenderly, tried calling Franks name twice more but when he spotted the unfocussed eyes staring along the carpet he knew Frank wasn't going to answer. He bowed down to hold a finger to his colleague's neck, and found a weak pulse.

Mick knew he should be rushing to a phone and calling for help. Yet he was still standing over Frank. He looked to the ceiling, linked his fingers around the back of his neck, and sucked air into his lungs in big gulps. He closed his eyes and forced himself to concentrate. He'd been in an eerily similar situation before. The key was to remain cool and focussed, in order to see the *benefits* which he could potentially gain.

A few seconds later Mick's eyes sprang open and he glanced to the shop door, then to the back of the betting office and around the ceiling. The shop didn't have any CCTV.

Mick shook a malicious grin from his face which had worked its way there during his contemplations, and adopted what he hoped was a worried expression, in case a passing pedestrian should peer into the shop door, left open by Sam Lewis. He had to work carefully and quickly.

His decision made, Mick trotted to the shop door and after a furtive look outside into the dimly lit street, he closed it as quietly as possible. Returning to Frank, it only took a quick pat of two jacket pockets before he found the keys; he tried not to look into his colleagues eyes. Mick went back and attempted to lock the shop door softly, wincing when the steel mechanism clanged noisily into place. Then he walked directly toward the bottom of the shop, stopping for a few seconds to stamp down on the duct tape Frank's fall had dislodged. He entered the staff area and went straight through the back door. The small back room consisted of a set of steep, thin stairs against the left wall and a small galley made up of a sink, taps and draining board. A partition wall encased a toilet whose door was emblazoned with the word 'The Office' written in black marker pen. His eyes narrowed as he searched the galley until he found what he was looking for: the kettle. Mick filled it to maximum, clicked it on, used the toilet, and waited patiently for the kettle to boil before making two cups of coffee.

Thirty minutes later Mick watched from behind a veil of crocodile tears as the ambulance crew took Frank away. He was alive, however, the paramedics had worked very quickly and wore serious expressions. Mick experienced mixed emotions as Frank departed. He hadn't liked the man particularly; however, Frank had been a decent financial controller. If he did wake up, he'd have to make sure…

His attention snapped back to the WPC beside him who was asking another question. The betting shop was awash with police officers. The shop door was open and blue light strafed the yellowing suspended ceiling tiles every few seconds. Beside him on the small stools in front of the bank of monitors, the police officer was sat cross-legged, making notes. Two cups of cold, untouched coffee sat on the steel shelf behind him.

'Mr. Kowalski?' the girl queried. Mick looked at her. He'd thought she was just a girl, but with her hair scraped back under her hat it was difficult to tell what age she could be. He looked a little harder and saw at least ten years of experience in her eyes.

'Yes, I'm sorry, it's been a bit of a shock,' he replied with a half smile.

That had sounded genuine enough he thought, but he'd have to control his smile. He forced his features to harden, ever so slowly.

'The two men who were in the shop,' the police officer restated, 'They'd left when you went to make the coffee?'

Mick nodded sadly. 'We'd had an argument about a bet. One of them had a vicious dog which they used to threaten Frank and me, so we asked them to leave. The whole thing shook Frank up, so I thought a coffee would help. I left him watching the seven o'clock race from Kempton.'

He stole a glance at the WPC who had her head down, writing as he spoke. No one else was close enough to hear their conversation.

'I suppose the shop door was still open...' Mick said airily.

'Could they have re-entered the shop?' she asked sharply.

Mick could have cheered. He rubbed his chin thoughtfully and sighed.

'Well, I suppose so... but surely they couldn't have...'

He'd answered with what he judged to be the right amount of uncertainty tinged with sincerity. He waited, rocking on his stool slightly, praying his words had worked.

The WPC stopped writing and looked into Mick's eyes. He blinked and flicked them away, choosing to stare balefully at the carpet instead. He cringed inside; he should have held her gaze for longer.

'Do you know the names of these two men?'

Inside Mick's head, another cheer went up.

****

Charlie stared gloomily out of the executive SUV's window as Scunthorpe and the BetMick betting shop became a fading blob of light at their backs. Charlie was debating whether to allow his anger to be released. He swallowing down this temptation but found himself screwing his face up in distaste as he recalling the hatred both men had shown, and the shock of Sam using Harvey as an instrument of extreme intimidation.

He took a sideway's look at Sam. He was wearing a contented, satisfied expression and appeared to be deep in thought. They had not spoken since climbing into the back seat of the car five minutes ago. Charlie examined the blind man's face in greater detail and shivered when he thought he detected a vengeful sneer creeping over Sam's features. He realised his pulse was racing and took a trio of calming breaths. They didn't help; he still felt uneasy. The celebratory atmosphere provided by the two winning horses had evaporated and his respect for Sam was also fading fast. But this wasn't a time to get angry he told himself; he needed to use Sam's post-revenge contentment to reassess his client and determine whether he was serious about pulling Cool Blue out of the Lincoln.

'I didn't realise your disagreement with Kowalski was this serious,' he said slowly and softly, his gaze locked on Sam, just in case the older man could read anything of his facial expression, 'I can't imagine how you must feel. The injustice must be hard for you to bear.'

Charlie paused, hopeful his words sounded believable and that silence would allow the appropriate sentiment to resonate with his listener.

'I can only assume there is a lack of evidence linking Mick Kowalski to your brother's disappearance, and this has motivated you to act in such a severe manner?' he asked, searching for the smallest grain of agreement.

'Perhaps I should have warned you,' Sam stated evenly following another period of silent reflection. He had seemingly returned to his former, amiable state.

'You've done a decent job, son,' he continued, 'But you don't know the history between me and Kowalski. The man only responds to threats, it's the way he does business.'

'That's okay, I understand that now,' Charlie agreed, nodding.

The car fell silent once again. Charlie used the time to assess his options. Just like any business meeting, the key was to plant your own idea or objective with the client in such a way they seize upon it and make their own. Meeting that requirement was then attainable, and hopefully, straightforward. Charlie steeled himself and made his move.

'Given what you've said Sam, placing further pressure on Kowalski may be the only way you will reach the truth.'

He waited patiently for his bait to be taken. Outside, the motorway banking scudded past, subdued road noise providing the only backing track as the blind man considered Charlie's words.

Sam grunted and turned to Charlie once more, his interest clearly piqued. However, he made a point of regarding his passenger for a few seconds before replying. Even though Charlie knew this was just posturing, he felt a shiver start at the top of his spine and shoot downwards through him. Sam may as well have twenty-twenty vision, Charlie thought, given the feeling of fear and revulsion his sightless eyes could elicit. Finally, Sam spoke, using a low tone.

'What do you suggest?'

Nineteen

Charlie emerged from Leeds Police Station and onto Park Street at midday on Thursday and was met by a knot of about a dozen media people insistent on firing questions at him. His solicitor departed, but Charlie stood firm, well versed in dealing with the press. He held up both palms, making a shushing motion and promised to answer their questions if the various reporters, cameramen, and photographers would calm down and form an orderly ring around him. There had been plenty of time during his wait inside the police station to anticipate their questions and he set about knocking them off one by one.

'No, I've not been charged with anything,' he told the first questioner, 'I was simply being eliminated from an inquiry following a horrible accident which happened last night in Scunthorpe. I had left the premises before the accident occurred.'

'Any comment on the fact that your coup partner Mr. Samuel Lewis is also helping the police?' asked a scruffy reporter with an unkempt full-set beard.

'Yes, I understand Samuel Lewis is facing similar questions up in Newcastle. Neither of us have anything to hide. This matter has no connection to Mr. Lewis's charitable betting advice.'

There was a general muttering in response to this answer. Charlie sensed the group's unease and tried to pick up on why this would be, getting a feeling he wasn't being believed. He decided to alter his approach.

'Do any of you know anything about Frank Best's condition?'

Charlie received a number of frowns and shrugs. However, a man in a long raincoat and a tweed flat cap standing at the edge of the semicircle of reporters cleared his throat. Several necks twisted toward him. He cast an appraising eye up and down Charlie, eventually locking eyes with him through heavily darkened glasses.

'I believe Mr. Best is recovering well. He has left intensive care this morning. I understand he is a bookmaker...'

He spoke in a clipped manner, with a light, faintly public school accent, pausing in order to hold the small group hanging for a moment.

'Why were you and Sam Lewis talking to a bookmaker in Scunthorpe?' he inquired.

Charlie examined the man more closely. He was in his late thirties, possibly early forties, and Charlie got the distinct impression he somehow didn't belong with this group. Beneath his thin, unbuttoned raincoat, he wore vintage clothes that Charlie found reminiscent of the nineteen forties. The only difference was this man wore large, dark glasses which almost obscured his eyes. His speech had been light and self-assured; however Charlie caught a sort of resigned, world-weariness in his stance. He retained a concerned expression and answered the man directly.

'Mr. Michael Kowalski wished to discuss the bets he had accepted from a number of charities.'

'Was there a deal done?' the man persisted quietly.

Charlie frowned, initially thrown by the directness of the question.

'No,' he countered forcefully, 'Besides, the bets are not ours. The charities hold the betting slips, not us.'

Charlie watched as the man attempted to halt the spread of condescension across his face. 'Yes, but Mr. Lewis owns the horse which will make all the difference to their winnings,' the man stated flatly.

It wasn't a question, the fact was simply rolled out for everyone present to consider. The questioner stared at him intently. Charlie got the impression the man was measuring him, quantifying his reactions in the micro-movements of his face.

'I can assure you no deal was brokered,' Charlie stated firmly.

The man pursed his lips and gave Charlie one slow, deliberate nod. His reaction gave no indication he believed the statement, on the contrary, the man was displaying a healthy scepticism.

Others now took up this line of inquiry. The questions continued and Charlie batted them off. Eventually the queries started to angle away from Mick Kowalski and Samuel Lewis and centre upon the bets placed by the charities and the Lincoln handicap at Doncaster in two days time.

'I've no idea whether the horse has even been declared by his trainer or whether Cool Blue has managed to make the cut,' admitted Charlie when he was asked if Cool Blue would definitely be racing on Saturday. 'I've been inside here for the last two and a half hours!' he added, hoisting a thumb over his shoulder toward the redbrick central Leeds police station building behind him.

'It's the first thing I'm going to check once I've dealt with you lot!' Charlie added lightly.

Inside, he felt anything but light-hearted. Charlie didn't trust Sam; he may have *already* pulled the gelding out of the race. Although he hadn't lied outright, Charlie now felt sullied, and compromised by his association with Sam Lewis. That was something he had to put right.

Charlie forced as benign a smile as he could muster, casting his eyes around the small arc of media types. He hoped none of them picked up on the worry that had been gnawing away inside him since the previous night. He scanned the crescent of reporters and discovered the man with the tweed flat cap on the end of the line had disappeared. Charlie peered up and down Park Street wondering why he would leave before the impromptu press conference was over. He thought he saw a pair of raincoated shoulders disappear around the corner of the street, but couldn't be sure.

'He has been declared,' the cameraman from Sky TV informed the group, his smartphone shining blue light onto his face as he checked the screen. 'Cool Blue managed to scrape in at the bottom of the handicap,' he added, a note of excitement present in his voice, 'He's number twenty-two of twenty-two runners.'

Charlie aimed a thanking inclination of his head at the man with a television grade camera on his shoulder. Tension flowed away from Charlie and he was able to allow an easy smile to brighten his features, this time without any effort.

'I'm delighted Cool Blue will be running on Saturday, and Mr. Lewis assures me his unexposed gelding is in good shape and will be trying his very best. With a little luck, Bluey's best could be enough to give a large number of charities a huge injection of cash.'

Charlie stated this in positive fashion, emphasising his last few words. Assessing the looks of satisfaction on the faces of the reporters, he determined they should now have a headline to submit to their editors.

'Okay, I think that's it for now, ladies and gentlemen,' Charlie told the group, sensing their thirst for information was sated. 'I hope to see you all at Doncaster on Saturday.'

The media people started to disperse, but the cameraman who had shared the news about Cool Blue's declaration hung back, clearly wishing to ask a question of his own. Charlie assumed he was a keen gambler, trying to gain inside information. However, he was suitably surprised when the longhaired, bespectacled youth simply wished to shake his hand and wish him the best of luck.

'My younger sister suffers from depression,' he explained, a couple of creases appearing around the base of his vibrant young eyes. 'She needs regular counselling, which is expensive. You sent one of your letters to the charity that supports her. They've lost their Lottery funding, and I don't know what our Lorraine would do without them. But you and Mr. Lewis could save them, or at least keep the charitable work they do going for a few more years. I just wanted to thank you and wish you the very best of luck. We'll be cheering you on!'

In order to thank him, Charlie had to swallow down a lump which had grown in his throat. The lad gripped his hand with obvious relish and pumped it up and down several times. As he smiled into the cameraman's face a thought struck him.

'I don't suppose you know who that reporter was, the one on the end there, the man in the tweed cap?'

'Reporter? Naa,' the lad said with a wrinkle of his nose. 'He's not one of us. I've never seen him before.'

After another round of eager thanks, Charlie watched as the cameraman scuttled off after his colleagues. He was left wondering about the number of charities who had placed the bet, and how many lives would alter for the better should Cool Blue win the Lincoln. In a sudden rush of realisation he also understood the depth of his problem. He had given that lad hope. There could be dozens, or even hundreds... Oh God, there could be *thousands* of people out there who now held the same hope. Hope that their lives could be changed for the better by something as frivolous as a horse winning a race. He'd created the conditions for that hope to exist, and despite Cool Blue's successful declaration for the Lincoln, that hope was hanging by a thread.

Twenty

Charlie took a few deep breaths, and tapped his phone to order an Uber taxi. He headed to the end of Park Street, his mind unclear and fuzzy. He needed time to sort out the confusion, to make sense of the differing strands which made up this mess. He'd not had chance to reflect on what had happened in the police station, so he concentrated on this first. It had been a shock when the two uniformed men had arrived at his office and asked him to return to the centre of Leeds for questioning.

The interview had turned out to be fairly procedural; the police had requested a statement about his visit to the betting office the previous night, and were particularly interested in Harvey's threatening behaviour toward Kowalski and at what point he and Sam had left the BetMick premises. His subsequent shock when learning of Frank Best's hospitalisation had certainly helped, as the interviewing officers seemed less inclined to believe he and Sam were potential assailants, after witnessing his genuinely horrified reaction. They'd gone on to quiz him about Harvey. Charlie had reported that the dog growled when it looked like something was about to be thrown at his master, and left it at that. His comments had been received by the two policemen with the sort of vacant disinterest civil servants reserve for form filling duties.

Charlie reasoned that Mick Kowalski had retaliated when the opportunity had presented itself. It appeared he had bent the truth in an attempt to implicate Sam, and also himself, in Frank Best's injury. It had been a pretty lame plan, decided Charlie. The loss of a morning had been inconvenient, however, this episode had given him a potentially useful insight into the mind of Mick Kowalski.

Dismissing thoughts of the bookmaker, Charlie became aware of a vibration on his hip. He realised his phone was buzzing in his suit pocket and found Stan's number blinking at him once he dug out the device.

'Is that Mr. Kray?' demanded a sarcastic voice. 'You been sprung from the clink yet?'

'Hello, Stan,' Charlie sighed.

'Now then, boss! You okay to speak? Has the Old Bill released you or did you have to bung 'em a bribe?' His questions were laced with joviality and Charlie thought he heard a quiet guffaw among the background of office noises. A weak smile crept onto his lips. He couldn't help having his spirits lifted by Stan's idiotic attempt at humour. It was so... *normal* for Stan. It provided a welcome oasis of normality in what had become an extraordinary few days. He considered providing an equally sarcastic reply, but couldn't conjure one up quickly enough, and in the end settled for a business-as-usual response.

'I'm in good shape and a free man, Stan. Thanks for your concern. I'm on my way back into the office.'

'Ah, well, that's good, because it's all kicking off here. We need you back pronto.'

Charlie ended the call a couple of minutes later, his spirits dampened once more. He concluded his stroll to the end of Park Street under a cloud of discontent and waited irritably on the street corner until his taxi arrived. He gave the taxi driver his office address and tried to relax into his back seat. The city centre and subsequent west Leeds roadside passed in a blur as he concentrated his thoughts on the whirlwind of events during the last twenty-four hours.

Sam Lewis was clearly nothing like his public persona, and Charlie winced when remembering his research into the man on the internet in Inkberrow. It had proved to be woefully lacking in depth. He should have picked up on the fiery relationship between Sam and Mick. There must have been some reports on their previous encounters, a court report, or a newspaper article. Had Sam managed to suppress them?

He opened his eyes and caught his reflection in the taxi's rear view mirror. Slumped in the back seat, he was shocked at how haggard he appeared; he'd not shaved that morning, intending to use an electric razor he always kept in his office. Being intercepted by the police and hauled off to Leeds before setting a foot in his office had killed that plan. He straightened in his seat and dusted himself off. He couldn't afford to become demoralised by Sam Lewis and Mick Kowalski. There had to be a way to come out of this situation winning.

Winning, Charlie thought bitterly. All of those people out there. The charities could be robbed of their chance of winning. His thoughts drifted to Joss Faraday in his small yard in Middleham and he wondered if Sam had already broken the news of Cool Blue's likely non-participation. Faraday would be devastated, thought Charlie. However he brightened a little when he realised that if Sam had his way, Cool Blue would be declared a non-runner on Saturday, perhaps as little as an hour or two before the Lincoln, allowing Sam to pile every ounce of possible pressure onto Mick Kowalski to reveal... well, to reveal what, if anything, Mick knew about Laurie Lewis's death.

Charlie curled his lip and leant a hand on his cheek, elbow on the car door window frame, disgruntled at the thought of Mick Kowalski. He'd already shown he wasn't beyond bending the truth, and what was there to stop him constructing any old story he fancied in order to placate Sam? How would Sam know? Sam had told him in no uncertain terms that he would *know* when the truth came from Kowalski's lips. Charlie wasn't so sure, he had the impression Sam was only after one storyline; the one that confirmed Mick Kowalski had been instrumental in his brother's death.

Charlie felt his phone buzz again and he eyed a number he didn't recognise. He sent the caller to voicemail, grimacing at the amount of missed calls, voicemails, texts and WhatsApp requests he had unread.

101

Back at Shipley, Graham Sutton met him as he climbed the stairs to his first floor office. It was intentional; his boss had been waiting for him.

'A word, please, Charlie,' he said in greeting.

Charlie tried hard not to roll his eyes. Instead, he traipsed upstairs behind the Managing Director and followed him into his office. Graham waited by the door and closed it behind Charlie.

'I have some good news,' Graham began.

Charlie remained silent. He came to a halt besides Graham's enormous mahogany desk and waited. He had a feeling he already knew what this so-called good news was going to entail.

'Samuel Lewis called me this morning.'

'Really? That's... unexpected.'

Graham curved his eyebrows downwards slightly at this response, but released them quickly and continued, 'He's offered us the chance to take over the Lewis's advertising account. It's worth about thirty million a year. That's significant turnover.'

Graham wet his lips with a rapid flick of his tongue whilst staring intently at Charlie. He was charged up, excited. 'All we need to do...'

'...is ensure Sam gets the result he wants from my project,' Charlie finished, blowing a long sigh out through puffed cheeks.

The spark in Graham's eyes dimmed. He flopped into his black leather executive chair and crossing his leg to the opposite knee, waggled his foot at the ankle.

'Why do I get the feeling there is something going on with this account that I don't know about?'

Standing in front of Graham's expansive desk, Charlie idly rubbed a couple of fingers on its shiny wooden surface, squinting down to avoid meeting his boss's eyes. He liked Graham. He was a good man; an honest businessman and a decent boss. The clients came first for Graham. Always. He would bend over backwards in order to retain a client or win a new one, and an account worth thirty million pounds would increase the company's turnover by twenty percent overnight. Sam Lewis was dangling a carrot so huge Charlie was sure Graham would go to great lengths in order to win the Lewis's business. Dashing the hopes of a few charities would be small beer to him.

'There's nothing going on,' Charlie lied, meeting the fifty-five year old's gaze, 'It's just become slightly... complicated.'

Graham shrugged. 'So you need more staff, that's not a problem...'

'No, it's not a staffing issue.'

'I assume your trip to the cop shop this morning isn't the problem?'

'No, that's all sorted.'

'So what?' Graham pressed.

'It's a matter of… timing,' Charlie announced after a pause, 'The right blocks falling into place at the right time. I've got a day to alter our plans and make sure everything goes like clockwork at Doncaster on Saturday. I just need time with my team, and to be allowed to get on with it.'

Graham contemplated this statement for a few seconds, scrutinising the best account director he'd ever employed with an appraising eye. He started to chew the inside of his cheek.

Charlie watched pensively. He'd seen Graham in this mode many times before. He was weighing him up, making his decision in his own time. It could go one of two ways; admonishment and then Graham's personal involvement in the issue, or measured, grudging acceptance that it was best left to others. Either way, there would be silence while he decided. This time the silence stretched out for longer than Charlie had ever experienced.

'Go on then, Charlie. Bugger off,' Graham said gently over forty seconds later, throwing two fingers toward the door to his office to indicate the interview was over.'

Charlie smiled gratefully. He knew thanking Graham would only embarrass him, but he did it anyway, and Graham reddened.

'Seriously, get lost!' he thundered, swivelling uncomfortably in his chair.

Charlie got lost.

Twenty-One

Suzie was the first to rush up to Charlie when he started to cross the mezzanine of the first floor. She looked flustered. Her usually immaculately brushed hair had clumps sticking out at right angles, and her make-up was applied heavily and smudged in places.

'We need to talk,' she panted, eyes wide. 'It's gone... crazy.'

Her voice tailed off and the hint of a tear welled slowly in the corner of her right eye. Charlie took the hint.

'Don't worry,' he said, cupping her hand gently into both his hands, 'We've got full control of the project. Graham's committed his support and we're going to get everything ready today.'

Stan appeared behind her. He rolled his eyes at Charlie's little speech and smirked. Behind him, a group of about fifteen other employees peered over open plan cubicles at him and traded intrigued glances.

'Where's the outfit with arrows on it?' Stan asked dryly.

Ten minutes later the three of them were in Charlie's office. His electric shaver hummed. Hot coffee and sandwiches arrived, the blinds were closed, and the three of them fell into comfy chairs.

'Okay, brief me. Suzie first,' Charlie instructed, as he scraped the shaver under his jaw and removed the last of his bristles. He flicked the shaver off and squinted into a small handheld mirror, sighing at a straightforward job, executed badly; he'd have much preferred a proper wet shave.

Suzie sucked in a breath through her nose and turned over the first page on her pad.

'The charity contact telephone number has received over seven hundred calls since Wednesday evening. At the last count we have one hundred and twenty one people who have reported placing the bet on behalf of their charity and provided us with the bookmaker's name.'

Charlie gave a low whistle. 'Wow!'

'Wow indeed,' Stan chirped in response, 'I estimate the bookmaking industry as a whole will pay out just over eighty million pounds to our people if Cool Blue wins the Lincoln tomorrow. I've checked; it'll be the biggest payout in British racing history.'

'How much for each charity?' asked Charlie, taking a slurp of coffee and hungrily eyeing one of the tuna and sweetcorn sandwiches on the platter at the other side of his office.

'Each bet should net around seven hundred thousand pounds, if they have followed the instructions we gave them in their letters.'

'And how many of them have taken up the offer of a free day at Doncaster races tomorrow?'

Suzie flipped a page on her notepad. 'The latest number is sixty-seven, almost all of them bringing a guest. I'm expecting we'll cater for around a hundred and fifty on the day. The room we've booked will hold two hundred, so we should...'

Her voice had started to waver, and Charlie held up a halting palm, aware something was worryingly wrong with the young woman.

'Suzie, what is it?'

Suzie's eyes welled and became glassy. Usually gregarious, she wasn't prone to mood swings or excessive displays of emotion, and especially not in business meetings, even informal ones like this. Inwardly Charlie kicked himself; the disturbed hair, her expression when she'd first approached him, the lack of finesse in her make-up. Sometimes his man management skills were woeful.

'It's okay,' he added, 'Whatever it is, you can tell us.'

Suzie blinked, dabbing her eyes with a paper tissue which appeared from inside the cuff of her blouse. She shuffled forward to perch on the edge of her chair and glanced nervously at both colleagues.

'I need to know. Have we broken the law?'

It was a simple question, but one which made Charlie stop and think. The harder he contemplated, the more complex the answer became. It swirled around his mind and every second longer it took for him to land on the answer, Suzie's worry lines deepened on her young face.

'Of course not!' Stan broke in, positive and serious, staring fixedly at her, his eyes full of concern. 'We've not done anything illegal, why would you think that?'

Charlie answered, 'I think when Suzie says 'we' she means ourselves *and* Sam Lewis.'

'Stan frowned and shifted his attention back to Suzie, who confirmed Charlie's assertion by closing her eyes and nodding.

'It's all the... stuff on social media,' she explained. 'That bookmaker, Mr. Kowalski, has said he was attacked by Harvey, you know, Mr. Lewis's dog. I just can't believe it, he was so nice... Then you were taken to the police station and...'

Suzie ran out of words and looked up at Charlie, her eyes ringed with redness. He considered moving across and giving her a hug, but decided against it. More than anything, she needed answers.

'The last twelve hours have been a bit of a blur,' Charlie pointed out, leaning an elbow on his desk and resting his cheek in his hand. 'That's no excuse though. You're right Suzie, you deserve to know what's gone on. I should have started with this, and I guess I was putting it off because I still don't have all the answers.' He ran his hand through his hair and ended by scratching the back of his neck thoughtfully.

Charlie spent the next twenty minutes running through the journey to Scunthorpe, meeting Kowalski and Best at the betting shop, Sam and Harvey's skirmish with the bookmaker and the journey back to Leeds, finishing with him being dropped off at his city centre flat in Leeds in the late evening. Then he quickly described how the police had interviewed him, and his short question and answer session with the press.

'The people in this room have done nothing wrong,' he emphasised, 'In fact, we should be proud with the job we've done so far.'

Stan and Suzie had remained quiet for the duration of the story, save for a few gasps or exclamations during Charlie's description of Sam's departure into rage at the Scunthorpe betting shop. Finally he told them about Sam's approach to Graham, and the offer of new business should everything work in his favour at Doncaster.

'That's a barefaced bribe!' Suzie exclaimed.

Charlie nodded sadly at the two of them.

Stan cleared his throat. 'We're mixed up in some serious bad blood between these two men. I've been digging deeper into them both and it doesn't make for happy reading. I'm only sorry I didn't discover this before we took the job, Charlie.'

'I took the job based on gut instinct. It's no one's fault but my own,' Charlie said quietly, staring into the distance, remembering the couple of days at his brother's yard, the thrill he'd felt in those first few hours. He snapped back.

'Come on then, what have you found?'

Stan looked down at a sheet of paper, filled with his small, spidery writing and took a breath.

'I don't think it would be going too far to say they hate each other,' Stan said with a shrug, 'It started after Kowalski's car went for a swim in the Tyne in summer 2016. Laurie Lewis had borrowed it to drive home to Ponteland in the early hours of the morning after being with Kowalski at the races and then at his city centre flat, but he crashed into the river just before the Scotswood Bridge, which is west of the city. The police fished it out just below the Tyne Bridge; it had travelled about a mile downstream. His brother's body was never found, but that's not as strange as it seems, the river is known to carry virtually everything out to sea.'

'Why was he driving Kowalski's car?' Suzie asked.

'The reports in the Newcastle Chronicle say they were friends and they would regularly drive each other's cars.'

'Drinking, perhaps?' Charlie suggested.

'Unlikely. Laurie Lewis was teetotal,' Stan said with a shake of his head.

He continued, 'Sam pestered the local police for months with claims about Mick Kowalski's involvement, suggesting he should be investigated for setting up the accident. The police did examine the car once it was pulled out of the river, but ended up cautioning Sam for repeated harassment of their officers. I imagine they just wanted him out of their hair. There was no evidence to link Kowalski to the accident and the car was sound.'

'Sam started to take things into his own hands and began hounding Kowalski. There's a report of an altercation in a city centre street in Newcastle, but no charges were brought. Then it went quiet for a few months until about nine months ago. Sam walked into Kowalski's business premises in Newcastle, found his office, and threatened to kill him unless he spilled what he knew about his brother's death. When the police got there, Sam was on his knees screaming and claiming Mick Kowalski had punched him.'

'Dear God,' Charlie said, shaking his head, 'That's… awful. What happened?'

'Well, here's the even crazier bit,' Stan replied. 'Sam tried to press charges against Kowalski, but the police wouldn't take it any further. They reckoned Sam fell or punched himself! It seems Sam was throwing himself around Kowalski's office, fell and smashed his teeth into a stone wall.'

At this news, Suzie emitted a startled whimper. The two men swung round and discovered her riveted to her easy chair, wearing an expression of shock mixed with a touch of fear. She had one hand pressed to her mouth, fingernails touching her bottom lip, gripping her teeth. She pulled her hand away once she registered their worried looks.

'I'm okay,' she assured them, repeating her assertion when Stan raised a questioning eyebrow. 'Really, I'm fine. It's just a shock after we had such a lovely day with Sam at the races yesterday. He and Harvey seemed so… normal.'

'It's bloody worrying,' Charlie agreed, happier Suzie was relaxing and breathing easily once more. Presently he added, 'Sam's managed to fool all of us, my brother included. It appears he's the same as Kowalski; quite happy to lie and use intimidation to get what he wants.'

He spun round to face Stan, who was back in his seat. 'So, come on, where on earth did you find all this information? I got the report on the accident from the local paper but never saw *any* of the Kowalski stuff when I did a search on Sam.'

Stan beamed, just about staying on the right side of smug. 'You need to know how to use the internet,' he confided, 'There were the local papers and a few mentions in court listings when I dug around, but most of the juicy stuff came from social media. Building up a network of friends in useful places like the police force helps a lot. Like my mate Joe.'

'Your mate, Joe,' Charlie repeated slowly with a sigh.

'I went to Uni with him. He's a DC on the force up in Teeside, Redcar actually. He, er... came up with stuff about Sam at Kowalski's office after I'd messaged him last night.'

'Did he?' Charlie stated flatly.

Stan tried a quick, hopeful smile. 'It all came up on their records, but the media never got hold of any of it at the time,' he said quietly.

Charlie planted his elbows on the slick wooden surface of the desk and started rubbing the bridge of his nose with both hands. Eventually he looked up, eyed his two younger colleagues for a moment, and then concentrated on Stan, who winced when their eyes met.

'I want to scream and bawl, and tell you you're out of order...' he said in an icy tone.

Pushing out his bottom lip, Charlie sucked air in through his nose.

'However, your information *is* extremely useful....'

Stan's frown slackened, only to return when Charlie completed his sentence, thundering, '...*Don't do it again*!'.

'Your actions now mean I have to alter my answer to Suzie's question about breaking the law!' he added.

Stan nodded sadly, accepting his ticking off with good grace. Meanwhile Charlie fixed Suzie with an apologetic look.

'Sam has definitely changed the rules of this project, but according to the company solicitor this morning, we've not broken any laws, and for the avoidance of any doubt, *you've* got nothing to worry about. Stan's indiscretion, whilst admirable in its results, shouldn't have any repercussions for us. I'm more worried about his mate.'

Suzie's shoulders dropped an inch as she relaxed, however tension still held her to the edge of her seat. Charlie noticed she was scratching the back of her hand; it was red raw. She appeared to be unaware of the abrasion she was causing and Charlie started to shape to speak. Before he got there Suzie had forced a brave smile onto her face, swallowed, and shot as determined a look as she could muster toward the two men.

'I've been talking with so many nice people from these charities,' she explained. 'They're all so excited, and I feel like I've been helping to build their anticipation for Saturday. We might not be breaking any laws, well, not much,' she aimed a weak smile at Stan, 'But I can't believe how callously Sam is going to treat these charities if he doesn't allow Cool Blue to race.'

She was gaining confidence and her voice was becoming more strident as she continued.

'I don't think we should allow him to do that. It's just not fair or in the spirit of the original project he asked us to create. I'm so angry with Sam, after selling all those good intentions to us; he's only bothered about his own self-interest.'

She suddenly balled a fist, shaking it as she spoke. Stan's eyes widened and he leaned away from her, transfixed by the energy the young woman was displaying, shock and fascination combining in her features.

'We placed the bet too... but I feel sick to my core about that now,' she continued. 'I'm passing my winnings on to a charity, I can tell you that for certain,'

Suzie's face was now filled with annoyance and indignation. The

108

tears were gone, yet dry streaks still ran down her cheeks. She got to her feet to make her final point, straightening, seeming much taller than her five feet four inches.

'If Sam's not going to run Cool Blue, we should tell everyone now, instead of them finding out at the last minute. If we don't, we're just as bad as him.'

Charlie and Stan stared open-mouthed at the small young woman who was standing with an arm outstretched, wagging an accusing finger at the two of them. She bristled with inner strength for a few seconds, the air around her electrically charged, seemingly conjured up through the sheer force of her speech.

A few seconds of silence greeted her final statement until Stan couldn't contain himself any longer.

'Bloody hell!' he blurted in exclamation. Charlie looked over, expecting a comic follow up. He was relieved to see there was an astonished sort of pride in Stan's face. 'That was… brilliant!' Stan added with an adoring sigh, seeking confirmation from Charlie.

Suzie dropped her arm, but still radiated defiance. Her eyes were glistening and she nodded a curt thank you to Stan.

'You're absolutely right,' Charlie said purposefully. 'Thank you, Suzie. Thank you for reminding us that the client isn't always right. You're spot on. We'll sort all three of those bets of ours here and now. And you can decide who should benefit.'

He paused, fixing Suzie with a brighter smile. 'So come on, we've got a day and a half. Let's get to work and make sure Cool Blue gets his chance to win the Lincoln and give the charities a run for their money.'

****

They worked solidly into the early evening on Thursday, only emerging from Charlie's office to replenish food and drink or to drag in extra whiteboards or flipcharts. All too soon it became dark and the open-plan office started to empty around them. They remained oblivious, having closed all the blinds around Charlie's glass office. At six o'clock there was a cautious knock and Graham poked his head around the door. He enquired how things were progressing, and received three positive replies in return. He bid them, 'Good evening and good luck,' before leaving for the night.

Two hours later Charlie drew two horizontal lines at the bottom of a flipchart page, stood back and let out a long breath. Suzie and Stan admired the page for a few moments and independently gave it their agreement. Then they cleared the room of every scrap of paper.

Once his younger colleagues had been despatched to get a good meal and a decent night's sleep, Charlie made three phone calls; to Joss Faraday, his brother Tommy, and Scunthorpe hospital.

Twenty-Two

Mick Kowalski's Thursday afternoon was proving to be no better than the rest of the week. The telephone handset travelled across his office as if launched from a trebuchet and Mick watched through tears of frustration as it exploded against the stone wall. Pieces of plastic and electronics cascaded onto filing cabinets and unopened cardboard boxes full of betting slips. He breathed angrily through gritted teeth, sending a shower of spittle onto the floor, grumbling as he wiped the white bubbles off the front of his AC/DC 1989 tour t-shirt.

The BetMick head office in Newcastle, down by the river in the unfashionable end of the city, wasn't the palatial steel and glass castle that most bookmaking firms preferred. This was an old mill building, close to the river and consisting of three floors of cheaply renovated, small, muddled rooms with high ceilings. Grey carpet tiles and whitewashed stone walls gave the place a sombre, and in some places, stark feel which was reinforced by the lack of any meaningful light; windows being small and unimportant in a mill at the turn of the century.

Mick didn't mind the lack of a view; it meant his employees concentrated on what was important – making him money. The staff and stock were stuffed in wherever they would fit. It was just about usable, and the rent and rates were cheap. The only thing he spent good money on was the internet link to his server cloud which enabled his staff to operate the BetMick website; the business's primary revenue and profit stream.

Mick inspected a red stain on the wall shaped like a pear. It was where Sam Lewis had fallen over the betting slips and smacked his face into the wall. He'd considered wiping it off, but found the mark left by the blind man's blood aesthetically pleasing, so he'd left it there to dry. What had the lunatic expected when he burst into his office and started threatening him? It wasn't his fault Sam Lewis had fallen over once he'd started throwing himself around the room. Mick recalled the moment the disoriented man fell. The memory troubled him, forcing him to shudder. He'd never heard screaming like that... Sam Lewis had smashed his front tooth on the wall, the pain must have been...

Mick closed his eyes tight shut, attempting to wash thoughts of Sam's howl of agony from his mind. He had weightier problems that were current and far more pressing. Twenty-four hours after being subjected to a vicious dog attack and losing his second in command to hospitalisation, he'd just found out that his ruse to implicate Sam Lewis for Frank Best's accident had failed.

What was it the officious sounding Inspector had said?

Mick lifted his backside onto the edge of his desk and sat facing a bank of six flat screens showing scrolling odds and muted live sports. He

110

tried to recall the phrase the policeman has used, Oh yes, that was it: 'A dubious pattern of evidence which didn't warrant further investigation.'

Mick scowled. Everything would have been fine if that bloody Sam Lewis just backed off. He was a constant irritant. He'd thought about pressing charges over the assault in his office, but he couldn't. His hands had been tied that time too, just like now. Mick growled audibly, jumped to a standing position, and started to pace the room, spitting Sam Lewis's name out over and over. He'd love to tell the twisted fool the real truth about his brother….

He snorted with laughter when he realised there *was* one small victory; apparently that bloody guide dog had been taken in by the police for monitoring; he hoped they'd put the damn thing down. Mick found himself blinking rapidly as he tried to rid himself of an unpleasant spasm which had started pulsing in his eyelid. When he thought of Sam Lewis's dog, all he could see was a huge canine mouth full of needle sharp fangs dripping with foaming saliva and the smell of rotten meat. He tried to rid himself of these thoughts, brightened momentarily when he realised the dog was now unlikely to be at Doncaster races on Saturday.

Mick soon fell back into his funk. His glazed eyes watched the odds scroll on the screens, unfocussed and unseeing. The only thing he could presently see were the numbers from a sheet of paper which lay on the desk behind him. They were burned into his mind. After canvassing all his shops, including the newly acquired set of Sutherland shops in West Yorkshire, a consolidated report had come through that morning from Frank Best's deputy, detailing their potential exposure to Lewis and his ad man's coup. Mick had been staring at it for the last hour; the potential payout if Cool Blue won on Saturday was forty-two million pounds.

He slowly ran the number across his mind once more and suffered similar reaction to its bulk again, his heart falling through his chest to his stomach and a hot, itchy rash started to burn at the base of his neck.

The price of the horse had plummeted as soon as the news had broken on Wednesday evening. Cool Blue was now trading at five to one second favourite in a field of twenty-two. There was no chance of laying off some of the potential payout. It was far too late for that.

Mick swung his legs over the edge of his desk, the rivets on the back pockets of his faded blue jeans scraping and creasing the surface of the desk. He hung his head low and bent his back forward, allowing his hair to dangle like a comforting black wall around both sides of his face.

The only way out of this mess was if Cool Blue didn't take part; if the horse was declared a non-runner. He considered there were several alternatives to simply forcing the horse to be *declared* a non-runner. Injury, now there was an option; a quick bash to the knee ought to do it. But he couldn't go around whacking horse's knees. He wouldn't know one horse from another. He didn't even know where the blasted thing was trained. Or how about a bribe to the race-day vet? For a few seconds Mick liked this proposal, before he realised he had no way of either knowing, or approaching whoever could make that sort of call. He wasn't an owner or a trainer; he knew little about the actual running of a racecourse. All he knew was how to squeeze profit from mug punters with deep pockets.

Perhaps he'd rejected the option of an injury too quickly? He allowed the idea to swarm around his brain. He did know a few people who might do it. Mick started to see daylight. But soon enough, the associated problems invaded his thoughts, snuffing the light out. He would have to find the right men, get them briefed, transport them over to wherever the trainer was located, then find the right horse and bash its knees…, all before tomorrow morning *and* without being caught… He shook his head in frustration, his hair whipping against his cheeks. Attacking the horse wasn't the answer.

In mid whip, Mick's face took on a serious expression and he halted his self-flagellation. A tiny sparkle crept into his steel blue eyes. He pushed himself off the desk and trotted to the door of his office, pulling it open.

'Vera!' he bellowed, trying to keep the excitement from his voice.

A thin, prim lady in her sixties, her head a swirl of pinned up hair, looked up sharply from her desk in the corridor.

'Get me the telephone number and address for… Hold on!'

Mick disappeared and his head reappeared around the door a few moments later.

'…Joss Fared… er, no,' he read from the biro marks on the back of his hand, vanishing from the door once more.

'Joss Faraday,' he related on his return, 'I think he's in somewhere called Coverham.'

'Middleham,' Vera told him.

'No, Coverham. Are you deaf or something?'

Vera took a deep breath, her tight, ribbed, turtleneck sweater expanding and contracting. She'd been Mick's secretary for twelve years and had already recognised her boss's current mood.

'Coverham is just outside Middleham, in North Yorkshire. It's a training centre for racehorses,' she reported patiently. 'I've taken my grandkids there to the Forbidden Corner folly. It's right beside…'

'Whatever!' he barked irritably, 'Just find his contact details will you. I've business with him.'

The door to Mick's office was slammed shut, only to open again seconds later. This time it was rather tentatively pulled open a few inches. Vera slid her gaze over when Mick's voice came through the crack.

'…and I'll need a new phone.'

Vera watched the door to Mick's office clank closed again before whispering, 'Tell me something I don't know,' under her breath and switching her attention back to the monitor on what was laughingly referred to as her 'workstation' by the IT department.

The monitor took up half her desk, being one of the old-fashioned, bulky square types; Mick refused to replace something that still worked, it had to be fifteen years old. She opened Google, found the trainer's details in seconds, wrote them on a scrap of paper, and hid it in the back of her diary. Crossing to a metal filing cabinet further down her corridor, Vera removed a brand new cordless phone handset. She noticed she was down to the last of her backup handsets; she'd have to order another three or four based on how many her boss had thrown across his room in the last month. The box was returned to her desk and placed on top of her diary.

She scooped up her mug from its coaster, made a mental note that she probably had at least twenty minutes before the belligerent and technically inept dolt in the next room started to wonder why he hadn't received his information, and headed off to the kitchen at the other end of the dimly lit corridor at a relaxed amble. Mick would get his replacement handset and trainer information, but in Vera's own sweet time.

Twenty-Three

Charlie's senses were heightened once he caught sight of the long, black, shiny Bentley parked directly outside the entrance to his office building on Friday morning. His concern increased when he spotted Sam Lewis's driver leaning against the rear of the vehicle, sucking on a cigarette.

His visit to Scunthorpe General Hospital on Thursday evening to speak with Frank Best had been relatively successful. He'd not secured a definite buy-in from the BetMick man, but it hadn't been the blowout he had feared. He'd found Frank propped up in bed on a mixed ward, something the man clearly found difficult, cowering slightly below his covers each time a female patient wandered past. A significant bandage had been wrapped around his head wound, and although he'd gone woozy once when he moved around too much, it seemed he was due to be discharged in a day or two's time.

Initially Frank had been in shock when Charlie appeared at his bedside at the start of visiting time, and it had taken a good ten minutes to convince the man his intentions were honourable. Frank's wife had arrived a few minutes later, which, on reflection, had probably helped. Charlie had got the distinct impression Mrs. Best wasn't a supporter of Mick Kowalski. They'd parted on cordial terms, Charlie handing over his business card, and Frank promising to give his suggestion some thought, bolstered by some significant prompting from his wife.

Once Charlie had bounded up the office stairs to the first floor, the few hours he'd spent visiting the hospital the previous evening were soon forgotten. There in his office he could see Sam, sitting with his back to him, his short silver hair making him easily recognisable. Graham was facing him, a set smile on his face, in stark contrast to the straight-lipped stares Stan and Suzie wore as they looked on from standing positions at the edge of the office, which significantly, were outside the hub of Sam and Graham's conversation.

Charlie spotted another man in the room; an older man. He was sitting in one of the easy chairs, but perched on the edge. He had a memorable profile: he held his chin up and seemed to be rocking slightly, perhaps in tune to someone speaking. A substantial adam's apple bobbed as he rocked and ancient hooded eyes gave a false sense that he was dozing. This was all rounded off with a bulbous nose. He was about the same height as Sam, but his thin frame, hunched posture and gaunt, unsmiling expression gave him the look of a preying mantis.

Suzie looked up and her face altered radically when she recognised Charlie. She burst into a radiant smile, supported by a release of tension which made her stand a couple of inches taller. Charlie gave her his best

114

twinkling grin and strode over to his office door, twisted the handle and walked straight in.

'My apologies, I can only assume I must have missed this meeting out of my diary,' he stated amiably, passing Graham to find Sam's hand in order to shake it. No one replied. It seemed Charlie had interrupted their flow somewhat.

He moved over to the old man, who cocked his bony chin up even further in order to track Charlie as he approached.

'Charlie Summer,' Charlie said, extending a hand.

The old man flashed a disgruntled sneer over at Sam before returning his half-closed eyes to Charlie. He lifted a liver spotted hand and wafted Charlie's greeting away, fixing him with a disdainful stare.

'This is my father, Reginald Lewis,' Sam rumbled in soft Geordie. 'We thought we'd drop in on our way to Doncaster for the races tomorrow, just to check everything was... under control.'

'Ah, I understand,' Charlie responded airily, 'That's sensible.'

Sam's brow dipped into a frown, just for a moment. Charlie suppressed a smirk as he watched the silvery pensioner trying to decipher his reply; whether it was sensible for him to travel the night before the race, or sensible to check Charlie and his team were doing their jobs.

'Graham and your team were filling us in,' Sam continued levelly. There was no accusation in his tone, however, it was also void of any joy.

'Really?'

'Yes,' Sam insisted. 'But now you're here, it would be good to know the plans are in hand. Graham and I seem to be in accord and I believe you're aware of the reward, should you succeed tomorrow.'

Charlie was still standing. He felt the urge to cross his arms and concentrate a cold stare back at the blackmailing little snake, but stemmed his flash of annoyance. Sam was spinning his thinly veiled web of deceit over the room, and a wrong word or undisciplined reaction now could bring the project to a halt right here. He wasn't going to give Sam, or his father for that matter, the satisfaction.

'The strategy is exactly as we discussed on the way back from Market Rasen on Wednesday night. The primary objective...' he purposefully took a deep breath, '...hasn't altered, and we will have everything in place to ensure a successful day for you Sam. Mick Kowalski has agreed to meet us at eleven o'clock in your private box in order to deliver his knowledge on your... situation.'

Sam blindly surveyed the room before settling on Charlie, as always, appearing to be staring at a space just over his left shoulder. He grinned, and Charlie decided Sam's wonky front tooth and one half-lidded eye gave him a slightly ghoulish appearance, now he knew which way the man preferred to work.

'We have considered every eventuality...' Charlie began.

'You think so, do you?' croaked Reginald from behind him. Charlie swung round to find Sam's father shaking his head contemptuously.

'Stop blowing smoke up my son's arse,' he crackled.

Charlie couldn't help allowing a faint smile to creep across his lips. He glanced up and found evidence of mirth on Stan and Suzie's faces; Stan's arms were crossed over his chest and they were bouncing up and down as he tried to stifle a laugh.

'What makes you say that, Sir?' Charlie asked sweetly. He sidled between the furniture to stand in front of his two colleagues at the back of the room, blocking Reginald's view of their amusement.

'Sam's got an unnatural obsession with Kowalski, and you are bleeding him for money with the promise you can nail the Polish bastard,' snarled Reginald in a Geordie accent much harder than his son's.

'Father…' protested Sam in a world-weary manner. 'I've got him pinned down. You've heard Graham and Charlie. Nothing will go wrong.'

'Nothing will go wrong,' Reginald countered, mimicking Sam in a childlike voice. 'That's what you thought before you tried to pin him down at his office. That worked well for you, didn't it?' he added in a darkly sarcastic voice.

All eyes sprang to Sam who immediately turned crimson and shot a filthy look towards his father. Charlie was sure he would react. His anger was clearly bubbling close to the surface. Surprisingly, Sam said nothing. Instead, he shook his head from side to side quickly for a second and emerged beaming, head held high. It was as if a different man had suddenly been switched, in place of the squirming, embarrassed schoolboy who had been occupying the same space only moments before. Charlie inspected him closely and caught a worryingly different darkness in Sam's eyes; one at odds with the plastic smile which graced his face.

'Oh bugger, you've done your smiley thing now,' groaned Reginald spitefully, 'Come on,' he growled, pushing himself to his feet, 'I've heard enough from these money-grubbing ad men.'

He was standing, hunched over, wearing an expectant look which soon slid into frustrated impatience.

'Come on then! Up!' he demanded. 'And this hotel better have some Newcastle Brown.'

Sam rose from his armchair, an inane smile still plastered to his face. It was only when he straightened that Charlie caught sight of Harvey; he must have been lying quietly at the other side of the armchair. The dog shook itself and yawned, displaying an impressive set of teeth. Charlie tensed for a few seconds before reminding himself to breathe. Sam's hand searched down the dog's back and grasped his harness. Charlie exhaled.

Graham jumped up and took Sam's elbow, guiding him out of Charlie's office and toward the stairs. Reginald shuffled behind them, but stopped at the door. He turned his head to one side so he could be heard, not interested in seeing a reaction, his hooded eyes elsewhere.

'You've made a fool of my son,' he growled angrily toward the floor, '…and shoved his insane obsession with Kowalski into public view. So, listen up you fucking leeches: protect him tomorrow, or I'll tear this entire business apart…' He paused, sucking in air through his doughy nose. '…brick by bloody brick.'

Stan, Suzie, and Charlie watched in stunned silence as the wizened old man shuffled to the landing. He grasped the handrail and descended the stairs a single step at a time, slowly disappearing downwards. An image of the underworld and *Dante's Inferno* suddenly filled Charlie's mind; each six inch step representing Reginald Lewis's gradual descent into wickedness.

'And we thought Sam was the weird one,' Stan noted sarcastically once the old man was out of sight and earshot.

'Imagine being undermined like that all your life,' Suzie mused in a quiet voice, still staring after the visitors, 'It's no wonder Sam is damaged.'

Charlie and Stan traded a glance. Suzie could always be trusted to see things differently. She was far more… forgiving.

'Don't start feeling too sorry for Sam,' Charlie warned. 'Do I need to remind you of how vicious Harvey was the other night, and who gave the Latin instruction to him?'

Suzie snapped her gaze back to Charlie, a frown developing.

'Surely Sam wouldn't set Harvey on someone in a public place!'

'Wouldn't he?' Charlie asked quizzically, 'You said yourself that Sam's damaged. The last thing we need around on Saturday is a guide dog capable of ripping someone apart.'

Stan grinned mischievously. 'I'm not sure Sam needs an attack dog when he has his father around.'

Twenty-Four

Joss Faraday knew he was demanding. He was demanding of his staff, and himself. He had learned success as a racehorse trainer didn't come if you accepted sloppy work. However, today he'd demanded a great deal of the people around him. On reflection, perhaps he'd demanded a little too much. As a result, he'd successfully managed to thoroughly hack off everyone with whom he'd come into contact. Night was drawing in, and his reward for battling through the day in a disgruntled grump, was a yard devoid of staff. He'd been left alone for evening stables. Both Chelsea and Brittany had departed as soon as the first opportunity arose.

A combination of lack of sleep and an inability to stomach anything resembling a decent meal recently, had meant he'd woken this morning stressed and operating on a short fuse. It was Friday, the day before the Lincoln at Doncaster, and he was pretty sure that among other things, he was suffering from nervous tension. The one positive from the day was Cool Blue, who had cantered well, eaten up all his grub and was currently enjoying a lie down in his box.

Faraday felt he and his yard were under the microscope. Last night *Look North* had referred to him as 'the northern trainer who could break the bookies', and he'd been buttonholed by several jockeys and trainers on the gallops this morning.

However, it was the telephone calls from three separate people over the last two days that had piled pressure onto him. A dark cloud had appeared the evening before courtesy of Mick Kowalski, or at least someone claiming to be the bookie from the BetMick chain of bookmakers. After that call he'd contacted Charlie Summers, although the ad man's reaction hadn't helped as much as he had hoped. Then this morning the dreary outlook had continued with a call from Sam Lewis, before growing in size after lunch thanks to Charlie Summer once again.

Faraday had finally realised how stressed he'd become after he'd found himself manically screaming at the feed man. He'd lost his temper with a lazy delivery driver, after discovering his order of expensive racing nuts left out in the rain, instead of the pallet being carried another few feet into the feed room. Not a huge issue normally, but then very little was normal around the yard at present.

As the last remnants of the day faded into night, Faraday was mindlessly shoving a brush around in front of the stables under the beams of a trio of small floodlights. His lack of concentration meant he wasn't making much of an impact; rearranging the dirt, rather than sweeping it up. His thoughts were elsewhere. Filling his mind were three men and a horse: Sam Lewis, Charlie Summer, Mick Kowalski and Cool Blue.

The call with Sam Lewis had been disconcerting, containing instructions that he might need to register Cool Blue as a non-runner late on Saturday morning or perhaps that afternoon. What sense did *that* make? Sam had rung off sharply, seemingly incensed at being asked for an explanation.

'It's my horse and I can do what I want,' had been Sam's final petulant words. Faraday had tried several times to call his owner back, but every attempted call was immediately dropped, with no option to leave a message.

The conversation with Charlie Summer had gone a little better. He'd offered an explanation for Sam's behaviour: media pressure. Yet it still struck him as slightly odd. Sam Lewis worked for a massive company didn't he? You would have thought he'd be used to plenty of attention. To be fair to Charlie, he'd been the only caller bothered to ask how he and Cool Blue were faring.

'The gelding is in far better shape than me,' he'd replied honestly.

Charlie had sounded relieved, then concerned, and promised to arrange some support - whatever that meant - he'd not been specific. Charlie had rung off, committing to find him at the track before the race on Saturday. This had also set Faraday worrying. Why the hell was there so much cloak and dagger stuff going on?

However the strangest call of them all had arrived late on Thursday afternoon, when he'd had to endure ten minutes of smarm from someone claiming to be Mick Kowalski. This joker had offered him fifty thousand pounds to self-certify Cool Blue as a non-runner; the cash to be paid if he didn't take the horse to Doncaster! Charlie Summer had been very interested in this conversation, peppering him with questions and unnecessary aggravation.

Now that it was early evening on Friday Faraday was holding the unshakeable view that the world was going mad. Training a horse to win one of the biggest handicaps of the season was hard enough, but now he had to contend with owners making no sense, their betting advisors confusing the situation, and a bookmaker apparently offering him a massive bribe. Getting rid of these sorts of distractions was one of the reasons he'd wanted to strike out on his own; for a simpler life.

'Huh, so much for making it simple,' he complained to a young filly who had poked her head out of her box to investigate his sweeping.

He pushed the weirdness of Sam Lewis's call to the back of his mind. It was *so* strange he reasoned his owner was confused, maybe he was going senile. He'd simply laughed at the Mick Kowalski caller; for all he knew, it was a prank. A thought struck him – could it be a newspaper trying to set him up? Faraday contemplated this, the sweat on his forehead suddenly turning cold, but he discarded the notion. He'd not taken the caller seriously and besides, he was a small trainer in North Yorkshire. It would hardly make headline news.

Would it though? His sweeping increased in intensity as this

119

thought spun around his head. Taking payments to effect the outcome of a race was bad enough in normal circumstances, but with Cool Blue being so high profile, thanks to Charlie Summer's charitable bets, you'd be committing career suicide even if you showed an interest in such a crazy offer. Faraday stopped sweeping and closed his eyes in the hope it would help clear his mind.

He was so busy trying to relax he hadn't heard them approach. They must have walked soundlessly into the yard down the pitch-black right-angled track, and he only became aware of the two men when one of them spoke.

'Ah! Joss Faraday? Mr. Joss Faraday?'

Faraday's eyes winked open and his heart jumped in his chest. Two small, almost identically sized figures were standing no more than ten feet away from him.

'Jesus Christ…' he blurted, backing away a few yards.

He caught his breath and squinted at the two men. Or could they be younger than that? They were standing beneath a floodlight, which shone down on them, sending their elongated shadows towards the paddocks. Their faces were also in shadow. Faraday took a step back, gripping his brush handle tightly and wielded it like a sword.

'Whooah there!' called the boy closest to him, his palms held up. It was of a deeper timbre than he was expecting. 'It's okay Mr. Faraday, we're here to help.'

The slight, yet sinewy figure stepped forward and now the floodlights revealed a lad of about twenty-two with short blonde hair, freckles, and a pair of ears that stuck out like wing mirrors. Faraday recognised him immediately.

'Peter Mountain?' he asked uncertainly, his eyes wide.

'That's me!' exclaimed the other lad, who now stepped up into the light to stand in front of Faraday with his hand offered out in greeting, 'And this is my brother Luke.'

The second lad waved, grinning from ear to ear. 'I guess we caught you a bit on the hop. I told him we should have shouted down from the top road,' he said, indicating his brother with his thumb.

The confusion still registering on Faraday's face prompted Peter to jump in again.

'I don't know if Charlie… that's Charlie Summer I mean, managed to explain, but we're here to lend a hand and make sure you get to Donny races tomorrow.'

They both leaned forward to shake the trainer's hand, yet Faraday still couldn't find his voice. The two top jumps jockeys, the famous Mountain brothers, identical twins, darlings of the media and stars of the National Hunt scene had just walked into his yard and announced they were here to *help him*?

120

'Why... er. Really?' was all Faraday could get out.

Peter chuckled and swapped a knowing glance with his brother.

'Yeah. I guess Charlie didn't tell you we were turning up eh!'

'I don't know,' Peter said with a comical shrug, 'You agree to pay back a favour and this is what happens. I'll be having words with Charlie.'

Peter raised his eyebrows in expectation and eyed the brush that was still in Faraday's hand. 'You got another one of those? Might as well get started, now we're here. Just point us in the right direction.'

Faraday frowned and eventually handed over his own brush, bewildered by what was happening. He watched in wonderment as Peter Mountain set off sweeping the strip of concrete and cobbles outside the boxes with energetic thrusts.

Luke fixed the trainer with an expectant stare. 'Now then, where's your yard star then?'

'Oh. Ummm... he's over here,'

Faraday led the lad over to a stable in the centre of the line of ten boxes. Luke took a quick look inside and found the gelding lying flat out in his bed of wood shavings. The four-year-old lifted his head and aimed a doleful eye at the grinning head poking over the top half of his stable door, snorted, and went back to sleep. Luke put his back to the box and surveyed the area. The stables looked out onto a grass paddock that ran about fifty yards downhill to a thin line of trees. Beyond was a field of rougher grass, which was for haymaking. To the left, another paddock stretched for about two hundred yards and was boxed off with a drystone wall.

'This isn't too bad!' he stated in businesslike fashion. 'Could have been much worse.'

Faraday scratched his head. 'You're here to protect Cool Blue?'

'Partly,' Luke admitted, 'Charlie was concerned for you, too.'

'Do my horses really need protection?'

'Charlie seems to think so, and from my experience with him, he tends to be right about these sorts of things,' Luke countered, inspecting the bags under Faraday's eyes. He whipped a mobile phone out from the back pocket of his jeans and touched it a couple of times before lifting the dimly glowing device to his ear.

'Charlie? Yeah, we're here in Coverham. Can you speak with Joss please...' he listened for a few seconds then looked up at the trainer.

'Yeah, I think he needs a good meal and some sleep.'

Luke passed his phone over and Faraday listened to Charlie Summer apologise for the lack of warning. Then he spent the next few minutes hearing how the two most popular brothers in jumps racing were going to sleep outside Cool Blue's box, but not before he and his fiancé were fed a takeaway of their choice and then sent to bed.

'You sounded in need of some help earlier today,' Charlie explained. 'You can trust these guys; they are rock solid. I've known them both since they were four years old.'

Faraday's shoulders loosened and he felt tiredness grip him. He did have a big day ahead of him tomorrow, and if you couldn't trust your yard to the Mountain brothers, who *could* you trust?

'Okay Charlie, you're probably right. I'll go with this.'

He was about to hand the phone back to Peter Mountain, when a thought struck him.

'Charlie, are you still there?'

'Yep, what is it?'

'What the hell did you do for these guys? It must be a hell of a debt...'

Charlie started to laugh. In front of Faraday, Luke grinned and he rolled his eyes.

'Put it this way,' said Charlie, 'It was something so huge this is only the start of the payback! Have a relaxing night and I'll see you and Cool Blue at Doncaster tomorrow morning, fit and ready to run,' and he rang off, half way through another laugh.

'Are we good?' Luke enquired, 'I guess there will be one more feed this evening, or are you only on a three feeds a day regime?'

Faraday nodded, 'Four.'

'Okay, so, you'll want to do that yourself in about an hour I guess. So get up to your flat, or house, whatever you've got here and Peter and I will tidy up and get ourselves sorted.'

Later that evening, after a grovelling apology to his fiancé for his poor temper, he jumped into a hot shower. Then the two of them polished off a Chinese takeaway delivered by Luke Mountain, much to the shocked amazement of Chelsea. Faraday went back to the yard, checked each of his horses, and did his final feed of the day. He left Luke and Peter reclining in old-fashioned deck chairs outside Cool Blue's stable. They were hunkered down beside a gas heater and as well as several layers of warm clothes, were wrapped in thick woollen blankets, all of which they'd brought down from their car.

'Are you two going to be okay out here?' he asked before he left.

'Sure!' the two Mountain boys responded, almost in unison.

Faraday grinned, shook his head, and wandered the short distance up the hill to the flat, making one last call of the day, back to Charlie, to thank him for sending the Mountain brothers. His day finally done, Faraday went straight to bed, fell asleep, and slept soundly until his alarm buzzed him awake at five o'clock the next morning.

****

As worshippers started to spill from the church, Charlie finished his conversation with Joss Faraday and rang off. He stowed his mobile

122

phone and remained in his car, watching patiently. He'd been sitting outside Inkberrow Church in the gathering gloom of Friday evening for about ten minutes now, but it was fine; after a two hour drive from Leeds, most of which he'd spent on his phone, finalising plans for tomorrow, he was now enjoying the quietness. The breeze and rustling leaves were the only sounds to puncture the silence inside the car. Almost all the ladies were pulling their coats tightly around them and rearranging scarves against the stiff breeze which was whipping around the churchyard. A couple of the men emerged holding a hand to the brim of their hats. He was pleased to see that none of the evening worshippers were hanging about too long, the chill wind was seeing to that. About a dozen members of the congregation had already headed towards him and passed his car. One or two of the nosier ones had gawped inside, their curiosity suitably piqued by a single man waiting in the dark. These unhappy connotations troubled Charlie a little, so he left the car and walked to the ornate churchyard gate, intending to wait beneath its tiled roof.

Sharon appeared in the church's vestibule, stamping her feet, her black smock flapping just below her hips. She shook hands, smiled, nodded, and waved people on their way. Charlie acknowledged a few of the parishioners as they passed him, trying to ignore the quizzically raised eyebrows his loitering engendered. One of the older ladies recognised him and flashed a knowing smile. It took Charlie a second or two, but was relieved when he placed her as being among the group of Women's Institute visitors to Tommy's yard the week before. He responded with a toothy grin, which he immediately regretted.

A group of parishioners were filing past him when he heard a female shout from the direction of the church.

'Hey! Yes, you! By the lychgate!'

Charlie looked up and realised Sharon had moved deeper into the vestibule and appeared to be hollering in his direction and pointing. He looked over his shoulder, then turned back and provided an animated 'What, Me?' mime, complete with finger gestures.

'Yes!' she shouted back, tipping her head skyward in what Charlie assumed was an exaggerated show of mock frustration.

He jogged the thirty yards to the entrance of the church and found Sharon sheltering inside with her arms crossed, eyes shining and her tongue stowed firmly in her cheek.

'You don't know what a lychgate is, do you?'

Charlie gave a self-deprecating shrug, 'So it seems.'

'Well, hurry up and come on in then, that breeze is raw tonight.'

Charlie followed Sharon through the vestibule and into the church and the two of them halted just inside. Charlie noticed they weren't the only ones there; a man and two women were chatting over a table stacked with hymnbooks and the remains of coffee and biscuits.

'I'll be over in a minute,' Sharon called to them. She spun round to face Charlie and he noticed her cheeks were slightly red, possibly from the change of atmosphere; it was surprisingly warm in the church.

'I wasn't expecting to see you until tomorrow, but I've a few minutes. Am I still on for my ride to the races?' she queried.

Sharon held both hands behind her back now, relaxed and her face tipped upward beatifically in order to lock eyes with him. He noticed her shoulder length bob was tousled, having been buffeted by the breeze and he had to resist the temptation to reach out and brush rogue hairs from her cheek. She wore what appeared on first look, perfectly standard black clerical garb. However on closer inspection her collar and smock were tailored to match her curves. A pair of tight black jeans emerged at the top of her thighs and plunged into an astonishing pair of heeled boots which started just below her knees. As vicars went, she was something of an eye-opener.

'Yes, of course we're still on,' he confirmed, 'I needed to run a few things by you, if that's okay?'

'Sure, but what sort of things? There's nothing wrong is there?'

'Well...'

Charlie watched Sharon's eyebrows pivot and dive into a concerned frown.

'I'll bring you up to date with what's going on with the owner and the horse on the ride to Doncaster tomorrow, but I wanted to make sure you'd be okay with sharing my car with two of my work colleagues. My plans changed and I needed to bring them down to Inkberrow with me this evening.'

'Sounds fine to me, although I'm intrigued to find out what's going on in your sinister sounding world of horse racing,' she quipped.

'It's actually more like bonkers than sinister,'

'Even better!' Sharon beamed.

He couldn't help it, Charlie broke into a hearty chuckle. The worries of the last few days fell away for a precious few seconds and he enjoyed the pleasure of connecting with someone who was totally removed from the chaos surrounding Sam Lewis. He came back down to earth with a thump when he realised she *was* involved. He'd ensured that by sending her a letter. She'd placed a bet for Saint Luke's Church.

'That's all it was really. Oh, and can I pick you up a bit earlier as well?'

'How much earlier?'

Charlie squirmed. 'About two hours earlier?'

Sharon rolled her eyes and then clenched them shut. 'So you need me suited and booted for...'

'Five thirty I'm afraid.'

'Gee whizz!' she exclaimed. Her voice was loud enough to elicit a concerned glance from the three people at the other side of the church.

'Let me explain,' he said grimacing, 'It's because I've been asked to appear on a live racing television show in the morning. They need me there for seven thirty.'

Sharon pouted theatrically for a few seconds and then blurted. 'Gosh, that's absolutely fine. Can I watch?'

'I'm certain that can be arranged,' he committed. In fact, he had absolutely no idea this would be fine, he'd *have* to make sure it would be. Besides, the TV company involved were desperate to feature him. The producer had called and already acquiesced to a few of his requests, the main one being that Stephen Jones hosted the interview. He'd done a great job at Market Rasen and Charlie thought he owed him the chance to be seen by a bigger audience. Most of all, he was simply relieved Sharon would still be coming along. It gave him a warm glow, like something had been lit inside him. Somehow this diminutive lady's attendance gave him greater hope for his plans on Saturday.'

'Great. Pick me up from the church?'

'Yes I'll be here. So it's a date!'

She examined him with slightly narrowed eyes and he suddenly got the dual meaning of what he'd inadvertently blurted. He felt himself blush. Now there was something he'd not done for some time.

'Yeeesss,' she said slowly, still staring up into his face intently, 'I guess it is.'

The two of them maintained eye contact in silence and Charlie found himself tingling. He hadn't felt like this since his college days.

Sharon broke her gaze first, casting her eyes to the stone floor, and biting her lip, seemingly a little embarrassed. She half turned toward her colleagues.

'I really must get things finished here, they're waiting for me,'

Charlie took a few steps backwards, making to leave.

'One last thing. Don't forget to bring your betting slip. You have to show it at the entrance to the racecourse to get into the room we've hired for the day.'

She regarded him quizzically. 'Isn't that a bit dangerous? It's already worth seven thousand pounds isn't it?

Charlie considered this, looking down the row of pews to a large arched window under which a small altar was positioned.

'Hmm, yes, I suppose it is,' he replied thoughtfully.

'No worries, I'll bring it.'

Striding back to his car through the icy breeze Charlie ran the math through his head. It had seemed an elegant solution to use the betting slips as a way of identifying the various charitable organisations as they arrived at Doncaster. If eighty of them turned up, there would be over half a million pounds worth of betting slips wandering around the racecourse. If

Cool Blue were to win, that would multiply to over sixty million pounds. Charlie felt a little sick as he feathered the car's accelerator, guiding it slowly down the single lane road leading away from the church. He now had another potential problem to deal with, this time of his own making. He'd managed to make every charity attending a target for would-be thieves.

****

Mick Kowalski rarely stayed in the office beyond four o'clock, but here he was, feet on his desk, trying to figure a way out of this mess at half past five on a Friday night. Truth be told, he'd never been in love with bookmaking or indeed any sort of hard work; he simply enjoyed the money. If his father hadn't left him that flea-ridden backstreet bookies office in Wallsend all those years ago, he'd never have considered it as a career. While he was being honest with himself, if Laurie Lewis hadn't come into his life when he did, the Wallsend shop would have folded. It was Laurie who turned it around, spent time in the business, and taught him how to make money from bookmaking. He'd been the driving force behind the website, bringing in technical and strategic people to run the online sportsbook and casino.

The BetMick website had soon become the cash cow, but Mick still played around with the betting shops. That's what he understood. The technology behind the website was way beyond his comprehension. He'd tried to get involved once and that hadn't ended well.

Mick grimaced. It was ironic that the website hadn't taken a single Lucky Fifteen bet containing those four horses. They'd all been struck at his betting shops. His shops produced less than two percent of his annual profit, and now they were on the verge of bankrupting the entire company.

He stared at the laptop which lay inert on his desk. It was rarely switched on as he had no idea how to operate it. As far as managing the website went, that was all left to Frank Best. He idly wondered how Frank was getting on. He'd been so busy trying to bribe that trainer he'd never got round to phoning the hospital yesterday. He rubbed the two days of stubble on his chin and decided he'd phone Frank later. Instead, he booted up his laptop. After screaming his obligatory curses when electronic devices didn't do things the way he expected, he eventually reached a browser window and managed to navigate to the *Sporting Life* website.

Right now he had to work out how he was going to play Sam Lewis tomorrow. Even the faintest thought of that man made cold pinpricks of sweat start to break out on his forehead. He'd been a thorn in his side ever since that night Laurie… Mick shook those thoughts from his head and instead ran his finger down the laptop screen's list of runners for tomorrow's Lincoln. There were twenty-two horses declared. At least one of those opponents must surely have the beating of Cool Blue, an unexposed four-year-old who had finished well beaten in his last two runs?

Mick shook his head. He couldn't afford to take chances. After all, this was his livelihood on the line. His finger stopped at Cool Blue and travelled along his line of form until he reached the jockey's name. Chris Hagar. He half recognised it.

Mick attempted a ham-fisted search for the jockey. His first two-fingered attempt at typing soon brought up results for 'Chros Jager'. He pounded the desk and swore before deleting the search and trying again. A correct list of documents for Chris Hagar, jockey, was duly produced; a couple of minutes, and two attempts, later. Mick clicked on a link dated 2018 and his eyes immediately lit up.

****

Sam Lewis felt his way around his queen-sized bed, naked apart from a damp Holiday Inn bath towel tied inexpertly around his midriff. He ran his hand over the length of the duvet, found a pillow and carefully levered himself onto the bed, ensuring as soft a landing as possible. The springs took his considerable weight without complaint. This achieved, he tried to relax. He pulled the large bath towel upwards so it covered the valleys of flab around his middle; the result of inactivity and lavish living. After getting comfortable, which took some doing thanks to the firmness of the bedsprings, he realised he didn't have his mobile phone and headphones. Grumbling, he felt all over the bedside table, but was unable to locate them. He was sure he'd left them there before he took his shower.

A cold, wet, yet familiar nose nudged his arm. Sam brought his hand around to pet his dog, only to find his fingers scratching on something plastic in the German Shepherd's mouth.

'What have you got there, Harvey?' Sam asked softly.

He gave a genuinely warm smile when he found he was proffering his headphones. He took it, hauled up the wire attached to his mobile phone and thanked him. The dog waited until he'd stopped patting and stroking his head, turned and silently padded off to his basket in the corner of the room, where he curled up.

The companionship of a dog had brought an unexpected joy into Sam's life at an early age. His adolescent stupidity had merited a brand new lifestyle when he'd lost his sight, one which he'd initially found shocking, frustrating and depressing; until the first of his dogs arrived from Austria. It was one of the last places in the world which trained German Shepherds as guide dogs, as opposed to Labradors, and where the family's wealth ensured he could buy the very best dog, trained to his specifications. Harvey was his third guide dog, and the best. Definitely the best.

127

Father hadn't allowed his children to keep pets. Mother had tried to talk him round when she was alive, but he and Laurie had to settle with each other. Sam hadn't had any contact with animals until his first guide dog arrived, along with a trainer who stayed for a month to teach the young boy how to cope with his new life in the dark.

Realisation had dawned slowly, growing stronger every day he worked with that first dog; he'd inadvertently created a relationship with his dog based on mutual trust. It was something he'd never experienced before with the people around him, apart from with his brother Laurie.

Thoughts of his brother filled Sam's head, as they often would. He felt his loss deeply and he could sense the anger wanting to rise to the surface. He swallowed it down, burying it for now. He missed his brother terribly, but finally, the truth might only be a day away. He had Kowalski exactly where he wanted him, and he would get to the truth, after which he was ready to exact his revenge. Kowalski is going to pay handsomely for his deception, Sam told himself.

He lay with the headphones still by his side, staring at the hotel ceiling, a shallow ring of grey invading the blackness of his sight. If he concentrated he could just make out where the ceiling met the wall. That was as good as his sight got now, and even that glimpse of reality would disappear soon, according to his Harley Street consultant.

He called softly to Harvey and patted the bed beside him. The dog didn't need telling twice, he trotted round and leapt onto the bed, settling himself down beside Sam. The room was warm and it had been a trying day; his father could be extremely testing. He needed to bring him though. His father needed to see his son succeed in forcing the truth out of that… criminal, Mick Kowalski.

Sam was drifting off to sleep when the door to his father's adjoining room clicked open and the octogenarian shuffled in.

'Oh,for heaven's sake, Samuel,' the old man carped, 'You can't seriously be sleeping with that dirty animal?'

Momentary confusion registered on Sam's face. He sprang forward on the bed, bolt upright and tensed, ready to give Harvey a command.

'It's sick, that's what it is,' Reginald continued, his face screwed up in revulsion.

Sam allowed his jaw to slacken. He recognised the detestation in the old man; that low, crackling tone which sought to demean, criticise, and belittle. Sam had lived with those sounds of derision all his life. At least his father was in no shape to physically bully… any more.

'Don't speak about Harvey like that,' Sam protested bitterly.

'Bah!' said Reginald, flicking a thin wrist in his son's direction. He took a robe off the back of the bathroom door, threw it onto his son, and walked towards the drawn curtains. 'He's probably the only thing who will sleep with you looking like that!'

The old man's disdainful eyes and curled lip didn't have any effect on Sam but they didn't need to; his father's words cut deep enough on their own.

Reginald swept the curtain back and he stared out into the blackness. From their position on the top floor, the white rails of the racecourse could be picked out thanks to the light the hotel threw onto the track. The finishing post was just visible, after which the rails disappeared into darkness.

'I don't like that Charlie Summers. He's a salesman. He'll only be out for himself.'

'I know what you think,' Sam sighed.

'I assume his company has placed bets?' Reginald sniffed.

'He and his two helpers had a bet at Market Rasen,' Sam confirmed, 'But that was just part of the fun. I trust Charlie, father.'

Reginald allowed a sly smile to grace his face before shuffling around to give his son a pitying look.

'We should let Summer sort things out on his own tomorrow,' the old man suggested, 'That's what you're paying him for. There's no need for either of us to be part of the drama. You're just showing off.'

'How?' Sam protested, 'Kowalski has had this coming for a long time. You and I need to be there to hear what *really* happened to Laurie. Don't you want to know how your son died?'

'Of course I do!' the old man spat back, 'But washing our dirty linen in public... it's demeaning. I've decided, I'm going home in the morning. Before the racing starts.'

'No, you're *not,* father,' Sam told him indignantly, 'I brought you here so you could hear for yourself what really happened to your son! We've both known for eighteen months that Kowalski is hiding the truth. Nothing adds up about that night of the car crash, and the moment I finally manage to box Kowalski into a corner, you're going to stay at home? He'll *have* to tell us, or lose his livelihood, and I'm sure he's far too selfish to allow that to happen.'

Sam was holding both his arms out in an imploring manner, palms up. He lowered his voice to a belligerent rumble.

'We've waited two years to finally get to the truth,' he said, crossing his arms and sticking out his bottom lip. 'Well, tomorrow I'm going to squeeze the words from Kowalski... until it all makes sense.'

Reginald Lewis turned to inspect his son, who was sitting draped in the bathrobe and wearing a sullen, almost disturbed expression. For a few moments the old man's craggy, sagging face betrayed his indecision, then it hardened once more. He turned back to stare fixedly out of the window.

'Alright, Samuel,' Reginald said gruffly, 'Let's see if, for once, you can make this happen, and not screw it up.'

Twenty-Five

Saturday 6-45am, Lincoln Handicap Day.

There is something magical about the morning of a big race-day Charlie decided, as he pulled up into an empty Doncaster Owners' car park. Something in the air pushes anticipation into the bloodstream, heightens the senses, and hints at the drama to come... and there was certain to be plenty of that today. Not all of it on the turf.

He switched the car engine off, checked the time was still before seven in the morning, and allowed himself a small smile when he looked over to Stan in the passenger seat. The young man's head was crumpled into the door, mouth open; he was fast asleep. In the back, Suzie and Sharon continued their conversation, apparently unaware they had arrived at their destination. Despite an age gap of what Charlie guessed to be about six years, the two of them had smiled, gasped, giggled, and talked for the entire two hour journey, Suzie updating her new pal on the story so far concerning Sam Lewis and Mick Kowalski. The two women were engrossed to the extent that Charlie had given up trying to follow their conversation, content to allow their words to wash over him.

There had been numerous pockets of mist as they had driven over from Worcestershire, but when Charlie pushed his car door open, got out, stretched and took in the skyline, it was deep blue and cloudless, providing a crisp coolness. Despite significant rain falling overnight, it was a perfect spring day without any hint of a breeze.

They were parked on a huge owners' car park opposite the mammoth Doncaster racecourse grandstand. Dampened grass twinkled where the low sun caught the dew, and Charlie sucked in a deep breath and stretched his neck and back muscles. Suzie joined Charlie outside the car and stood admiring the back of the grandstand, as the early morning sunshine made the steel roof sparkle. The racecourse buildings cast long shadows beyond the racecourse perimeter and the three of them stood in silence for a few seconds, simply gazing at the monster grandstand.

So much of horseracing was about the anticipation; it made you feel alive. Charlie could feel a crackle of electricity coursing through him and realised it wasn't nervousness. He was excited. This day's racing could go down in the history books as the greatest betting coup, or it could be a damp squib. Even though Cool Blue had to run his race, his actions would play a huge part in determining whether the day as a whole was a success. God, he hoped he was up to it, he thought, rubbing his middle finger and the thumb of his right hand together as if he were testing the air, trying to ground himself.

Sharon slid ungainly from the backseat of the car and out onto the grass, immediately noticing Charlie's nervous tic. No, she decided, correcting herself, it was more of an aid to concentration. She remained silent. It seemed this was an important moment for him.

Suzie sensed the same thing, stepping quietly over to the passenger door of the car and rapping smartly on the window. Stan's eyes opened and he jerked in his seat, before waving an acknowledging hand at her. Rubbing his face and pawing his hair back into shape, he joined them outside the car a few moments later.

'There it is,' Charlie whispered as the four of them drank in the still morning air, 'This is our playground for the next eight hours. We need to be sharp today. We've no idea what surprises Sam, his father, and Mick Kowalski have got up their sleeves, but we have a few tricks ourselves. Kowalski doesn't want Cool Blue to reach the starting stalls, Sam may be the same if he gets the information he wants, and Reginald Lewis is the wild card. We've got to ensure Cool Blue gets his chance to run. To do that we've got to stay two steps ahead of them, every step of the way...'

Sharon made a muffled snorting noise. Charlie glanced over and found the vicar holding both hands to her mouth.

'What?' he asked

'Nice speech,' she said apologetically after wiping away the evidence of her mirth, 'That's an awful lot of steps.'

Suzie was similarly amused, 'Is that it, Charlie, or are there more steps?' she laughed, unable to prevent herself from adding a dollop of sarcasm.

The two women giggled at each other and Stan joined in with an amused look. Charlie rolled his eyes. There was nothing wrong with having someone around capable of pricking your bubble of pomposity, and Sharon was apparently adept in this regard. After all, he reflected, what happened today at this racetrack wasn't a case of life and death. It was a horse race, some bets and some people pursuing their own selfish goals, him included. When you looked at it that way, it seemed far less important, less... serious.

'I knew it was going to be a bad idea getting you two together,' he said to the two girls, adding a sigh for effect. He tried to place a self-deprecating look on his face, which he hoped would indicate he had appreciated their attempt to cut him down to size. He received smiles in return and immediately felt better.

They took in the view for another few seconds. 'Right, breakfast?' he suggested, clapping his hands together with relish.

'I'm in! I could murder a bacon sandwich,' Sharon agreed quickly, flashing an impish smile at him.

Suzie glanced at Stan and flashed him a warning look. He bit back the sarcastic remark he was about to make, simply raising a pleading eyebrow back at her.

'I can't be expected to keep quiet all day,' he complained to Suzie as they fell in behind Charlie and Sharon.

'Keep it zipped,' Suzie maintained, giving him a serious, tight look, 'She's quite a woman, you know, quite… different. If you hadn't fallen asleep you'd already know that. Did you hear how she came to be a vicar?'

Stan looked nonplussed. 'She was a thief,' Suzie continued in a low voice, 'She loved the thrill, but her life was out of control, until one day… well, she got caught. Ask her about it. She's definitely got something about her, I think that's what Charlie is drawn to.'

Stan had to admit he'd been taken aback when Sharon had introduced herself earlier that morning at the church. She had playfully pulled him out of the back seat of Charlie's car, insisting she would rather get to know the organ-grinders, than the monkey in the driving seat! Suzie was right. Sharon was definitely a marked departure from the usual specifications Charlie chose in his female friends. Stan had met a few of Charlie's previous girlfriends over the past two years; virtually all of them had looked like they belonged between the covers of *Vogue*. They had also been rather one-dimensional and strangely vacant.

Stan watched Sharon speaking with Charlie, pointing up at the grandstand as they crossed the dual carriageway outside the racecourse. She only came up to Charlie's shoulder, was – Stan tried to come up with the right word – 'rounded', albeit in all the right places, and her clothes were conservative, yet stylish. Sharon was as different as Charlie could get from his normal choice of companion, but Suzie was right again; she exuded a type of energy, a thirst for life, but also humour, yes, definitely a sharp sense of humour, Stan decided.

Ten minutes later they were inside the Holiday Inn hotel which stood as high as the grandstand, looking directly up the track from behind the winning post. All four of them attacked a decent breakfast, although Charlie noticed Suzie pushed her food apologetically around her plate after a few minutes, and kept checking her watch. He smiled inwardly; she hated to be late for anything.

At eight o'clock they left and walked the hundred yards back to the main entrance to the racecourse. Charlie halted and asked his little group to huddle.

'Before we go in, we all know what we're trying to achieve today?' There were energetic nods all round. 'We have to try and appease our client, whilst ensuring Cool Blue gets to come out of the stalls in the Lincoln. After that…'

'…we're all in God's hands,' Sharon finished brightly.

'Exactly!' Charlie exclaimed. 'We've got a few things up our sleeve if we need them, so let's try make this fun. And remember, we're dealing with the Lewis family who are… *difficult* to say the least. They are used to anger and conflict, so let's kill them with kindness and sincerity.

They won't know how to cope with that!'

'Seriously?' Stan queried.

'Oh yes! If they scream and shout, we will be calm and collected. If they direct us to do something that will stop Cool Blue running, we'll quietly direct them elsewhere...'

'And if they set their attack dog on us, we'll run,' Stan added with a thin-lipped smile and wide eyes.

Sharon giggled, and set Suzie off. Charlie lifted his eyes to the sky but was smiling all the same.

'Come on then. Let's do this.'

They approached the entrance to the racecourse and found a line of darkened glass doors, all of which were locked. A bit of knocking and door shaking attracted an officiously mannered middle-aged woman, and after an introduction explaining he was appearing on the live breakfast television show, Charlie and his colleagues were allowed to enter and were directed up a set of escalators to a room on the third floor of the grandstand.

Sharon walked in after Charlie and whistled at the view over the racecourse. The room was a large, bare, magnolia box, apart from a mass of camera paraphernalia, lighting, and black leads running across the dull, carpeted floor. Against the wall was a small set, consisting of a semi-circular bench behind a round glass table covered in Channel Fifteen logos. A group of four people were in discussion to one side of the room, while on the opposite side a lone technician was fiddling with some photography equipment. However, the stark quality of the room was instantly forgotten, as the vista beyond the set, through the floor to ceiling glass wall, provided a jaw dropping view over the empty racecourse. Beyond the flat and jumps tracks the view extended past the corporate village into the deep distance where the racetrack eventually faded into a darkly emerald line of trees. The four of them stepped forward to take in the majesty of the landscape but were soon swinging around one by one, their attention drawn to the raised voices behind them.

Charlie spotted Stephen Jones among the knot of men and women. The racing pundit was easily half a foot taller than anyone else, and Charlie tried to catch his eye. He was in animated conversation with a short, earnest, middle-aged man with a shaved head who was grasping a set of papers and shaking them up at the significantly taller man's chest. Stephen didn't look best pleased, barely managing a weak smile when he looked up and recognised Charlie. The small man waggled his fist of papers into Stephen's stomach again, demanding attention, and appearing to issue an ultimatum whilst glaring up at him. There was a final exchange of views before the small man stalked away, pushing past Charlie's group and leaving the room without bothering to make eye contact.

Stephen covered the ground between them quickly and produced an apologetic smile. He was introduced to Sharon, and recognised Suzie and Stan, but seemed distracted.

'Thanks for this, Charlie, it's great for me, but that was the floor manager. He's not happy with me being your sole interviewer,' Stephen explained.

Charlie shrugged. 'Well, he's going to have to like it or I won't give him his interview. Given the amount of interest in the bets and Cool Blue, I would have thought he'd bend over backwards to secure a live interview?'

'That's the problem,' Stephen grumbled, 'It's such a hot interview, the main talent is complaining.'

'Main talent?' Sharon queried.

'Paul Prentice would normally do the…' Charlie halted mid sentence, preoccupied with something over Sharon's shoulder.

'That's right, Paul Prentice,' called a light Irish accented voice behind her. Sharon spun round to find a wiry man, no taller than her, standing with his hand out in greeting. Unlike Stephen, who was well turned out, but slightly ruffled around the edges, this media man was immaculate from head to foot, and it made her shudder. When she didn't take up his offer of a handshake, Prentice's leathery, tanned face broke into a grin which revealed a string of perfectly straight, pearly-white teeth.

'I assume you must be the clever people behind this wonderfully executed coup?' he ventured, his hand still outstretched, waiting.

Charlie stepped forward and shook the ex-jockey's proffered hand, while Sharon remained stock-still, eyeing him pensively. At least Stephen radiates some warmth, she thought. This man had shallowness written all over him and there was something lurking behind his eyes she didn't trust. She held back a little, watching Prentice hawkishly.

'I believe Stephen and I will be conducting a two-handed interview with you, Mr. Summer,' Prentice breathed, still hanging onto his grin.

'No, I'm afraid not Mr. Prentice,' Charlie responded levelly.

Prentice's grin didn't move. He drank in Charlie's group before alighting on Sharon, meeting her gaze for a few seconds.

'Perhaps Stephen hasn't explained.'

'Yes, he has.'

'And the floor manager has confirmed the arrangement?' Prentice queried, raising one perfectly manicured eyebrow.

'Not yet, but he will.'

'That would be such a shame,' Prentice said, ever so slightly pushing his bottom lip upwards, 'I think with *both* of us investigating your intentions with the charitable bets, we could make your interview far more entertaining.'

Charlie swallowed. A bitterness had developed in the back of his throat which he couldn't seem to shift. He'd never met Prentice before, and already he was choosing his words with care. Prentice had garnered a reputation as a bully in the weighing room, and Charlie wondered if the same approach in the media world had served him well, as his rise up the ranks had been impressive, if somewhat bewildering.

'No, Stephen's background in handicap ratings and bookmaking, really does make him my preferred option. I'm not convinced your more populist approach would serve your viewers on this occasion,' Charlie replied sweetly.

This clearly riled Prentice. The grin faded and the creased face of the forty-five year old turned sour.

'I'll just get that rubber-stamped by the powers that be, as it's not my understanding of the situation,' said Prentice, making for the door.

'Please do,' Charlie advised, 'I'll be here with Stephen getting ready.'

Presently a short, balding man whom Charlie presumed was the floor manager, wheeled into the room. He called out Charlie's name, barely masking his irritation. Behind the floor manager, Prentice ambled back into the room with a satisfied smirk on his face.

'Perhaps if we took this outside,' Charlie stated, tapping the small man's arm, then walking into the corridor and closing the door after him. The floor manager looked to the ceiling, shook his head, and followed.

Two minutes later the floor manager re-entered the room and crossed over to the window where Prentice was standing, leaning against the glass. He had a short, hushed, and intense conversation with his talent.

****

An hour later, 'Racing Breakfast', hosted by Paul Prentice, began with some energetic introductory music and a montage of racing from the Lincoln meeting in previous years.

Charlie leaned his back against the wall and watched over a couple of camera and sound people as Paul Prentice read his pre-prepared spiel over the top of the all-action video tape. He finished the minute long introduction with twenty seconds devoted to the Lincoln. As the videotape died, Prentice dropped his crib sheet to the floor, straightened his tie, and looked into the camera lens, adopting what he imagined was a welcoming gaze but to Charlie's critical eye, came off as a self-satisfied smirk.

'Welcome to Lincoln day at Doncaster. It's the start of the flat season and don't forget,' Prentice warned his audience smoothly, 'Today's big race has the added spectacle of a runner who may bring a change of fortune for dozens of charities. If the Joss Faraday trained four year old Cool Blue can defy his odds and win the Lincoln, bookmakers could be set for the biggest payout in history.'

Prentice had been joined by two more presenters on the other end

135

of his long elliptical sofa, whom he now introduced; an ex-bigwig from a bookmaking company and a younger chap from a speed ratings and handicapping company. They batted some chat backwards and forwards before Prentice took up the role of anchor once again, moving the show on.

'We are also delighted to be bringing you an exclusive, live interview with the man responsible for setting up and executing this incredible coup, Mr. Charlie Summer, the brother of National Hunt trainer Tommy Summer. And all of this is coming up later on the Racing Breakfast show...'

Low-key chatter between pundits, three minute breaks for bookmaker adverts, and various taped features filled the next thirty-five minutes. Charlie remained in his standing position at the back of the room, getting a feel for the rhythm of the show and watching Prentice operate. Prentice had become distinctly frosty once he'd been instructed the channel could lose the interview if Stephen wasn't allowed to conduct it alone. Stephen also looked on, sitting beside him, studying his interview notes. The rest of Charlie's team had been banished to watch the show from a room further down the corridor, despite Sharon's disappointed protests.

Stephen had insisted he ran through his interview questions with Charlie, partly to make sure the flow of their conversation made sense, but also to determine whether he was going to be allowed a free hand with his questions. Charlie liked Stephen, who had an honest, professional approach, knew his topic in minute detail, and more importantly, he always listened to the answers he was getting back and would drill down to a greater depth, something which was sorely lacking in many of his colleagues who seemed more interested in filling the air with their own views.

At nine thirty five, the channel went to an extended break and Charlie and Stephen took their place on the sofa in front of the two cameras. Prentice glowered at them, standing with his arms crossed behind the two cameras, just out of shot.

They went live, and Stephen took over. The first few minutes went well, covering the request from Sam Lewis, the work that went into sending the 'donations' out to the charities and the day at Market Rasen. Charlie was delighted to find Stephen was injecting some of his sense of humour into their interview, a facet he felt would be popular with viewers, and would do his own career no end of good too. Charlie also hoped the more popular this 'coup' became with the public, the less likely Sam Lewis would be able to force Cool Blue to be a non-runner.

'Perhaps you could explain why you placed an unnamed favourite into your suggested bet for the charities? To a normal gambler that would seem outrageously risky,' Stephen pressed, warming to his task.

Beyond the cameras the door to the room opened a crack. Charlie was already well into his explanation of why a totally random selection had been placed within the bet, when the door opened another few inches and to Charlie's amazement, Reginald Lewis slipped inside. The old man stood, shoulders hunched against the back wall, his half-lidded eyes peering over the lights, cables and cameramen... and directly at Charlie. There was the faintest muscle spasm in Reginald's upper right lip; a flash of distaste. He blinked hard, and his steely gaze moved on.

Charlie suddenly ran out of words. He'd been transfixed by the aged interloper who now wore a look of poisonous satisfaction. He snapped back, took a quick sip from a glass of water, and gathered his thoughts. Whatever reason Reginald Lewis had for being here, it would have to wait until he'd finished his interview. He owed that much to Stephen. Meanwhile, Stephen had skilfully picked up the slack and bought him a little time to compose himself. Charlie shook Reginald Lewis from his head and concentrated.

The next few minutes were probably even better in terms of entertainment value than the opening to the interview, as Charlie found his stride and pushed Reginald to the back of his mind. Stephen had arranged for the last twenty seconds of each of the three races to appear on a monitor on the floor and Charlie talked through the last few strides of each race, describing the increasing tension on the day, generated from each winning run. There were audible gasps from the crew when Charlie had revealed the number of charities confirming successful bets had been placed. Stephen converted this to potential payout and the conservative headline figure of seventy million pounds was confirmed by Charlie. The figure had been guessed at in the press and was the subject of heated debate online, but this was the first time Charlie had been given a specific figure and agreed it was more or less correct.

The last advert break behind them, they reached the final eight minutes of the interview and Stephen steered the conversation to whether the bookmakers would actually pay out such a huge sum.

'In every coup of this kind, bookmakers have had to be taken to court in order for payment to be forthcoming. Put simply, will they pay out?' Stephen prompted.

In response, Charlie raised both his hands and shrugged. 'Why wouldn't they?' he queried, 'Sam Lewis and I are no different to the tipsters you find in every newspaper and on every racing website.'

'Ah, yes. But tipsters don't pay for their readers' bets,' Stephen pointed out in a tone which was more investigative than accusatory, 'By funding these bets aren't you colluding as a group, something which is illegal according to every bookmaker's terms and conditions?'

Charlie nodded and considered for a few seconds, hoping to add to the gravity of the query. 'That's a fascinating question,' Charlie replied in a measured voice, 'If every charity we wrote to had placed the bet, I would agree that it would appear that Sam Lewis and I had colluded with these third parties in some massive coup.'

Charlie waited, hoping Stephen would allow the moment to extend in order to heighten what he knew was coming next. Stephen merely nodded, playing along with the game.

'However, over *seventy-five percent* of the charities decided to take the fifty pounds enclosed in their letters and bank it as a simple, straightforward donation. That choice was theirs alone, with no pressure or persuasion applied from anyone. They acted as individuals. The others walked into their local bookies and placed a bet on their charities behalf, knowing that any winnings would benefit their charity, and their charity alone.'

'I find it difficult to believe that such a clever, well planned and lucrative coup would be just for charity…' said an Irish accented voice off camera.

Stephen and Charlie whipped around and saw Paul Prentice picking his way towards them. Behind him, the floor manager was waving whilst whispering vehemently into his headset. Prentice stepped onto the set and took a seat on the end of the sofa. He softly crossed his legs, and when he was settled, provided the primary camera with his trademark grin.

'I'm sure the viewers would love to know what *you're* getting out of this coup, Mr. Summer. It's a simple question, surely one you can answer?'

Charlie and Stephen's eyes met. Stephen's face was wreathed in rage, which he was barely suppressing. Charlie watched as the six foot four presenter turned slowly to face down the man who had hijacked his interview. Prentice stared steadily at Charlie, although the presence of Stephen glaring down at him from close range did have an effect; a bead of sweat glimmered on his forehead. It started at the corner of his temple, built into a sparkling drop and began its journey down his leathery cheek. Charlie watched it descend until it dripped off Prentice's chin. It must be killing him not to wipe it away, thought Charlie, momentarily fascinated.

'It's okay,' Charlie said quietly toward Stephen. He switched his gaze onto Prentice and hoped his expression showed the pity he felt for the man. Then he turned to speak directly into the primary camera.

'I wanted to ensure this interview was conducted properly, which is why I asked for Stephen Jones to chair this question and answer session. I was concerned that the interview could become just about the money.'

He turned to face Prentice again before he continued.

'Sam Lewis had one objective; to allow charities to share in something quite wonderful – the knowledge that he had three horses with exceptionally good chances of winning their next race. He needed someone to co-ordinate this for him, and so he came to me. I will not benefit from Cool Blue winning the Lincoln, but Sam Lewis has paid my company a fee to cover myself and my excellent team's time. That bill will total less than five thousand pounds, and I can confirm that the company I work for has committed to donating this to a local hospice in Leeds.'

Prentice smirked. 'So you and your team will not benefit from Cool Blue winning the Lincoln?'

Charlie didn't reply. There was something about the way Prentice had said 'will not benefit', as if it had some hidden meaning. Charlie wracked his brain and suddenly knew where this line of questioning was leading.

'Absolutely not,' Charlie stated clearly, narrowing his eyes. Prentice licked his lips, clearly about to land his killer blow. He opened his mouth and sucked in some air.

'So what about the three bets your team of helpers placed...'

'Each member of my team placed a bet on behalf of all those charities who decided against joining in the 'coup', as you call it.' Charlie interrupted loudly, maintaining his steady gaze on Prentice. 'It was an excellent idea by a member of my team, Suzie Wu, and if Cool Blue wins today those charities will enjoy a further donation, a share of about two million pounds, as long as BetMick agrees to pay out.'

Someone had got to Prentice and primed him, Charlie reasoned. They had given him sensitive information which he was using to try and paint the charitable bets as nothing more than a shady corporate deal. He'd expected me to wilt in front of him, Charlie thought. Thank goodness for Suzie's outburst the other day. All three of them had signed their winning betting slips over into the care of the company and signed statements which guaranteed any winnings went to the non-participating charities.

A slightly deflated Paul Prentice stared angrily at Charlie. He'd patently been expecting a different answer. Nonetheless, he ploughed on.

'I'm also informed that some of the 'charities' with winning bets are in fact just a front for you and your company, a clever way to secure a payout. Can you...'

'Yes, I can,' Charlie interrupted smoothly, 'Every single charity Sam Lewis contacted with his donation is registered with the Charities Commission. We only wrote to charities who had been registered for at least three years and I would advise any bookmakers to ask for confirmation of this before they pay out. This means there is no way a bogus charity could be just a front – a call to the charities commission can confirm this. Furthermore, three-quarters of the charities with winning bets are arriving here today to cheer on Cool Blue. You're welcome to meet them this afternoon.'

Paul Prentice scraped a hand over his increasingly sweat-lathered forehead. Charlie realised Prentice couldn't have been too certain of his ground before he made his move; he'd been nervous before he sat down and had tried to wing it. Charlie really hoped the second camera was getting this, as the man looked like a rabbit in the headlights, not knowing where to run. Prentice's eyes dropped to the floor and Charlie imagined the presenter's brain was pulsing, desperately trying to find a way of preserving his dignity.

The room was silent, the crew statues. The floor manager was the only person to move, spinning his index finger violently in a circular motion in an attempt to force someone to break the silence. Finally, Stephen spoke up.

'Where did you get the information regarding Mr. Summer's bets, Paul?' Stephen asked quietly but firmly, daring his subject not to answer. Charlie was impressed; Stephen had caught on quickly. He'd also asked the most pertinent question of the entire morning.

'Yes, I'd be fascinated to discover this too, Mr. Prentice,' Charlie reiterated in a helpful tone, 'This was a private matter and we had hoped to surprise all those non-participating charities after the Lincoln result was known. It's rather disappointing that someone has spoiled their surprise. Who was it that gave you such bad information?'

The question appeared to penetrate Prentice's being like a poison tipped arrow, deflating, and then pervading him. In a moment which Charlie found deliciously revealing, Prentice proceeded to betray his accomplice. He leaned back, parted his lips, and drew his eyes up and over to the back of the room for a split second... where Reginald Lewis looked on with a disgusted leer.

'I must apologise, I'm sure you can appreciate, I...' Prentice started.

Stephen turned his back and addressed the camera, making it clear that he was no longer interested in what Prentice had to say.

'I imagine the question which is *actually* on everyone's lips this morning is will Cool Blue win? Charlie, can you help us?'

Charlie beamed, forcing his questions regarding Reginald Lewis's involvement into the background for the time being. 'Yes, he can win,' he replied succinctly. Stephen seemed to be asking for a little more, so he embellished his answer.

'It's the most difficult leg of the bet, and the most important. As I'm sure your viewers will know, we believe most of the charities managed to get an antepost price of 100/1 for him. The horse wouldn't be a part of the bet if he didn't have a great chance. I'm sure you will be speaking with his trainer, Joss Faraday, who will give you his professional opinion. But from my perspective, I understand the gelding is fit, healthy, and ready to run a competitive race.'

Prentice rose silently from the sofa during Charlie's answer and trod carefully between the lighting rig and cameras until he was well beyond the mechanics of making television. He straightened and stared angrily around him, scouring the room. His head twisted in the direction of the door as it clicked shut; the object of his search had already left.

Twenty-Six

Saturday 10-08am

Charlie and Stephen found Prentice in the grandstand's third floor washroom, his hands gripping the sides of a washbasin. He was staring into the mirror, watching the tap water drip from his face.

'You were set up by Reginald Lewis,' Charlie stated baldly.

Prentice winced, shutting his eyes so tightly his face crumpled into a sea of wrinkles. 'You two didn't make it any easier,' he shot back bitterly.

Stephen gave a pitying grunt and glowered at his colleague.

'He assured me...' started Prentice.

'Reginald Lewis told you we were somehow collecting all the bets?' Charlie prompted.

Prentice turned and leant against the basin, his head down, inspecting the floor. His perfectly sculpted hair was ruffled and his shoulders slumped forward.

'He said there were only a few real charities and the rest were fronts for your company. He said his son was a patsy and didn't realise you were conning him.'

'And you thought you could break the biggest betting con of the century on live television in front of millions. But it all fell apart when you weren't anchoring the interview,' Stephen concluded.

Prentice didn't react, prompting Stephen to deepen his frown. Charlie caught Stephen's expression and was surprised at how resentful he was of this apparently broken man. They locked eyes for a moment and Stephen read Charlie's concerned look.

'He was quite happy to ruin both of our reputations a few minutes ago, on the flimsiest of evidence,' Stephen said hotly. 'I'm not about to forgive him for that just because he's a self-pitying mess in a toilet!'

Charlie couldn't help smiling. It hardly seemed possible for a man who already stood at six foot four to grow, but Stephen seemed to be standing taller.

There was no use talking to Prentice any more, Charlie had confirmation it was Reginald Lewis who tried to smear him. Now he needed to know why, and he doubted Prentice was going to be party to that sort of information. He and Stephen made to leave but almost immediately Charlie came to a halt, struck by a new potential positive.

'Have the production company got one of those roving cameras, you know, the ones that mean they can follow presenters around?'

'Yeah, we'll have at least two here today.'

Charlie spun back. 'Hey, Prentice,' he called in a voice which

141

echoed slightly around the ceramic urinals, 'Are you willing to give up the anchor this afternoon in return for redemption?'

'You want me to give up...'

'Listen you idiot,' Charlie interrupted, allowing his patience to run thin, 'You've just looked inept in front of four million racing fans.'

'Four million?' Prentice gibbered, his bottom lip quivering, 'We only get about half a million at most on a Saturday morning.'

Stephen grinned, starting to enjoy himself. 'That's right, the early indications show Charlie's interview increased our viewers to over four, perhaps even five million. There could be twice, or even three times as many watching this afternoon. It could be the biggest racing TV event of the year; there's already talk the race may be broadcast live abroad.'

'With your little performance this morning, chances are you've already lost the anchor,' Charlie intimated. He had no way of knowing whether this was true or not, but Prentice's wide eyes indicated his suggestion had struck a chord.

'And I'm sure social media will be alive with plenty of less than sympathetic Prentice hashtags.'

Charlie let that thought sink in for a few seconds. Prentice held a shaky hand to his cheek and started to scratch, contemplating how his error in judgment may have come across to all those viewers.

'What I'm offering might, if you do a proper job, get you the anchor back,' Charlie said, allowing a hint of hope to enter his tone. 'But more importantly, I suppose it could allow you to put your mistake behind you straight away.'

Again, Charlie paused. Just long enough to allow his words to filter through the man's mind.

'You're probably wondering why I would help you, which is fair enough. So I'll tell you; you'll be helping me to service my client. I really don't think you're going to get a better offer,' Charlie concluded.

Prentice eyed the two men uncertainly, but desperation got the better of him. He nervously flashed his tongue across his lips and jerkily sucked in a breath.

'Alright, what do I need to do?'

****

Saturday 10-15am

Cool Blue gave a sharp kick to the partition in his horsebox and a concerned whinny came from his diminutive companion. The horsebox had stopped and been stationary for a few minutes. The gelding was getting restless. However, his travelling pal had exhibited enough discontent with his kick for the thoroughbred to calm down and settle himself. He blew a snort of breath through his nose to indicate his impatience, but this time refrained from kicking.

A few more snorted complaints ensued before the back of the two-horse transport cracked open and the spring sunshine poured in. Joss Faraday cast an eye over his two travellers and was satisfied with what he saw. Pedro, the donkey, was aiming a doleful eye up at his much younger travelling partner. Cool Blue towered over him and sensing his friend was about to leave, the four-year-old brought his nose down to tap the donkey's rear. Pedro, five years his senior gave a little shake of his mane and trotted down the ramp and onto the grass. Without any prompting from Chelsea, he immediately dropped his head to get a quick rip at the turf. Cool Blue stamped a foot and followed his soul mate a few seconds later, Faraday holding the gelding's lead rein tightly as his hooves clanked noisily on the ramp.

'What a difference!' Faraday exclaimed in a low voice to his fiancé, patting Cool Blue's neck as the gelding took a pick of grass.

'I told you it would be worth bringing Pedro,' said Chelsea, 'He's a calming influence on Bluey.'

Joss and Chelsea led their charges into the racecourse stables, followed and preceded by one of the Mountain twins. The strange group received one or two querying looks, not least due to two top jump jockeys acting as security men. Once the two equine members of their party were safely ensconced in their stable, having been fed, and their water supply checked, Luke parked his back up against the stable door and slid his backside to the floor; an immovable object.

'You two can go get some lunch. I'll stay and look after them. Besides, Bluey is that popular there are two racecourse guards patrolling up and down the stables today.'

'Okay, great, so where's Peter?' Faraday asked, looking up and down the long rows of stabling; the second identical twin was nowhere to be found.

'Oh, he's okay. He's had to run an errand for Charlie,' Luke explained with a meaningful look. Faraday raised a questioning eyebrow. However, once it became clear no flesh would be added to the bones of this explanation, he let it go. He thanked Luke anyway, and taking Chelsea's hand, headed to the stabling staff's café where they could get an honest meal for a fraction of the price the racecourse would charge its racegoers.

Twenty-Seven

Saturday 11-10am

'He's not coming,' Reginald Lewis reminded Sam for the third time, 'Kowalski is playing you for a fool!'

Sam was sitting in an ornate wooden armchair at a round oak table, taking his father's abuse stoically. 'Five more minutes,' he stated firmly whilst running his hands softly over his dog's ears.

Charlie remained silent, as he had done since joining the Lewis's in their private room at the top of the Lazarus stand. It afforded them a superb view of the racecourse and waitress service, although it looked unlikely father or son would be making much use of either. Below them on the third floor, Sam's one hundred and fifty-seven invited guests were busy arriving and being seated at the sixteen round dining tables in the huge room funded by the Lewis organisation. Having taken over a large number of the private rooms on the third floor, the racecourse had renamed its Mallard Room the 'Lewis Room' for the day.

The racecourse was starting to hum to the sound of conversation, punctuated by sporadic announcements on the public address system. The footfalls and echoes of exuberant racegoers in the concrete base of the stand drifted up through the floors and every now and again a burst of female laughter came through the wall from the private box next door.

The joyous sounds contrasted starkly with the atmosphere in the private box. Charlie remained straight-lipped, leaning against a partition wall, head down, regarding the gaudy carpet whilst his insides churned. Sam was sitting, idly fondling Harvey's ears, causing the German Shepherd to angle his head to one side and close his eyes. Meanwhile Reginald paced the room with arms crossed, ensuring his impatience wasn't lost on the other two men by issuing regular deep sighs and unintelligible grumbles. Another two minutes ticked by before Charlie silently dialed a number and finally broke the nervy silence.

'I've tried to call him twice,' he announced, 'Mick Kowalski's mobile is currently going straight to his answering service.'

'What a surprise,' Reginald said sarcastically, 'I tell you, this day is going to end badly. I really don't know what you expect Kowalski to tell you about Laurie anyway.'

Sam ran his tongue over the top row of his teeth and he sucked at his wonky front tooth before answering. His glum expression bore tiny signs of resignation, although this feeling was currently swamped with the irritation he directed at Reginald. Charlie wondered how many times the son had travelled this circular conversation with his father.

'There's something about Kowalski that isn't right, father. I can

144

just tell – he's always been evasive every time I've tried to get any sense out of him about the night Laurie died. There's a malicious streak in the man, and I feel like I'm the only one that can see it. I'm sure he was either with Laurie the night he disappeared or he manufactured the accident himself. Either way, he knows more than he's letting on. The police won't listen…'

'And we know why not,' castigated Reginald.

Sam took a breath and exhaled slowly before continuing. Why his father wasn't supportive of his pursuit of the truth, he couldn't fathom. Accessing Kowalski's office and demanding an explanation from him had been useful, even if he'd ended up in hospital as a result. He'd ended up in hospital through no fault of his own before…

'Any sane man would have pressed charges against me for barging into their place of work, but he didn't!' Sam persisted, 'He's got something to hide and doesn't want the police involved. I now have Kowalski cornered. If he's ever going to talk about Laurie, today is the day.'

'So where is he then?' the old man bleated.

'There's over three hours to the race. There's time.'

'If this circus hasn't finished by two o'clock, I'm leaving.'

'No, you're not!' Sam responded in sharp rebuke, 'We'll go about our business and let him come to us. Knowing Kowalski, he'll leave it until the eleventh hour. Stop being so negative, father.'

I'm counting on that late play from Kowalski, thought Charlie. The Lincoln runs at three thirty-five and with any luck Reginald Lewis will be correct. Kowalski won't even turn up. That was the best scenario all round. He nudged himself off the wall with his elbows and straightened. 'I'm sorry, gentlemen, but we have a rather well attended lunch downstairs and Sam and I have some entertaining to do. Shall we go?'

Charlie held the door of the private box open for Reginald, Sam, and Harvey, and they filed out. Waiting for the lift, Charlie standing behind the father and son, he noticed Reginald start nervously picking at the wick of his manicured fingers. The elderly gent appeared to be genuinely stressed. Even so, Charlie couldn't feel a shred of compassion.

****

Saturday 11-15am

The *Whitby* Fish and Chip restaurant situated opposite Doncaster racecourse had opened its doors fifteen minutes early, it being a Saturday race-day, yet his potential client was already sat down at a table surrounded by a high-backed red vinyl booth. That's where he'd said he'd be.

Chris Hagar crossed the tiled floor without waiting to be seated, his riding satchel slung over his shoulder.

145

'Mick Kowalski?' he asked, making to seat himself opposite the bookmaker.

'Yeah that's right,' the man replied. A pair of hard piggy eyes, far too small for such a wide face, inspected Chris.

'You're not Mick Kowalski. Do you think I'm stupid?' he complained in a steady Yorkshire accent, not waiting for a reply, 'I'm out of here.'

Before he made to turn around, his expression altered markedly and he stared hard at the fake Mick Kowalski. The man watched the colour drain from the jockey's face. Chris scanned the empty restaurant, his jaw tightening.

'If this is a set up, I'll bloody…'

'It's not,' said a voice from behind the man, from the opposite side of the booth, 'Just calm down or you'll attract attention.'

The large, piggy-eyed man smirked and jerked his head upwards and to the right. Chris walked a few steps and peered around the back of the booth and found the real Mick Kowalski on the other side, absorbed in the perusal of a menu. He was wearing a grey three-piece suit and his hair was scraped back over his head and into a straggly black pigtail that started far too high up his head to look anything other than infantile.

Without looking up, Mick released a pudgy finger from the menu and pointed to the long vinyl seat beside him. Chris threw his satchel down on the end of the seat and slid in beside the bookmaker. Mick immediately moved across to him until their thighs were touching, making the jockey fight the effects of a shudder.

'This used to be a fire station you know,' Mick said in a low voice, still staring at the large plastic menu card. 'Now it's another bloody restaurant.'

'What happens if there's a fire down the road now, eh?'

Chris examined Mick's profile and saw the flat bulb at the end of his nose, the black hairs extending from his nostrils and the folds of skin around his neck. He was far too close for comfort and tried to stifle another shudder of revulsion but couldn't manage it, not that it mattered, Mick Kowalski was still staring fixedly at the menu. Chris grunted a non-committal reply as he shivered.

'Hah,' Mick continued, 'I've got a fire I need putting out and you're the fireman,' he said, slapping the menu onto the table and turning to eyeball the jockey.

Chris tried not to react, even though Mick Kowalski's leering face was only a couple of inches from his. Mick reached into his suit pocket and produced an envelope. He waggled it against the table for a second then surreptitiously tucked it between the crack of space between their legs and the seat.

'Finish where you want, but don't win,'

146

Chris didn't look down. He concentrated on the space between Mick's eyes and didn't blink. 'I've been thinking,' he ventured, 'This is worth more than five grand to you. I've read in the *Racing Post* this morning it will save you millions if the rumours are true.'

Mick's gaze faltered and he looked the jockey up and down. Chris could smell the man's aftershave and wondered for a fleeting moment whether it was the aroma of fear; it was sharp and salty.

'How much?' Mick growled, 'We agreed five.'

'Fifty,' squeaked Chris, his mouth suddenly dry.

Mick glared down for a couple of seconds, then snorted out a resigned laugh.

'You bent little shyster,' Mick observed light-heartedly, shifting a little away from the jockey. Chris marvelled at this reaction, Mick had clearly been expecting the increased demand.

'You've been caught doing this before. I read up on you,'

It was Chris's turn to focus his gaze elsewhere. He dipped his chin and examined the floor of the restaurant.

'Okay, you'll get twenty grand,' Mick sniffed, 'It's worth it to me. You do your job and don't get caught doing anything stupid. I need Cool Blue stopped good and proper.'

'I only got *accused* of cheating once,' Chris pointed out, slowly lifting and turning his head to lock eyes with the bookmaker, 'And those charges never stuck.'

Mick held the jockey's gaze, studying the thirty-two year old.

'Fair enough,' Mick sneered, 'You're a bent jockey who doesn't get caught. That's what I need.'

Chris's heart thumped harder as Mick Kowalski started to produce envelopes loaded with cash from his jacket. He dropped them onto the seat between them. Chris didn't know whether to pick them up or not. Mick was producing envelopes from his pockets with only cursory checks to their contents. Finally he nodded at the pile of five manila envelopes between them.

'Go on then, there's ten grand. You'll get the rest afterwards. I'll arrange for you to place a winning bet,' Mick said with a smirk, 'That'll make sure there's no comeback for either of us, and of course it's tax free.'

Chris tried to breathe out and it came in heart thumping gulps instead of a steady flow. He rammed the envelopes into his satchel and started to slide away from the bookmaker, however a large hand shot out and tightly grasped his race hardened bicep.

'Don't screw up, otherwise my mate on the other side of this booth will be paying you a visit.'

'No need to worry,' Chris replied, forcing a smile and prizing Mick's fingers from his arm, 'Cool Blue won't even get out of the stalls with me on board.'

Mick watched the jockey's back disappear toward the restaurant exit. He picked up the menu once more, licked his lips, and couldn't help but allow himself a satisfied smile. He'd not expected to enjoy this foray into the dark side of racing quite as much as he had. The kick to his ego really was intense; he realised his fingers were tingling. A wave of self-affirmation surged through him; he'd bought the result of a race, probably the betting race of the decade, and it felt… incredible.

His mobile buzzed inside his jacket and he dutifully fished it out, smiling once again, this time at the missed calls and specifically the current caller's name. He replied by text message and knocked on the booth's wooden surround. Once his beefy friend had joined him the two of them ordered fish and chips with mushy peas and bread and butter, washing it down with a couple of pints of lager each.

Twenty-Eight

Saturday 11-20am

Charlie's phone beeped twice with text message alerts during the short lift journey down to the third floor. He waited until the doors opened so he could step out into the corridor before opening the messages, not wishing Reginald to have any chance of reading the contents over his shoulder.

Once he'd read both messages he called over to Sam. 'Mick Kowalski has sent me a message. He says he'll speak with you before the race. He's coming to the Lewis Room on the third floor at half past two.'

Sam pushed out his bottom lip in contemplation, 'I don't think he's going to tell me the truth about Laurie's death. He's decided to let Cool Blue run and take his chances.'

'Well, there are twenty-two runners,' Charlie pointed out, 'Maybe he fancies the odds are in his favour.'

'For Christ's sake!' Reginald exploded through gritted teeth, 'You two are like naïve schoolboys. He's obviously got something planned, otherwise he'd have turned up twenty minutes ago to buy himself some time.'

Reginald had been leading the three of them and Harvey down the corridor. Now he stopped, turned to face them and began wagging a bony index finger up into Charlie's jaw.

'I didn't build a billion turnover bakery business without knowing something about game theory!' he ranted, 'He knows something about the horse, and he's going to arrive at your big party in time to watch the two of you suffer in front of a bloody audience! I tell you, Sam, you're going to look an absolute fool.'

Charlie remained silent, allowing the pause to settle for long enough that Reginald dropped his accusing finger. There was no one else on the carpeted corridor and the only sound was from Reginald, who was panting from the vehemence of his rant.

'Or Sam could be a hero,' Charlie stated crisply, maintaining a steady gaze into Reginald's watery blue eyes, 'He could be hailed as the architect of the biggest winning racing bet in history. Even better, he will be recognised as one of the world's greatest philanthropists.'

'That isn't an accolade I would be proud of,' Reginald scoffed.

Charlie cheered inside. If he was right, here was a chance for Sam to grab redemption from the jaws of indulgent, small-minded obsession; to commit to running Cool Blue and also hit back at his father.

'What do you think Sam, shall we confirm he's running?' Charlie asked.

149

He waited for Sam's rebuttal. Silence reigned; it stretched out, awkward and longer than Charlie had anticipated. Charlie stole a look at Sam. Harvey must have sensed the gravity of the situation as he chose that moment to sit down and twist his head up to regard his master quizzically.

Sam was stony-faced, unreadable. None of the reactions Charlie was hoping for were written on the blind man's features. He stood mute, unable, or unwilling to offer a reply or display even a flicker of emotion.

Reginald scowled, turned his back on the two men, and shuffled flat footedly down the corridor, muttering his continued discontent out of the side of his mouth.

Twenty-Nine

Saturday 11-25am

He couldn't believe his luck. Mick Kowalski had been sitting there, as bold as brass in the restaurant, eating a plate of fish and chips. They'd seen him through the window as they passed the restaurant on the way to the racecourse entrance. He had to make the most of this chance encounter, it could save so much... *hardship* later on. They requested a table on the other side of the restaurant, ensuring Mick's back was to them, ordered a couple of coffees and waited for the opportunity to act. He was bound to get his chance, with a little luck, and patience.

There was a burly man with Mick who he didn't recognise, but that didn't matter, the two men looked content, relaxed, and that made them vulnerable. They couldn't stay together forever and they weren't expecting him.

He'd visited the washroom as soon as they'd been allocated a table, to get a lay of the land. Despite the racing starting in a little over two hours time, the restaurant wasn't too busy yet, plenty of time for things to play out in their favour. If they waited patiently, their chance would present itself.

He watched Mick order another pint of lager; not too long now, he thought. The bookmaker had completed his main meal and rubbed his plate clean with his fourth slice of buttered bread. He would surely now... On cue, Mick stood and cast his gaze around the restaurant. He headed toward the stairs which led to the washrooms. Once Mick rose, he was on the move too, careful to remain out of sight. He checked the large man was still seated in the booth, and allowed himself a tight smile when he saw the bruiser's head was buried in a dessert menu.

He watched Mick lift himself up the stairs two at a time, cross the tiled floor and enter the gentleman's washroom, his ridiculous ponytail wagging itself as he walked. He followed, opened the first door, waiting behind the second in the small three yard long anti-room, both of his hands on the sculpted metal push plate.

Downstairs, his companion paid for their drinks and strolled over to the bottom of the washroom stairs to loiter and if necessary, delay any further users of the facilities above.

He waited for a minute in the small, ill-lit anti-room, listening to patent leather shoes squeaking from one side of the washroom to the other, the sound of running water, a hand dryer. More footsteps on the ceramic tile; they were approaching the door. He waited until he could almost sense Mick Kowalski's hand on the washroom door's pull plate. The door moved a crack, applying a miniscule amount of pressure onto his fingertips.

It was a solid door. When he thrust it inward with the full force of his arms and body it caught Mick Kowalski's knee and his face first, followed by his forehead and stomach. The bookmaker let out a sharp scream of pain as cartilage in his nose split and tipped him backwards. His assailant stepped forward and aimed a steel-toed kick at his right shin and Mick Kowalski's stagger backwards became a fall, howling in pain as he toppled.

He leapt onto the larger man, expertly using his foe's own weight to whip him over onto his stomach and kneeling on his neck, he wrenched the bookmaker's right arm up his back. Kowalski pounded his free fist on the stippled yellow tiles of the washroom floor and squeaked an expletive as his face was forced down, enjoying a glazed, sideways view of the inexplicably old-fashioned urinal basins set against the wall.

'Make a sound and I break your arm,' a growl close to Mick's right ear threatened.

Mick Kowalski whimpered, his eyes darting around, trying desperately to catch a glance of his assailant. His nose and shin ached with a throbbing, insistent pain but it was his right shoulder which sent white-hot jolts of agony along his arm and down his spine. It forced him to relax and accept the situation. His cheek was being forced onto the ice-cold tiles, their raised dimples biting into the flesh.

'Listen carefully,' the voice close to Mick's right ear told him, 'This is a… *friendly* reminder. I've been asked to ensure you don't forget the consequences of breaking the agreement you made on the banks of the River Tyne two years ago.'

It took a few moments for Mick's brain to rationalise this statement. When it did, he attempted to jerk his head off the floor and upwards to get sight of his attacker. He glimpsed a wide brimmed Fedora and a finely sculpted jaw line before the pressure of a sharp knee in his neck intensified and another shock of pain was sent juddering around his body, its epicentre in his shoulder joint.

'Ah, you *do* remember,' the man remarked in a tone not entirely devoid of humour. 'So you will be reminded of the consequences of breaking that agreement?'

Mick croaked a quiet, 'Yes,' in reply, his cheek flat to the tiles, staring frustratedly at the Armitage Shanks logo on the basin opposite.

'That's what I needed to hear. Every time your shoulder twinges today, be reminded of that agreement. Whatever the consequences, Sam Lewis's charitable bets have on your business, they won't be as serious as breaking the agreement with our mutual friend.'

The pressure on Mick's neck lifted and instead a knee joint in the small of his back made him squirm. Suddenly all of the bright, sharp pain was gone from his shoulder and a dull ache took over. He gingerly rolled over onto his side and tentatively looked up, initially fearing more retribution. The washroom was empty.

Mick pushed himself up into a sitting position and his vision blurred for a moment, a wave of sickly sweet nausea swamping him as the smell of fish and chip bile reached his battered nose and an acid taste stung the back of his throat. He struggled onto all fours and crawled desperately toward one of the white ceramic basins on the wall before depositing his barely digested jumbo cod and chips into its foul smelling urinal trench.

****

Saturday 11.45am

Stan's facial muscles were aching. The meet and greet at the grandstand entrance to the racecourse had been enjoyable. But, he wasn't used to all this smiling. Sharp-witted sarcasm was his meat and drink, which was in low demand from the middle-aged men and women he'd encountered so far. In fact, the women outnumbered the men significantly, producing beatific smiles when they entered, winning Lucky Fifteen betting slips being produced from purses or bags with childlike zeal. It seemed to Stan the average charity pitching up with their winning betting slip was already so excited with their free VIP day at the races and the potential windfall for their charity, his primary role was to calm them down. However, their heightened expectations were infectious and drew a ready grin each time a new customer approached.

He could spot his charities a mile off. They were the ones entering the racecourse concourse looking around like tourists, some giggling maniacally. It really was a sight to behold. They beamed at you from start to finish. He couldn't help responding with a similar excitement and a smile which had been clinging to him for the last hour, hence the reason he was now rubbing both cheeks in a circular motion in an attempt to ease his previously underworked muscles.

With his technical skills largely surplus to requirement today, apart from a few Tweets and Facebook posts, he was processing the charity, church, and good cause arrivals, giving them their Premier Badges, and providing instructions to the third floor where Suzie was waiting to meet, and then seat them. Since ten-thirty just over a hundred and thirty of Sam Lewis's guests had passed through the turnstiles and the queue had only just started to dissipate.

Stan finished his face massage and rolled his jaw around, his eyes closed. When he opened them, two men were waiting at his desk, having popped into existence right in front of him. The smaller of the two was dressed in a vintage black velvet suit, a light raincoat over his arm and a tweed flat cap, the brim of which he was holding between finger and thumb and twitching in greeting. His colleague was older and wore an

153

immaculate black suit, yellow tie with small black markings and a white handkerchief protruding at right angles from his top pocket. A pair of calm, blue eyes, almost hidden by dark glasses, met his gaze. They were highlighted by darker than expected eyebrows, one of which rose as Stan cleared his throat. He wore a Fedora, which appeared to be rammed impossibly tightly to his head. Stan was reminded of Trevor Howard in Brief Encounter, right down to the high, prominent cheekbones and his down-turned mouth.

'Good afternoon young man, we're here for the Cool Blue race,' the tweed cap wearer offered smoothly before Stan could find words of greeting. He inclined his head towards Stan expectantly, which allowed sunlight to bounce off his shiny receding hairline and give him a warm glow. Stan uneasily perused his list of attendees and the man's eyes fell to the document.

'Mr. Harrison Saddington,' he said, producing a helpful smile, 'And my colleague is Mr. David Hayton.'

Stan was somewhat relieved to find the man's name on the second page of his list. He followed the line across to where the charity's name was printed: The Refuge, Teeside. He met the men's gazes again and realised the overarching quality the two men exhibited was actually their stillness. Or at least, he decided, a sort of quiet, unspoken purpose.

After providing the two men with his stock spiel, he watched as they entered the grandstand concourse, their chins held upwards to take in the magnitude of the building. They dissolved into the growing race day crowd before re-appearing alongside each other as they boarded an escalator travelling upwards.

There had been a number of memorable characters during the morning, including an incredibly excited lady called Jeanne Stream, the chairwoman of a cancer charity who had provided him with her racing tips for the other six races, as she was apparently already an owner of several racehorses. She spoke authoritatively about the day of racing and was clearly used to public speaking, resulting in a huddle of about twenty charity guests and a smattering of other racegoers massing around her to take notes in the queue. Then there had been a very talkative and warm-hearted couple from Darlington who ran a greyhound rescue charity. They had invited Stan to 'Come on up to see us one weekend! You can watch our fifty ex-racing greyhounds tear around the fields at home, it is such an experience! You could bring your girlfriend, I'm sure she'd love it. You must have a girlfriend, a good looking young man like you…' And so the stream of words had continued, the wife picking up when the husband took a breath and vice versa.

Perhaps one of the more bizarre and touching encounters had been with Jill Newberry, a teenage girl who, hand in hand, had approached his desk with her seventy-six year old grandfather. They had taken a taxi, two trains, and a bus to reach the course from the south coast, having set off very early that morning. The bright-eyed, switched on sixteen-year old had explained she had been chosen to represent a Caring for Carers charity in her town, whose secretary had received the Sam Lewis letter.

'They didn't know what to do, but I've been running my grandad's bets to the local bookies for years,' the girl had explained happily. 'It was just luck the woman from the charity called on Tuesday evening and I was there to explain what a 'Lucky Fifteen' was! I put the bet on in my school dinner hour the next day, along with my grandad's bets.'

It transpired her grandfather, who had a number of medical issues, had always lived with her. Jill had become his sole carer at the age of fourteen, when her mother had died. With no father or siblings around to help out, the young girl managed the household single-handed.

'Aren't you too young to bet?' Stan had asked.

'Oh, they know me at the bookies,' Jill had laughed, tossing her long brown hair over her shoulder, 'I get one of the old boys there to place my grandad's bets for me. The betting shop manager understands.'

The grandad said very little, preferring to allow his grand-daughter to light up those around her with her exuberance and vitality, although it was clear to Stan he was just as excited and possibly a little bewildered by the experience. Stan had sorted their badges filled with awe for Jill's fortitude and a strange pride that he had, in a small way, helped to bring about their attendance on Lincoln Day.

Stan checked his watch. It was almost noon; time for him to leave the racecourse entrance. There were still a mix of four charities and a church on the list who hadn't arrived, but he was now needed up on the third floor. He collected his paperwork together, shouldered his laptop, and gave the last few names to the two ladies running the *Owners and Trainers* reception. As he moved off a young man nimbly crossed the reception hall to intercept him. He was wearing sunglasses and a baseball cap which proclaimed he supported the *Racing Welfare* charity.

'Nothing untoward to report,' Luke Mountain said under his breath as he joined Stan.

'Did you follow all of the charities upstairs?'

'Yeah, as best I could. I've not seen anyone approach the winners, or bump into them, at least on purpose. If there are pick-pockets around, I didn't spot any of them.'

'Okay, I'll let Charlie know. He was really worried someone would try to steal their betting slips.

'No problem,' Luke nodded, 'I'm away back to the stables to help get Cool Blue ready.' Before Stan could reply, the top-flight jumps jockey had pulled his cap down low and drifted away from him, heading to the west entrance of the grandstand and the stabling area beyond.

Thirty

12-30pm Saturday

Charlie arrived at the entrance to the third floor function room, after skipping past Reginald, in order to manage their entrance properly. He was greeted by a slightly flustered Suzie who was standing behind a collapsible lectern. Stan was with her, fresh from his stint at the ground floor entrance. He caught Charlie's eye and confirmed all had gone well downstairs with a thumbs-up gesture.

Suzie, her head buried in a seating plan, was blowing frustrated puffs of air upwards in an attempt to push her fringe back from her face and cool her forehead. She was being supported by Sharon, who currently had her back to him, standing hands on hips. She seemed to be surveying the room. She whipped round on hearing his voice and he noted with interest that the vicar was now wearing her clerical collar. He wondered for a moment why that might be. Perhaps it was for an added air of authority?

The double doors to the room were fastened back and Charlie caught sight of several circular tables within, each presented with silky white tablecloths and an array of cutlery and sparkling glasses. An extravagantly tall display of glass and flowers provided the centrepiece to each table, and the necks of several champagne bottles poked out of silvery buckets. The tables appeared to be fully occupied with guests and the burble of good-natured conversation spilled into the corridor.

'Everything is fine,' Suzie told him, her eyes betraying her relief that the cavalry had arrived, 'It's just that Prentice chap, you know, the TV presenter,' she angled her eyes through the doors, 'He's been asking for you, *constantly*, for the last thirty minutes.'

'He's become a right pain in the rear,' agreed Sharon quietly lifting her eyes to lock them with Charlie, 'I'd have decked him by now. This girl is a saint.'

'Oh, it's not been *that* bad,' Suzie insisted. Then her eyes hardened, 'Oh blast, here he comes again.'

Prentice's fingers appeared first, gripping the door jam, then his head and neck poked around the corner of the entrance and his eyes widened when he caught sight of his prey. Charlie struck an expectant pose and Prentice strode up to stand right in front of him, demanding attention. He didn't notice that Charlie's attention was torn between himself and Sharon, as Suzie was now introducing the vicar to the Lewis family.

'Mr. Summer, I'm so glad you're here!' Prentice exclaimed loudly, looking up at the object of his consternation, 'Perhaps we could share a few minutes so you can explain exactly *what the hell* it is I'm doing up here?'

'Please call me Charlie, Mr. Prentice,' he told him amiably, unlocking his gaze from Sharon and dropping his eyes downwards to the small, agitated man. 'You have my undivided attention! I'm all set to provide you with an array of opportunities which, with your personal touch, should have your audience on the edge of their seats.'

Prentice regarded him nervously for a few seconds, not quite sure what to make of Charlie's charming declaration. His desperation quickly got the better of him.

'Well, please explain!' he said, producing a false laugh to try and cover his impatience.

'All in good time,' Charlie replied, pre-occupied with how Sam and Reginald were getting on behind him. A glance backwards found Suzie hugging Sam, who looked very happy, and also slightly abashed. He found himself wondering how many times Sam was hugged these days. Meanwhile, Sharon smiled sweetly at Reginald whilst engaging him in conversation. Suzie then transferred her affections to Harvey, bobbing down and showering the dog with pats and delicately folding his ears between her hands. Sharon then shifted her attention to Sam. They're both good at this, Charlie decided. In fact, they're quite the double act.

Charlie guided Prentice back into the Lewis Room. He'd helped plan the layout with Suzie and Stan, however this was the first time he'd seen the real thing. It was a large oblong room with the far wall consisting entirely of shining glass ceiling to floor, providing a fabulous view of the final two furlongs. Glass doors were evenly placed to allow guests to venture outside onto the grandstand steps, and if they wished, into a private viewing and seating area. Several large flat-screen televisions hung on the walls and from the ceiling. The huge round tables were impressive and another triumph for Suzie. He took all this in, eventually scanning to the back wall where he found a cameraman leaning with a bored look on his face. He nodded to him and indicated he'd be ready in a couple of minutes.

It started with a few whispered asides, followed by a scratch of chairs being pushed back on the tiled floor and then the round of applause started, then grew, as the architect of their Lucky Fifteen bet was recognised. Prentice had the presence of mind to step back and allow Charlie to take in the entire room, and the hundred and forty people who had just got to their feet. A sea of happy, and in some cases, ecstatic faces beamed at him from every direction. A few seconds into the applause Sam, Harvey, and Reginald entered and the applause became cheers. Prentice groaned and retreated to the wall, allowing his cameraman to record the welcome. Reginald slipped sideways, shrinking from the attention, holding a few fingers to his forehead as if he was suffering from a headache.

Charlie took Sam's hand and bent close to the man's ear.

'Your public is pleased to see you.'

Initially shocked, Sam soon found a smile expanding across his face. Charlie seized the moment, raising Sam's free hand above their

157

heads, an action which, as Charlie had hoped, served to increase the fervour around the room. Sam listened to the sounds of appreciation growing and then reverberating around him and couldn't help himself. He laughed and thrust his hand higher.

At the zenith of the cheering, Charlie carefully released Sam's hand and palms up, asked for hush.

'Thanks for that tremendous welcome, it's great to see you all here,' Charlie started, which got another smattering of applause. He introduced Sam, Suzie, Stan, Sharon, and himself, returning to Sam in order to emphasise his importance and fluff his client's ego.

'You are, as you know, honoured guests of Sam Lewis today, and he is delighted to welcome you to Doncaster racecourse for the Lincoln and our attempt to raise *over seventy million pounds* for your charities.'

This got a roar of approval and a few whoops, particularly from the tables already enjoying the complimentary champagne. Charlie made a mental note of where most of the noise was coming from, just in case he needed some unadulterated support later in the day.

'We've got a couple of hours before racing starts, so please enjoy your lunch, which will be served very soon. We have complimentary champagne (another roar of approval), and we'll also have today's race caller coming down to mark your card. We've got Mr. Paul Prentice, presenter from Racing Television, here to conduct interviews with you and to capture the excitement of the race…'

This received a muted response which left Charlie impressed. It seemed a good proportion of the charity guests had either caught the early morning show, or had already heard about it.

'… and before Cool Blue's big race, Sam and I will be around every table to meet with you all.'

Sam frowned and shot an uncertain glance Charlie's way. He hadn't been aware of a requirement to meet the people. He would have to nip that idea in the bud. His line of thought was interrupted by a woman's voice a few yards from him. She was speaking with another lady.

'…and so noble. They will surely write a book about this, it's… such clever philanthropy.'

The warmth of Suzie's welcome had been unexpected, and now he was being cheered and spoken about in terms he could never have imagined. These people really *liked him*. Sam allowed his smile to broaden and he waved a hand once more.

'Put that down, you moron,' growled his father from behind him, 'You're not a bloody rock star. Can't you see that sycophantic ad man has you lapping up his drivel?'

Sam tried to ignore the comment, feigning loss of hearing, however his expanded heart started to contract and the smile which had continued to grow over the last few minutes faded accordingly in degrees.

158

As if to order, Suzie arrived at his side. He recognised her particularly fragrant floral perfume, and his smile rebounded.

'There are a number of the charities who wanted to thank you personally, but only if that's okay with you?' she asked Sam sweetly.

Before he could refuse, Suzie was introducing a lady from a dogs re-homing charity. The line of charities wishing to meet their benefactor quickly expanded and Sam was kept busy shaking hands and making small talk for the next twenty minutes. Charlie looked on, dipping in every now and again as required. He stepped back after rescuing Sam from the attentions of Mrs. Jeanne Stream, who had been determined to run through the form of the Lincoln in minute detail, leaving Sam glassy-eyed and bemused. If Sam could remain engaged until the race, they could just about pull this off, but it was imperative he was enjoying himself. If it meant fluffing up his ego, then it would be duly fluffed.

Reginald was on another level though. Charlie cast his eyes around the room and spotted him leaning against an internal wall, arms crossed, watching his offspring with disdain, bordering on contempt. Charlie hadn't broached the attempt to derail the breakfast interview with Reginald. He'd considered asking Reginald to explain himself upstairs in their private room when they were waiting for Kowalski, but had thought better of it. He doubted he'd have received anything more than a derogatory sneer. Quite why the old man was so keen to see his son fail was a head-scratcher, but it clearly marked the old man out as a firebrand who needed monitoring closely.

Prentice sidled up to Charlie again and this time he engaged with the presenter immediately.

'First things first, you need to apologise,' Charlie started.

Prentice looked hurt. 'But I thought... in the washroom...'

'No, no,' Charlie said, waving this reply away, 'You need to apologise *on camera*. It's how you're going to rescue your career. Come on. Let's speak with your cameraman.'

Prentice followed Charlie over to where the cameraman was standing, looking a little less bored and irritable, but needing to be won over. They spent the next five minutes listening to Charlie explain the potential events that afternoon. Prentice's well-plucked eyebrows rose and fell for the first few minutes before settling into an engrossed, concentrated stare. The cameraman began with a sleepy look which soon developed into open-mouthed interest. The two of them eyed each other excitedly once Charlie had left them, turning to regard the seated guests with renewed interest. Prentice picked up a hand-held microphone, inserted an earpiece, and started a discussion with his director.

Charlie returned to the entrance, pleased with how his discussion had gone. Sharon was standing waiting for him wearing an expression which screamed, 'What on earth have you been up to?'

'That seemed to go well,' she challenged, 'Forgive me for being nosey, but would I be right in assuming you were cooking something up?'

Charlie grinned 'Mmm... sort of. I have to admit that Prentice's desperation to land an exclusive this morning has presented us with an unexpected opportunity. We did have Stan all set up to film everything today, but if we can keep Prentice fed with worthy material it means we're potentially broadcasting to millions of people direct, rather than via a YouTube channel.'

Sharon studied Charlie. He was unaware of her attention, engrossed in Prentice getting ready and monitoring Sam's current conversation with another charity boss. Eventually she slipped her arm through his. He accepted it, albeit absentmindedly, his focus on the room.

'Do you ever tire of using guile, manipulation, and exaggeration in the pursuit of your goals?' she inquired, trying to ensure there was a hint of mild amusement in her voice, on the off chance she had read Charlie completely wrong.

He looked down at her, slightly surprised, but his interest piqued. She was teasing of course, and he realised her question was tantamount to a backhanded compliment, yet there was something far more serious happening behind her eyes. He adopted a mock-horrified expression.

'Yes, of course,' he admitted, as if he'd been caught out. He inserted a dramatic sigh afterwards for extra effect.

'It's all rather tiresome, actually,' he continued airily, looking nonchalantly out into the room once more, 'Behaving like a conniving, two-faced liar is fine, but actually realising you *are* a conniving, two-faced liar is a major failing in my line of work. It's rather insightful of you to have noticed my inner turmoil,' he added with a pained expression.

'I really *must* do something about it. What would you suggest?'

He peered down at Sharon, this time purposefully adopting a daft, inquisitive pose.

'Oh, I wouldn't worry too much, you'll cope,' she laughed, finding the sight of a single eyebrow so high on Charlie's face rather funny. She was about to add something but Charlie started speaking again.

'Sam isn't my primary client today,' he said with a serious edge, 'These guys are,' and nodded toward the tables full of noisy, chattering people enjoying their day at the races.

160

Thirty-One

Saturday 1-20pm

Charlie's interview with Prentice was conducted outside in the red, fold down plastic seats in the stands, with the camera's low angle catching all the charities in the background. It was pre-recorded and would go out at the start of the afternoon's coverage on the primary channel, which allowed everyone to get the piece right.

It went well and Prentice was back on form again. Charlie had reminded the ex-jockey of a set of impromptu interviews he'd seen him host at the Derby meeting a number of years back, well before he had settled for the comfy indoor anchorman sofa. At the time, Charlie had been genuinely impressed with how Prentice had allowed members of the racing industry and the public to express themselves as he moved among the Derby-day crowds, yet maintaining the pace of his five minute pieces with precision. On being reminded of this moment in his career, Prentice had positively glowed and produced a wonderfully honest piece to camera without any of his previous pomposity or rancour. Charlie accepted the heartfelt apology with what he hoped, was a good degree of finality, aiming to close down most of the upset Prentice's mistake had created.

Charlie re-iterated his suggestions for what Prentice could film during the build up to the Lincoln and declared he was leaving them to it, apart from one last introduction.

'Follow me to the bookmakers' table,' Charlie instructed the cameraman. To Prentice he added, 'There's talk that many of the bookies won't pay out if Cool Blue wins today. They will try and drag us through the courts, arguing we've colluded for group gain. Well, your opening pre-recorded exclusive can be the news that we've convinced four bookmakers to guarantee they will pay out if Cool Blue wins.'

Prentice's surprised look turned to one of anticipation when Charlie informed him he'd invited the bookies representatives to join him, and they were currently waiting for them at a table in the Lewis Room. In fact, none of these bookmaking firms stood to lose more than three million pounds each. However, it was great PR for them, and Charlie reckoned it should make a few minutes decent television.'

Back inside the room and with Prentice and his cameraman following, Charlie looked around and found who he was looking for: Sam was still shaking hands and had a knot of guests around him. Sharon and Suzie hovered close by. Meanwhile, Reginald had found a spare chair, which he'd pulled over to the wall, well out of the way. He sat, arms and legs crossed, his hooded eyes peering across the tables which were now being served lunch. He reminded Charlie of a vulture, waiting for the last breath of a beast before swooping down to gorge itself.

Charlie crossed over to the old man. 'Before we have lunch,' he gestured to an empty table set a little apart from the rest to their left, 'I do need to introduce your son to one or two of his special guests. But feel free to start without us.'

Reginald sniffed but didn't move or bother to look up. Charlie tried for a few seconds to feel some empathy for the man. It didn't work. Reginald was almost certainly a lost cause, thought Charlie. His views hardened, his impatience, rudeness, and disenchantment with his world already ingrained. Charlie recalled Reginald had lost his wife and he wondered how much her suicide, and the loss of his eldest son, had contributed to the bitterness which clearly crippled the old man. Even so, the sheer level of scorn and vitriol he poured onto his remaining son, and his treatment of everyone else around him, made it difficult to feel anything other than a miniscule amount of pity for the man.

Whilst dwelling on his thoughts of Reginald and how a man of so little warmth could have created such a behemoth of a bakery company, a tall man wearing vintage clothes and a hat brushed past him. It wasn't until he had disappeared into the corridor that Charlie placed the man. It was the gentleman with the pertinent questions outside the police station in Leeds. Perhaps that was why he'd been there, Charlie reasoned, he was a charity guest and had placed the bet.

He didn't know why, but he wanted to know more about this enigmatic individual. Charlie made to go after him through the scrum of guests, intending to be re-introduced, but by the time he'd reached the entrance to the Lewis Room, the corridor was empty. An expectant Prentice popped up at his side again and Charlie determined he would have a word with the Trevor Howard look-alike later in the afternoon. At the moment he had a bit of positive PR to organise.

Charlie rescued Sam from his adoring press of guests, who were being carefully presented one by one by Suzie and Sharon. He took Sam's arm and guided the blind man, along with Harvey, to a table at the far end of the room. Prentice followed. Charlie whispered a few helpful phrases in Sam's ear as they walked and presented him to a table which consisted primarily of dark suited middle-aged men. If the empties were anything to go by, the table was onto their fourth bottle of champagne. The men shambled to their feet as Charlie, Sam and Harvey reached them.

Still in his warm place after the reception and subsequent chatting with guests, Sam moved around the table making positive noises and thanking the men for their commitment to pay out should Cool Blue win in a couple of hours time. This was all captured by Prentice and the cameraman, much to the bookmakers' delight.

Charlie watched as Prentice moved in and started to interview Sam and the bookmakers. The media makers would get what they wanted from this little encounter, no doubt billing it as when the punter met the enemy, and the bookmakers would get plenty of kudos for being good enough to promise to pay out to the charities.

Charlie was reminded of that Sunday in the hotel in Inkberrow, where he had written the phrase; 'shame them into paying,' on the whiteboard. He allowed himself a small congratulatory smile. Many of the companies at this table had already published newspaper adverts and bombarded their social media accounts with the news that they intended to pay out to the charities without quibble or delay. This was the result of work by Suzie and Stan, systematically contacting all the major bookmaker head offices with this suggestion and pointing out the potential positive coverage. Charlie also calculated this TV coverage should help to heap pressure on the bookmakers who were keeping quiet about their intentions. Bookies like BetMick.

****

Joss Faraday welcomed Luke Mountain back to Cool Blue's box in the stabling area with an; 'Ay up, Howd'ya get on?' and received a smile and a, 'Not too shabbily,' reply in return.

'How's Bluey?' Luke inquired.

'In good shape.'

'Good enough shape to win?'

'Of course,' Faraday replied matter of factly.

Peter Mountain was still sitting unmoving underneath Cool Blue's stable door. Luke offered his twin brother a hand and pulled him to his feet.

'Go on, get yourself some lunch. I'll take over here. I've got some emailing I've got to get on with now anyway, may as well be sat here doing it than anywhere else,' Luke told him.

Peter didn't need telling twice, and strode off toward the staff canteen. Faraday, a set of blue and yellow silks in his hand, took a look over the stable door and clucked at the two unlikely friends inside. They both had their heads down, carefully picking through the straw on the floor, sucking up the last remnants of their horse nut lunch which had spilled out of their mangers.

'Okay, I'm on my way to drop these colours into the weighing room and pick up Chelsea,' he told Luke.

'Ah, lunch with the knobs!'

'Yeah, not my favourite, but it has to be done.'

Faraday took a few steps, but then stopped and turned back to Luke, displaying a quizzical frown.

'Come on, tell me what that favour was that Charlie is making you and your brother pay back.'

Luke unexpectedly shone a delighted smile back at the trainer. 'Has it been bugging you?' he asked, to which Faraday responded with a shrug. 'I bet Peter wouldn't give you an answer either?'

Faraday scratched the back of his neck and frowned, 'No,' he grumbled, 'Your brother is pretty tight-lipped. Did Charlie set you up with girlfriends?' Faraday ventured.

'Nope. Sorry, wrong again,' Luke grinned, plugging a set of earphones into his mobile and attaching the ear-buds. Faraday took this as a signal that the conversation was over, sighed heavily, and set off to the weighing room.

Thirty-Two

Saturday, 2-15pm

In the washroom on the third floor of the grandstand, Mick Kowalski adjusted his tie in the mirror and inspected the yellow stains on his shirt. A tweed waistcoat wearing young man moved up to use the sink on his left, but upon sniffing the air, screwed his nose up. Eyeing Mick up and down with disgust, he opted to leave without washing his hands. As the washroom door was pushed back, the roar of the crowd rushed through. The second race on the card was in its closing stages.

Mick was alone, having fallen out with his associate on his eventual return to the restaurant table. He took Big Jimmy with him on his trips to the races when he was entertaining high rolling customers. Luring big money punters to the races with the promise of some VIP treatment in a private box was an enjoyable exercise for Mick. He would entice them to increase their stakes, and win or lose on the day he knew a taste of that lifestyle was intoxicating. He always won big in the end. Jim's bulk was usually enough to dissuade a disgruntled customer from having a pop at him. However, Jim had seen nothing of his assailant, probably because he'd been tucking into a huge ice cream dessert. Mick had seen red and promptly pushed Jim's half-eaten bowl of brightly coloured assorted ices into his pal's lap and left him in the restaurant.

Mick checked his watch. There was just over an hour until the Lincoln. Even though he wasn't looking his best, and the smell of sick still wafted around him, he wasn't going to miss the opportunity to watch Sam Lewis fail. He rolled his shoulders, attempting to ease the dull ache his attacker had promised would be with him the rest of the day. He was reminded of the man's words; the agreement.

In an effort to rid his mind of the encounter Mick pulled in his stomach, adjusted his belt, and inadvertently caught his reflection in the mirror. A tired man in his late-thirties with stringy, unkempt black hair examined him. His doughy face had a grey pallor which made the slack skin around his eyes and the bottom of his cheeks look like it had melted and set. He inexpertly tied his hair back and grinned back at his image, keenly aware that his appearance was unimportant. His mother had been stunningly good looking. She'd died too young, however he had photos, each one precious. In every picture, from every angle, his mother had been beautiful. Conversely, his Polish father had been like him; only a short few steps from being downright ugly. Mick had come to terms with his looks a long time ago, and used them to his advantage. After all, who cared if their bookmaker was good looking? The uglier the better! At least he was memorable. A love interest? Well, if he wanted a woman, the right sort didn't mind how repulsive he was, as long as he had money.

Entering the third floor corridor Mick sucked in a deep breath, narrowed his eyes, and prepared for the afternoon ahead. He was determined to enjoy every single minute of Sam Lewis's embarrassment.

****

'I'm going to go and get his saddle and weight cloth as early as possible. We'll saddle him here and then take him to the pre-parade ring,' Faraday explained to the Mountain brothers. The three of them were standing outside the gelding's box, checking their watches and phones.

'Why not saddle in the pre-parade boxes?' Luke queried, opening the stable door and pushing the gelding back so he could get in and lock the door behind him.

'Too many people. I don't want him getting fractious when he sees the size of the crowd,' Faraday replied.

'Yeah, and we've already had a steady flow of owners and trainers passing his box interested in the big gamble horse. It could be a bit full on when we get in front of the public,' Peter agreed.

Faraday leaned on the door to the stable, pondered this comment a little more before adding, 'That said, he's such a prima donna, I wouldn't be surprised if he revels in the attention.'

Inside the box, Luke made a chuckling noise, 'I can confirm he likes being brushed. He's standing here like he's a king and I'm the boot boy.'

'Naa, you're the court jester!' Peter quipped.

'Just make sure you brush his pal a little as well. He gets jealous,' warned Faraday, 'We don't want Pedro taking a chunk out of you.'

The trainer watched Cool Blue getting brushed down and tried to relax. He'd surprised himself with how relieved he felt when the Mountain brothers had returned from their latest errand for Charlie. Standing around the racecourse stables with little to occupy him had allowed his worries to grow. Right now, he was waiting for Paul Prentice to arrive. He was due to conduct an interview with him; his first for network television. This mental reminder had the effect of turning his mouth dry.

He'd had a degree of his concern relieved when the Mountain brothers had offered to lead the gelding up instead of Chelsea, which meant she could help him out in the parade ring with all of Sam Lewis's guests. His nerves had been jangling since this morning, ever since he woke to hear his own name mentioned on TV bulletins and radio. He wasn't the best at meeting new people. Having Chelsea beside him in the parade ring would help, and he'd gratefully accepted their offer.

Faraday leaned onto the stable door, watching Luke's rhythmic movements of his brush down the four-year-old's flanks. He checked his phone again and began to tap his finger sporadically on the steel on the rim of the door.

'Go for a walk around the stables,' Luke suggested, 'You'll go daft waiting around here for another fifteen minutes.'

Faraday didn't need telling twice; he set off at a jog, the breeze cooling his brow and his footfalls on the chalky surface removing the sound of his heart banging against his ribs.

Thirty-Three

Saturday 2-40pm

Cool Blue poked his head through the V-shaped grille of his racecourse stable and snorted at the little gathering outside. The gelding seemed irritated and Luke Mountain moved toward him, cupped his chin, and rubbed his whiskers while speaking softly. The four-year-old blinked a few times, retracted his head, and joined his stable companion in the murky depths of his box.

Luke Mountain sniggered, turning to share with his brother what an uptight ball of muscle the gelding was.

A few yards away Joss Faraday finished speaking with Paul Prentice and his cameraman, wishing them well before turning back to the stable where the two Mountain brothers and Chelsea had been watching. He walked over to the box and clucked at Cool Blue, who dutifully came back, shoved his head out of his stable, and plonked his chin on Faraday's shoulder. Prentice nodded to his cameraman and they rushed over to add a few extra questions while the trainer and his horse enjoyed an intimate moment, the horse blowing hot breath into his trainer's ear and onto the camera lens at the same time.

'Thanks for that, Joss,' Prentice told Faraday with genuine warmth, 'The audience will love those extra few questions.'

Faraday shrugged, not sure whether to admit it was the first proper television interview he'd ever done. 'I hope you got what you wanted.'

Prentice screwed the corner of his mouth up and frowned, 'Of course we did. You were great! I'm looking forward to talking to you again after the race.'

As Prentice walked away from the stables, he exchanged a few comments with his cameraman. Both of them were of the opinion that Faraday had come across really well, given his age and lack of media training. Prentice walked on a few more steps and as they turned at the end of the row of stables he suddenly realised he'd missed this interaction as an anchor; actually creating the content, rather than managing lightweight, staged conversations between so-called racing experts. A weight had been lifted. His blowout this morning had been coming for months, the pressure had been getting to him, he'd been trying too hard, desperate to impress, to protect his position at the top. When that gnarled old man had caught him outside the filming room this morning, he'd been too quick to believe, too desperate to take time to question him. The old man had told him what he wanted to hear.

Before the two men reached the transfer point to the racecourse Prentice took a sideway's step and tugged at his colleague's jacket, bringing him to a halt.

'Be honest, I think that was a decent interview. What did you think?' Prentice asked earnestly.

The cameraman was experienced, ten years older than Prentice. He inspected the presenter for a few seconds, weighing up how to present his response.

'I think that Summer chap has done you a massive favour,' the cameraman confided, 'You were going crazy on that sofa and it was starting to show. If you take my advice, you'll take the drop in salary and stick to your interviews with non-media people. That's what you're good at, and by the way, I can already hear them in the mixing truck talking about that Faraday chap. They're going to run the entire interview before the big race. Does that answer your question?'

Prentice nodded thoughtfully, 'You're right, Charlie Summer could have got me fired today. Instead, he's released me.'

The cameraman remained silent. Prentice was unaware he had become the butt of every joke within the production team during the last few months. There was even an office pool on when he would get fired. Yet the man was great with trainers, jockeys and members of the public. It was when he tried to foster discussions with his peers that he became unwatchable.

A few more seconds ticked by, both men in contemplation.

'Thanks again for that,' Prentice said suddenly, his cheeks flushing pink as he did. He vaguely remembered sharing conversations like this when he started as a presenter, but not so much, if at all recently, 'I know it sounds crazy, but I find talking to some people difficult sometimes.'

The cameraman gave Prentice a tight, but genuine smile, 'No problem. Come on then, if what Summer has told us is true, you'll have plenty more rich pickings.'

Prentice examined his colleague for a second, suddenly unsure of himself. This morning he'd been so obsessed with the anchor he wouldn't have even countenanced speaking with any cameraman, never mind this one. Instead, here he was, producing a self-deprecating smile back at him, and discovering it made him feel better about himself. To his horror, he realised he didn't even know the cameraman's name, and resolved to remedy this by the time they were back on the third floor of the grandstand.

Thirty-Four

With Sam's tour of the guests completed, he and Charlie had joined Stan, Suzie, Sharon and his father at what equated to the 'top' table. It was identical to every other dining table in the room, apart from being set five yards apart from the rest, to the far left of the room. Joss Faraday had popped in for fifteen minutes with his fiancé, before making it clear he needed to be with his horse. He'd left to do his final preparations with Cool Blue and to conduct an interview with Paul Prentice. The Mountain brothers were staking out the gelding in the stables and the only person missing was the one Charlie and his team would be pleased never to encounter today; Mick Kowalski.

With the racing underway, if felt the temperature in the room had risen and the anticipation for the Lincoln at three thirty-five was palpable. There was one race left to run, a quality mile race due off in a minute or two. The Lincoln would follow thirty-five minutes later. Charlie couldn't wait for the time to tick down. The closer they got to off time, the less likely Sam could demand the horse was declared a non-runner.

Everywhere you looked around the Lewis Room there were people chattering excitedly, nervous laughter sporadically punctuating the general hubbub. Watches and mobiles were checked far too often. Jackets, jumpers, and cardigans were being discarded as nervousness turned to sweat and blood pressure's rose. The tension was stemmed for some guests by the tapping of pens on race cards, scrutiny of anyone coming and going from the room, and of course, most importantly, movements on the top table. Legs jangled nervously under tables and hands were clasped and wiped clean of perspiration above. The room felt like electricity was coursing through the people, sparking from one to another. The pressure was tangible, and no one was immune from its effects, even the racecourse staff serving lunch were caught by the atmosphere in the room, drawn into the drama of whether Cool Blue could pull off the biggest ever bookmaker payout.

The televisions around the room currently showed the runners for the three o'clock entering the stalls down at the mile start, the split screen detailing horses, prices, and jockey's silks. The screen held the attention of most of the guests.

At the point where the runners jumped raggedly from the stalls and began settling into the race, Mick Kowalski strode purposefully into the room. He halted a few yards in, standing legs apart and hands on hips, like a comic book hero minus his cape billowing in a breeze. He surveyed the tables with disdain. Stan saw him first and brought Charlie's attention to

Mick's arrival. All of the top table twisted and stretched their necks to take in the bookmaker who stood to lose over forty million pounds if Cool Blue won his race in just over half an hour's time. The interest in Mick was also picked up by a few of the guests who started to examine the disheveled figure who resolutely glared at anyone strong enough to lock eyes with him. In the corner of the room Prentice nudged his cameraman, nodding in Mick's direction. The presenter grabbed his handheld microphone and set off toward the top of the room.

Charlie slipped his mobile phone out of his trouser pocket and from under the table he carefully sent a short text message before getting to his feet. He approached Mick with a broad smile clamped to his face and held out a hand in greeting. Mick saw Charlie coming. He gave him a nod of recognition and started to head towards him, but instead of taking the proffered hand, he sidestepped smartly past and stumped up to the top table. Mick slapped both his hands onto the tablecloth, leant forwards, and while leering gracelessly at Sam Lewis, announced in a loud, triumphant voice, 'I'm here Lewis. You ready to do the deal?'

The pale skin on Sam's cheekbones immediately flushed and he turned his nose up in disgust as the smell of fish and chip bile crashed over him like a wave. He did his best to glare over at Mick, as ever, missing his pitch slightly.

Sitting beside him, Suzie noticed the blind man roll Harvey's harness under the table, moving his fingers down to grip the release mechanism. A small roar came from the terraces outside the room as the race reached its closing stages. Mick sniggered, pulling a chair out from under the table and he sat down heavily, his legs wide apart. Hidden by the white tablecloth draped over the edge of the table, Harvey felt the movement of nervous fingers and stood, the hair on his back rising.

As soon as Mick had made his declaration, the last of the chattering died away in the room as a new, inquisitive mood descended on the guests. One by one, they peeled away from the drama of the race outside. A number of them stood to get a better view of what was happening on the top table. To Suzie's relief, Charlie slipped smoothly into the vacant chair beside Mick and tried to engage the bookmaker in conversation, allowing Sam to catch his breath.

During this lull in the excitement created by Mick's entrance, Stan took the opportunity to observe the faces around the table. He was struck by Reginald's body language. He was slumped forward, his elbow leaning on the table, while thumb and forefinger moved in a massaging motion across his forehead. If Stan wasn't mistaken, the old man seemed to be cringing with embarrassment.

'Thank you for joining us, Mr. Kowalski, I see you are alone,' Charlie started smartly, having to raise his voice over the sound of the commentator calling the last furlong of the race outside, 'Sam and I were

171

wondering how your colleague was coming along since taking ill?'

Mick hadn't taken his eyes off Sam and Reginald since he'd sat down, and continued to stare intently at the two of them across the table. His obstinacy was unnerving Reginald, whom Mick recognised from a fleeting introduction engineered by Laurie Lewis years ago. Given the disturbance the Lewis family had caused in his life over the last few days, he was going to enjoy this feeling of domination for as long as he could. He'd heard the question from the marketing man, deciding to ignore him, besides, he didn't know the answer. Frank Best could be dead for all he knew, he'd forgotten to find out.

Outside, the crowd noise increased to a roar as the mile race reached its conclusion, two of the fancied runners flashing past the winning post together. Inside the room, all was quiet.

'Yes, I understand the police wanted to speak with you both. For a day or two they got it into their heads that you had caused the injury to my number two,' said Mick, producing a wan smile which made Charlie narrow his eyes for a moment.

The excited background chatter created by Mick's arrival had disappeared and the top table now boasted an audience of about a hundred people. This was increasing as guests flowed back in from the private viewing area outside. Some had edged forward to surround the table, others were standing, straining their hearing and asking what had been said after each exchange. It was hardly surprising; a good sixty percent of the charities in the room held a BetMick betting slip and had a vested interest in what their bookmaker was discussing with the architect of their potential good fortune.

'Get a shot of this!' Suzie whispered to Stan in the seat beside her.

'No need!' he replied from the corner of his mouth, pointing a surreptitious finger over to where Prentice was speaking quietly into his handheld microphone while his cameraman recorded, the red light on the top of his camera blinking. Stan wondered whether this was going out live. It could be, there was undoubtedly more drama in here than there was on the racetrack at the moment.

Sharon leaned back in her chair. She wasn't a player in this game so it allowed her to take in each of the players at the table. It did seem like a game of poker. She'd played that game many times in a previous life and she could recognise the plays, the stances, and the bluffs. She took time to look, and process, and consider. She compared the major players once more: Sam, Mick, and Reginald. Then an idea popped into her head. Sharon placed a hand over her mouth to disguise a giggle.

Sam cleared his throat. 'I imagine…'

'I've no interest in what you imagine,' Mick cut in with a cocky, condescending tone. He pushed his chair back and in an even louder voice he continued, 'I'm interested in facts. For example, do your guests know

172

you have offered to pull Cool Blue out of the Lincoln in return for some privileged information I possess about your family?'

The public address system crackled into life and stated 'Here is the result of the photo for first place…' An incongruous roar of approval went up outside the room as the favourite was declared the winner of the three o'clock.

Sam's mouth fell open and Reginald groaned behind his hand. Sharon, Suzie, and Stan immediately looked to Charlie for a reaction. He remained rigid, seemingly unfazed by Mick's declaration. An initial ripple of gasps among the guests soon became a set of disgruntled conversations.

Mick was pleased. He sent a sneer around the table, adding 'Well, your charities don't need to worry because *I like a gamble.* I'm going to take you on. You can stick your offer Lewis, instead, we'll find out whether Cool Blue can win, or if I'm going to be lucky!'

Charlie couldn't help it; the faintest of smirks crept onto his lips. He quickly wiped it away, and clicking back into his professional host mode, he stood up to address the growing crowd.

'Ladies and gentlemen, I'm sure this news the Managing Director of BetMick, Mr. Mick Kowalski has just delivered may be a little confusing. However, I can confirm that Cool Blue is set to run in the Lincoln.'

As if to order, the public address system sprang into life once more, this time with an official sounding announcement. Charlie paused, hoping it was going to be what he expected. It would certainly help cool the audience if it was. One or two of the guests were showing definite signs of concern. He could do without his audience turning into a mob.

'We have news from the stewards concerning the next race, the Lincoln Handicap, due off at three thirty five,' stated the announcer, 'The trainer states that number twenty-two on your racecard, Cool Blue, is subject to a late jockey change and will now be ridden by Ben Plumber who will also claim a three pounds allowance.'

****

'Okay, let's get him to the parade ring,' Faraday told the Mountain brothers when they passed him on their next circuit of the pre-parade area. Luke nodded and instead of setting off on another round of the squashed oval walkway, he shared a quick word with his brother and they angled Cool Blue towards the parade ring path. With over twenty runners, they joined the middle of a long line of single file racehorses and handlers as they walked, snorted and jig-jogged their way out past the smaller grandstand at the bottom of the course.

Faraday checked his phone. No missed calls. That was a relief. He really didn't want to explain the jockey change to Sam Lewis. He'd not

173

really understood why Charlie had insisted he switch jockey bookings from Ben to Chris Hagar on Thursday, only to revert back to Ben at the last moment, but the ad man had been insistent. He consulted his phone; still no communications. Perhaps Sam had missed the announcement? As instructed by Charlie, he switched his phone off, casting thoughts of Sam Lewis away.

'What's it like having the weight of expectation on your shoulders then?'

Faraday found Vince Herring standing beside him. A long-standing fellow trainer based in Middleham, Vince was a constant source of good advice, which Faraday called upon on a regular basis. Vince was giving him a reassuringly comic smile.

'Oh, well, it's been… *different,*' he managed in reply.

'It's only a horse race,' Vince pointed out, 'A great inconsequence, as a man brighter than me once put it.'

'Tell that to this lot!' Faraday replied, waving a hand at the ten deep crowds circling the pre-parade ring, and he tried to force a smile, 'I've been hounded by well-wishers all day. I'm usually the face in the crowd, not the centre of attention. God help me if he doesn't run well.'

'They'll forgive you,' Herring replied lightly.

'Really? And how long do you think that will take?'

Herring chuckled, 'Oh ten, maybe twelve *years*. They have long memories in Yorkshire.'

Thirty-Five

Charlie, Suzie, Stan, and even Sharon had known the content of the announcement well before the horse's name was confirmed by the clipped, well-spoken voice over the public address system. Mick Kowalski was about to be cut down to size.

Stan and Suzie shared a look of relief before directing their gaze onto Mick. It took the bookmaker a few seconds to join the dots, but once he did, his reaction was truly memorable. His nose, still reddened by his washroom encounter, twitched and his face lost its glow, becoming a pallid, grey colour. He visibly crumpled.

It didn't take much for Charlie to convince Mick Kowalski and the Lewis's that retiring to their private box upstairs would be a sensible move, given the mood in the Lewis Room. Reginald appeared positively entranced by the suggestion. Sam's face was a mask of confusion.

On the way up in the lift Charlie watched Reginald closely. He wore a look of fierce concentration that Charlie imagined was the old man trying to consider the ramifications of the jockey change. Harvey was also sensing the atmosphere, giving a low-pitched whine when the seven of them entered the Lewis private suite.

Once inside the room, Mick, Sam, and Reginald all started talking at once. Stan stayed close to the door and Suzie and Sharon tried to fade into the background.

'Enough!' Charlie demanded after listening to half a minute of bickering. In a softer tone he continued, 'I'd like you to meet someone who will help explain why we made this last-minute switch of jockey,' and he beckoned to Stan, already with his hand on the doorknob. He opened the door to the private room and a short, slim, well-dressed man with a pinched face stepped inside.

'This is Chris Hagar,' Charlie told his audience, getting the impression from their reaction that they were mostly confused. However, at least they were being quiet. He cast his eyes down to his side, where Mick Kowalski was sitting. He was peering in open-mouthed horror past Charlie, at the jockey standing with a confident, almost challenging stance.

'Up until a few moments ago, Chris Hagar was due to ride Cool Blue.'

Charlie pointed to Mick, 'However, late this morning Mr. Kowalski attempted to ensure Cool Blue would not win, by paying Mr. Hagar ten thousand pounds to throw the race, as he assumed Chris would be riding the horse.'

'That's rubbish,' Mick blustered desperately. 'It's not true! It's a bare-faced lie!'

'As you would expect, we have evidence,' Charlie added, nodding to Hagar. Staring stony-faced at Mick, Chris Hagar stepped forward and dipping into his inside jacket pocket, one by one, he threw five envelopes onto the table. Charlie took one and ripped it open, tipping out the contents.

Mick's mind swam, grasping for options. As his cash fluttered dramatically onto the table and a gasp of incredulity issued from Reginald and Sam, he tried desperately to see a way through, seizing upon the only angle he thought would make sense.

'That's not proof,' he countered gruffly, 'I've never seen that money before, and I've never met this… this, jockey. He's a liar.'

'Are you sure, Mick?' asked Charlie, carefully moving around the table so that Stan, and more importantly, the camera he was holding could get a clear view of Mick's reaction, all the time maintaining his gaze on the bookmaker.

'This is Chris Hagar. He's a professional jockey. He was accused of taking back-handers two years ago. Does this jog your memory?'

Mick shook his head energetically, his ponytail whipping around at the back of his neck.

'At the time, there were lots of reports online, and in the newspapers, accusing him of throwing races, of cheating his owners, the public, and the horses themselves….'

Charlie paused, allowing this to register with his audience, still staring fixedly at Mick. 'However, it was all untrue. The trainer and the owner of the horses were found guilty and Chris was subsequently exonerated. The trouble is, mud sticks, and it's been difficult for Chris to re-start his riding career after the eighteen months the case took to be settled. So when I asked him to help us catch someone who wanted to stop Cool Blue from taking his chance in the Lincoln, he jumped at the opportunity,' Charlie gestured to the cameraman, 'It will hopefully help Chris get his riding career back on track.'

Charlie paused once more, glancing back to the table. Sharon had got to her feet and was sharing a quiet word with Suzie and Sam, her arms around their shoulders, her head bowed. Stan had produced a laptop from his bag and was grinning. He had anticipated Charlie's questioning look and nodded his readiness enthusiastically.

'We'd like to show you this photograph. It's one of many taken this morning at a restaurant just over the road from this racecourse,' Charlie said as he moved to position himself between Kowalski and the door.

Stan tapped his laptop and spun it round to face the room. Mick read the situation immediately. He recognised the décor of the fish and chip restaurant in the image, Chris Hagar's back and his own face. He was gleefully brandishing an envelope in the photo, just like the ones lying on the table.

'I've had enough of this!' he muttered angrily, throwing his arms in the air in exasperation. He stood and started toward the door.

'This is entrapment... you'll be hearing from my...'

Mick's threat remained unfinished, further words wrenched from his mouth by the sound of a vicious growl behind him. There was a scraping of chairs and a joint intake of breath as all seven people in the room, apart from Sam, obeyed a primal instinct to place as much space as possible between them and the animal hunting them.

Turning slowly, Mick found Sam Lewis standing five yards away, but it was the set of gnashing teeth and evil eyes in his companion that rendered Mick numb with terror. He told his legs to turn and run, but somehow his brain wasn't in sync with his muscles. He remained stationary, frozen to the spot. Sam's face was twitching uncontrollably, reddened with rage, a feeling he was managing to transmit to Harvey. The dog was pawing at the floor with his claws extended, saliva dripping from his bottom jaw and being propelled into the air when his growl became a piercing bark.

Mick had forgotten about the dog. It must have been by Sam's side all the time. He'd just not... registered. He was dimly aware of Charlie speaking sternly to Sam, but he didn't register the exact words. Holding out his hands, fingers wide, he managed a dry swallow and tried to speak.

Sam responded by holding up a palm to Charlie, who fell silent. Over the sounds of people moving away and the continued gnashing of Harvey's teeth, Mick started to speak.

'You were going to ruin my company...'

'I've heard enough,' Sam interrupted, issuing an almost inaudible Latin command to his dog and releasing his harness.

However Harvey remained standing beside his master, blissfully unaware Sam had commanded him to bring Mick Kowalski down.

'Deleo!' Sam cried again, his voice bouncing around the private room. Harvey looked up at him, cocked his ear, sat down, and started to scratch the back of his head with a rear paw in an agitated fashion. All of his aggression was gone, having vanished as quickly as it arrived.

Charlie stole a look at Suzie. She was standing a little apart from the others, staring down at her mobile phone for a second and then up at Harvey, intermittently tapping the screen of her device. The German Shepherd continued to ignore his master and now started to roll over on the floor, flailing his paws as if swimming through the air.

Sam was waiting for the sounds of canine attacking human, but instead he was treated to Mick shouting 'Ha!' followed by the crackle of his condescending laughter. Without his hand on Harvey's halter Sam felt his power ebb and a sense of loss and helplessness gripped him. Mick's laughter rang loud in his head as his foe's amusement grew. It occurred to Sam that today had been *his day*, his chance to bring Mick Kowalski down.

He centred his concentration on the laughter, which had now turned callous, homing in on the horrible nasal rasp which indicated the position of his target. Without thinking any further and without warning, he rocked back on his heels then rushed toward Mick, head down, covering the few yards between them by literally propelling himself blindly forward.

Mick didn't register what was happening before it was too late; a surge of silver beard, forehead, and hair cannoned into his jaw, married to the sound of teeth cracking together as heads collided.

Caught out by Sam's sudden movement, Charlie, Reginald, and Stan watched in horrified fascination as Sam Lewis ran headlong into Mick Kowalski, their heads bouncing sickeningly off each other. Mick's neck was forced backwards as Sam's head made contact, and the two of them tumbled to the floor in a single ungainly heap.

Sam's considerable bulk landed squarely on Mick's chest and with the element of surprise still on his side, and no worse for his head butt, his hands found Mick's neck. He started to squeeze. Mick felt nothing. Dazed, he was dimly aware of a weight on his chest, making it difficult to breathe, and his head sang as he faded in and out of coherent thought. He did nothing to fight back for those first few seconds, blissfully unaware of the threat lying upon his chest.

The sweet, nauseating smell of bile, combined with a pungent sweaty odour filled Sam's nose as he tried to exert pressure on Mick's neck. It felt fat and rubbery. He could feel the man's day-old whiskers biting into his fingers.

'Sam, get off him,' demanded a voice. It was his father.

The request didn't even register. Sam's mind was so full of hatred for the accursed wretch on the floor. This man had taken his brother from him and refused to tell of his hand in the death. This was a man who was prepared to cheat and lie; a man who through his chosen line of work, set out to ruin people with gambling addictions.

Words skimmed over Sam's brain: 'Even now, like this, you won't tell me how you killed my brother. You'll never get caught will you...' Sam paused momentarily, a sudden resigned quality to his thoughts. 'I'm better off putting you down...' he decided.

'Stop this lunacy, Sam!' bellowed a voice from behind him. Reginald was at Sam's shoulder, both hands gripping his son's shirt collar, a wild, torn expression on his face. Showing surprising strength, the old man wrenched his son off Mick. Sam landed on his backside and sat panting. A few yards away Mick was coming to his senses whilst battling with a hacking cough.

'No, father,' Sam screamed, his annoyance at the interruption to his act of revenge lifting his tone an octave, 'He's scum, he's worse than scum... he's...'

'He's your brother!' howled Reginald.

178

Thirty-Six

Sam glared at Mick, his jaw grinding as he considered his father's words, no longer needing restraint. Mick was on all fours, trying to bring a coughing fit under control. It was taking time to subside and he could hardly focus as fluids streamed from his eyes and nose.

Reginald circled Sam, placing himself between his two sons.

'Get up, Sam,' he hissed, 'Stop making a scene!'

Charlie was standing a few yards away. Close enough to see the derision in Reginald's eyes as he tackled Sam. He winced as Reginald started to shake his head and sigh, fearful Sam would see red once more and renew his attack.

'He's your half brother! You will get up and act like a man!' Reginald insisted. It was such a patronising tone, it made Charlie, now consumed by the drama, groan inwardly.

'My brother,' Sam repeated in a ghostly voice, 'Mick Kowalski is my brother…' He muttered a command toward Harvey and gave him a little hand gesture.

Harvey looked up, his tongue lolling out. An expression of joy hung on the dog's face, or what Charlie believed approximated to canine joy. The German Shepherd pushed himself up to his feet and padded over to Sam's side, dutifully plonking himself down beside his master.

The room collectively exhaled. The TV screens around them showed pictures of jockeys for the Lincoln mounting their horses and a commentary burbled over the top.

Reginald glanced at one of the screens, his face hardening.

'Sam, we have to stop your horse from racing,' he demanded, 'If it wins, you will ruin your brother's business.'

Charlie had heard enough. He stepped into Reginald's line of sight, using an arm and shoulder to push him back a few feet. He turned to Sam, 'You can't do it, Sam. You have to let Cool Blue run.'

Sam shrugged expressively. He looked bewildered. Charlie found himself feeling sympathy for the man, which didn't help. He shot a pained look to where he expected to find Sharon and Suzie, only to find their seats vacant. He continued to search before realising they were already at his back.

'Leave him for a moment,' Sharon insisted, 'Let me speak with him.'

'He's not religious, girl. You're not going to help,' Reginald snorted in derision.

Sharon gave Reginald a withering stare which made him swallow back the follow-up comment he had been readying. Even Charlie took an involuntary step away, relinquishing his leading role to allow her to take control.

'He needs to make sense of your bombshell,' Sharon stated in a tone which dared Reginald or Charlie to question her, 'And so does he!' she added, pointing to an equally bewildered looking Mick, who was now up on his feet, being closely monitored by Stan. Any question of whether Mick had missed Reginald's declaration could be dismissed; he was inspecting Reginald as if he were a specimen in a jar.

'The three of you need to talk,' Sharon continued with authority.

She saw Charlie make as if to say something and gave him a warning stare. He stepped back from the small group and mimed a zipping motion across his mouth.

'This is bollocks,' Reginald snarled angrily, 'We have to stop that horse racing, otherwise…'

'Show some compassion for your sons, Mr. Lewis,' Sharon cut in exasperated, her arms tightly crossed over her bosom. She glared up at the agitated old man, completely dominating him, 'Sam can speak with his trainer on his phone if he decides on that course of action.'

With that, Sharon manhandled the three befuddled men and Harvey toward the corner of the room. She sat them down in a triangle of chairs and returned.

'Is Cool Blue okay to run? They have to be running out of time?' Stan asked Charlie in a whisper.

'It's ten minutes until the off-time and the horses are being led out of the parade ring,' Charlie answered, pointing a finger up to the television monitor closest to him, 'Once they are going to the start the only thing which will stop Cool Blue racing is if he is injured or he won't go into the starting stalls. I don't think there's time for Cool Blue to be removed from the race now.'

'Those micro *Bluetooth* earphones Suzie managed to plant on Harvey earlier today worked perfectly!' Stan murmered, 'The music stopped him in his tracks, he couldn't hear Sam's commands.'

Charlie turned to Sharon and she beamed up at him. 'Mission accomplished?' she asked, slightly frustrated by the fact he still wore a worried look.

'I didn't consider their phones,' Charlie replied, turning and surreptitiously indicating the three men, 'I thought I'd considered everything, but there are people they could contact. My worry is that Sam or his father decides to phone the Stewards direct. Sam could be swayed by them. I told Joss Faraday to turn his phone off after the announcement so he couldn't be reached, but…'

'I wouldn't worry.'

Charlie caught the impish grin on Sharon's face and some of his worry was released. 'Why?' he inquired, fearing he wasn't in full grasp of the situation.

'Because unless they can run down four flights of stairs, fight their way through the crowd on the grandstand concourse, find the weighing room and then the stewards, all in under four minutes, there's no way they can stop Cool Blue racing.'

As she spoke, Sharon dug deep into the pockets of her smock. She produced three mobile phones.

'I did tell you I found God after being involved in some pretty naughty stuff, didn't I?'

She said this, brandishing the phones like a hand of cards, holding them up to her chest, her lips curled in mock embarrassment. 'Well, I thought if they couldn't communicate, how can they make Cool Blue a non-runner?'

Charlie's astonishment gave way to an admiring grin. In response Sharon produced a relieved smile.

'But when… how?' Charlie said, bemused. Sharon's grin broadened in response to Charlie's brows rising.

'Picking pockets was the first thing my father taught me.'

****

Luke Mountain was finding it hard to remove the grin from his face. He'd ridden at Doncaster only a few weeks before at their final jumps meeting of the winter season to a crowd of no more than a couple of thousand. It had been a quiet midweek meeting. He'd ridden in three races and won on his last mount, coming back into the winners enclosure to nothing more than a few handshakes and a polite smattering of applause. Such was the scale of Doncaster, a small crowd, no matter how feisty, made the place look and feel desolate.

Today the Town Moor was… he searched for the right word, eventually settling for 'buzzing'. The carnival atmosphere swirling around the track was intoxicating and Luke received confirmation he'd chosen his descriptive noun well when he glanced over to his brother on the other side of the gelding. They were both leading up, Peter closest to the rails was giving left-handed high fives to dozens of outstretched palms as he made his way around the parade ring, his right hand firmly gripping the gelding's lead rein. Cool Blue was taking all the attention in his stride, Faraday's view of his gelding's character being confirmed as soon as the horse set foot in the parade ring. Cool Blue was puffing out his chest, pushing off his feet as he walked, and lifting his head to eyeball the crowds.

Peter caught his brother's glance and grinned back, 'This is crazy,' Luke laughed, 'But bloody brilliant!'

As if to remind the brothers of their pre-race roles, Cool Blue chose that moment to throw his head back and roll his shoulders, transferring his weight to his hind legs. His front feet left the spongy surface of the walkway for a moment and the brother's walk came to an abrupt halt. The gelding shook himself, returned his head to its previously high, imperious position and he settled once more, before walking on again as if nothing had happened.

'I think he agrees,' Peter shouted over the gelding's head.

Faraday, Chelsea, and a group of about a dozen charity guests who had been granted permission to enter the ring, watched the gelding stride on again. The parade ring was an oasis of normality, the one place where the jostling for a position to view the horses, or the race, wasn't an issue.

'No need to worry,' Faraday assured the group as Cool Blue swaggered onward, 'That's just the way he is; he likes to make sure you know who's in charge.'

The group's attention was soon directed to the top of the ring as a peel of applause and numerous shouts of encouragement went up. One by one, jockeys started to emerge, some of them appearing to be propelled into the ring after having to fight their way through the forest of well-wishers. The calls of encouragement increased in number, becoming a rumble as Ben Plumber appeared, his arms raised and a huge smile on his face. Faraday winced inside as Ben turned back to the crowd and shook his clenched fists at head height, shouting, 'Come on!'

This elicited a delighted roar of approval from the large knot of his supporters.

'Looks like we've got more than one prima donna on our hands today,' Faraday told the small group of charities drily.

'Now then, boss!' Ben said in greeting, his face still in the grip of a broad smile, 'This place is jumping!'

Faraday had to agree. He'd never seen a racetrack as busy, or as highly charged. Royal Ascot may be the pinnacle of achievement to which every flat trainer aspires, but he doubted it could match the raw emotions which were on show here today. Everyone associated with Cool Blue were the centre of attention. He'd drilled the riding instructions into Ben the night before, but for the benefit of the attendant charities he would do so again. Before he started, Faraday took a breath and a moment to take in the scene around him.

There were people making use of every conceivable vantage point. The hundred-year-old stands beyond the furlong pole were stacked full, the lawns in front of the track, usually a place for kids to play football or littered with family picnic rugs, had racegoers crammed in so tight there wasn't a single patch of grass visible. On the rails adjacent to the track, racegoers were already ten or twelve deep in places, and around the parade ring there was a pulsing sea of people, almost every face sporting a wide-eyed sense of anticipation. Every now and again their nervous tension broke into group conversations or laughter, which rippled through the crowds. Race fans lucky enough to be on the parade ring rails were being forced to hang over them due to the press of people behind them and looking up into the two major stands, there wasn't a space to be had, standing or sitting.

The centre of the racecourse, once full of working class spectators unable to afford the Tattersalls or Silver rings on race days in the fifties and sixties, now catered for companies and sponsors. The corporate tented village had been invaded by the same people who used to stand on its uncovered steps sixty years ago. The Great British public, tempted by the spectacle of bookmakers getting a good thrashing for a worthy cause, had entered the public space in the middle of the track in their thousands. Unhappy with the lack of a good view of the action down at the two furlong pole, someone had flattened the flimsy fence which protected the white tented village, and now a thousand members of the public had joined the businessmen and women at the finishing post. The inside of the racetrack now resembled an infestation of bees, all buzzing around the edges of the track, and specifically attracted to the finishing line.

Faraday started to rattle off the riding instructions and before he had completed them the 'Jockeys please mount,' announcement came over the public address system.

Thirty-Seven

Saturday 3-30pm

'Forget it, it's too late,' Reginald barked angrily at Sam, 'I can't find my phone and we'll never make it to the parade ring or the stewards room, there's too many people out there. It's a bloody farce!'

Reginald Lewis's sons peered at their father who was leant on the glass windows, one hand holding his back, staring out over the racecourse from their fourth floor box. The last few minutes had consisted of a monologue from the old man detailing his affair with Mick's mother. He'd cut it short to demand Cool Blue should not run in the family's interests.

'I want him to race,' Sam stated quietly from an armchair.

'Well I'm with your… *my* father,' Mick chipped in. He was sitting on a table, his feet on the seat of a chair. He jumped down and continued, 'I stand to lose a lot of cash thanks to you. And you can't be bothered to stop him running,' he told Sam angrily.

Sam didn't reply, unmoving in his chair.

'Mind you, win or lose, I'm made now,' Mick cackled.

Reginald had been pacing the room. Now he spun around and eyed Mick with a mixture of anger and disdain.

'And why would that be?'

'You know why,' Mick replied haughtily. He rubbed the angry red marks on his neck and then slid his hand up to a golf ball sized lump which was throbbing just under his hairline.

'Quite apart from the fact I have grounds to take Sammy boy here to court for assault, I've just joined a family worth over a billion,' he said smugly, 'Whatever happens to Cool Blue, I'll be fighting for my slice of that gigantic pie. It will be like I've lost a penny and found a pound, regardless of whether that bloody horse wins.'

'Why, you little…'

'Shut up father!' Sam barked at his father, 'I've had about as much of you as I can stomach. You disgust me.'

Reginald turned to face the room, his half lidded eyes bulging, taken aback by his son's challenging tone. Phlegm crackled in the back of his throat as he started to shape a response, only to be beaten to it.

'All I want to know…' Sam's voice caught and he swallowed, '…All I've *ever* wanted to know, is what happened to Laurie.'

He tipped his face upwards, as if addressing the entire room. 'I don't know why you didn't press charges against me all those times I confronted you. I don't know why you've kept lying to me. But now your future is assured… *brother*, why not tell me what really happened the night Laurie died… Did you kill your own brother?'

Mick was stunned into silence. He inspected his half brother and opened his mouth to answer, but was distracted by a television screen in the corner of the room which burst into life to inform its audience that there were only a handful of horses left to load into the stalls for the Lincoln.

'Well, hang onto your seats everyone, take a deep breath and don't leave your television screens,' Stephen Jones cooed excitedly from the television monitor as another horse was loaded, 'Will Cool Blue complete the biggest multiple racing bet of all time and win the charities he's running for over *seventy million pounds*? Everyone here on Channel Fifteen certainly hopes so, and it looks like the racing public does too, as he's now been backed down to be the four-to-one favourite.'

There was a cut back to the studio in the stands where Stephen, plus two other pundits were sitting on the edge of their sofa like excited schoolboys, captivated by the monitors behind the camera.

'We've heard some wonderful stories from the charities enjoying Sam Lewis's hospitality on the third floor of the grandstand this afternoon, and we're going over to get a final word from Paul Prentice before the off.'

Prentice appeared in the middle of a group of charity guests in the private, open-air viewing area. Around a hundred people surrounded him and all of them were on their feet.

'In all my years of covering horse racing, I've never witnessed tension quite like this, Stephen,' Prentice began, 'I'm among the seventy charities waiting for the race to get underway and the anticipation is becoming unbearable. If you're nervous watching this at home, imagine what it's like for the people around me: they each have around seven hundred thousand pounds of funding for their charities at stake! But everywhere I've gone around this racecourse the story has been the same. Everyone wants Cool Blue to win.'

This received a little roar from the twenty or so guests nearest to him. As it died down, the camera on Prentice began to close in on the presenter as he spoke his last few words.

'I admit, I was sceptical about this whole situation, and very vocal in my condemnation of what I believed to be a sham; a cleverly orchestrated corporate coup. I now know I was wrong. This is far, far more than a coup, and believe me, there is a greater story to tell about the background to this race. But that's a story for later. Right now, I want Cool Blue to win this race. To win for Sam Lewis. To win for his charities. But most of all, to win for the sport of horse racing.'

The director allowed the camera to linger on Prentice. It stayed on him a few more seconds, longer than the presenter could realistically have expected. For many days later this footage would be pored over by millions on the internet, trying to decide for themselves whether the awestruck look on Prentice's face, followed by his crumbling descent into tears of raw emotion was brought on by the moment, or incredibly well

185

crafted fakery.

The next cut was back to the anchor and a close up of Stephen's head and shoulders. He appeared slightly shocked for a moment before gathering himself, gazing into the camera, and steeling himself.

'Wherever you are, whatever you're doing, keep your eyes on your television screen for the next ninety seconds as you could witness horse racing history being created. Sam Lewis may become a philanthropic legend... or the hopes of millions of people could be dashed. It's time to go over to our race commentator for the Lincoln Handicap...'

Sam got up from the armchair where he'd listened to his father speak of his infidelity to his mother and grasping Harvey's harness he shuffled disconcertedly over to the window. He felt old, and even more alone than when he'd lost Laurie. He stared blankly up the track to where he imagined the start of the straight mile lay. All he could make out was a blurry crescent of green, coloured by a tiny fragment of white.

'Please, someone. Take me outside,' he asked in a quiet, quavering voice, 'I want to listen to the people in the stands.'

Suzie crossed the room and took the blind man's arm. Once outside, she took in the view and couldn't help but gasp at the huge numbers of people who were swarming around the racetrack. The strip of bright green turf bordered by shiny white rails which bisected the sea of people seemed to glow in the weak spring sunshine. She was joined by Stan, Sharon, and Charlie who together leaned out over their small, private area of the grandstand and enjoyed the experience of being above, looking down on the packed enclosures. Suzie inspected Sam more closely and thought he looked washed out. Within a few seconds she found herself describing the scene to the blind man, the other members of the group listening as they took in the vista.

'One hell of a turnout,' remarked Charlie once Suzie had fallen silent. He glanced down and recognized a large group of the guest charities on the floor below, all of whom were on their feet, the flip-up seats rendered redundant. Standing allowed more guests to squeeze onto the open-air terraces and share in the atmosphere.

Sharon placed a hand on Suzie and Stan's shoulders. 'Your work over the last week has brought them all here.'

Charlie considered, 'Yeah, whatever happens now, you guys should be proud. You're going to go places after this.' He checked his watch and then one of the large TV screens and was relieved to see the last two of the twenty-two runners being loaded into the stalls. The tinny clang of starting stalls pinging open came from the televisions hung around the inside of the room.

'And they're off!' exclaimed the announcer, 'They are off and running in the Lincoln handicap...'

Thirty-Eight

Ben Plumber was used to handling his nerves. This was his second season as an apprentice jockey and any anxiety was now confined to the big races, or when he was riding for prestigious owners. Now he was milling around at the start and he'd had a chance to think; always a negative. He'd been interviewed by the media as Cool Blue had walked down the chute and every single shout or call from the public side of the track had been wishing him good luck; hundreds of them. He'd not heard one shout for any of the other horses. This was a ride of a lifetime, and he'd been lucky to keep it, being a three pounds claimer and relatively inexperienced. Mr. Faraday had been good to him. What if he was to let him down? What if he dropped his whip, or clipped heels, or heaven forbid, fell off? He'd never live it down.

A stalls handler jogged up to him with a lead rein. He was a small, pudgy faced ex-jockey who glanced up at the twenty-year-old lad in the saddle while he was checking the gelding's girths.

'This is Cool Blue ain't it?'

'Yeah, that's right.'

'Ha! You must be bricking it m'laddo,' the handler observed.

'No, I'm fine,' Ben lied. The handler locked eyes with him for a couple of seconds before looking back to the horse's midriff, smiling to himself.

'Don't worry what your instructions are. This is a cavalry charge. Just make sure you get some open ground in front of you over a furlong and a half out so you can give him a chance to get a good run to the line, and you'll be fine.'

'You've ridden in the Lincoln?' Ben asked.

'Four times. Was second once, but the first time is the one I remember. I was bricking it… best of luck lad.'

The handler moved on and Ben realised half the field had been loaded up during the two-minute exchange. Two minutes where he'd forgotten to worry.

Ben kept Cool Blue moving, keen for the four-year-old not to boil over. The gelding was sweating slightly under the saddle, but that was normal. He'd done that before every race as a two and three-year-old. Drawn in stall twenty, he was loaded into his berth fairly late on the stands side. Cool Blue slid into his stall without the need for any shoving. The same couldn't be said for the last two, who needed blindfolds and man-handling. The gelding was forced to stand and wait for two minutes, during which time Ben stood up on the frame of the stalls to take the weight off the horse's back. Finally, the starter called, 'One to go,' raised his flag and shouted, 'Jockeys!'

The front of the stalls opened and Cool Blue jumped smartly out with Ben digging his toes into his irons and gripping the reins firmly.

The straight mile at Doncaster provided a level, fair surface with very little in the way of undulations. Cool Blue got a clean start and, with only two horses on his outside, Ben enjoyed open turf in front of him for a few seconds. He looked between the horse's ears and the green strip narrowed into the distance, the finishing line denoted by two closely positioned blobs of red on the horizon.

Ben sensed Cool Blue was travelling a little too exuberantly and after the first half furlong, angled him left to get greater cover. The entire field had congregated around three leading horses by the seven marker, with Ben towards the rear. He wasn't concerned. The gelding had settled into a steady gallop, churning through the good to soft ground with mechanical precision.

In the parade ring, Joss Faraday, Chelsea, and a dozen of Sam Lewis's charity guests watched the race unfold on the huge television screen in the centre of the course. There was no way any of the owners and trainers could leave the parade ring, as fighting their way through the crowds to watch in the grandstand was an impossibility. Faraday watched the yellow cap bob up and down at the rear of the field as the TV provided an almost head-on angle. Aware the media were likely to be tracking his own reactions, he remained as stoic as he could, blocking out as much as possible, concentrating on the image on the screen.

On his fourth floor balcony, Sam Lewis gripped the rail and listened intently, eyes closed, his face tilted toward the sky. Suzie, Sharon, and Stan were alongside him. Charlie was on the end of the line, trying to concentrate on what was happening out on the track as the field reached the six furlong pole, but instead found his thoughts absorbed by the Lewis family revelations. Discovering Mick Kowalski was Reginald's son had almost turned today's plans on their head, although on reflection it had only been Sam who greeted the news with negativity. There was certainly more to the Lewis family once you scratched away at that rough, fragmented surface.

An unexpected tiredness descended onto Charlie. After all, his job was done, he'd completed the client's requirement, and Cool Blue was racing for the charities. He couldn't influence the race result. However, he soon regained his motivation when he considered the treatment of the charities, their payout, and what would happened if Cool Blue won… that was still all to play for and very much in his hands.

Inside the private room, Mick was standing with his hands in his pockets, keeping a doleful eye on the race. From time to time he glanced over to Reginald, secretly assessing his face, noting the blunt end to his nose and for the first time, recognising other similarities to his own features, even down to the old man's stance. He'd been sure the man he'd called father as a boy hadn't been his real father; his mother had told him as much before she died of pneumonia when he was twelve. He'd never *felt* Polish, but failed to share this with his father. Mick also found his thoughts drifting to Laurie. Laurie, the man who had entered his life, picked up his failing little bookmaking business and turned it into a profitable enterprise. Had Laurie known? Did that explain Laurie's actions that night…?

Reginald Lewis stared pensively at the television monitor and scowled when Cool Blue's name was mentioned again on the commentary. He watched for his son's racing colours, picking out the yellow and blue, kicking himself for allowing Sam to indulge his love for this pointless, frivolous sport. To his horror, this pastime which parted weak minded people from their money had become the conduit for his bastard child to be unmasked, and now it could ruin his son's company and more importantly, the family name; his legacy. He'd been following Mick's progress of course, supported his mother enough to keep his secret quiet, and made sure his lowlife surrogate father had made enough to bring his boy up when she died. Yes, he'd done his bit.

Reginald scratched his jaw with manicured fingernails, baring a bottom row of dull grey teeth. He recalled the day Laurie had pitched up at the house with Mick, declaring Kowalski to be his new business partner. He'd stared at the young man and seen his own cold blue eyes staring back, and as for that nose… Reginald winced. What were the odds that Laurie would fall in with Mick Kowalski, a relationship that would ultimately lead to his death. He'd lost a wife and son to that river. They'd dragged the Tyne for weeks afterwards; searching for his son's body so he could lay him to rest, but to no avail.

Reginald recalled with bitterness the effort he'd put in to try and distance his remaining son from Kowalski, but Sam couldn't let go. He'd hoped to stop Sam from meeting Kowalski today, but he wouldn't listen. Getting that odious TV reporter to expose Summer on that breakfast show could have nipped things in the bud if the ad man wasn't so slippery. Sam had selected his coup accomplice well, not that he'd ever admit it.

The Lincoln runners became a smudged mess on the TV as Reginald considered how he'd reached this state of affairs. He'd been drawn into Sam's feud with Kowalski, making it impossible to untangle his illegitimate son from his life. Now the little bastard was after a slice of his estate and his business. It occurred to Reginald that he needed a son to carry his legacy forward, and once again he had two to choose from. The thought of Kowalski running his company sent an involuntary shudder through him which made him shake. He determined it wouldn't be Kowalski. Alone in his thoughts, Reginald sighed angrily at his own misfortune and also at the TV screen; Cool Blue had moved up into mid-division.

With the ground riding 'Good to Soft', Faraday had given his jockey one overriding instruction: ride Bluey to come home. There was bound to be a blistering pace, so sit behind, cover him up, and then push the button over three out. You should be able to pick them off one by one. Ben watched the four furlong pole drift past him, the trainer's words regarding the three pole at the forefront of his mind. Cool Blue was still travelling strongly, relentlessly carrying him forward. Ben could sense the untapped reserves which still lay in the muscle, tendons and bones beneath him. In front, the familiar sight of weighing room colleagues shifting from a poised crouch into rhythmic pushing broke out at the head of the pack and the field started to splinter and spread across the track. Bluey is loving this ground, thought Ben, allowing the joy of experiencing a quality horse pointing his toe, and powering through rain-softened turf, to fill him for a few seconds.

Ben was shaken from his reverie when he felt a surge in the gelding; a gap suddenly opened up in front of them and Cool Blue went to make the most of the opportunity. Too soon, his rider communicated through his reins, and the gelding allowed Ben to angle him behind a group of three runners racing abreast, conserving energy for another few strides. That surge forward had taken them into midfield, closer to the pace, and Ben watched as a grey to his right started to labour, his rider's efforts altering from energetic push to frenetic rowing. Cool Blue eyeballed his competitor as the grey horse slid past, maintaining his gallop, regular breaths undisturbed.

On their left, through the forest of pumping fists and whip cracks, a shape moved forward. Ben picked this up, only because the horse's rider, a vision in shocking pink, was motionless, guiding his mount through beaten horses. He glanced to his right and saw nothing but flailing arms and horses under pressure. His decision was made quickly, even so, the three furlong pole had already flashed past.

Despite being on the stands side of the course, Ben switched Cool Blue left, losing precious momentum to find a path through horses under pressure. The course commentator boomed Cool Blue's name, communicating the view that he'd been caught on heels and was now on the move toward the inside rail. Fifty thousand people reacted with a mixture of disappointment and eroded hope. A chorus of concern rang from the stands and was matched from the inside of the course.

Charlie, standing on his toes, and leaning heavily against the balcony railing groaned in unison with everyone around him. The television pictures showed the gelding moving sideways toward the inside of the track, navigating around weakening animals while three others, already lengths ahead, had struck out, already making their bid for glory. A warm hand unexpectedly squirrelled its way around his arm and looking around, he found Sharon beaming up at him.

'He can do it, can't he?' she demanded excitedly, her eyes

190

switching to peer down the track.

Charlie gave her a brief smile, 'He has lots of ground to make up.'

'Come on, Bluey,' insisted Sharon, desperately squeezing Charlie's arm, and jiggling on her toes like an excited schoolgirl.

The two furlong pole was a blur as Ben collected Cool Blue together after switching him, and instructed the gelding he could now lengthen. The four-year-old joyfully extended, immediately consigning half a dozen of his competitors to a lower finishing position. Ben gasped as the raw energy left in the gelding was converted to ground gained.

'Go, Bluey!' Ben screamed and Cool Blue responded by bursting through the scrum of horses into third position over a furlong out, persuaded to do so by nothing more than a rider content to keep his charge balanced. Ben didn't reach for his whip; he could feel the horse stretching. Reminders were surplus to requirement and could be detrimental now. Balance and momentum would be his saviour.

The renewed hope as Cool Blue rushed into contention connected with the crowd, drowning out the commentary as a deafening burst of released tension fizzed into the air. Half a mile away, Doncaster city centre reverberated to the sound of the race-day crowd, as Cool Blue attempted to reel in the two horses three lengths ahead of him.

With ears flat to his head, Ben urging forward, Cool Blue broke his breathing pattern. Ben felt him suck in a huge gulp of air at a hundred and fifty yards out and the four-year-old held his breath. The gelding's head pushed lower, his stride grabbed an extra few inches of grass and his competitors loomed large. To his right the challenger in second shortened his stride and Ben became aware of that dark shape leaving his vision. Now he concentrated on the sickly pink and white britches pumping up and down in front, to his left. Still straining, Cool Blue pushed on again, drawing his head up to the flanks of his final rival. Ben maintained the synergy, at one with his horse, dimly aware of the circular red finishing post no more than a few strides ahead. The sound of a whip cracking onto the backside of his rival felt close. Then suddenly he was alongside him. Ben, barely aware of where he was in relation to the finishing line, felt his outstretched hands push nothing but air for a moment during that last unnerving microsecond, where Cool Blue's nose strained to cut the beam of the finishing line camera.

The gelding took a breath; a necessary refuelling of his lungs with wonderful, life preserving air. Two strides after the finishing post, Cool Blue faltered, his back legs wobbled, and he collapsed.

Thirty-Nine

As David Hayton and Harrison Saddington exited the grandstand lift on the fourth floor, the screams of encouragement around the racecourse rushed at them. The sound grew as he and his colleague paced the corridor, searching for the private box door emblazoned with the Sam Lewis name. The excited shouts reached a crescendo, and cheering rang out for a short time, cut short by a jarring howl of horror.

Standing still outside the door to the Lewis box, the two men each readied themselves. David tilted his head from side to side, careful to ensure his Fedora stayed firmly in place. Harrison took a breath, grasped David's hand and squeezed it softly. Pursing his lips and with a slight narrowing of his eyes in concentration beneath his dark glasses, David quietly pushed the door open and entered. Walking confidently into Sam Lewis's box, he found Reginald Lewis sitting in an armchair, watching the immediate aftermath of the Lincoln on a flat screen wall-mounted monitor. Mick Kowalski stood close by. Both had their backs to him and were engrossed with the images on the screen.

David Hayton scanned the room and spotted five people standing outside on the balcony. All of them were leaning out, facing the bottom of the racecourse, straining to see something, their faces taut.

Ignoring the loud, hyperbolic voice on the television, David and Harrison shared a confirming glance and converged on the bald dome of the old man's head. Its pink skin dappled with liver spots and wisps of hair protruded a few inches above the back of the armchair. David halted at the seat back and looked down onto Reginald's head and shoulders, flexing his fingers.

'Hello again, Reg!' he exclaimed, as his hands closed firmly around Reginald's scrawny neck and started to squeeze.

Forty

Ben Plumber inspected a blurred green mound surrounded by blackness. Rolling his head, he shook mud from his face and helmet and caught a glimpse of a blue sky and wispy clouds. Something trembled beside him, something warm. He was aware of shouting and the thud of hooves some way off in the distance, but knew better than to immediately try to move. Instead, he waggled his fingers and his toes. That was good, they all responded. Tempted to try more, he pushed himself up on his elbows, easing himself into a sitting position, legs straight out.

An echoing voice shouted, 'Photograph, photograph.'

People were running toward him, and he heard a snort close by. He looked to his boots, blinked a few times, and realised a thick brown leg with a hoof for a foot was lying across his legs, along with some leather reins. He swivelled his head and swallowed hard as he took in the wall of horseflesh which lay alongside him.

Ben Plumber got shakily to his feet, reins in his hand. He was covered in mud and grass stains right down his right hand side, the slide across the Doncaster track making his britches stick to him. Cool Blue was lying prone, flat out on the grass, his chest heaving. Suddenly, the situation coalesced in Ben's mind and he bent down onto one knee to place both hands onto the horse's neck in an attempt to keep the horse on the ground where he was less likely to injure himself further.

Cool Blue opened one eye. The whites rolled around then settled to look at Ben, then snapped shut. The horse snorted and Ben released some of the pressure he was applying to the gelding's neck. Cool Blue responded immediately. His eyes focused and he rolled onto his chest, collected one front leg, then the other under him, got to his feet, and shook himself. His mud-encrusted tack had been wrenched around and the saddle was hanging off the gelding's flank. Cool Blue looked sheepishly at Ben, breathing deeply and regularly. Transferring the rein to his left hand, Ben stepped forward and gave the gelding a pat and stroked his neck a few times.

It was only then that Ben became aware of the crowd. A cheer rose from all sides of the racecourse, so loud it shook the grandstand. Hats, newspapers, and racecards were thrown. Plastic beer glasses joined the airborne tribute, and a few seconds later a round of applause started on the inside of the course, and went on as Ben led Cool Blue across the racetrack. The grandstand picked up on the clapping, joining in the appreciation as the lone horse and rider walked in front of the stands on their way back to the parade ring which doubled as the unsaddling area.

Now that horse and jockey were up and walking unaided, the television screens around the racecourse that had been holding off showing the closing stages of the race for fear of serious injury, now burst into replay mode. Head-on, side-on and long shots from drones slowly rolled through the last stride of the Lincoln, and Cool Blue's final thrust for the finishing line, his head stuck out long, and low. Then a stutter two strides later, horse and jockey hitting the ground together and sliding fifteen yards across the track, followed by the rest of the field doing their best to avoid the stricken partnership.

Ben spotted the Mountain brothers running down the chute towards him, Joss Faraday in behind, trying to keep up. Luke reached him first and after shouting a few compliments, and making sure Ben was okay after his tumble, busied himself with the gelding's tack. As Faraday drew closer Ben realised the young trainer had tears rolling down his cheeks. The trainer grabbed hold of him, and once satisfied his rider was in command of all his faculties, Faraday turned his attention to Cool Blue, inspecting him from every angle.

'Did we get up and win on the line?' Ben asked wearily.

'No idea!' Faraday responded, relieved his inspection of Cool Blue had yielded no major issues, 'Great ride by the way, you were right to switch him onto the pace. Christ, the way he dived at the line… this horse wanted to win and knew where the finish was.'

Cool Blue continued down the chute, now awash with the other returning runners. Ben and Faraday waved at the crowd, trying to avoid the television cameras and ambulance men, arriving all too late on the scene. The horse held his head high. Still no result was announced.

As they approached the parade ring, Luke Mountain rearranged his grip on Cool Blue's saddle and tack. He hefted the saddle up and down again, concern starting to build in him. He called to Peter and the brothers shared a short few earnest words, the result of which saw Peter take a few bouncing steps before springing over the running rail in one lithe motion. He hared off down the track toward the finishing line.

'What's that about?' Faraday asked, watching Peter run off.

'Probably nothing,' Luke shrugged, 'Just checking something.'

They had almost reached the entrance to the parade ring when the public address system crackled back into life and as one, fifty thousand people were hushed into silence. Ben and Faraday shared a hopeful look.

'Here is the result of the photograph for first place,' stated the announcer, before pausing to take a breath.

'First, number twenty-two…'

The roar from the crowds drowned out the rest of the announcement. As soon as the first 't' of twenty came bouncing down from the stands, Doncaster racecourse erupted. Rendered mute and unable to continue, the announcer started again ten seconds later.

'First, Number twenty-two, Cool Blue…'

A second burst of appreciation was sent up by the Yorkshire crowd. '…the winning distance a nose, and three lengths.'

Forty-One

'Oh stop complaining Reg, you know you deserve this,' David Hayton told Reginald calmly. Mick whipped around, suddenly aware there were another two people in the room, and found Harrison Saddington blocking his path to the old man. He considered trying to push past, but the man looked younger, fitter, and seriously steadfast. Mick quickly decided he didn't really care. Besides, when he looked into the man's face he sensed he recognised him, despite the dark glasses and cap.

Reginald gurgled an unintelligible reply as he pawed and scratched desperately at the steel-like fingers around his throat. Squirming in the well-worn seat of the armchair, his bony backside sliding on the shiny leather, he was unable to escape the grip of his attacker. David Hayton squeezed a little more, ignoring the pain and blood from the lesions created by Reginald's clamouring fingernails biting into his skin. He smiled down at the old man, as if giving him a soothing massage.

'Did you ever wonder how it felt when you did this to me?' he asked smoothly.

Reginald didn't reply. His vision was swimming and spiralling. He tried to speak but all he could manage was a garbled whine. Through his fingers David felt the old man's crazed scrabbling weaken and his neck muscles sag.

'That's enough,' Harrison told his colleague.

'Oh dear, losing some of our fight are we?' David commented conversationally, releasing his grip on Reginald. The old man coughed violently and pitched forward, belly flopping onto the carpet. He slowly raised himself to his hands and knees. He stayed there, sucking life back into himself, coughing hoarsely and clutching his throat, his thin bony legs bent and splayed.

'You look like an insect,' David commented, a hint of amusement in his voice.

'What do you want? My wallet, take it...' Reginald rasped between shallow breaths. He pushed himself up onto one elbow and drew his legs in, fearful of more violence. David circled him.

'Your first thought is for money,' he scoffed, 'Not *who I am*?'

Reginald's forehead furrowed and he peered up from the floor at the man now taking a seat in the armchair opposite him. He narrowed his eyes, trying to measure the man and determine whether he knew him, whether he could place him. A disgruntled work colleague perhaps? Or a business associate with a grudge? His face was masked by glasses and a hat, however the man's jaw line was vaguely familiar...

A metallic squeak of a hinge on the balcony door caught the attention of the four people in the room. David acknowledged the entrance of Sam and Charlie's colleagues with a smile. They quietly fanned out into

195

the room. David turned back to Reginald, deciding it was the right time. He raised his right hand and removed his large tinted glasses, revealing a set of soft, azure eyes with full lashes.

'Hello again, Reg,' he said, his voice suddenly rising a full octave from the husky tone he'd adopted previously. Finally, he removed his Fedora, pulling out a barely visible hatpin which had been holding up his hair inside.

Sarah Lewis placed her hat on the arm of her chair, shook her shoulder length hair, and allowed it to fall across her face. She brushed it aside with practised fingers, leant forward, and the fifty-nine year old woman grinned at her cowering husband.

'Remember me?' she asked in a light northeastern accent.

The fear fell away from Reginald's face to be replaced with a contemptuous sneer. Sarah watched the reaction with interest, examining the eighty-year-old with the sort of dispassion a scientist might have for his laboratory rat.

'You scheming bitch...' Reginald started, 'How dare you...'

'Shut up, Reg, I'm not interested. You're going to listen to me.'

Reginald got shakily to his knees, then to his feet and rubbed his neck thoughtfully. 'The day I do that...' he lurched toward her, a hand intent on a blow raised above his head, but didn't get any further than his second step. Using the arms of the chair Sarah pulled herself to her feet, her forward momentum allowing her to thrust out a clawed fist into her husband's chest. Reginald reeled backwards. His back slapped against the partition wall and once again his backside met the carpet. He sat like a rag doll, arms and legs temporarily useless, mouth open, tongue lolling as he fought the burning sensation in his chest. Sarah, standing hands on hips, inhaled through her nose and blew a satisfied sigh out through her mouth.

'I've no time for your bullying and threats,' she told him, 'I've moved on. I've learned how to deal with men like you. In fact, you prepared me well. I'm helping other women to deal with their misogynist, manipulative, and psychotic partners. Of course you were the master, Reg, but you took it to another level by topping off your control of me with a broad streak of evil.'

'Who the hell are you?' Mick asked Sarah. She ignored him and returned her attention to her husband, who despite his age still had some fight in him and was trying to clamber to his feet.

Reginald blinked a few times, found the use of his limbs, and tentatively pushed up against the wall to achieve a standing position.

'She's my wife,' he muttered slowly and spitefully, his chest heaving with the exertion of standing. Reginald locked eyes with Sarah.

'If your life is so wonderful, why are you here?' he hissed.

She smiled brightly, 'It was Sam. He sent me a letter, quite by accident of course, telling me to place a bet for my charity. I run a number of women's refuges, helping subjugated women to rid themselves of men like you. Seeing you again made me realise, I couldn't leave him with you any longer. We're here to rescue Sam.'

Reginald produced a sneering cackle, which soon developed into a contemptuous laugh.

'You seriously think Samuel will leave all this?' he jeered, throwing a hand wildly around in an arc, 'And Mick is like me, he'll not give up a fortune for you! You always were stupid, Sarah, but now you are deluded.'

'I'm not interested in your illegitimate son,' Sarah countered with a derisive snort. 'I'm here for *my boys.*'

Reginald stared at his wife in bewilderment, trying to make sense of her. She was so different... Sarah watched the old man intently, revelling in his inability to grasp the situation.

Mick switched his attention to stare into Harrison Saddington's face once more. The man was still ensuring no one interfered with Sarah Lewis's conversation with Reginald. He received a grin back in return. It was the grin that did it.

'Laurie?' he said, half querying his own assertion.

Laurie Lewis removed his glasses and cap and turned to look at Sam, who stood uncomprehendingly only a few yards away.

'You haven't got it yet, have you, Reg?' Sarah said grimly, 'I am still your wife... come back from the dead... and I want a divorce.'

Now Reginald got it. He understood. This bitch was about to tear the family apart and take his business with her. Sarah watched as realisation stretched across the old man's face and hatred built in his eyes.

'There you go, Reg! You've got it now. So it's time to set the wheels in motion... I have a son here I haven't hugged for far too long.'

Sarah turned toward Sam, whose features were contorted in bewilderment. Her own face softened as soon as she laid eyes on him.

Reginald was lost for words. Anger filled him quickly; it had been his servant throughout his life, and it would serve him once more. He scanned the room. As soon as Sarah's back was turned, Reginald pulled a half drunk bottle of champagne out of its cooler bucket and closed the short distance between them, lifting the bottle into the air.

'I'll sort you...'

The moment before he brought the heavy, green Moet club down onto the back of Sarah's head, a malicious thin grin slipped onto his lips.

As if Charlie, Stan, and Suzie's horrified faces weren't enough, Sarah had caught Reginald's movements in the reflection in the glass wall. She whipped around, ready to defend herself, only to find it wasn't necessary. A clear shout of 'Custodio' had rung in the air and Reginald's evil grin became a surprised grimace as an airborne canine landed on his chest with a snarl, sending him sprawling. The champagne bottle slipped

197

from his grasp and sprayed its foaming contents over the floor. Harvey had his front two paws on Reginald's chest and was growling with teeth bared, close to the man's face.

'Good boy,' Sam praised, before adding, 'Harvey's back!'

His mother gave Sam a hug and Laurie joined them.

Forty-Two

Ben Plumber and Cool Blue re-entered the parade ring together at a leisurely walk, Ben with his hands aloft. Faraday had been joined by Chelsea to lead the gelding in and Luke Mountain followed, carrying the saddle and tack. A thin tunnel of applauding people was created to allow them to cross the parade ring and lead the gelding into the winner's enclosure. Ben realised there were jockeys, trainers, and owners of the other Lincoln runners among the cheering throng. Television cameras, excited charity guests, and a variety of racing and national press reporters soon descended onto the winning connections amid the sound of cheers. Outside the Lewis Room on the private terraces, it was bedlam, with the guests hugging, bouncing, and whooping with delight, calling their congratulations down to the winner's enclosure below with little hope of their messages ever reaching the intended recipients.

Luke offered up a bucket of water to the four-year-old, which Cool Blue buried his head in and thirstily slurped, to the delight of the knot of people around the winning horse. Faraday and Ben were interviewed, with Ben particularly of interest, being asked for his reaction to the last-stride winning lunge by Cool Blue and his subsequent dramatic slide across the turf.

A racecourse representative hovering on the edge of the growing group of well-wishers, consulted his watch and moved in to have a quiet word with Ben regarding the need to weigh in. He nodded and looked around for his saddle. Locating it, he scooped the saddle up and with more congratulations ringing in his ears, started to make his way across to the parade ring exit.

Peter Mountain was immediately at his side, out of breath and speaking in bursts. Ben stopped and Peter continued, before placing a hand on his shoulder. Ben smiled uncertainly back at his fellow jockey, turned, and started toward the weighing room once more. As he left the parade ring and climbed the half dozen steps onto the walkway he stopped, clutching his saddle across his chest with his right hand, holding his forehead with the other. His legs buckled and the Lincoln's winning jockey fell forward in a dead faint.

Peter was the first to the jockey's side and for the next five minutes chaos reigned around them. Within six minutes Ben was on his way to Doncaster Royal Infirmary in the back of an ambulance.

Forty-Three

Paul Prentice was straight to his feet with his cameraman in tow once Charlie appeared at the entrance to the Lewis Room. Charlie was met by a barrage of delighted guests who broke into spontaneous applause. Sharon, Suzie, and Stan followed him in. Charlie made a short speech of thanks and told them he would try to visit each guest table before the close of racing.

'I've been asked to get your feedback on one more topic,' Prentice pressed, once the rest of the room backed off Charlie for a few moments, 'Can we get what we need?'

Charlie caught an unexpectedly anxious look from Suzie. 'It has to be quick,' he insisted.

Prentice nodded at his cameraman and closed in to stand beside Charlie, his microphone in hand, and spoke directly into the camera.

'I'm here at the post race party for the charities who have benefitted from what people are now calling the Cool Blue Coup. I have to say, there's a great atmosphere here and as you would expect there are some very happy people around. We'll speak with some of them later, but just now I have the architect of the coup, Mr. Charlie Summer with me.'

Prentice switched position and Charlie could sense the camera closing in on him. 'First of all, congratulations, Mr. Summer', Prentice started, but retained the microphone, uninterested in gaining a response, 'The whole country has been fascinated by your coup but the big question now is: will the bookmakers pay out your big win?'

The microphone was directed toward Charlie and Prentice stared expectantly. Charlie pursed his lips and rubbed his chin thoughtfully.

'Firstly, it isn't my win. Each charity placed their bet independently and they will be the ones to benefit from their bet. But in answer to your primary question I can tell you that you and your viewers should stay glued to your screens over the next few days. I can reveal that out of the seventy-six million pounds the charities have won today, almost forty million of it is due to be paid out by one bookmaker; BetMick. I can tell you that I expect him, and the rest of the bookmakers to pay out.'

Prentice gave a crooked smile and shaking his head, stated, 'You certainly have all the answers Mr. Summer.'

'What's up now?' Charlie asked as soon as he rejoined his colleagues. His query was met with glum expressions.

'You need to speak with Peter Mountain,' Suzie told him anxiously, He's been trying your mobile.' Her voice seemed to be breaking and Charlie couldn't be sure whether it was due to shouting Cool Blue home at the top of her lungs, or something was desperately wrong.

Ten minutes later, after a call to Peter, apologies to the charity guests and a mad dash down the grandstand and back to the car park, Charlie jumped into the drivers' seat of his car. He bashed the postcode for the Doncaster Royal Infirmary into his satnav, waited impatiently for Suzie, Sharon, and Stan to buckle up, and gunned the engine.

'Did Peter say Ben was okay?' asked Suzie.

'He was busy with a doctor, he just told me to get down to the Infirmary. He said he'd go through everything when we got there.'

Suzie made a soft grumbling noise which Charlie correctly guessed was irritation.

'That fall was horrible,' Stan chipped in, 'Bluey must have skidded ten or fifteen yards when they went down. And Ben went down hard in the parade ring by all accounts… delayed shock I heard someone say.'

A thoughtful, pensive silence descended as the occupants of the car considered this information.

'The Lewis's sure are a broken family,' Sharon stated reflectively after the car had barrelled around the first few corners.

'You have to hand it to them, those disguises were pretty good though, especially David… er, Sarah Lewis's,' Stan offered, trying to keep the conversation going. However, it withered into silence.

'We're here,' Charlie announced a minute later, turning the car into the Park Hill Hospital entrance. He swore under his breath and said 'Hold on!' before pulling a u-turn and heading back out.

'Wrong entrance,' he explained, 'We need to be further down for Accident and Emergency.'

Sharon pushed back into her seat again, consumed in her own thoughts. There had been many things about Reginald that had chilled her that afternoon, but none more so than when Sam had explained how he lost his sight. She shuddered as she replayed Sam's terrible story in her head.

It was after Reginald had stormed out of the private room following the reunion of the Lewis family. Mick Kowalski had set off after his newly discovered father, not before shouting a torrent of abuse back at Sam. Stan had set off in pursuit of the two men to ensure they didn't cause a scene with the charities on the floor below.

Clearly emotional, Sam's beatific expression on finding his mother and brother alive had suddenly darkened once the two men had departed. He had become tearful and had started to tremble.

'I'm tired of the lies,' he had told Laurie and Sarah as they comforted him. He'd seemed oblivious to the fact that Charlie, herself, and Suzie were still present.

'Only my father and I know the truth…' Sam had stated flatly once the room door had been flung shut by Mick and the sound of his ranting had subsided, '…which is, my father blinded me. I'd like to think it was unintentional, but as time passes…'

Finding strength, Sam had paused, thought for a moment, and

grimaced, ahead of telling his family the truth.

'You remember the junior scientific set I got for my eighth birthday…'

'We know, Laurie had said softly, you don't need to relive it, we know it blew up in your face and blinded you.'

Sam had shaken his head. 'No, it didn't. That was just a cover, a lie my father forced me to keep.'

He continued 'I was disappointed with the lack of chemical reactions, I guess I wanted to create an explosion, so I took my test tubes and beakers into my bathroom. I raided the cleaning cabinet, and started to mix things up. You can imagine the mess and smell. I mixed all manner of fluids and sprays together and spilled them all over the bathroom floor and furniture. My father found me amid all my mess, and lost his temper. His punishment was to hold my head down the toilet before he flushed it. Unfortunately, one of the many fluids I'd poured into the toilet bowl was a bottle of drain cleaner. It immediately reacted with my eyes and face, blinding me. My father threatened me never to tell a soul, warning me he'd be sent to prison if I did. He was my father and I was only eight…'

Sharon stared out of the window at the shiny lines of parked cars and modular hospital buildings whizzing past, but didn't really see them. She was replaying Sarah's reaction in her mind, wincing as she recalled the horror of the mother learning of her son's abuse at the hands of his father. Not that Sarah's life had been any different; she'd endured years of similar treatment from the same man. It was the pervading sense of guilt Sharon had recognised swimming in Sarah's eyes which had been heartbreaking. As the stories continued to be told, the magnitude of Reginald's abuse had flooded her senses and rendered her mute. She could only look on in stupefied awe as Sarah, Sam and Laurie came together.

Sharon was shaken from her thoughts by Stan in the backseat.

'So why did Sarah Lewis marry a man like that?' he asked.

'Sarah told me she'd met 'Reg' when she was only twenty and been swept off her feet by him, a successful, powerful forty-year-old man,' Sharon answered. It comforted her somewhat that Stan was also trying to come to terms with what they had learned that afternoon.

'I suppose the fact Reginald was a billionaire may have added to his attraction!' Charlie said, attempting to maintain a straight face.

'Indeed,' Suzie agreed ruefully, 'Once they were married, Sam was born, then Laurie straight after. Reginald lost interest soon after and started to treat her terribly. She stuck around until the boys were old enough to make their own decisions, but needed Laurie to help her start a new life.'

Charlie broke in, 'It turns out the only person to witness her early morning dive off the Tyne Bridge fifteen years ago was her twenty-year-old son, Laurie.'

202

'It must have taken a huge effort for Laurie to lie to everyone in order to help his mother get away from Reginald,' Sharon said, 'She told me she'd tried twice to leave him, but Reginald found her and forced her back, threatening further violence if she left him again. It was as if she was his property.'

Suzie was nodding in agreement, 'Anyway, Laurie's account of his mother's death was finally enough to stop Reginald from trying to find her. But you can't help being impressed with how Sarah fought back! She changed her name and went on to rediscover her identity.'

'It took ten years, and she received a lot of help from charities along the way. However she became stronger, more self-assured. She trained in self-defence and rebuilt a life for herself,' Suzie added.

Stan looked a little puzzled, 'So how did she afford to live?'

'Laurie had been salting money away from his trust fund and business interests and kept Sarah solvent,' Suzie replied, 'His money helped her to start Sarah's first woman's refuge in Gateshead. Her charity has a dozen locations all over the North now. Quite by chance, she received Sam's letter. It was the catalyst for her to decision to confront Reginald, and the day of the race was perfect for that...'

'Oh!' Charlie blurted suddenly, slapping the driving wheel and in doing so making the other three jump in their seats.

'Sorry,' he added, 'I... remembered something... Anyway, we're here. We'll find a parking space and go look for Ben.'

'So Laurie's death was a setup too?' Stan prompted.

'Not quite, it was a spur of the moment thing apparently,' Sharon replied, 'After his mother died, Laurie quickly rose through the ranks of the Lewis family bakery business. He came across some of his father's accounts and discovered he was gambling regularly and losing large amounts to a bookmaker in Newcastle.'

'Mick Kowalski?'

'Well, originally it was Mick Kowalski's father. When he died, Mick took over the family bookmaking shop. Laurie knew Reginald didn't gamble; he was losing on purpose. He must have made sure he never backed a winner, it was just a way of supporting his secret son. Laurie followed the paper trail, visited the bookies and when he saw Mick and his physical similarity to his father, he worked out the link.'

'All the Lewis men seem to share that weird flat end to their noses,' Charlie added as he maneuvered the car around the packed hospital car park.

Sharon picked up the story once more, 'Laurie was a bit vague about his reasons; I guess he wanted to get to know his half brother. So he ended up putting money in Mick's business, renaming it BetMick and building a hugely successful and profitable betting and casino website at a time when online gambling was starting to explode. Eighteen months in, the two of them had a big fall out and one night Laurie told Mick he was going to sell his share of the BetMick business.'

'Personally, I got the impression Laurie decided Mick was just as bad as Reginald, and wanted to get away from him,' Sharon said thoughtfully, 'Apparently Mick would goad his punters into betting more and more when he took them to the races and Laurie eventually found the whole business distasteful.'

'When did you lot get all this extra information?' Stan challenged.

Sharon looked over at Charlie as if to prompt his input.

He sighed, checked his rear view mirrors, 'Laurie was pretty talkative while Sam and his mother were getting acquainted again. He explained quite a bit while you were busy following Reginald and Mick out of the racetrack.'

'But the juiciest bit about his own escape is still to come,' said Suzie, her eyebrows raised.

'Well you're going to have to walk and talk then,' Charlie told her, engaging the handbrake and switching the engine off, 'We need to find out what's wrong with our jockey, our trainer and the lead up men.'

Stan threw a few pound coins into a parking meter and the four of them jogged into the accident and emergency unit. A large, mostly glass box turned out to be the reception and Charlie clanged a hand bell on the counter. A small, chunky, middle-aged lady appeared behind the steel reinforced glass and peered at them over the top of a pair of reading glasses perched on the end of her nose.

'We're looking for Ben Plumber, he's a jockey and was brought here about an hour ago?'

'Are you all family?' she asked in a broad Doncaster accent.

'Err, well, no.'

Sharon bustled Charlie to one side with an arm and a pleasant smile before beaming at the lady. 'This is Ben's brother and his girlfriend,' she said sweetly, indicating Suzie and Stan, standing behind her, 'They really are worried, you know, hyper-ventilating in the car on the way here,' she explained, fanning herself with a palm and sucking air over her teeth as she spoke. 'It would be helpful if they could get to see him. I'm their parish vicar. Could you possibly help?'

The woman eyed the two youngsters doubtfully, returning to Sharon to take in her clerical collar and give her an appraising stare. After a couple of seconds she sighed and then tapped on a keyboard.

'He's already gone through triage. You'll need to go to Ward A on the Lincoln wing. Back out of here and round to the left.'

'How apt,' Sharon commented as the four of them toured around the hospital perimeter, 'Ben wins the Lincoln and gets to spend the afternoon in a ward named after the race.'

The Lincoln Ward had its own reception, but this time their search for Ben was unceremoniously halted. He'd gone for tests and a starchy member of admin staff told them in no uncertain terms they'd have to wait until Mr. Plumber was back on the ward.

'No arguments, there's the waiting area,' a stern middle-aged nurse instructed, daring any of them to counter her proposal.

To Charlie's relief the waiting area was virtually empty. He had worried the press might have beaten them to the hospital and he really wasn't in the mood for more interviews. They chose a set of two bench seats facing each other.

'Come on, then,' urged Stan, 'What happened that night when Laurie drove Mick's car into the Tyne?'

'Laurie wasn't driving, Mick was,' Sharon revealed, 'Mick was taking Laurie back out to the Lewis family house in Ponteland. Apparently it's one of those big, modern mansions. They'd been arguing most of the evening and into the night, and it continued in the car. Mick started to get really angry, as Laurie insisted he was going to force a sale of BetMick. Laurie hadn't lost his two million pounds trust fund betting with Mick, he'd been *investing* in BetMick and building it into a large, profitable company, until their relationship went sour. Anyway, they were so caught up in their spat, Mick wasn't concentrating and when he looked up there was something in the road, Mick swerved to miss it, and the car ended up bursting through the iron posts on the bank and went over the edge, becoming half-submerged in the river. The car got caught on the riverbank railings and hung headfirst from a rear wheel and its back axle.'

Sharon took a breath and continued, 'We've only got Laurie's word on this, but he told me Mick got out and reached the safety of the bank, then started to kick the back of the car,' Sharon said, her eyes growing large. 'He made Laurie promise not to sell the company, or he'd send him into the river with the car!'

'Jesus!' exclaimed Stan, 'That's a murder threat isn't it?'

'I guess so, but get this!' said Sharon excitedly, 'Laurie agrees and gets onto the riverbank with some help from Mick. They both sit in the dark, getting their breath back when Laurie gives Mick a new alternative to him selling his part of the bookmaking business. Laurie tells Mick he wants to start a new life and won't sell his share of BetMick as long as Mick doesn't reveal their secret! Together, the two of them heave the crashed car into the water and it gets taken by the current. Laurie tells Mick to get his story sorted so it looks like Laurie went into the river and died alone, and Laurie heads off to start a new life with his mother and most importantly, without the contaminating influence of Reginald or Mick ...'

Sharon threw her head back and took in a lungful of peculiar tasting hospital antiseptic air, as if relating the story had exhausted her.

'So Sam Lewis was never going to get his answers from Mick, because otherwise he would lose his business,' Suzie surmised.

'Bang on,' Charlie confirmed, 'It also explains why no matter what Sam did to him, Mick wouldn't take any direct action, or bring any charges against him, for fear of Laurie popping up with a 'For Sale' sign for BetMick.

'It also came out that Sarah had an altercation with Mick in a restaurant restroom earlier on the day of the race, reminding him not to say anything about Laurie's involvement!'

'Oh…is that why he stank of…' Suzie trailed off, searching for the right combination of words.

'Fish and chip sick?' Charlie offered.

Stan was shaking his head slowly downward from side to side. 'It's a bloody mess,' he said quietly when his eyes reached the floor. He looked up at the other three, 'I can't believe I'm saying this, but the Lewis's make my own home life look positively boring!'

'And they've got plenty more fun to look forward to,' Charlie added, 'Sarah is going to divorce Reginald and try to take half his fortune, which is fair enough I think, given what she went through. Mick was threatening to sue for a share of the Lewis money and Sam was warning him if he did, he'd make sure Mick's attempt to fix a race and defraud the charities of millions in winnings would be made public.'

'I don't think Sam will have a say in it,' Charlie pointed out, 'Mick will be getting a knock on his door from the racing authorities pretty soon, whatever happens with his newly found family. As a jockey, Chris Hagar is bound by the conditions of his riding licence to report anyone attempting to compromise him.'

'What about Reginald?' asked Suzie.

Charlie gave a gruff laugh, 'Tell them, Stan.'

'I tracked Reginald and Mick down to the bottom of the grandstand. They had an argument on the basement concourse and Reginald walked off into the crowds. Mick was trying to catch up with him, but both of them kept getting recognised by race-goers. Every few feet they got stopped. People were telling Mick to pay out to the charities. He got swamped!'

'He deserved it,' Suzie said with feeling, 'I feel a bit sorry for Sam. He seems to have come off worst out of all of this. He's been lied to by virtually every member of his family, including the brother he was grieving for. Now I know how badly his father treated him, I can see why Sam might think having a big dog around is a good idea.'

As the others contemplated this, a set of double doors pushed apart close to the reception desk and a tall young woman wearing a white knee-length consultant's gown walked confidently through. She had long brown hair whipped up in a bun and a perfectly symmetrical face that was topped off by intelligent brown eyes looking through small, round glasses.

Sharon noted with a shade of disappointment how Charlie's eyes grew round and his irises expanded as he took in full impact of the doctor.

'Are you the friends of Benjamin Plumber?' she asked, removing her glasses, pushing a stray strand of hair to the side of her face, and blinking slowly.

Sharon caught Suzie's eye and the two of them shared a silent understanding. Sharon bit back the urge to query under her breath how many times the doctor had practiced that move in the mirror at home.

'Yes, that's us,' Charlie answered, standing to greet the doctor, 'How is Ben?'

'Come and see for yourself,' she said, smiling in Charlie's direction and ignoring the rest of the group.

Forty-Four

Sharon, Charlie, Suzie, and Stan trooped into a shared ward where curtains gave scant privacy to its bedridden inhabitants. Ben, still wearing his shiny blue and yellow silks and riding breeches was sitting up on the bed with Faraday and Luke sitting either side of him, legs straight out, apparently enjoying a rest. All three of them grinned goofily at the new arrivals.

'Why do I get the impression you're absolutely fine,' commented Charlie as he and his colleagues surrounded the bed.

'Right as rain,' whispered Ben conspiratorially.

'What the hell is that doing here?' Charlie queried, nodding at a mud encrusted saddle and tack which had been dumped on a bedside table.

'Luke wouldn't let it out of his sight,' Faraday explained with a comical shrug and the other two laughed. Sharon surmised these three had been doing quite a bit of laughing.

'A racecourse attendant came up and offered to carry it for me after I went down and Luke told him there was no way it was leaving his arm because it was now the most valuable saddle in Britain!' Ben explained.

This prompted another torrent of guffaws from the three of them, leaving Charlie scratching his head.

'So why did I need to get down here so fast?'

Faraday got up from the bed, adding a little whimper for effect, 'We thought we'd need you to help buy us some time, but thank goodness, we won't need it anymore.'

Charlie stuck his tongue into his cheek in exasperation and gave the trainer a hard, quizzical stare.

Chastised, Faraday held up a hand, 'Right, right. I'll fill you in. Once Ben had got up and Cool Blue was on his feet, Luke took the saddle off and carried it back to the parade ring. But the weight cloth was light.'

'He's talking about the cloth that holds the extra weight in lead the horse has to carry,' Charlie explained to the other three.

'It didn't feel right,' Luke said, taking up the story, 'When I checked, the press studs were undone. They must have popped open when the horse slid across the track. He only had seven pounds in each side, as he was bottom weight in the race, but one of the lead weights had fallen out.'

Charlie's face broke into a grin as he realised what Luke and Ben had cooked up on the spur of the moment, but he allowed Luke to continue.

'So Peter runs off to try and find the lost weight, as we can't send Ben to weigh-in without it or the Clerk of the Scales will disqualify him for

208

weighing in light. Can you imagine?... So time's ticking on and there's no Peter. The parade ring attendant gets a message telling him he's got to get Ben to the weighing room.'

Luke's eyes were sparkling now, and Charlie guessed he'd already run through the story more than once.

'There's only one way a jockey can win a race and not weigh out afterwards, and that's if they are injured.'

Luke fell silent, his eyes dancing between the newcomers standing around the bed, eager for them to reach the only possible conclusion.

'You pretended to drop unconscious in the winners enclosure with your saddle in order to be brought here?' Sharon asked Ben in a bewildered tone, 'Isn't that cheating though. You must have carried the wrong weight?'

'No!' countered three voices at once, making Sharon jump.

'The weight must have come out of the cloth after the winning line. But racecourse officials, being officious types, aren't going to go looking for lost weight, they'd just disqualify the horse...'

'However *there are* people who will scan the whole of the racecourse until they find it!' a voice behind them called out cheekily.

'Peter!' Faraday exclaimed, beaming at the young man. Suzie, Sharon, and Stan did a double take as Luke's identical twin brother joined the group and tossed a rounded off square of lead onto the bed.

'Found the little sod,' Peter stated triumphantly. He placed his hands on his hips, and grinned before dramatically wiping a dirty hand across his temple, as if he was a hero returning from battle. 'It must have fallen out when I was carrying the saddle, as it was about forty yards away from where Ben fell off. Took me a blummin' age to find it.'

'Quick thinking, Luke,' Charlie commended, 'Nice acting Ben, I can't wait to see a replay. And good foraging skills, Peter. I'll give you a call the next time my mobile phone goes missing. Talking of mobile phones...' Charlie fixed a questioning gaze onto Sharon.

'They mysteriously reappeared on the table up in Sam's private box during their rants at each other,' she reported.

'Ah, excellent, then I only have Suzie and her doggy earphones to thank for ensuring Harvey didn't maul anyone apart from Reginald, Stan for drawing my attention to Hayton and Saddington, and of course Mr. Faraday here for pulling off a cracking training performance!'

He nodded to each of them in turn before adding in a low, commanding voice, 'Against *all* the odds, Cool Blue won!'

Forty-Five

'Do you think they will just pay us out, without any complaints?' the anxious woman beside him asked quietly, 'It's just that it will mean so much to my charity. We're ever so small you know...'

Aware there were at least ten press reporters and two television cameras surrounding them, most of whom would have heard her question, Charlie placed a comforting arm around the middle-aged lady.

'Please don't worry, Helen, this bunch of media people being here should help ensure your bookmaker has no other option.'

He indicated the gaggle of reporters standing around them on the pavement of a busy Leeds city centre street. It was Thursday morning, five days after the race, and his third day of helping charities to get their payouts. He'd spent so much time with these press people he'd got to know many of them on first name terms during the last three days. The scene had become familiar to Charlie and his team. They were outside a betting shop, ready to demand payment because the bookie had refused the charity earlier in the week. This particular bookmaker was an important one, as it belonged to one of the powerful high street bookmakers. The bookmaker had laid thirteen of the winning Lucky Fifteen bets and they were refusing payment to every charity.

Charlie looked down at his mobile to check the time. It was ten fifty-five. They had warned the bookmaker that Charlie, Helen Gant, and the media would arrive here to demand payment at eleven o'clock. When he looked around Charlie was pleased to note that the numbers of people waiting outside the betting shop to support Helen had swollen considerably in the last few minutes. Several people had come up to congratulate the two of them already, and it looked like they now had about a hundred people milling around outside the shop.

'Shame them into paying,' Charlie thought. It wasn't the first time this week he had reminded himself of the phrase he'd written on that flipchart back in Inkberrow only eleven days earlier.

With his team taking a rest on Sunday, the job of supporting the charities had started again first thing on Monday morning. With tens of millions of pounds due to be paid out to the charities, the almost inevitable refusals to pay had started as soon as the betting shops opened on Monday. Bookmakers had a long history of stalling big wins, and in some cases, refusing to pay completely. A number of famous coups had ended up in court and eventually resulted in some grudging bookie payouts, but there were just as many cases where the bookmakers had simply refused to pay and crushed the punter into submission with spiralling court costs.

This was day four of Charlie, Suzie, and Stan's payout tour. Each of them had travelled the country supporting those charities that needed help in cashing in their winning betting slips. When Stan had correlated the final numbers, one hundred and fifteen bets had been placed by charities, plus the three they had struck in the BetMick on-course betting shop at Market Rasen, making one-hundred and eighteen bets. With each bet totalling winnings of just under seven hundred and sixty-eight thousand pounds, the total takeout of bookmakers coffers was set to be almost ninety million pounds. But only if every bookmaker paid.

On the whole, the bookmakers had seen the advertising potential of a goodwill payout and with those who had committed to pay out before the Lincoln, a total of fifty-four bookmakers had produced cheques for the charities concerned on Monday or Tuesday. To Charlie's delight, the media had been full of stories of local charitable organisations, both big and small, enjoying the benefit of the 'Cool Blue Coup'. In fact, the response to the winning bets had received such wide coverage, Charlie's own team had been able to dedicate their time to personally assist those winning betting slip holders who had encountered negative responses from their local bookie.

Some of the non-paying bookmakers had only required a phone call from Charlie or Stan to point out where the money would be going, and how their stance could produce bad publicity and potentially ruin their business. For those bookmakers with harder hearts and even tougher skins, Charlie had already visited fourteen betting shops in the last few days, along with the charities concerned, in order to cajole, and in a few cases, read the riot act to shocked betting shop managers, Area Managers, Regional Managers, and in some cases, Chief Operating Officers and Managing Directors.

It had helped enormously that Charlie was now able to conjure up a dozen reporters with a simple text message request. The story was still front-page news and continued to be discussed on all the social media channels, in Britain and abroad. The press had become his entourage, delighting in being called out to betting shops to report how some bookies, including several of the bigger chains, were trying to wriggle out of paying out to well-deserving charities that had joined in Sam Lewis's huge slice of good luck. There were now only seventeen winning betting slips which hadn't been paid, although this excluded the forty-two bets that had been struck with BetMick.

Charlie was reminded that the latest battle in the war with BetMick was due to be fought later that day. However, ahead of that encounter he had this large bookmaking chain to confront on behalf of Helen Gant and her small team of volunteers. If this bookmaker would pay, a further twelve charities would also get their money.

'My daughter, Catherine, died of sepsis,' Helen was telling one of the reporters. She went on to describe in greater detail how she set up her charity in her daughter's memory and how it had grown from handing out leaflets about the condition, to raising awareness in local schools and local government, to now, where she was involved with supplying hospitals, doctors surgeries and many other public places with materials to help aid early identification of the condition.

'It's just so terribly expensive,' Helen continued, 'As well as our information service, we organise professional bereavement counselling for families all over the country. The money from Mr. Lewis's bet could keep that service going for the next six or seven years. It would be a godsend.'

Helen had returned to this betting shop on Monday morning, only to be told that her winnings were being withheld. It had been a similar story with the other twelve holders of winning betting slips with this company. Their head office had refused to put Charlie through to anyone in authority, so he and Suzie took to social media and via the company's Facebook and Twitter feeds, informed them he, Helen, and a few friends, would be arriving at their shop in Leeds at eleven o'clock on Thursday morning to discuss the matter.

As the crowd grew larger, hands started to appear through the crowd requesting to be shaken. Shouts of, 'Good on you, Summer,' and 'About time the bookies got a good whipping!' increased in number as it got closer to eleven o'clock. With his arm still around Helen, the two of them pushed the glass door open and entered the betting shop at exactly ten fifty-nine.

Reporters and cameramen scrambled to follow Charlie and Helen into the blue and green corporately decorated shop, and then the general public pushed in behind. Charlie was thankful it was a large city centre betting shop. Had it been a smaller space the hundred and fifty people behind them might have caused a stampede. There were already a good hundred people inside the shop. Most smiled or nodded their appreciation as he and Helen passed and Charlie realised they must have been waiting for them, rather than being punters there to gamble. That's the power of social media, Charlie thought as he and Helen slowly made their way toward a huge blue coloured counter populated by five tills and two nervous looking female cashiers.

Charlie gave the cashiers a broad smile and eyed the space behind the counter. He'd already done enough of these approaches to know what to look for. However, on this occasion the two or three white, middle-aged men wearing lounge suits (virtually all the bookmaking executives had fit this description so far) didn't appear to be in attendance. Charlie's confidence dropped a few notches. Perhaps these businessmen really couldn't be shamed into paying?

Charlie brought Helen to a gentle halt a few yards in front of the counter and gave her a quick morale boosting wink, then went into his Advertising Director mode. He took a breath and turned to face a ring of reporters and cameras. Behind them it was standing room only. Charlie gulped when he realised that people were still pouring into the shop, pushing the standing hoards forward. Yet there was pretty much silence apart from the hum of the monitors around the shop and the shuffling of feet.

It was as he was about to launch into his pre-prepared speech that a small, wiry man of about seventy using his elbows, pushed between two reporters and jostled a cameraman in order to stand in front of Charlie. He had thinning hair but a winning grin, and he immediately struck Charlie as the sort of individual you would find in every single betting shop up and down the country; a small stakes punter who loved his daily bet. Charlie considered brushing the man off, but only for a split second, there was something terribly genuine about him. The man shrugged off complaints from the reporters and gathered himself for a moment, before beaming at Helen and thrusting out a bony hand.

'Really well done,' the man said in a light, warm voice, 'Can I see the bet love?' The punter's eyes seemed to mist over as Helen produced the Lucky Fifteen betting slip from her handbag. He squinted at the betting slip and crackled with laughter. It was a victorious laugh, the sort which is infectious and it soon caught to the forty or fifty people able to witness the man's joy at a stranger's winning betting slip.

Once the laughter subsided, the seventy-year-old looked up and gave Charlie an appraising stare.

'I've been betting for fifty-five years,' he said in a steady, louder tone, enough for the whole shop to hear him. 'I've had my winners, but I reckon I've probably lost to bookies what you've won in that one bet.'

There was a twinkle that appeared in the old man's eyes and Charlie wasn't too sure where he was going to go next, but didn't act upon an urge to speak. The man was somehow managing to hold his audience of two hundred people spellbound.

'So I feel...' he continued, '...it's a winning bet for *everyone.*'

There were murmurs of agreement in the crowd and the reporters started to pay the old man more attention; a few camera flashbulbs went off and one of them asked the man his name. He ignored them.

Very quietly, almost growling to himself in anger, the man said, 'Pay her.'

Helen glanced sideways at Charlie not sure how to react.

'Pay her,' the wiry man said again in an insistent tone, balling his fist and bouncing it off his chest as he spoke each word.

He turned to the crowd and paused for a few seconds before shouting, 'Pay her. Pay her. Pay her!'

Behind the reporters a voice joined the punter, 'Pay her!'

Within seconds three, four, now a dozen, and before long, two hundred people were chanting together in a steady, regular rhythm to the beat of the punter's fist as he pounded his chest. The betting shop reverberated to the sound of the insistent refrain.

Charlie breathed in the atmosphere for what felt like a long time, all thoughts of his own speech well and truly quashed. The punter had handled it perfectly. He turned around and faced the betting counter. To his absolute delight the two cashiers had been replaced by three perplexed looking men in black and grey suits. Presumably they had been hiding in the back office. One of them beckoned to Charlie and he dutifully approached the counter.

'Could we discuss this?' the bookmaker ventured.

Charlie grinned, and turned to regard the chanting betting shop before returning his gaze to the grimly unimpressed Regional Manager.

'You really think it warrants a discussion?' Charlie asked above the noise, 'Perhaps you should swallow your pride, accept you're wrong, and pay the lady what she's owed.'

****

'Can you believe they tried to pay out only fifty thousand at the Royston Bookmakers in Birmingham?' Stan told Charlie and Suzie as they drove across the Tyne Bridge.

'I was in there with a local homeless charity and the bookie tried to make out he had terms and conditions which limited a lucky fifteen payout to only fifty thousand. It was laughable.'

Suzie rolled her eyes encouragingly at Stan. He had been amusing her and Charlie all the way from Leeds with his increasingly tall stories of the payouts he'd been involved with. All three of them had attended bookmakers this week to help charities to force a payout, almost exclusively due to the press involvement and aided here and there by a bit of punter power.

'What happened when you got the photograph out?' she asked.

'It was glorious!' Stan exclaimed, 'That was pure genius, Charlie. There is no way they could argue with an image showing all their terms and conditions on the day you placed the bet. I can't believe how many bookmakers changed their betting terms and payout limits literally the day after the Lincoln and then claimed they didn't have to pay the full amount.'

'Bookmaking is a business,' Charlie replied levelly, 'They are trying to make a profit. Bookmakers don't have to accept a bet, and if they have the right terms and conditions, they don't have to pay one out that breaks their rules.'

'But you made them!' Stan trilled from the back seat.

Charlie gave a wan smile, but remained silent. He was acutely aware that what transpired over the next few hours would determine whether the other forty-two BetMick winning betting slips would indeed be paid out. The victory over the major chain this morning had been a good one, and he'd managed to ensure the charities got paid and the bookmakers

214

emerged with as little damage to their reputation as possible.

'Then there was that betting shop in Stoke that tried not to pay the bonus!' Stan piped up, 'The charity I was with ran a hospice. She was beside herself when her winnings jumped up by ten percent!'

Suzie giggled to herself in the front seat of Charlie's car. One of the facets of a Lucky Fifteen was that if you managed to select all four winners a bonus of ten percent of the entire winnings was usually added. Some of the bookmakers had 'accidentally' forgotten to add the extra ten percent, as stated on their terms and conditions of the bet.

After visiting Ben in Doncaster Infirmary, Charlie, Suzie, and Stan had returned to the racecourse later in the afternoon and spent time giving pay out advice to all the charities who had attended. The primary advice was to know exactly what they should expect as a payout and to have their photos of the bookmaker's terms handy. Virtually all of the charities had followed the advice in Sam's letters and taken a photo on their mobile phones whilst they were in their chosen betting shop. Once a copy of their own terms was shown to bookmakers as evidence, most of the bookies had capitulated immediately and added the bonus; the camera didn't lie. The ten percent bonus amounted to another seventy thousand pounds being added to their winnings.

'Now we need to make the biggest payout of the lot happen,' Charlie stated, 'So it's time for the big guns.'

Charlie found the BetMick head offices behind the Newcastle upon Tyne train station. At four o'clock, Charlie, Suzie, and Stan entered the glum stone-built building. It boasted a small vestibule where a secretary sat behind a built-in desk from the seventies. It reminded Charlie of office furniture from a Reginald Perrin set. Mick was clearly tight with his money.

They were shown into a bare meeting room with the very minimum of facilities; an oblong painted chipboard table and twelve chairs, two of which had ripped upholstery. The walls were dirty and several long, single line cobwebs hung down from the ceiling, wafting as people moved around. The only natural light came from two small windows covered in metal grills.

'Mr. Kowalski will be... down,' the secretary told them. She knew the score, Charlie reasoned; Mick would see them when it suited him. They could be in for a bit of a wait. He settled in, carefully placing his paperwork in front of him.

Twenty minutes later, Mick burst into the room unannounced, making Suzie jump and turning her cheeks scarlet. If anything, the man was more ebullient when he was under pressure, Charlie noted. He tapped a couple of icons on his mobile phone before welcoming the bookmaker. Mick ignored the introduction, rounded the table, and sat at the opposite end to Charlie and his colleagues, a good four yards away. He was wearing an AC\DC Back in Black T-shirt which was at least a size too small. Mick leaned back in his chair and glared down the table, adopting a fixed, disdainful grimace.

Silence descended on the room. Charlie waited.

'So, you're here to collect your money?' Mick asked presently in an overly sweet, sarcastic voice.

Charlie reached out to a neat pile of papers he had purposefully placed onto his notepad on the table. He twanged the elastic band which held copies of the forty-two BetMick Lucky Fifteen betting slips. It made a pleasant thwacking sound which, he was pleased to see, annoyed Mick.

'Yes, I'd like forty-two cheques for seven-hundred and sixty-eight thousand pounds each please,' Charlie replied with a benign smile, 'Made out to these people.'

Suzie jumped up, placed the cheque instructions in front of Mick and returned to her seat.

Mick produced a hollow laugh which died almost immediately. The room seemed to suck his joviality from the stale air.

'You think you're the clever one, don't you? Well, you won't be shaming me into paying you like the rest of those spineless bookies. It won't hurt my brand; if anything, we'll get more revenue. Mug punters are already flocking to my shops, just to try and get me back for not paying out. I've already got an advertising campaign mapped out; 'Get Mick back. Back with BetMick'

Mick had leaned forward as he delivered his diatribe, the pace of his delivery becoming more and more frenetic the longer it went on. He leaned back and took a breath.

'The public will love to hate me.'

'I'm impressed,' Charlie replied airily.

'You'll have to spend years, if not decades pursuing me through the courts,' Mick continued, 'I'll tie you and the legal system up in knots. You'll never get even a single penny from me.'

Suzie and Stan shared a nervous glance. Charlie remained silent for a short while and pushed his bottom lip out, as if in contemplation.

'Allow me to make a counter-offer,' Charlie stated, piercing Mick with his own hard stare and pinging the elastic band once more, 'It might place a different... slant on things. Just give me a moment.'

Charlie consulted his mobile phone and nodded.

'Ah good, they should be arriving just about now.'

Charlie fixed his gaze on the door to the room, and to his relief, it opened fifteen seconds later. Laurie Lewis and Frank Best entered. They wore serious expressions and neither of them looked at Mick. Both chose a seat at Charlie's end of the table.

Mick eyed the two men nervously and slanted a filthy look at Frank Best, sensing the man was about to turn traitor. He had hoped that bravado would see him through this meeting. The only reason he'd agreed to it was because his legal people had insisted. It would apparently help his chances when the case came to court, having 'listened' and 'entertained' the plaintiff's side of things. The last few days hadn't been enjoyable for him. He'd been castigated in the media, harangued in the street by strangers, and his betting shops had been virtually empty.

'Get on with it then!' Mick demanded, 'I'm a busy man.'

'Indeed, but I think we might be able to solve that particular problem,' remarked Charlie with a touch of irony. A curt nod across the table resulted in Stan producing a recording device, checking the levels and placing it in the centre of the table.

Stan took on a businesslike tone, 'I'm sure your legal people will be interested in hearing this. I will of course provide you with a copy after the meeting.'

Mick silently waved the issue away. It was of no consequence, he'd said as much as he was going to say. It was just a case of listening to them whine about the lack of payouts for the next few minutes, perhaps with a few threats if he was lucky. Either way, he would throw them out of his building within ten minutes. Job done.

'According to BetMick Ltd's latest set of accounts, you now have sixty-five million pounds in reserves, more than enough to pay out the charities you owe. Will you be willing to do so? I'm asking just for the record you understand...' asked Charlie.

'Of course not, I've already told you...'

'Very good,' Charlie interrupted, 'Well, I need to inform you that as of three o'clock this afternoon I own forty-nine percent of BetMick Ltd.'

Mick felt light-headed. He shook a little and looked befuddled for a few seconds before recovering his composure.

Now, Laurie Lewis steepled his hands, cleared his throat and locked eyes with Mick.

'I became disenchanted with bookmaking after spending eighteen months working with you, Mick. So I have sold my shares in the company to Mr. Summer... for one pound. I want nothing else to do with BetMick. The sale of my shares has only one proviso; all profits derived from Mr. Summer's percentage will be donated to charity each year. The primary beneficiaries will be organisations that support victims of gambling addiction, although Mr. Summer has kindly insisted my own mother's charity also receives a sizeable annual donation.'

On cue, Suzie stood, and once again walked the few yards to the end of the table and placed a legal looking piece of paper in front of Mick.

Mick stared incredulously at the figures and signatures on the piece of paper and then down to the end of the table, trying to grasp what was going on.

Laurie continued, 'You may also remember that when I recruited

217

Frank, that's Mr. Best here, as a part of his remuneration package he was given a two percent share in the business. Well, I believe Mr. Best and Mr. Summer have reached an understanding...'

As Laurie continued to explain, Charlie watched Mick Kowalski disintegrate as the magnitude of Laurie and Frank Best's actions hit home. This was no longer about paying out a few Lucky Fifteen bets, it had become a corporate takeover.

'... which means that Mr. Summer and Mr. Best now own a controlling fifty-one percent of BetMick Ltd.,' Laurie concluded.

A long silence filled the meeting room. Mick remained seated, his hands and forearms lying flat to the table. He glared at Charlie, his face flushing and he started to tremble with rage.

'My first action as the controlling owner of BetMick will be to pay out each of the forty-two outstanding winning charitable bets,' Charlie said, 'It will place a little pressure on the company's cashflow, but Frank assures me it can continue to thrive.'

Mick looked set to explode.

After a pause, Charlie added thoughtfully, 'Also, I do think a change of Managing Director and a rebrand will be in order. BetCharlie has a nice ring to it...'

Mick exploded.

Forty-Six

Charlie and Sharon strolled the two hundred yards from her church to the nearby pub, taking their time and enjoying the warmth of the lunchtime sun, sharing a conversation about the spring flowers in the graveyard, the scent of the hawthorn bushes, and discussing how Suzie and Stan were getting along since Lincoln day. The Old Bull in Inkberrow had become Charlie's favourite haunt in recent days. They ordered sandwiches and a basket of chips at the bar, finding a table in the corner where they wouldn't be easily overheard.

This was the first time they'd met since the day at Doncaster, partly through Sharon being away from the parish on church business for a few days, but also because Charlie had been busy with the subsequent fallout from Cool Blue's success. In the two weeks since Lincoln day Charlie, Ben, and Faraday had been hounded by the media. Sam Lewis was refusing to speak with anyone from the press and even Suzie and Stan had been approached with interview requests.

'They want to do a documentary?' Sharon queried.

'Yep, so far we've had four production companies, including an online streaming business, as well as Channel Six, showing interest.'

'Are you going to do it?'

'Good God, no!' Charlie laughed into his pint of beer. Sharon gave him an expectant stare and he mouthed a, 'Sorry.'

'I did get one of the media guys quite excited when I suggested I could possibly get Sharon Stone to take one of the roles though…'

Sharon shook her head, 'Not going to happen,' before adding 'I'm guessing they knew *which* Sharon Stone?'

She glared at Charlie and catching his single raised eyebrow, realised he had been joking. He confirmed this with a cheeky smile.

'Come on then,' he cajoled, 'Have you had the press of anyone else around at the church asking questions?'

'No, but then I don't suppose anyone would remember me. Wearing a clerical collar tends to makes most people look away these days,' she sniffed.

'Well if you hadn't liberated those phones from the Lewis's, it may have been a different story, so in my book you were integral to our success.'

Sharon inspected Charlie's face intently across the table and for a moment he felt a little uncomfortable.

Their lunch arrived and the conversation veered away from Doncaster and Lincoln day. Sharon spoke about being confirmed as the resident vicar in Inkberrow for another three years. Charlie congratulated her and revealed he'd handed in his notice. He'd reached a decision the night of the race; he needed a new challenge. Charlie also revealed he intended to leave his flat in Leeds.

'I might go to Newcastle for a while,' he told her between bites of his hearty sandwich, 'It's taken a few days for Mick Kowalski to calm down after our meeting, but he's accepted five million pounds for his share of BetMick. Frank has asked me to be a consultant on a short term contract, to help smooth the transition of BetMick into new ownership and build the brand back up now Mick has gone.'

'I was wondering about that. How *did* you pull off that little scam so quickly after the race?'

'I think *scam* is a rather derogatory way to describe a well executed plan,' Charlie responded, feigning offence.

'Well?' she asked, ignoring his theatrics.

'When I was investigating BetMick right at the start of this, I noticed someone called Saddington owned forty-nine percent of the business. I didn't think anything of it at the time and assumed it was a sleeping partner or a corporate investor. But I noticed Frank Best owned two percent. Laurie knew Frank was excellent on the internet side, and the share was a way of getting him to join the company. I think Mick had forgotten about it after Laurie went, and Frank isn't the sort to boast about his small percentage.'

Charlie paused to spear a chip with his fork and munched on it thoughtfully, chewing with more vigor when he caught sight of Sharon's exasperated look.

'I got Frank on board before the race. He and his wife weren't great supporters of Mick,' he explained, 'Initially my idea was to force a board meeting and try to make the other forty-nine percent shareholder back me and pay out to the charities, but of course that all changed substantially for the better when Laurie and his mother gate-crashed the private room.'

He stared wistfully at his sandwich, 'You know, I hadn't made the link between Saddington the shareholder with Saddington the charity guest.' He shook his head, 'That was a light bulb moment I had in the car on the way to the hospital.'

Sharon cast her mind back to that journey but it was the celebrations in the hospital afterwards that were more vivid for her. She gave up trying to remember. After all, there were more pressing questions.

'I was wondering, with that huge charity pay out and with Mick gone, will BetMick survive?'

'Money will be tight for a while, but Frank is confident,' Charlie confirmed. 'Half of the money they paid to the charities was from reserves the company never touched because Mick was so tight. Frank is hoping to make the most of the fact they are the only bookmaker in the world where at least half their profits will go to charity. It will be my job to convince the betting public it's a great reason to bet with BetMick.'

'What about the others?' Sharon asked, 'What's happened to Sam?'

'Laurie told me that Sam has left his father's house and gone to live with his mother. That's left Reginald to rattle around his mansion on his own with his five members of staff. Mick Kowalski has gone to ground. No one has seen him since the meeting in Newcastle. I'm guessing it won't take long for him to pop up again though. I imagine he's got his sights set on Reginald's millions.'

'Hasn't Mick been charged with race fixing?'

'I heard the racing authority integrity team had tried to track him down, without any luck. It's going to be a tough one to pin on him without it looking like entrapment, but I've been asked to send the details to the British Horseracing Board. I guess they will weigh up whether it's worth pursuing him. It should also help Chris Hagar too. He's not been getting the rides he deserves since being wrongly accused.'

'Oh yes, I'd forgotten about him,' Sharon admitted.

'Chris is a nice chap. I met him at Tommy's yard a year ago and heard how he'd been struggling to get rides on the flat even though he was totally blameless in the cheating scandal he got caught up in. I got Joss Faraday to alter the riding arrangements as soon as I found out Mick Kowalski had tried to buy Joss off. I couldn't quite believe how well it worked, Mick was on the phone to Chris the next day! Luke Mountain was filming everything in the restaurant on his phone, so that was sent to the BHA too. Actually, *The Racing Post* did a nice piece on Chris the other day, and I see he's been riding for a couple of new yards this week.'

Charlie stabbed another forkful of twice-fried homemade chips from the basket in front of them and dolloped a healthy portion of *HP Sauce* onto his plate.

'So you've been paid out?' he enquired through a mouth filled with tuna sandwich.

Sharon produced a satisfied smile, 'I was lucky, my bet was with one of the bookmakers who guaranteed to pay up. My Bishop was speechless when I produced my cheque. Inkberrow church will be receiving one or two much needed upgrades over the next few years.'

Charlie nodded his approval and took another bite out of his sandwich. The two of them ate and drank for a minute, the lull in their conversation easy and relaxed.

'I don't suppose I could tempt you to come up to visit me in Newcastle for a few days?' Charlie asked, looking up from his plate pensively.

Sharon locked eyes with Charlie for a few seconds and he sensed she was making her decision as her eyes bore into him. She broke away, concentrating instead on pushing a couple of chips around her plate.

'I don't know if that's such a good idea,' she admitted in a tentative tone, rolling her gaze back up to him momentarily.

'Oh, why's that?' Charlie replied, trying to keep things upbeat and relaxed.

'Well, on only the second occasion I met you, I managed to get embroiled in a gambling coup which resulted in me stealing and lying.'

Charlie gave a gentle laugh, 'Yes, I'm afraid I can't promise you that much excitement every time we meet!'

Placing her fork on her plate and leaning back, Sharon held the base of her wooden chair with both hands, frustration building in her dark brown eyes.

'And that's the problem,' she sighed, 'I enjoyed it a little too much.'

'I can have that effect on people,' Charlie admitted, maintaining what he hoped was a light, jokey persona. Sharon tilted her head to one side and produced a serious stare which drained all the light-heartedness from him. He wiped the smile from his face, placed his own fork carefully onto his plate and was about to give his 'that's okay, I understand' speech, however Sharon beat him to it.

'I think it's best if we don't become too… involved. I left all the lying and stealing behind me some time ago and I don't want to return there. To be honest, I don't know whether we're that well suited.'

There was a definite sadness behind her eyes now and as she searched for more words, Charlie felt a rush of feelings course around him, most of which he didn't quite understand.

Charlie raised both eyebrows. 'A bad influence and I'm not your type,' he stated quietly with a shake of his head. He mulled this over, trying to plot a path out of the gloom which had descended around the table.

Sharon was at a loss of what to say. Charlie had summed it up almost perfectly. The Bishop, while welcoming the injection of a considerable donation, had been less enamoured with her involvement at the racetrack. She had been walking on air for a few days after Doncaster, returning to ground with a bump when some of her parishioners pointed out the stark reality of hanging around with someone like Charlie. Her smiling face had figured in a number of photos which were circulating in the newspapers and on the internet.

One of the reports had linked her to Charlie as his possible love interest, which had thrilled her at first, then angered her. Her flock had been less than thrilled with the exposure. A roving young vicar wasn't an ideal fit with a sleepy, conservative village where the average inhabitant was aged fifty plus. She might get away with her funky clothes, and less than holy language on occasions, but that was probably as far as she could push it. Besides, she'd become attached to the parish. She wanted to stay.

Then there was Charlie; handsome, funny, and most of all, exciting. That said, he did get bored easily and it surely wouldn't be too long before he became bored with her, and she wasn't sure she could cope with that sort of rejection... again. Besides, fending off the advances from all those tall, perfectly formed models Charlie seemed to attract would be tiresome. She looked down at her smock, knowing it covered a body more akin to mothering than modelling and gave a little sigh.

'Friends it is!' Charlie exclaimed without rancour, 'And I promise to keep you out of any... er, *funny business* I might get involved in.'

Sharon considered this for a short time before allowing her cheeks to bunch into a smile.

'That sounds perfect,' she agreed, raising her glass of mineral water.

They clinked and Charlie smiled back, trying to hide the relief he felt at not losing Sharon's friendship completely. He took the hit to his ego and recovered quickly, silently regarding the quirky, strong-willed woman with her shady back-story. It struck him that he'd never had a proper female friend before, or at least one which didn't turn into a romantic quest, or wasn't linked to work. His brother was always teasing him about his lack of guile with intelligent women.

He was challenged by her, he realised, and if he was being truthful, a better person when she was around. If he could make their friendship work, now that really would be... he searched for the right words and couldn't help smiling when they came to him.

It would be a bit of a coup.

Author Note

Many thanks for reading 'An Old-Fashioned Coup', I do hope you enjoyed this racing story. If you did, I'd be really grateful if you would visit Amazon and provide a rating and review, it really does help my stories reach a wider audience.

You can reach the review page at: **https://amzn.to/2SJiqWC**